THE
HOSPITAL
MAKERS

THE
HOSPITAL
MAKERS

Irwin Philip Sobel

1973
DOUBLEDAY & COMPANY, INC.
GARDEN CITY, NEW YORK

There never was a McKinley Hospital. The men and women in this book never lived. Only the devotion, the discipline, the loyalty, and the striving are real.

ISBN: 0-385-00567-9
Library of Congress Catalog Card Number 72–79426
Copyright © 1973 by Irwin Philip Sobel
All Rights Reserved
Printed in the United States of America
First Edition

To Jake and Minnie, my parents,
Margaret and Michael, my family,
and Gladys Romanoff, my audience.

THE
HOSPITAL
MAKERS

PART
ONE

"O, call back yesterday,
bid time return!"

ONE

THE ANGEL OF DEATH, they called him, and although he was a physician, he was proud of the title. Those were the days when diagnosis was the giant, treatment the dwarf, and he the greatest consultant in the City of New York. It was said that no prominent patient would agree to die until Dr. Rintman had examined him and said that he must.

At precisely three o'clock of a September afternoon in nineteen hundred and thirty-three, he walked into McKinley Hospital's Male One and nodded curtly to the attending physicians standing respectfully near the entrance to the ward. It was a gesture performed less out of politeness than to call attention to the Mephistophelean hair tufts he carefully tended every morning. The interns huddled in a corner he dismissed as nothing more than a white mass of inexperience. Ignoring them, he looked with satisfaction at the fifty beds evenly spaced along the sides of the rectangular room and the gleaming parquet boulevard running down the middle, an arrangement that provided an excellent bird's-eye view for the nurses but little privacy for the occupants. Each patient could at all times be seen by the other forty-nine except when the screens were rolled around him so that he could properly perform the daily act of getting rid of excreta or the once-in-a-lifetime act of dying. Rintman did not stop until he reached the nearest bed. Then he faced his audience, and without a word of greeting began to teach.

"Which of the five senses is the most important to the diagnostician?" he asked the attending physicians and the house staff. "Is it sight, as represented by inspection; hearing, as represented by listening through the stethoscope; touch; or perhaps even smell or taste?"

The doctors were too intimidated to answer. Besides, they knew that he was about to embark on an anecdote, as was his custom on the first Grand Rounds of the season.

"I learned the answer long ago at one of Professor Plautner's lectures at the University of Leipzig. He was sitting in front of the senior class in the amphitheater of the old medical school, a beaker full of urine on the table before him.

"'It is really not necessary to use complicated laboratory methods to discover a case of diabetes,' he began mildly, 'or to find sugar in the urine. Do exactly what I do, and you will see.'

"He dipped a finger into the beaker, sucked his finger with obvious enjoyment, murmured, 'Sweet, quite sweet,' and passed the specimen around. The students imitated him, and then either spat into their handkerchiefs or gagged." .

Rintman paused for a moment and smiled his twisted smile. "When the beaker was returned to him, Plautner stood up in a towering rage (he was a small man like me, but at the moment he seemed a giant) and shouted,

"'Schweinhunde! Do you realize what you have done? For all you know, the urine you just tasted may have been swarming with virulent germs, typhoid bacilli or plague. Didn't that occur to you? Now please watch carefully what I do, only this time use your eyes. Brains you can't use because you don't have any. Use your eyes, then, your eyes!'

"He dipped his index finger into the beaker, held it up before the class, and then slowly put his *third* finger into his mouth."

Rintman looked hard at the interns. "From that day on, I have never wavered in my belief that a wise pair of eyes are a diagnostician's greatest asset."

There was an impressive silence.

"Wasn't the right finger ever used?" asked an attending bent on currying favor.

Rintman sniffed and his eyes glowed. "Yes, once," he said, holding up the third finger of his right hand. "This finger." He paused to let the effect sink in, and continued: "One year Plautner pulled this stunt on the senior class for the benefit of the Professor of Medicine of Oxford, who was visiting him at the time. Deciding to show off his knowledge of English, he turned to his guest and said, 'In the words of your St. James version, "They have eyes, but they see not."'

"To which the Englishman suavely replied, 'I would rather say, "They have eyes, but for pee—not."'"

Everyone laughed except the nurses. They smiled, the supervisor rather sourly.

As Rintman walked slowly up the ward, he saw out of the corner of his eye an unshaven patient who was rinsing his mouth into a kidney basin. To his intense delight, he noticed that the fluid was blood-stained.

"To the internist, sight is king of the senses," he continued, "but that does not mean that the others are unimportant. For example, certain diseases with unique odors often betray themselves to the physician with a keen sense of smell."

Undisturbed by the fact that he knew this to be completely untrue, he raised his head and inhaled deeply a few times as if to show that the air he was now sampling would lead him to something that would confound them all.

"There's scurvy in this room!" he announced softly. "The scent is clear." Turning to the House Physician, he said, "You smell it, of course."

Too flabbergasted to answer, the chief intern just shook his head.

Rintman smiled his crooked smile. "Perhaps I'm expecting too much. It takes a certain talent."

He resumed his deep breathing, trying to create the impression of a bloodhound closing in on its prey. Suddenly he whirled around and pointed accusingly at the unshaven patient.

"There's your man!" he cried out.

The House Physician gulped and dropped his stethoscope. Just a few hours before, he had admitted a case of scurvy, and this was indeed the man. Of course, he was unaware of Rintman's secret custom. Every afternoon about fifteen minutes before rounds, he would drop into the admitting office, where the big ledger was kept, and study the names and diagnoses of all the patients who had entered the Hospital, together with the wards to which they had been sent. Today he had pounced on the fact that a man with scurvy had gone to Male One. He also noticed with satisfaction that an experienced outside doctor had made that diagnosis and the referral. Although the head clerk knew the purpose of Rintman's visits, she never gave him away. After all, he had once pulled her through a vicious attack of lobar pneumonia. But even without this, she would never have betrayed him. Whatever increased his prestige added luster to the Hospital.

Rintman picked up the stethoscope and handed it to the embarrassed intern with a sardonic bow. Then, as if unveiling a monument, he jerked the covers off the patient and pointed to the red flecks on his legs.

"Hemorrhages," he announced. "They are characteristic, quite characteristic."

For the first time, he decided to pay some attention to the patient instead of to his disease. "For weeks you've had pain in your knees, *nicht wahr?*"

The man nodded, and then winced as Rintman bent his leg

14

slowly. "And you have had no fruits or vegetables, only scraps and booze."

Again the man nodded, and a smile came into his bleary eyes.

Rintman stroked his chin. "And you have little blue bags above your front teeth, *nicht wahr?*"

The man smiled delightedly and said, "*Jawohl, Herr Professor,*" as if Rintman's detailed knowledge of the inside of his mouth was only to be expected. After all, when a magician is doing tricks, why be surprised?

Before Rintman would raise the patient's lip, he insisted that his audience step closer. There were the blood-filled sacs in the gums just above the upper central incisors, just as he had predicted.

"Please observe that the gums are friable and bleed easily." He sniffed. "Characteristic, quite characteristic." He turned to the House Physician. "And of course his urine is loaded with red blood cells?"

All the intern could do was nod.

Almost as an afterthought, since his primary interest was in diagnosis, not treatment, Rintman barked, "I want this man to have orange juice, more orange juice, and still more orange juice!" accenting each "orange juice" with a jab of his forefinger. As he walked away he looked over his shoulder and asked the House, "What is he?"

"A derelict, a waterfront derelict."

Rintman turned around and smiled. "An interesting case. For us on rounds, better a waterfront derelict with scurvy than a bank president with the common cold."

Then he continued on his way, the House Physician at his heels, the silent retinue a respectful distance behind, until he reached the next to the last bed.

"I hope you are beginning to see how important each of the five senses—even smell—can be to the diagnostician." Again he took a few deep breaths. "This time the scent leads to a case of rheumatic heart disease." He pointed to a young man in the bed nearest him.

The House Physician's look of amazement was too much even for Rintman. He laughed and patted him on the back, a little low down and rather lingeringly.

"Come, come, Doctor, that was easy! You can smell the oil of wintergreen as well as I. Now, look at the patient, at the flushed cheeks, the cracked lips, the expression on his face. He's obviously feverish, acutely ill, and in pain. Now, when do we use oil of wintergreen in this Hospital? Either for the joints in rheumatic fever, or for a sprain." He paused. "Does that boy look as if he has a sprain? And at his age, he can't be more than sixteen, rheumatic fever usually involves the heart."

He took out his stethoscope, the silver plating of which had long before worn down to the brass, and listened to the patient's heart. All he heard was a blowing systolic murmur, and so knew that there had been only early damage to the mitral valve, which was allowing some of the blood to leak back. The rumbling presystolic murmur had not yet made its appearance. That would come later and would signify that the valve had been seriously damaged. Rintman put his stethoscope in his back pocket and turned to the House.

"Did you hear the rumbling presystolic murmur?"

"No, just the systolic murmur."

"Listen again."

The intern, a singularly honest young man, listened and shook his head. Rintman patted him on the back, a little lower down than before, and said,

"Oh, well, it takes a certain talent."

He motioned to his attendings, who filed by and one by one listened to the patient's heart. Although a few said they heard the rumbling presystolic murmur, none of them actually did. And for a good reason. It was not there. Rintman was merely laying the foundation for a future performance. He knew that perhaps in six months, perhaps in a year, but inevitably, the

16

boy would return with a second or third attack of rheumatic fever, one that would further damage the mitral valve so that this time the ominous narrowing, with its telltale rumbling presystolic murmur, would really be there. Then he would turn to his attendings and say in an offhand way, "When I first listened to this patient's heart, some of you were unable to hear the rumbling presystolic murmur. I think all of you should be able to hear it now."

But today he was careful not to belabor the point. He merely shrugged and said, "I want salicylates given in massive dosage." Then he walked to the opposite side of the ward and said banteringly, "So all your puzzles are solved, your mysteries dispelled, your diagnoses established. There is nothing for me to do, is that it?"

The House Physician smiled. "There are two cases that might interest you. We can't figure them out."

Rintman's eyes glowed as the chief medical intern guided him to a bed near the middle of the ward and whispered to one of the junior interns to recite the history.

"Not today," said Rintman, anticipating the presentation. "For years I've preached that a detailed history is the foundation on which a good diagnosis must rest. But not today. Let's see what we can do without it. Just a brief summary, please."

The House Physician cleared his throat. "Five days ago this forty-two-year-old man noticed swelling of his right testicle, a swelling that has increased and been accompanied by some pain. There has been no discharge. He feels he may have been a little feverish for a few days, but his temperature is now normal. His past and family histories are negative except for the fact that his mother and father both died of cancer."

Rintman pulled the sheets down gently, and lifted the short hospital nightgown. The man's genitals rested on a hammock of adhesive tape slung between his upper thighs, and the right side of his scrotum was the size of a grapefruit. At the first rustle of the bedclothes all the nurses had pointedly wheeled in the opposite direction, because just as it was the religious duty of a Mohammedan to turn his face toward Mecca five times a day, so it was the ladylike duty of a McKinley nurse to turn her back on the phallus whenever it was displayed—and to do it militantly, lest her virtuous action be overlooked. The head nurse, who had had sexual intercourse twice the night before (with the same man, of course), saw nothing strange in a philosophy that encouraged her to make amorous contact with the male organ at three in the morning, only to prohibit her from looking at it, even professionally, twelve hours later. Jim, a junior intern who as yet knew none of the nurses, wondered if they harbored a secret fear that some catastrophe would overtake them if they peeked, like being turned to stone, the fate of those who dared to look at the snakes on the head of the Gorgon Medusa. Medusa had at last been vanquished, he remembered, when Perseus had had the wit to gaze at her image in his polished shield while he lopped off her head. He wondered what would happen if someday while a nurse was helping him dress a postoperative hernia wound with her back to the patient, he handed her a mirror and whispered diabolically in her ear, "Take a chance! Look!" They would probably throw him out of the Hospital. When he looked around again, the nurses were still staring at a spot on the wall directly opposite the patient, and Rintman was completing his examination.

"Well, what do you think it is?" he asked the House.

"A tumor of the testicle."

"Malignant? Almost all of them are."

"Yes."

Rintman turned to one of the junior interns. "What do you think it is?"

"Gonorrhea."

"With no previous discharge?"

"The patient may not be telling the truth."

Rintman looked at the junior intern scornfully. "Why should he lie? It is you who are not telling the truth."

He beckoned to Jim. "Come here and look at it, Dr. Morelle. You're a junior, too, but you may do better." After giving him a moment, he asked, "Well, what is it?"

"I don't know," said Jim, shaking his head.

Rintman smiled his lopsided smile. "Good. You're going to be a surgeon, and a surgeon should be a doer, not a knower."

He motioned to Stanley. "Well, Dr. Levinson?"

"I don't know either," confessed Stanley.

Rintman sighed. "You should know, because you are going to be a pediatrician."

He looked at his retinue and said, "This man has a disease most of you have already contracted. Even you," he added to a big, bony nurse standing near him. Since she was flat-chested, faintly mustached, and had misconstrued his remark, she blushed violently.

Walking slowly up to the patient and fixing him with his basilisk eyes, Rintman shouted, "Why didn't you tell the doctors about the swelling in front of your ears?"

The man began to tremble. "It was just swollen glands, Professor, swollen glands. I didn't think it had anything to do with down there." He pointed to his scrotum.

"Swollen glands, you idiot, what do you know about swollen glands! That swelling you had in your neck two weeks ago was mumps!"

He turned to his retinue. "It's a mumps orchitis. One out of every three adult males with the disease gets involvement of the testicle as a complication."

The patient's color was returning. "Then I won't have to have the cancer cut off, Professor?"

"The only thing we'll cut off is your tongue—for withholding information."

Rintman pulled the man's nightgown down and covered him gently with the sheet. "After a couple of weeks, when the swelling goes away, you may notice that the involved testicle is much smaller than the other. Never mind. You'll be able to have a hundred sons"; he bent down and whispered in the man's ear, "by a hundred different women, of course."

The man looked up and his eyes were shining. "God bless you, Doctor, God bless you!"

Rintman straightened up and smiled. "For what? For giving you immoral advice?"

As he walked away, leaving his retinue immobilized by the unexpectedness of the diagnosis, the ward burst into an excited hum. Before the House could recover, there was such a distance between him and the Director of the Medical Service that he decided he would have to run to catch up. Rintman looked over his shoulder and frowned. Hurrying and bustling were perfectly proper, even commendable on rounds, but running, never. The House slowed down, pointed to an empty bed, and said, "Right here, Dr. Rintman."

By this time the head nurse had come up. The House Physician turned on her sharply. "If I've told that old man once, I've told him ten times to stay in bed for rounds."

"I know you did, Doctor," answered the nurse, "but he has spells when he doesn't remember."

Again the sanctity of Grand Rounds was broken, this time by the shuffling steps of an old man in a gray flannel bathrobe, who, like a swimmer breasting a strong current, was struggling to reach the empty bed against the combined force of thirty pairs of hostile eyes. When he at last reached his goal and crawled up on top of the mattress, no one helped him, even though he did everything to call attention to his frailty and weakness. He reminded Jim of a puppy who, after making a mess on the floor, relies on its helplessness to avert punishment. The House advanced on the man. Rintman held up his hand. "No reprimands, no detailed history, and no laboratory reports, please. Just a brief summary."

The House nodded and cleared his throat. "This seventy-four-year-old white male was admitted yesterday with the presenting symptom of painless jaundice, which has increased steadily during the past three weeks. He has had almost complete loss of appetite, and according to the people who sent him here, the Wiesendorfer Home for the Aged, he must have lost over ten pounds. There has been no fever."

"How long has he been at the home?"

"Only a month."

"Where did he live before?"

"With one of his married sons."

Rintman turned to the old man. "Did you want to go to the home?"

The patient shrugged. "An old man has got the right to be a burden only up to a certain point. When that's all he is, when he's no father, no companion, no counselor any more, when he's just nothing, then I suppose he's got to go to a home."

Rintman turned back to the House. "Excuse me for interrupting you."

The House nodded. "He's noticed that his stools have turned white during the past two weeks, and this has disturbed him. The chief physical findings are the yellowness of the skin and eyes, a slightly tender liver four finger-breadths below the coastal margin, and a firm mass about three inches in diameter in the left lower abdomen—at least I felt it there today. Everyone who has examined him feels he has a carcinoma of the pancreas pressing on the common bile duct."

"And what about treatment?"

"Well, we'd like to have him operated upon—just an exploratory, of course, to confirm the diagnosis. That is, if it meets with your approval."

"I know what you're saying," said the old man in a soft voice. "You're saying that I got cancer and you can't do anything about it. You'd think a hospital of this size could do something." He coughed a loose, old-man's cough.

"Did I say we couldn't?" said Rintman sternly.

"My children will act so sad when they hear the news," continued the patient, ignoring Rintman's last remark, "but it's going to be a relief to them just the same." He coughed again. "I don't know why it is that children always hold it against a parent for living too long. Is it my fault? Of course, in my case it means they have to come up to the home once a week, rain or shine, especially rain. A rainy day they must never miss." He smiled. "It shows how devoted they are. It means they got to bring me little things I don't want, and run little errands I never sent them on. It means they got to walk in with a big smile and say, 'Pop, you look great!' But the real smile doesn't come into their eyes until later, when they stand up and say, 'Sorry, Pop, but we have to go now!' And it means they got to make me out a bigger burden than I am. The funny part is that all I really want out of life now is to see a couple of ball games next spring."

"You'll never get to those ball games unless you let me examine you," said Rintman gently.

He took out his stethoscope and went over the patient, pulling his lower lid down at the end of the examination.

"He's not very anemic for a malignancy," he murmured.

But his mind was already working on something else, on a scent, this time a genuine scent, which was leading him to the faded bathrobe draped over the chair. To everyone's amazement he began to smell it all over, and as if this were not mystifying enough, to trace with his forefinger the faint rings on the flannel evidently left by amateur application of cleaning fluid. It was at this moment that the man coughed again. Rintman tilted the patient's chin and smelled his breath. He did not say anything, but his eyes glittered.

"Have you done a rectal?" he asked.

"Not yet," replied the House.

Rintman took off his coat and handed it to him with a reproachful glance, making a little ceremony afterward out of undoing his links and rolling up his stiff cuffs. By the time he was finished, a student nurse was standing in front of him holding out the rubber gloves every other doctor used when performing this procedure.

"What are you handing me these for?" Rintman asked. "How can I feel the bowel with gloves on?"

It was known around the Hospital that he never wanted anything between him and the rectum, not even rubber gloves. He held out his right forefinger toward the frightened nurse, who was now shaking so badly that most of the lubricant she squeezed out of the tube landed on the floor. Holding up his hand like a torch, a drop of jelly glistening on top of his extended finger, he gruffly ordered the patient to lie flat on his back, knees flexed and thighs spread far apart. As soon as the great internist pulled up the covers from the foot of the bed it became apparent why a Rintman rectal examination was recognized as a remarkable ritual. He pushed and stretched, grunted and clicked his tongue, glanced up at the ceiling and down at the floor, looking at one point, when the bedclothes reached his shoulders, like an old-time photographer about to take a picture under a cloth. Strangely enough, none of this violence was communicated to the patient, who lay flat on his back placidly staring at the wall. After a minute, Rintman worked himself loose and walked over to the sink at the end of the ward. When he returned to his retinue, he was already clicking his cuff links into his turned-down sleeves.

"Do you know what that mass is?" he whispered confidentially as the House Physician helped him on with his coat. "The one you felt?"

The intern had a premonition of disaster and said nothing.

Rintman's face grew even paler. "Stool!" he shouted. "That's what it is! Stool, pure and simple!" He lowered his voice and smiled his twisted smile. "That is, if stool can ever be pure or ever simple."

The dreadful silence was interrupted by the patient's

coughing. Rintman sat on the edge of the bed and took one of the old man's hands between his own.

"I must disagree with you, my friend," he said firmly. "I am sure you don't have cancer."

"Well, you're the great Dr. Rintman," the old man said. Rintman laughed. "This time I must agree with you."

The old man laughed, too. "That's why you are the great Dr. Rintman; you know when to agree and when to disagree."

Now everyone laughed.

"What are you doing for his cough, Doctor?" Rintman asked the House Physician, but his eyes never left the old man's face.

"I'm sorry, but I haven't given him anything. I guess this is one of those days when I can't do anything right."

A sly look came over the old man's face.

Rintman slid up toward the head of the bed. "What are you taking for your cough?" he asked like a fellow conspirator.

"You just heard," protested the old man. "They're not giving me anything."

"I know. But what are you *taking?* Maybe we could use it. We doctors don't know everything."

"You're sure you won't scold me?"

Rintman patted his hand. "Of course not. I only scold doctors."

The old man opened up the drawer of his bedside table and took out an unlabeled bottle half full of a clear, colorless liquid. Rintman pulled out the cork and smelled it.

"This isn't cough medicine. This is cleaning fluid," he said gravely.

The old man looked confused. "Is it?" he shook his head, bewildered. "Then, why did I take it?"

"Why *did* you?"

"I don't know." A strange look came into the man's eyes. "It smells like a cough medicine my mother used to give me when I was a little boy. Only, it couldn't be the same cough medicine. That was so long ago." He sighed, and added by way of apology,

"Anyway, I've only been taking it since they sent me to the home."

Rintman stood up and tapped him on the chest. "Do you know why you're sick, why you have the yellow jaundice, a big liver, and white stools? It's because of this." He pointed to the bottle. "Your nice cough medicine, the cleaning fluid in here, is a liver poison. Let's make an exchange. You give me the bottle, and I'll give you . . . your life."

He turned to the doctors who were now clustering around the bed. "This is undoubtedly Carbona, a cleaning fluid composed principally of carbon tetrachloride. Now, just think things over for a minute, gentlemen. How do we produce liver damage, liver destruction, in experimental animals, in guinea pigs and rabbits? Isn't it by giving them small daily doses of carbon tetrachloride, the standard liver toxin? What we have here is the reproduction of a classical animal experiment in a human being." He sighed and said, "I like this colorful old man. He has courage, imagination, and a sense of humor. He's stolen a little of the divine fire and, like Prometheus, he's having trouble with his liver."

He took out his blanks and wrote out a prescription with a big, black Waterman fountain pen.

"This is a cough medicine I have been very successful with in my private practice," he said to the old man, handing the paper to the head nurse at the same time. "You won't swallow any more cleaning fluid, will you?"

The old man shook his head.

"And you won't use my fashionable cough medicine to take the stains out of your bathrobe?"

"Never!" said the old man.

"If you keep those promises," Rintman continued, "I'll see that you get to the Polo Grounds next spring."

"Do you really think it's worthwhile saving an old man like me?"

"Especially an old man like you." Rintman looked around

the ward that had been so carefully preserved for seventy-five years. "You say you're old? So is McKinley Hospital."

He handed the House Physician the bottle of cleaning fluid. "There's your cancer of the pancreas," he said, and walked away, slowly.

To everyone's consternation, the old man climbed out of bed and put on his bathrobe. Rintman stopped and turned around when he heard the shuffling steps. The old man was trying to catch up with him. Everyone waited quietly.

"Thank you, Doctor, thank you," said the old man, standing up very straight. "It is *you* who have stolen the divine fire!"

The great internist bowed and walked briskly to the door. That was one thing about Rintman, everyone agreed. He knew when to ring down the curtain. As he crossed the threshold of the silent room, it was as if he were being ushered out by a thunderous applause.

Only the House Physician dared accompany him to his locker in the Doctors' Lounge.

"I'm sorry I pulled so many boners today," he said as he handed his chief the black Homburg and the Inverness cape.

"You'll learn. I wasn't built in a day."

The black Pierce-Arrow was waiting for him, the chauffeur already standing by the open door. He could never understand why the chief was always pale and drenched with sweat after the first Grand Rounds.

"The usual?" the chauffeur asked, as if he were a bartender.

Rintman nodded and climbed into the car. When they reached Central Park, he shivered and drew the Inverness cape around him. The auto rolled up the East Drive and came to a halt at a quiet spot just beyond the lake. It was illegal to stop here, but then the police always granted special privileges to the license plate with the lonely R. Rintman walked across the grass, sat down on a bench behind a bush, and put his face in his hands. Well, it had been a virtuoso performance all right, but, God, he had taken some awful chances. If anything had gone wrong, he would have looked like a posturing charlatan. He raised his head from his hands and smiled. But would he? A clinician's great diagnoses live after him, his mistakes are interred with his bones. Like a statesman's. Nobody cared about the times Babe Ruth struck out, but everybody remembered the homers. He sighed, and wondered how long he could keep up the bedside magic. Ten years? He would not ask for more. That was all he had left at McKinley. Then let it come—after him the deluge, the deluge of laboratory discoveries that would engulf and obliterate bedside medicine. He sat there for a few minutes, waiting until his hands stopped shaking. Then he took out his big, black Waterman and some three-by-five file cards, the foundation stones of his renowned memory, and made a note. There would be quite a to-do at the home next spring when the old man got his tickets for the Polo Grounds. How could such a famous man remember a little thing like that? they would say. He smiled. A man had to live up to his legend, didn't he? He took off his cape and walked to the car.

He looks better already, the chauffeur said to himself.

Rintman sank back against the cushions and picked up the phone. "The first consultation is at 993 Fifth Avenue," he said. The car was already in third.

TWO

As LONG AS they practiced medicine, which they hoped would be until the very day they died, Jim and Stanley felt that they would never forget the morning of July 1, 1933. It would be memorable not because of dramatic occurrences, but because it was the day they first reported to McKinley Hospital. When they entered the Superintendent's office, proud at being fifteen minutes early, they found the fourteen other interns already seated on camp stools in front of the desk. No one said a word. At precisely eight o'clock Mr. Stahlhelm sat down behind the desk with a sigh of disgust and took off his glasses, as if to indicate that although he had to talk to them at least he was not obliged to see them. Huge, ponderous, and loosely made, he had fierce, flickering eyes and a flame-tipped walrus mustache. He put his glasses in the top drawer of the desk and glared at the young doctors contemptuously like a lion tamer who had entered a cage full of pussycats by mistake.

"Interns are a dime a dozen," he began coldly, "but a good porter is hard to get. Since the medical schools accept only one out of every fifteen applicants, the men we get should be nonpareils. You obviously are not. Can you imagine what kind of doctors the rejected fourteen would have made if the medical schools had been less choosy?" Here he hunched his shoulders and shuddered as if he found the room too chilly. The interns, on the other hand, thought it uncomfortably hot.

"The rules for interns are simple," continued Mr. Stahlhelm. "Each of you will be off duty every other night and every other Sunday. On your nights off you are to be back in the Hospital by two in the morning—exactly. If we had to make a choice between your coming back at a quarter *past* two because you had been home in bed dreaming of the twelve apostles, or your returning here at a quarter *of* two after an evening of fornication, we would much prefer the latter. That is because we treasure promptness. Furthermore, although we do not care whom you sleep with, one of our major concerns is where you sleep and how long. Under no circumstances will we countenance your spending the entire night at home. You will not live part time at the Hospital and part time with your parents. We will not share you with any other institution, even the family. Your eleventh commandment is, 'Thou shalt have no other home but McKinley.'"

Everyone was impressed by the part about fornication. Most of the interns, including Jim and Stanley, were virgins; the rest, with small experience.

"Secondly," Mr. Stahlhelm continued, "we cannot have a married man on the intern staff. At the end of two years, you will receive your total accumulated back pay, twenty dollars, the exact price of a blood-pressure apparatus. With this in your pocket you may *then*, of course, marry if you wish. Not much of a salary, you think? Well, there will be people here who will feel that it is more than you are worth. Be that as it may, anyone who marries while he is an intern will upon discovery be summarily dismissed, receiving no credit for the time spent here even though he may have completed twenty-three of his twenty-four months. This means he will have to start all over again at another hospital, and probably not a very good one, since he will be both married and without a recommendation from us."

The audience was not disturbed. This was a lash stroke that had landed too far away to raise a welt. Marriage during an internship would have openly proclaimed to the world that the couple was being supported.

"Some years back," Mr. Stahlhelm went on, "a member of the house staff did get married. He was, of course, instantly discharged, and today," here his stolid face glowed with satisfaction, "is practicing in the suburbs!" He made it sound as if the former intern was working out of a shack on Devil's Island.

"Third, this Hospital was established for the treatment and care of the sick," the Superintendent said gravely, "not in order to provide you with an education. True, you have an obligation to learn, but our attendings are under no obligation to teach, especially the unwilling, the unpleasant, and the smug. For the intern who already knows everything, instruction is obviously unnecessary. For the rest, who at least have the grace to realize that they know nothing, it is a prize to be earned, not an inalienable right, like life, liberty, and the pursuit of happiness. Here you have one function only—to help the patients. Anything you learn is a by-product of this function. Nevertheless, he who serves us well will find to his delight that in the end he will have received an education which in depth and richness surpasses anything he believed possible in medical school. When you have completed your internships, do not ask, 'What have I gotten out of McKinley?' but rather, 'What have I done for her?' It is from those who ask the second question that our future attending staff will some day be chosen."

Mr. Stahlhelm rose. "You will report for duty at nine o'clock —precisely. I suggest that after consulting the bulletin board, you use the remaining time to acquaint yourselves with the Hospital." He smiled coldly. "There will be no guided tour."

By nine o'clock Jim and Stanley had seen very little of the Hospital, but it was enough to make them fall in love with it.

McKinley's five hundred beds filled the entire city block between Sixty-ninth and Seventieth streets and Park and Madison Avenues, a piece of real estate as valuable as any residential plot in the world, and one that was responsible for much of the Hospital's unique charm. Sister institutions must have chosen slum neighborhoods in order to make it easy for the poor to reach their doors, but McKinley, operating on a different principle, seemed to proclaim, "Make the effort! Travel a few blocks farther! Then you, like the rich, will live on Park Avenue, pampered by our nurses, guarded by our doctors, and warmed by the glow of our quiet elegance." Although a few trustees thought it cruel to introduce patients to such a heaven only to send them back to the tenements as soon as treatment was completed, most members of the board felt that nothing was too good for the poor—as long as they were sick.

The visitor's first impression on entering the Hospital was of an active, obtruding, militant cleanliness, a cleanliness that was no more a mere absence of dirt than valor is a mere absence of cowardice. Everywhere there was painting and touching up, mopping and scouring, dusting and polishing. A McKinley painter did not quick-spray a wall with one ear cocked for the twelve o'clock whistle. He used grave and measured strokes, and leaned back from time to time like an artist assessing his canvas. A McKinley charwoman did not do her floors with a mop. She got down on her hands and knees and scrubbed until the hard wood glowed with an antique patina. And a McKinley porter did not wipe a doorknob as if it were venetian glass. He rubbed until the brass took on a martial air. Cleanliness was everywhere, intangible yet powerful like Time. It was McKinley's fourth dimension.

Originally founded by wealthy Germans, among them those great brewers of New York who had had the imagination seventy-five years before to buy inexpensive land that the northward growth of the city had made priceless, the Hospital had been officially christened the Allgemeines Krankenhaus, an unwieldy name that the staff, the patients, the personnel, and even the inhabitants of neighboring Yorkville had long since changed unofficially to "the German Hospital." Only, since most of them had an accent, they did not pronounce it that way. They called it "the Sherman Hospital."

In 1917, when war was declared against Germany, the telltale title, Allgemeines Krankenhaus and anything like it had to go. The Hospital was renamed "McKinley," not after the President but after the mountain, and not because it was the highest peak in North America, but because it was far away and non-controversial. Rintman often said that they should have named it the Sherman Hospital, since everyone was used to calling it that anyway, and Sherman was a non-controversial figure, up North at least. In those days everybody agreed that war was hell.

Seen from above, McKinley was a hollow square with a small courtyard inside. Medically it was as solid as a rock. And that was exactly what the interns called it—the Rock. The great German clinicians of the previous generation had had their own private pet name for the Hospital—pretentious, perhaps, but certainly affectionate. They called it, only among themselves of course, Valhalla, not because of the obvious implication that they were the gods of medicine, although they were certainly that, the old German gods of the medical world, but simply because they felt that their Hospital was *fit* to be the home of the gods. But although every one of them had heard the *Ring*, sat through *Götterdämmerung*, seen the flames, none of them for one moment believed that their Valhalla would ever be engulfed by that deepening twilight. They would die, they knew, but what they had taught would never perish. Others would arise from their loins, created in their image, others through whom they would pass the sperm of their immortal knowledge, others indistinguishable from themselves, medically divine, who would abide in Valhalla forever. So they thought.

There was Frederick Treuler, the founder of thoracic surgery, who built a negative-pressure room on the third floor of the main building the better to operate on his chest cases. Frederick the Great, they called him, after the Kaiser pinned the decoration on his chest at Potsdam. "A meeting of the two emperors!" the American ambassador had said, but softly. There was Wilhelm Gerhardt, the Director, or rather the Czar, of the Medical Service, a pioneer in gastroenterology and the first man to pass a tiny bucket from the mouth into the intestine. People used to come to him from all over the civilized and even the uncivilized world (he used to say that sometimes he found it hard to tell the difference between the two) for diagnosis and treatment. His fees were so high that he was able to bequeath a million dollars to the Hospital. And there was Hauser's predecessor, after whom the children's pavilion was named. Imprisoned in Germany during the Revolution of 1848 because of his enlightened views, he escaped to New York, where he founded the specialty of pediatrics. When, thirty years later, the most treasured of all prizes, the incomparable Professorship at Berlin was laid at his feet, he rejected it, preferring the country of his rebirth to the country of his birth, the land that had offered him the company of its children to the land that had introduced him to the loneliness of a prison cell. But principally he refused this, the most important of all university chairs, because he could not bear to tear himself away from the hospital he loved so well, a bit of New York earth, a group of buildings, a hollow square—his Valhalla.

All this, Jim knew. He had heard his father recite Tales of McKinley too often ever to forget. And if music had been needed, his mother certainly could have supplied it—Wagner, of course, not Offenbach. Stanley, too, was familiar with the history of the Hospital, having learned it from Dr. Morelle

33

over the dining-room table during those wonderful roast beef Thursdays in the house on 122nd Street.

Both of them also knew that an internship was a stern discipline. Before the young doctor could assume his houseship in the second year of McKinley's two-year rotating program, he had to serve as a junior for the first six months and a senior for the second. A junior was a slave. What few technicians there were remained rooted to the laboratory and never came down to the ward to help the new men with their routine tasks. Blood counts and urine analyses, chores that today are everywhere performed by paid female workers, were then done by the overworked juniors, who realized quite well that the thousands of such examinations they would have to struggle through in their first half year could not possibly benefit them later in their careers. This was scut work, pure exploitation, and one of the bitter facts of medical life every new doctor had to face. That the scut work plus emergency duties left him very little time to sleep was of no interest to the attendings, who assumed that he had come to McKinley not to sleep but to work and keep his mouth shut. Especially to keep his mouth shut. On rounds he was not supposed to express an opinion about a patient or a disease but only to have memorized the clinical and laboratory data in all the bedside charts so thoroughly that he could recite a piece of information contained in any of them the moment it was requested. Although some of the charts were an inch and a half thick, it was considered worse than cheating at cards to peek inside to answer an attending's question. The first six months were evidently designed to humble the recent medical-school graduate. But a year would make dictators of the oppressed. The gulf between a house man and a junior was as great as the one between a junker lieutenant and a Pomeranian cadet.

One evening in August, after a day devoted entirely to blood counts, the two friends confronted each other after supper across a small table in the interns' dining room.

"Can you knock off now?" asked Jim, picking up a piece of pound cake.

"Knock off! I've got twenty bottles full of urine sitting next to the sink. Some of them must have been there for two days."

Jim nodded. "Me too. My place looks like the Liebfraumilch wine cellars." He got up and walked away munching his pound cake.

At ten o'clock, when he entered the room he shared with Stanley, he found his friend lying on top of the bed staring at the ceiling. He walked over to him.

"It didn't smell like Liebfraumilch when I got those bottles open. I think I'll take a shower."

He came back in his shorts with a towel slung over his shoulders looking just the way he used to when he climbed into the ring at Stillman's. Stanley was still staring at the ceiling. Jim walked over to him again and looked down.

"It's not like the day you won the Intercollegiates, is it, Stan?"

For the first time, Stanley smiled, thinking of the way his flat forehand drives had flicked the chalk lines, and of how he had gone to the net after his first serve to put the ball away in the corners. And of Mr. Huegenon, to whom he had sent the best seat in the stadium, looking down at him with cold, satisfied eyes.

"I didn't see a patient all day; just fingers, Jim, fingers. Over and over again I kept saying, 'This finger, please. The fourth finger is the one you use the least. And I'll stick you just once.'" He struck his head. "Just once! One poor bastard I had to stick three times. He just wouldn't bleed."

"You should have come with me if you wanted clinical experience. I saw an operation." He paused for effect. "A nurse cut a patient's toenails."

"I can see that it's going to be tough getting ahead in this place. Look at your father. Handsome as a king, a born diagnostician, the poor-man's Rintman, and where did it get him?

After fifteen years he's still a third-class citizen around here, doing scut work in the dispensary until the end of his days."

"My mother thinks it's because of an interview he had with Rintman long ago. He never talks about it. There's one thing you can be sure of. They won't appoint a Harlem general practitioner to the medical service at McKinley."

"Why didn't he become a specialist?" asked Stanley.

"Because it takes training to become a specialist. And training means time off from work. He's been a good breadwinner and I've had the best, but on what he earned and what he spent on us he couldn't save a nickel." Jim looked away. "My mother hasn't helped much either. She loves him. She's beautiful, a music and literature buff beyond compare. She's wonderful, but she just isn't worldly. She's not a schemer. It would have been totally beyond her to do the entertaining and socializing necessary to ease him into a fashionable practice."

"Maybe. But if you don't get ahead at McKinley, you won't be able to blame it on heredity. Or on environment, either. That house on 122nd Street where you were raised still seems like paradise on earth to me."

"Sure. I'm explaining, not kicking. I couldn't have chosen better if I had had my parents made to order. 'Only the brave deserve the fair' must have been written in their honor." He chuckled. "I'll never forget the day the drug addict came to the office on 122nd Street, pulled out a gun, and ordered Pop to give him an injection of morphine. My father nodded, went to the medicine cabinet, and pulled out apomorphine instead, his favorite drug for making poison victims vomit. Using his thumb to cover the first three letters of the word 'APOMORPHINE' on the label of the bottle, he showed it to the man, who, seeing only 'MORPHINE,' growled, 'Hurry up, Doc.' Pop gave him a stiff injection of the emetic, and after he started to throw up, disarmed him. It took Dad fifteen minutes to clean up the mess. Then he gave the man a grain of morphine by mouth so he wouldn't go into a cold-turkey convulsion, paid him ten dollars for the revolver, and sent him to a rehabilitation center. And the man went."

There was a sharp knock at the open door. They both looked up, nettled by the interruption. A stocky intern in a sharply creased, fresh white uniform was standing on the threshold.

"I'm Aims Blair, the House Obstetrician," he announced, as if he were introducing Kitchener of Khartoum.

Born in Calcutta, where his father was the American consul, Aims had been exposed to the English language as spoken by storybook Englishmen for the first thirteen years of his life. Although the same age as Jim and Stanley, he looked ten years older with his square, florid, perfectly shaved face, expressionless blue eyes, bristly brown mustache, and glazed brown hair that had one searching for the gray streaks that were not yet there. So short that he had to tilt up his chin when conversing in the Hospital corridors, he managed to give the impression that he was looking over everyone's head. His very shortness served him as an advantage, however, because his low-slung, broad-shouldered, shield-chested physique let you know at once that he would not be easily overturned. When he came toward a group of people with that slow, measured tread, they got the irrational feeling that there was nothing in the world that could stop him. His father had once remarked that when he saw his son marching down the street, he was reminded of the old British hollow square, which, indifferent to grapeshot and musketry, continually re-formed without losing a step and pressed inexorably onward until the enemy threw down their weapons and fled. But Aims's most striking characteristic was his elegant diction, especially his "r's," his beautiful "r's," or rather their emphasized absence. When he announced, "My name is Blay-uh," the name had two syllables and ended in a soft, deep sigh of an "uh." If someone had said, "Heard 'r's' are sweet but those unheard are sweeter," he would

37

have replied, "Isn't that from the 'Ode to a Grecian Uhhhhn'?" His parents, whose New England diction had been exposed too late to anglicizing influences in India, were as impressed as everyone else by their son's. They did everything they could to insure his worldly success, sending him to the right schools and exposing him to the right people. Although never rich, they took good care to act as if they were, and this more for his sake than for their own.

After many years abroad, Mr. Blair, a career diplomat, was transferred to Washington, where he held a moderately important position in the State Department. But Aims never forgot Calcutta, and still treated people with a good-natured lordliness, as if they were natives back in India. Although on the surface he was a hail fellow well met, a good sport and a good mixer, in the depths was a hard, unfissionable core of well-thought-out snobbishness. He felt that the more people you knew, the more you could manipulate; the more friends you had, the more favors you could ask; the larger your circle, the larger your influence. He was determined that his influence would someday be great. No one could deny that he had the tools, a State Department background, a perfect diction, and an intuitive ability to assess a man's worth—by his own standards, of course.

"Are the P and S hotshots on exhibit?" he asked, as he walked into the room in his slow, unstoppable way.

"We're on exhibit to anyone who doesn't order a blood count," answered Jim.

"I rarely do," said Aims. "A house man who has to lean on the laboratory is a pretty weak sister. When you're struggling with a breech delivery, a blood count doesn't help you very much. When the backside comes out first instead of the head, that's reality, boys, not theory."

He sat down heavily, careful not to mar the crease in his trousers by crossing his legs. "Theory and the laboratory go together like two wallflowers waltzing around the floor. The trouble with medical schools is that they are theory-wise and practice-foolish. You know that the Chinese say one picture is worth a thousand words. Well, for an intern, one operation is worth a thousand books. According to the schools, if it isn't in the books, it doesn't exist. But although those sanctimonious bastards know all about their scientific heaven, there are more things on earth than are dreamt of in their philosophy, Horatio."

"The name is Jim."

Aims chuckled indulgently. "Well, I'm no Hamlet." Suddenly his manner changed. "We've got a little dossier on you two boys, all about your academic didos at P and S. I'm afraid you're in for a comedown here. Honor men always are. You might as well learn right now that AOA keys are just considered costume jewelry in these quarters."

He picked up a pencil from the desk and held it like a swagger stick.

"You think they gave you all the answers in medical school, don't you? Just let me ask you a question to see how good you are."

He put the pencil down. "What is the first sign of recovery in a man getting over an operation?"

Jim and Stanley regarded him stonily.

"Don't look so surprised," he said, misinterpreting their expression. "An obstetrician knows a few things about men, too. Doesn't obstetrics start in the testicle? Well, to get back to the question. You'd know the man was on the road to recovery after his operation when he started to get morning erections again. There's something you won't find in the textbooks."

He picked up the pencil again, and finally crossed his legs, taking good care that the creases were not mussed. "I learned that from an old man on the ward. It's quite a story."

Aims had noticed that many of the obstetricians told dirty stories while they were in the Hospital. And that they told more than any of the other specialists. Just as little boys who play

39

only with girls fear that other little boys will regard them as sissies, so specialists who treat only women have similar misgivings about their colleagues' attitudes. That was why, Aims felt, so many of the obstetricians took refuge in the genital joke, the scatological skit, the slightly husky voice, and the hard-boiled manner, all of which when kneaded together made an excellent mask of virility.

Rintman had once said that no one must try harder to be a man than he who sits forever between a woman's thighs. Less than a hundred years ago, he had emphasized, such an occupation was deemed fit only for a midwife.

"Once when I was a senior on the surgical service," continued Aims, as if it were during the time of Hippocrates instead of two months previously, "an old man who had had his gall bladder out a couple of weeks before, called me over to his bed and said, 'Doctor,' and by the way, gentlemen, never let them call you 'Doc,' 'Doctor,' he said, 'I'm well now. Do you know how I can tell?' I shook my head. 'I had a hard-on when I woke up this morning,' he went on, 'the first one in two weeks. I been operated before, and when I start getting hard-ons every morning I know I'm on my way.'

"A faraway look came into the old man's eyes. 'When I was a young feller, we used to have a farm up by Honesdale.'"

Aims turned to Stanley and interpolated pleasantly, "That's excellent dairy country, but I don't imagine you'd know that, Levinson. None of your folks were ever farmers, I daresay."

To Stanley, who was as sensitive to an anti-Semitic insult as litmus paper to acid, this was like saying, "I don't blame you fellows for going in for usury. You certainly couldn't have gone in for farming. You'd have had one hell of a time tripping over your kaftans in the country."

He grew pale, and Jim frowned.

"The old man seemed to be getting interesting," Aims continued, "so I pulled a chair close to his bed and sat down. "'When I was maybe sixteen, seventeen,' the old codger confided with a reminiscent glow, 'I'd wake up early in the summer while it was still dark, pull on a shirt and a pair of pants, and nurse a good hard-on all the way to the barn. And while I was sitting on the stool, I wasn't thinking of no *cow's* tits, neither. After I finished milking I'd stand up in the half light, fill out my chest, and lift up the pail. You ever tried to lift a full milk pail, Doctor? Well, never mind. I'd lift it up and hang it on my old bazook, right through the pants and everything, and you know what, Doctor, you know what? I'd never spill a drop. And I'll tell you something else. When I was fifty-one, I went back to the farm one summer right after I had my appendix out. My younger brother and the kids were running the place then. I sneaked out to the barn one morning about five to do a little milking and a little experimenting and, by George, the old bazook could still hold up a good half a pail of milk without it slipping off. And I'll tell you something else. The way I'm feeling today, and I'm seventy-five, it's good enough to hold up a quarter of a pail, any morning!' "

No one said a word. After a moment's pointed silence, Stanley looked up and asked, "Where do you fit in, Blair? Are you the tenth-of-a-pail type?"

"You're wrong, Stan," said Jim, turning toward his friend, "completely wrong. He's strictly a Lily-cup man, one paper cup—empty."

Aims's ruddy face grew a little more plethoric. "It's a pity, gentlemen, that you had to read the Declaration of Independence in school. You evidently were overly impressed by the part that said all men were created equal, a palpable absurdity to anyone who has ever delivered a Mongolian idiot. But even you must admit that all men don't remain equal. A junior is not the equal of a house man, a fact you are bound to discover before long."

He uncrossed his knees and stood up. "The sooner you get those rough edges worn off," he counseled, "the better off you'll be." He walked to the door.

"Thanks for all the wise precepts, Dr. Polonius," said Jim. "And here is one for you. Never hide behind an arras. Somebody will sure as hell run you through."

As soon as Aims was halfway down the hall, Stan said, "Now that we've antagonized that bastard, I suppose they'll give us the works."

But the reverse was destined to be true. On the following afternoon a case would be admitted that would catapult them to the attention of the entire Hospital.

THREE

At four in the afternoon the admitting office sent the woman up to Female Three with a note from Emmerich, then one of the greatest surgeons in the world, to prep her for operation the following morning. She was a lady, and obviously out of place on the ward, but on her librarian's salary she could hardly have been expected to pay for a private room with nurses around the clock.

Too humane to accept her on a charity basis, the administration set her rate at ten dollars a week, all medical expenses included. It was clear that she had devoted a great deal of thought to getting ready for the Hospital. Her light-blue, out-of-date velvet dress was obviously her best; her blue-felt cloche hat was of an old but elegant design; and her blue shoes, cut from good Italian leather, looked as if they had been polished a thousand times. Only her accessories were new, a suede bag and suede gloves, both jet black. There was a peculiarly disturbing atmosphere of neatness about her. Although she was a walking lint trap, not a fleck could anywhere be seen. That was because she had been sitting at home among her clothes, a pathetic Lorelei in reverse, brushing, just brushing, while she mused over the suddenness with which her own life had gone on the rocks in Emmerich's office.

The nurses guessed that she was in her late forties. Actually she was a tense thirty-five. After helping her undress and get into bed, the head nurse slumped into a chair in the treatment room and said, "Poor thing!" The patient was clearly that—since all she had in the world was one hundred and eighty-four dollars in the East River Savings Bank and a cancer of the left breast.

Jim was called to take the history. The woman was sitting up in bed, prim hands on her lap, staring straight ahead with a well-bred smile. It turned out to be a difficult history, not because it was complicated, but because, although she answered all his questions politely enough, she volunteered no information at all. She was either dried up, he thought, or else desperately holding herself in, perhaps even trying to hold her cancer in, lest it break through its wavering bonds and destroy her. But he dismissed these thoughts as figures of speech. There must be something else.

The history proceeded slowly. When had she first noticed the lump? Four months ago. Why hadn't she gone to a doctor earlier? Well, you know how those things are. Had it grown much? No. Hurt her? No. Had she lost any weight? No. Had she had any cough or pain in the back? No. Were her parents alive? No. What had they died of? Her father had died of cancer of the stomach. When? When she was fifteen. And her mother? Of cancer of the breast. When? Six months ago. Had any other relatives had cancer? No. How did she feel as compared to a year ago? Quite well, thank you. Had she ever been married? No. Did she live with relatives? No, alone. She had lived with her mother until her death. Did she have any questions? No, thank you, none at all.

Jim had a floor nurse move the screen around the bed before he examined the woman. Her breasts were small, with pale little nipples, and there was no asymmetry. But in the upper, outer quadrant on the left side he could feel a hard, walnut-sized mass, foreign and ominous. Even so, if there were no axillary nodes, he said to himself as he slid his hand into her armpit, she would have a chance. He encountered none. The remainder of the physical examination was completely negative.

"The mass is localized and you don't have involvement of the glands under your arm," he informed her as the nurse helped her put on her hospital nightgown. "It's going to sound strange to you, but you're a very lucky woman."

She smiled her meaningless smile. "Oh, I know." But she did not seem particularly interested. Then she added with a cheerful irrelevancy, "Everyone seems to be so pleasant in this hospital. Are you all trained to behave this way?"

He leaned over and whispered, "I could mention a few people around here who must be out of training, but you'll probably never meet them."

There was a book on the bedside table, which he glanced at, less out of curiosity than to learn something about the woman's tastes. On the female wards the reading matter was pretty much limited to foreign-language newspapers, the *Ladies' Home Journal* and *The Saturday Evening Post*. To his surprise he saw that she was reading *Leaves of Grass*. As he reached for it with a perfunctory "Do you mind if I look?" the hitherto polite creature brought her hand down and shook her head.

"I'm very sorry," he apologized, staring into her frightened eyes.

"It's perfectly all right," she answered, recovering quickly and smiling. But she kept her hand firmly clasped on the book.

That night at ten, when he went to Female Three to do a blood count, he stopped near her bed for a moment. She was sitting up, reading her *Leaves of Grass* with a terrible, twisted smile on her face.

For the rest of the evening he could not drive her from his mind. When he went to bed at midnight in the room he shared with Stanley in the interns' quarters, he decided to tell his friend about the case.

"What disturbs me, Stan," he concluded, "is that she doesn't seem at all interested in the operation or the results of the operation. But she has made up her mind about something, for sure."

Stanley shrugged and turned out the light.

At two o'clock in the morning, the muted buzzing of the telephone jolted Jim out of a sodden sleep. He listened for a moment and then said sharply, "Now, how can that be! I just saw her a little while ago." But he added that he would be down as soon as he could get his clothes on.

"How can what be?" asked Stanley, turning on the light.

"Some nurse thinks the woman in Female Three is unconscious."

"Unconscious! How can she be unconscious?" asked Stanley, sitting bolt upright in bed. "She was perfectly all right a couple of hours ago, wasn't she?"

"Of course. I saw her."

"How come they call you for a thing like this? All of a sudden you're promoted from blood counts?"

"The House Surgeon and the Senior are doing a perforated gastric ulcer in the O.R."

Stanley lay down again. "Call me if you need a shot of brains."

Jim raced for the old hydraulic elevator, buttoning his white clerical collar on the way. The floating-bubble ride only intensified the night's unreality, but when the heavy, open-work metal gate slid back and he rushed through, the true situation hit him. It was impossible, simply impossible. No cancer ever acted this way. Maybe he had overlooked something. Well, what? The physical examination had been completely negative. The heart? Normal, and there was no pain. How about a stroke? At thirty-five, with a low blood pressure, no headaches, and soft radial arteries? He shook his head. All at once he re-

46

alized that he was only a few steps from Female Three. He stopped running, opened the door, and walked, through the silent ward, the block-long parquet boulevard with the twenty-five evenly spaced beds on each side, in what he hoped was a dignified manner.

The patients were sleeping quietly, but there was one who slept more deeply than all the rest. Attached to an enema stand, a naked electric light bulb bathed her and the nurses clustered around her in the disenchanting illumination a theater-goer sees backstage at the end of a performance. She was unconscious, all right, responding not at all when he shook her by the shoulders, slapped her cheeks and called out her name. Suddenly it dawned upon him that she had stopped breathing. For interminable seconds he stood there and stared, paralyzed by disbelief. When finally she took a short, shallow breath, he breathed, too. Only then did he break loose from his lethargy and time her respiratory rate. It was an impossible five to the minute and getting slower all the time. As he feared, the physical and neurological examinations he rushed through, helped by nurses who turned the woman on her side and then on her back again, told him nothing. He asked one of them to ring Stanley.

His friend got there so fast that Jim knew he must have dressed the moment he was alone. The first thing he said when he saw the woman and heard about the physical examination was, "How about poison?"

"In front of forty-nine patients and five nurses!" exclaimed Jim. "And where would she get it?"

But he went through the drawers of her bedside table very carefully just the same. There was nothing at all. By this time, the head nurse, who had run out when she heard the word "poison," came rushing back again.

"I went through her clothes and her handbag, Doctor, and I couldn't find a thing. Not a vial or a bottle. Nothing."

But Jim was not listening. "She doesn't look good, Stan,"

he said staring at the woman's lips, which were now turning blue. "She's getting cyanotic!"

Stan nodded and raised her upper lids. "Boy, are her pupils clamped down!"

Jim bent over the woman and all at once thought of the story his mother had told him when he was a boy—the story of how his father had disarmed the man with the pin-point pupils. "And when Father saw the man's pin-point pupils," she would say, lingering on the alliterative phrase, "he knew."

"That's it, Stan," he cried, unable to control the excitement in his voice. "Pin-point pupils, depressed breathing, and unconsciousness. Someone gave her an overdose of morphine, and it must have been a pip!"

"That's it," said Stanley grimly.

Jim turned to the head nurse. "Who did it? Because whoever gave her that injection pulled a terrible boner."

"Maybe I can help you, Doctor."

He looked around and saw the Night Supervisor, blond, statuesque, and amazingly big-bosomed, a Brünnhilde with a built-in shield.

"I hope so," he said. "We're not blaming anybody. We don't want to pin anything on anybody. We just want to verify the diagnosis so we can go ahead and treat her."

The Supervisor took all the nurses to the center table for a brief inquisition, and then ran through their notes on the chart.

"She's had no morphine, no medication at all, Doctor," she said, shaking her head.

Jim sighed. "Now where do we go?"

She caressed his inexperience with her tired eyes.

"Maybe you ought to call Dr. Emmerich," suggested Stanley.

"At two-thirty in the morning?" Jim glanced apprehensively at the patient. "Besides, I don't think we're going to have much time."

They looked hard at each other for a few seconds. "O.K., let's go," said Jim. "What have we got to lose?"

"Only her life if we're wrong."

"We ought to look for needle marks."

They searched her arms and thighs, but there were none. "It's still morphine," said Jim quietly. He turned to the nurse. "I'll have to wash out her stomach while one of you gives her a hot coffee enema." He looked at Stan. "Would you mind writing an order for caffeine and camphor by hypo? And make them step on it, Stan."

Stanley whipped out his gold Waterman, a Bar Mitzvah present from Uncle Yosh, and wrote the orders while two student nurses looked over his shoulder and then rushed off. That was one thing you had to say for Uncle Yosh. Irreligious, yes, but he certainly gave wonderful presents. Stanley stood up to hurry the nurses, but they were already boiling the syringes. When he returned to the patient, the stomach washing and the hot coffee enema were in progress. "Poor thing!" he said, looking at her sadly. "She's getting it from both ends."

"She didn't even gag when I passed the stomach tube," said Jim.

As soon as the two procedures were completed, they turned the woman on her back. She had stopped breathing.

"She's very blue!" the head nurse called out in alarm.

A continuous murmur could now be heard from the other patients in the ward.

Jim vaulted onto the bed, straddled the woman's hips, and began artificial respiration. Twenty times a minute, through stiff arms and outstretched palms, he leaned against her motionless ribs, and twenty times a minute as he straightened up, the decompression of her chest sucked air into her empty lungs. Stanley was already in the supply room wrestling with an oxygen tank as tall as he. Nothing is quite as unmanageable as an oxygen tank when you're in a hurry, he thought. By tipping it gently on one edge he tried to roll it straight ahead, but succeeded only in making it veer hopelessly from side to side. Fortunately a student nurse appeared from out of the darkness to take the other side of the tank between her hands. Suddenly expert, the two steered the tank to the head of the bed, where the head nurse was waiting with a moistened rubber catheter. Only too aware that he had never performed this procedure before, Stanley pushed the tube quickly through the woman's nostril until it almost touched the pharynx behind. The instant this was done, the nurse anchored the catheter to the patient's cheek with a strip of adhesive tape, attached the open end to the gauge, and turned on the oxygen.

For the next few minutes Jim rocked back and forth with the precision of a crewman, while the patients, now sitting up in bed or propped on their elbows, watched the ghostly regatta. Even the least imaginative felt that Death was in the other boat.

"She's not doing any breathing by herself," said Jim, "but she seems a little less blue. Or is it my imagination?"

"She's definitely less blue," announced Stanley. He looked up at his friend on top of the bed. "We'll alternate every half hour, O.K.? You've got twenty-two minutes left."

Jim nodded.

"How long can you keep this up?" asked the Night Supervisor.

"Until she regains consciousness or dies," answered Jim.

"Don't the police have a pulmotor for emergencies like this?"

"If we used a pulmotor on this woman, we'd blow a hole in her lung." He paused. "Let's try another shot of caffeine."

The head nurse ran out and returned with a hypodermic syringe and needle, which she snapped into the patient's thigh as if she were playing a game of darts.

At the end of thirty minutes, Stanley tapped Jim on the shoulder and said, "Do you mind if I cut in?"

For the first time, Jim smiled. They managed to exchange positions without losing the rhythm of the procedure.

After he had worked on the woman for a quarter of an hour, Stanley called out, "She just took her first breath."

Jim walked over and looked down at her. "It's like the first breath of spring."

"With birds."

Soon the woman was taking an occasional breath without help, and some of the tension in the room lifted. The Supervisor raised her Wagnerian-soprano head, said something sharply, and the student nurses all left the glare of the spotlight and faded into the darkness. She, herself, did not remain much longer.

"I feel like a heel opening this," Jim confided as he sat down next to the bedside table and reached for *Leaves of Grass*.

He began to turn the pages carefully, one by one. In the dead center was a two-inch-long paper packet folded meticulously as if by a pharmacist. It looks like a Dover's powder, Jim thought. Then he saw the white crystals.

"Stan!" he called out so urgently that his friend stopped the artificial respiration for the first time. "Here it is!"

Stanley leaned over and looked at the powder. "She couldn't attempt suicide at home on her own time," he lamented. "Oh, no. She had to come to the Hospital for that, and pick our night on."

He went back to the artificial respiration.

"I'm going to sample it," mumbled Jim, touching his little finger to the tip of his tongue.

"Don't be an idiot!" shouted Stanley.

But Jim transferred a granule to his tongue. "It's got that bitter alkaloid taste. It must be morphine."

"Save the rest for the lab," said Stanley, looking down at the woman, who was quite pink by now.

Twenty minutes later, the House Surgeon walked in, sweat-soaked operating-room jacket clinging to his body, his face white with fatigue. Jim told him what had happened.

"Dr. Emmerich hates to cancel an operation," said the House, "but somebody will have to tell him."

"Are you going to call him now?" inquired Jim politely.

The House Surgeon gave a bitter laugh. "Am *I* going to call him—at half past three in the morning? *You're* going to call him. She's your patient." He left without looking back.

"I'm glad I'm on the medical service," said Stanley, continuing with his task.

Jim walked to the center and picked up the telephone. Emmerich's "hello" was a little testy but he said nothing during Jim's concise report. There was a long pause at the end. Then the famous surgeon said, "No one could have done more," and hung up.

By now the woman was breathing on her own, three or four times a minute, but an ominous complication had appeared. Each time she took a breath, a dreadful rattling issued from her throat. Jim took out his stethoscope, listened to her chest, and shook his head. The gurgling was caused by a collection of mucous and saliva, and every minute it grew louder and more terrifying.

"She's drowning in her own secretions," said Stanley.

"I'm afraid if we don't get suction to her, she's through," said Jim, taking off for the operating room, which fortunately was on the same floor.

"O.K., O.K.!" said the instrument nurse wearily, as he burst through the door. "We've canceled the operation already. How is the crackpot?"

"Punk. She's choking to death." He began to push the suction machine toward the door. "Is it all right to take this out?"

"Don't you know we've got A.C. here and D.C. on the wards?"

He looked around desperately and saw a big coil of rubber tubing, a hose, in fact, resting in the corner. "How long is that?"

"Two hundred feet."

"I hope to God it reaches."

"It will," she replied calmly, opening up the medicine cabinet and giving him the suction tip.

He handed her one end of the tubing, and then played it out rapidly, walking backward all the way to Female Three. She had been right. When he reached the woman's bed, there were five feet left over.

"Tell them to turn it on!" he called out to one of the student nurses.

Before he had the metal tip securely in place, her footsteps were already fading away toward the operating room. There was an agonizing wait. Stanley sighed, and suddenly as if echoing his sigh the blessed hiss of suction was heard in the room. Jim pulled the woman's jaw down and slid the tip far back into her throat, moving it gently from side to side. She did not gag or swallow, but immediately the rattling stopped.

All through the night they worked over the woman, exchanging positions regularly every half hour. Sometimes she breathed well for a few minutes, so they could suspend artificial respiration; at other times continuous resuscitation was necessary. But she remained pink, and they were finally able to remove the oxygen catheter.

Just before dawn they had a strange visitor, the oldest nurse on the registry, who had taken the long trip from the private pavilion in order to borrow some milk of magnesia for her sleeping patient. Since age had slowed her movements and robbed her of strength, she was regularly assigned to convalescent patients who slept soundly through the night. Pushing one foot ahead of the other as if caught in a great snowdrift, she entered Female Three just as Jim was bending over the woman, his hands perilously close to her breasts.

"In my day," the old nurse thought to herself, horrified but excited, "this would have been impossible. No doctor connected with German Hospital would have gotten into bed with a female patient, much less on top of her."

She plodded over to the bed and stared into Jim's face, which was outlined by the droplight on the enema stand. Then, to his amazement, she patted him gently on the cheek and said, "My apologies. With a face like that you could do no wrong."

In a moment she was gone, plowing through her private snowdrifts toward the milk of magnesia at the end of the ward.

By now the woman's color was so good that suction was rarely necessary, and artificial respiration was suspended for increasingly longer intervals. At exactly seven, the day shift came on and the ward was flooded with nurses. Jim looked up, and to his surprise saw that the bulb on the enema stand had been taken away. It was sunlight that was shining into his eyes. A swelling tide of conversation engulfed him. The night nurses, too possessive to leave the field of victory, insisted on telling and retelling the story of the attempted suicide; the day nurses, too inquisitive to go about their ordinary assignments, insisted on asking and reasking probing questions; and the patients, too thrilled to wash themselves or have their temperatures taken, insisted on reliving the night's excitement. The noise continued for a few minutes in a steeply mounting crescendo, and then suddenly ceased as if a giant hand had been clamped over the mouth of the ward. Jim glanced up and saw Emmerich standing in the doorway. Patients and nurses froze as if they were children playing a game of "statues." Ignoring them, the illustrious surgeon walked briskly to the head of the bed and observed the woman's breathing for a minute.

"Schwester!" he called out without taking his eyes off the patient. The head nurse came running up. "I want specials put on this case around the clock. The Hospital will pay."

He darted a glance at Jim and Stanley. "And I want you two to stay here until you are relieved."

He walked away without another word. Just before he reached the door, he turned, arm raised, two fingers extended, looking, thought Jim, a little like the statue of Augustus in the old mythology book, and snapped, "I'm going to take her breast off next week, just the same."

Then he was gone. For a few seconds no one uttered a sound,

but almost at once the hubbub broke out again. Jim turned and saw Aims Blair standing near him, straight, stocky, and very British, mustache bristling, blue eyes sparkling, a wide smile lighting up his face—his blue-eyed smile, his mother called it, adding that it was reserved for important people. He looked as if he were ready this very minute, Jim thought, to join forces with Clive and help destroy the Nawab in the mango grove at Plassey.

"I think you engineered all this, Morelle," he said with a chuckle, "just to get out of doing blood counts." Then he gave Stanley a junior version of the blue-eyed smile, said, "Good work," and walked out.

"At least he didn't say, 'Good work, *men*,'" said Stanley as he climbed upon the bed to take his turn.

In half an hour, as soon as they had exchanged places again, everyone was electrified by a strange newcomer. Looking a little like a soubrette out of *Fledermaus*, a maid in a black satin uniform and a lacy apron sailed in carrying breakfast on a silver-laden tray, which she deposited on the center table as if such service were an everyday occurrence on the ward. In response to her insistent "Bitte," Stanley sat down, sure that he was hallucinating until he saw the Old English "E" on every piece of silver. The patients were quiet now, watching the performance as if they were witnessing the birth of a baby. Next, she served him a glass of orange juice in a silver bowl packed with shaved ice. Rising melodramatically to the occasion, he lifted the glass toward the unconscious woman and drained it at a single draught. It was a hot day, and an appreciative "Ah!" went up from the audience. When he looked down, the silver bowl was gone and the maid was putting a plate of bacon and scrambled eggs in its place. She poured the coffee, added cream, and even buttered the toast, which had been concealed in another linen napkin on the side. Only after he had drunk a second cup of coffee did she reluctantly pick up her things and leave. Twenty minutes later, she was back with another

55

breakfast. As Jim sat down, he noticed a letter next to the silver bowl, but when he picked it up, the maid intervened.

"Please, everything will get cold."

"This wouldn't get cold in a week," he said, waving away the steam; but he put down the envelope.

Jim, too, had to drink a second cup of coffee before she would leave. Only then did he dare stand up and open the letter. There was absolute stillness in the ward. Even the nurses stopped what they were doing.

"Dear Dr. Morelle and Dr. Levinson," he read aloud. "I hope this breakfast gives you the strength you need. You see, I want to have a part, if only a tiny part, in helping you save your patient. Irene Emmerich."

He paused and examined the stationery fully. "Tiffany's!" he announced, looking up.

The patients burst into applause.

"That will be enough of that!" sang out the head nurse. "What do you think this is, two a day at the Palace?"

They were quiet, but when the medications were passed around, most of them had a faraway smile on their lips.

From now on the young doctors' task was much easier. The woman began to breathe slowly but fairly regularly by herself, and needed artificial respiration only on those rare occasions when the interval between inspirations grew too long. During the morning, attendings and interns from every service dropped in to see the case. Even Hauser came, all the way from the pediatric pavilion.

Shortly before noon, Jim, who had been straddling the woman for the past twenty minutes without giving artificial respiration, said, "Stan, she just swallowed. I think she's conscious now."

"One swallow doesn't make a summer," said Stanley.

But in this case it did. She opened her eyes, and the head nurse cried out happily, "She's awake!"

The woman lay there looking up and focusing on Jim. To

everyone's surprise, she smiled and murmured, "So handsome, so very, very handsome!"

The head nurse squeezed her hand. "You should see him after he's had a shave and a good night's sleep."

The woman sat up and, propping herself on her hands, leaned forward and brushed Jim's cheek with her lips. It was like being kissed by a well-bred child, he thought. Then she sank back on the pillow, turned her face to the side, and fell asleep. This time no one applauded. Instead, a low, satisfied hum filled the ward. Jim got off the bed carefully, as if afraid of waking her, and shook hands with Stanley.

"She made it."

One of the floor nurses walked over and handed him a report. "You're experts on morphine poisoning."

"I don't know about that," replied Jim, "but we're certainly authorities on Walt Whitman."

He read the laboratory report. "Specimen consisted of a small amount of white powder wrapped in paper. Analysis: Morphine Sulfate."

That afternoon at two the nurses sat the woman up in bed and fed her broth and crackers. An hour later they swung her feet down so that Jim and Stanley could curl her arms around their shoulders and march her up and down the ward. With Jim so tall and Stanley so short, she looked a little lopsided, but soon they had her walking by herself. The relief intern arrived at six o'clock promptly.

The next morning when they visited the woman on Female Three, they found her sitting up in bed reading *Leaves of Grass* just as if nothing had happened. She regained her strength rapidly. The following week, Emmerich removed her breast, working with tremendous speed and communicating as always a peculiar sense of excitement to everyone in the operating room, even though he himself regarded a mastectomy with its unavoidable clamping and tying off of innumerable arteries as something of a mechanical bore. In contrast to her stormy first days in the Hospital, her postoperative course was unusually smooth. She made no more suicide attempts, perhaps because her masochistic drives had been temporarily sated by so close a brush with death and a mutilating operation as well. To everyone's relief, the microscopic examination demonstrated that the glands in her armpit were free of cancer.

Almost every day during her convalescence, Emmerich dropped by, less to check her general condition than to learn something about her mother, whose adventures seemed to fascinate him. A willful and gifted person, she had managed after years of inactivity during her marriage to recapture her place as one of the country's leading commercial artists. But her second success brought her no comfort. At increasingly frequent intervals she found it necessary to drop everything and rush off on a cruise to some distant part of the world. When her daughter pointed out to her the inadvisability of going off to places such as Hong Kong and Madagascar by herself, she would laugh and say, "I'll try anything once."

It was on just such a trip that she decided to apply this cliché to opium, only to learn too late that "once" had no place in the vocabulary of drug addiction. Just before she died of a painful cancer made bearable by medically administered opiates, she said with that silly little laugh of hers, "I could have gotten all the dope I wanted from the doctors and saved over thirty thousand dollars in the bargain if I had only had the sense to get cancer a few years earlier."

She left nothing to her daughter except eighteen grains of the morphine she had acquired in the old days. At midnight, eight hours before she was to be operated on, the heiress, who had never taken anything stronger than aspirin in her life, swallowed her inheritance while the ward slept.

Well aware that the operation was but the first step in the woman's rehabilitation, Emmerich persuaded her to go to a friend of his, a young psychoanalyst, as soon as she left McKinley. Her three and a half years in therapy were quite stormy, but that they were worth the struggle even the most skeptical could not deny. For in the end, when she met Joe Alternyk, she was ready. He was sixty at the time, a childless widower whose wife had died eight months before. He had not always been wealthy. On the contrary, he had been brought up in degrading poverty by a violent father and a loving but ignorant slattern of a mother. In later years, when he had amassed a fortune, Joe would say, "My mother was not only a good woman and a fine cook. She was a genuine slob." Only, he would say it not as a wisecrack, but to emphasize an attribute so important that it could not be omitted from an honest portrayal.

When he decided to get married, at twenty-one, he felt much too smart to wed the girl next door. There would be no Hell's Kitchen bride for him. He chose a girl from the Bronx, pretty, but six years older than he. It has been said that in marriage a man either embraces or flees from his mother. Joe evidently did the former, because his wife turned out to be as sloppy and ignorant as the poor woman who had brought him into the world. Even thirty-five years later, her overdecorated Park Avenue apartment always looked as if it had just been evacuated by a convention.

Joe's rise in the construction business had not been easy. It had been a slow climb—brick by brick. And even when he became financially important, his goal still eluded him. The refined, the cultured, the well-informed people, the ones with the neat homes and the nice voices, still rejected him. They laughed at his unfortunate grammar, his disordered house, and his impossible wife. In the end he pursued the only course he felt remained open to him. He kept to himself, dressed with compulsive neatness, and read good books. His method was to buy the collected works of an author he had heard about in grammar school and read him straight through. By the time he met the woman, he had read Scott, Dickens, Thackeray, and George Eliot from cover to cover.

She was sitting next to him at Carnegie Hall following the "Prelude to the Meistersinger" in a big score she had borrowed from the library. Her orchestra seat had been sent to her by Irene Emmerich; his had been gotten from a speculator. What fascinated him from the first was the way she pointed to different parts of the music, just like someone reading a blueprint. He could tell she knew what she was doing, because whenever she put her finger on the page, something was sure to happen on the stage, like the brasses blaring or the strings singing a melody. As soon as intermission came, he decided to take a chance. After all, he was sixty. What did he have to lose? He pointed to an alto clef and asked her what it meant. When she saw the look in his eyes, she knew exactly what she was going to do. Without any introductory small talk, she set about to explain the music to him, humming the three themes, telling him what each stood for, and finally showing him how they were woven into a fugue. After they were separated by the crash of the orchestra, he sat there feeling as if he had been hurried through fifty years of culture in fifteen minutes. At the end of the concert he asked her if she would like to go out for a sandwich and a cup of coffee. She slipped into the coat he held out for her and smiled without bothering to reply. He took her to the St. Regis, a place she had passed a hundred times but never dared to enter. Instead of coffee and sandwiches, he ordered Piper Heidsieck 1927, which the maître tasted and served himself. Before he had drunk a glass, Joe knew he was going to marry her—this woman who was everything he desired: cultivated, neat, refined, and young—young enough to be the daughter he had never had. And as for her, she sat there smiling at the bubbles, flushing under his gaze, thinking how strange and wonderful it was to be admired. She, admired! A thirty-eight-year-old librarian with one breast and a psychoneurosis! Maybe he would take her out again, but in case he didn't, this was good enough. She could live on it for years. But he did ask her out again, night after night, in fact. Two weeks later, after a talk with her analyst, she told Joe that her breast had been removed by Dr. Emmerich. As usual, the analyst had been right. Joe felt not only that the operation made her more precious, but that perhaps it would make her feel inferior enough to marry him. When he proposed to her two months later, she accepted, not because she felt inferior, but because he had made her feel superior, and not because she admired him, but because she loved him. On their wedding night, Joe, who had been impotent for years, managed to summon the passion to deflorate her, helped by the feeling, as he penetrated her body, that he was screwing the whole God-damned neat, refined, and grammatical world that had always eluded him. Afterward, he felt a tremendous surge of gratitude toward this woman who had given him back his manhood. He hoped that he would have enough years left in which to repay her. And as for her, lying next to him naked except for the brassiere she felt she had to wear, she nursed her pain joyfully, accepting it as a proper punishment for the undeserved happiness she knew would now be hers.

Two days later, Emmerich received the first of a series of belated but magnificent gifts, each accompanied by a Tiffany card on which was die-engraved "Mrs. Joseph Alternyk." Their exquisiteness did not surprise him. After all, she had always been a cultivated woman and was now a very rich one. But their profusion did. After the fifth, a Rembrandt etching, "The Goldweigher's Field," he decided that he would have to call a halt, reminding her that "zu viel ist ungesund." His telephone call bewildered her. Basking in the joys of her marriage, she had not thought about McKinley, her operation, or Emmerich in weeks. Certainly she had sent him nothing. Suddenly she realized that it must have been Joe who was doing all this without telling her; Joe, trying to relieve himself of the burden of his gratitude in the only way he knew. That night they made love again, and this time she rose to a wonderful climax.

Soon after the woman left the Hospital, Jim began to realize that he would not be permitted to treat any more patients as long as he was a junior. In another month he wanted nothing more than to put this part of his internship behind him. It was not merely the blood counts, the scut work, and the exploitation that were so distasteful. It was the fact that he was not allowed to have any real contact with the sick on the wards. He was reminded of that first deadening year in medical school, the reign of rote and trivia. And then suddenly his six months of slavery were over. It was New Year's Eve and he and Stanley were resting in their room. The procession of contused and lacerated drunks would not stumble into the accident room until later. At five minutes to twelve he opened the window and let in the voice of the city, the whistles and the bells, the laughter and the shouts, the sad, seductive calls from the ships on the rivers, and the muted roar that seemed to rise from the earth. A little of the noise, he thought, must be coming from hotels downtown where young men in tuxedos were saying wonderful things to girls who were leaning against them in brand-new evening dresses. He wondered what his parents were doing. Probably drinking a bottle of champagne in the library of the house on 122nd Street before quietly going upstairs to the bedroom to make love, just as if he were a little boy again, fast asleep on the third floor, and they were afraid of waking him.

He went to the cooler in the hall and came back with two paper cups filled with ice water. He handed one to Stanley.

"To never another blood count!"

"Oh-main!" his friend responded in the classical Hebrew "Amen" intoned after the Friday night Kiddush.

The hooting and the noise of the factory whistles were growing louder. It's the Depression, thought Jim, and New York is whistling in the dark.

FOUR

When Mr. Levinson walked into the office on 122nd Street that raw March day in 1920, Jake Morelle could tell at once that he was seriously ill. He helped the patient into the chair next to the desk, and then sat down himself. Mr. Levinson came to the point at once.

"I've been praying you could do something for me," he sighed.

"What is wrong with you, Mr. Levinson?" Jake asked gravely.

"Cancer. Just cancer. In the stomach."

"How do you know?"

"How do I know?" Mr. Levinson laughed bitterly as he pressed his fingertips repeatedly against the pit of his stomach. "I can feel it here, that's how I know. Of course, the doctors didn't tell it to me in exactly those words. But I know that they are thinking it. Besides, they told it to my wife already."

"I'm not a surgeon, Mr. Levinson. What do you want me to do?" Jake asked gently.

"I want you to tell me it's not cancer. What else?"

"Even if it is?"

"Even if it is."

"First, tell me about your illness. From the beginning."

Mr. Levinson took out a clean but unpressed handkerchief from his back pocket. He was beginning to perspire. "Gladly. Well, I was always in A-one shape until a year ago. Oh, maybe a little indigestion, who hasn't?"

"How old are you, Mr. Levinson?" Jake interrupted.

"Forty-five," answered the patient. "So, about a year ago I began to lose my appetite, first for meat, then for everything. I was pretty well upholstered once, about one hundred and eighty pounds. You know what I weigh now?"

"I can see it's not much."

"One hundred and twenty-six. And it's no wonder. I can't eat anything. I've been vomiting maybe three, four times a day for a whole month now."

"Blood?"

"Yes, blood."

"How about the stools?"

"Blood. Only there it's like tar."

"Do you have any pain?"

"I never had so much as an ache until a few weeks ago. Now I got cramps maybe two, three hours a day."

Jake began to write down the history in his elegant, Spencerian handwriting.

"You don't write much like a doctor," said Mr. Levinson, peering across the desk.

Jake looked up. "Are your parents living?"

Mr. Levinson shook his head.

"What did they die of?" asked Jake.

"Cancer."

"Cancer of what?"

"Who could tell? It was in Poland years ago, and a poor Jew couldn't afford a fancy diagnosis."

Jake resumed his writing. Finally Mr. Levinson asked, "It's what you would call a classical case, huh, Doctor?"

Jake did not answer him. "What do you do for a living, Mr. Levinson?"

"I work in a furrier's establishment, sewing, cutting, piecing, putting the skins together. Eighteen years I've been at it now."

Jake sat back and toyed with an idea. Suddenly he stood up and said abruptly, "Take your things off, please."

Lying on the oak examining table with the black leather top, Mr. Levinson looked startlingly pale and emaciated. In the upper abdomen just below the inverted "V" of the rib cage, Jake could easily feel the tumor—hard, implacable, and as large as a croquet ball, but, strangely enough, movable, freely movable. He pulled down the patient's eyelid and looked at the pale conjunctiva lining its inside surface. Anemic, yes, that he was, but not possessed by the indescribable sallow, marked-for-death look he should have had if a carcinoma of this size were eating at his vitals. Jake thought of Miss Riess, the nurse who had taken care of Jim when he was a baby, and the Blickärzte whom she had served under in Germany. If he were one, he felt the first glance would have told him that this man did not have cancer.

He went to the medicine cabinet, picked up a salmon-colored rubber stomach tube, and dropped it into the sterilizer. Mr. Levinson raised himself on his elbows.

"I had that already, Doctor. There's no acid in the stomach juice. Everything fits."

"I'm not looking for acid," Jake answered.

He cooled the tube on some cracked ice that the Polish girl had brought up from the kitchen, and quickly passed it into the mouth and down into the stomach of the sitting patient, who accepted it stoically without gagging. It took longer to suck a specimen of gastric contents into the oversized syringe attached to the other end of the tube, but soon that, too, was over and Jake was squirting the turbid, amber fluid into a kidney basin on the sink. Fighting an overpowering impatience, he waited until some peculiar filaments rose slowly to the surface. Only then did he pick them up between his thumb and fingertips and carry them to the light. It took him almost a minute to decide that they were indeed what he was looking for—hairs, short hairs of different colors.

He started to wash his hands in green soap. "Put on your clothes, Mr. Levinson. We're going to the place where you work."

As they walked down the stoop, Mr. Levinson asked, "The doctor has a machine?"

"No, we'll go by subway."

It took them over an hour to reach the little back room in the Bronx where Mr. Levinson made his living. Jake sat down on an empty crate in a dark corner and crossed his legs.

"Go about your business just as if this were an ordinary day. Do the sewing and the cutting and all the other things you do with the furs. Just forget about me."

Mr. Levinson was very self-conscious at first, but he was such a sincere craftsman that eventually he lost himself in his work and put the doctor's presence from his mind. Then at last came the moment that Jake had been waiting for. Mr. Levinson brought his fingertips up to his lips and quickly stroked the front of his tongue. Approximately once a minute he repeated the gesture, and each time left a few hairs inside his mouth. Jake noticed that he never spat them out. Completely immersed in his craft and ignorant of his habit, he always swallowed them. After ten minutes of this, Jake stood up, walked over to the light, and patted the furrier on the shoulder.

"I've seen all I need."

Wearily Mr. Levinson put the skins away. "Well, Doctor, what's the verdict? Is it cancer?"

"No, it's not."

"It's something worse? Is that it?"

"No, again. It's completely curable. You'll soon be as good as new. Better, in fact."

Mr. Levinson looked up at Jake skeptically, and for the first

66

time a sarcastic note crept into his voice. "I hope it has a fine impressive name, at least."

"It even has that. It's called a trichobezoar." Jake sat down on the table and smiled. "English translation, a hair ball."

"Like in a cat, you mean?" Mr. Levinson asked incredulously.

Jake nodded. "You don't realize it, Mr. Levinson, but you have a dangerous nervous habit. Almost once a minute you lick the tips of your fingers and transfer a few hairs from the fur to your tongue. So unconscious are you of the act, that instead of spitting out the hair, you actually swallow it. You've been doing it a few hundred times a day, week after week, for eighteen years, and now it's caught up with you."

Mr. Levinson grew even paler, and then a very faint flush spread over his face. Jake was surprised that he could summon up even that much color.

"You can't eat much, Mr. Levinson, because you have a big, slime-covered mass of matted fur in your stomach. You vomit, because it blocks the exit, and when the stomach contracts, there is no place for the food to go but up and out. You have lost fifty pounds because very little nourishment can enter the intestine, where it is absorbed by the body. Everything fits this way, too, you see."

There was a long silence. "But where is the blood coming from, Doctor?"

"From an ulcer, a bleeding ulcer. This hard hair ball of yours has been resting against the delicate mucous membrane, the lining of the stomach, for so long that it has finally eroded a small area."

Mr. Levinson thought this over. "Thank God I told you I was a furrier." He laughed quietly. "If you had asked my wife, she would have told you I was a Talmudist earning a few dollars on the side in the fur trade so we could eat."

"Mr. Levinson, you've lost a good deal of blood. I want you to go to Dr. Emmerich as soon as possible."

"Emmerich! Please, Doctor, where would I get the money to have him operate on me?"

"You don't need a lot of money. He'll charge you twenty-five or at most fifty dollars for the consultation. Then he'll put you in McKinley on his ward service and operate on you himself for nothing. I'll take you to his office as soon as I can get an appointment."

"Thank you." There was a pause, and then Mr. Levinson added reverently, "Doctor." He began to walk up and down with his hands clasped behind his back the way he did when he was expounding a difficult Talmudic text. "And I really mean both parts. First, the 'thank you.' That was for my life, whatever it's worth. Second, the 'Doctor.' That was not merely a fact, but a recognition. For you are truly one, not only in the oldest sense, a teacher, but also in the best sense, a healer, a doer, and a bringer of hope."

There was no trouble about the appointment. In fact, Jake was a little surprised when the nurse told him to bring the patient in the very next day. The office was on the ground floor of a quiet, solid, fifteen-story apartment house facing McKinley Hospital on the other side of Park Avenue. When the secretary swung back the heavy brass door, polished so that it shone like 18-karat gold, Mr. Levinson was deeply impressed, not so much by the massive metal gate itself, as by the promptness with which it had been opened. In most of the flats he visited, he was accustomed to ringing the bell endlessly until from somewhere in the depths a shrill voice would scream, "Wait a minute, will ya! I'm coming already!" To his further surprise, Dr. Morelle and he were the only ones there. Dr. Emmerich did not favor a noisy waiting room filled with restless patients who had all been scheduled for the same time so that they would be impressed by the size of the doctor's practice. His fees, usually from five hundred to five thousand dollars for an operation, were so large that he could afford the luxury of a quiet office. In less than five minutes, his veteran nurse, gray-haired, ninety-eight pounds, sweet, even roguish, but tough as a traction cable, walked in briskly and whispered, "Will you follow me, please. He is ready for you now." Her tone implied that "He" was spelled with a capital H.

No one ever forgot his first impression of Emmerich's consultation room. Running for fifty feet along Park Avenue, its six leaded windows were so cleverly curtained that their dim, filtered light created an artificial dusk which obscured the walls at the far ends and made the room stretch into a mysterious infinity. When Mr. Levinson entered from the brightly lighted foyer, he turned to the left and saw only the twilight. But when he turned to the right, he saw silhouetted against the pale silver lamplight, like the face on a Roman coin, the profile of Emmerich, already, at forty-three, one of America's greatest surgeons. He was seated behind a beautifully carved walnut desk, on a plain, high-backed chair, which Mr. Levinson was sure must be a throne. The surgeon turned, and without standing up, motioned them to chairs.

Herman Augustus Emmerich had devised the operation for radical removal of the breast used everywhere in the country and was universally acknowledged to be a master of general surgery. He possessed that legendary, loyalty-compelling quality which once had made the grenadiers of the Old Guard proud to lay down their lives for their Emperor. His head movements were quick, his prominent blue eyes warm and darting. Although only of middle height, he seemed much taller, because his sparse, gray hair was swept upward as if by the rush of erupting ideas. Today, as always, he wore a suit of some dark, subdued material, but no one could sit with him for more than five minutes without realizing that it was cut from the imperial purple.

"Start from the beginning, Mr. Levinson," he ordered, giving the patient a quick smile and ignoring Jake.

Skillfully and very rapidly he elicited from Mr. Levinson a sharp résumé of his symptoms. Next, he pushed a button under the desk, and when the nurse appeared, inclined his head to the right. She led Mr. Levinson into the adjacent examining room, which was brilliantly illuminated and filled with the most modern equipment, including a hospital-sized autoclave for complete sterilization of instruments. Emmerich followed them, observed Mr. Levinson for a moment, halfheartedly palpated the tumor, and returned to the consultation room without a word. Jake was amazed at the perfunctoriness of the examination, even though he knew that Emmerich prided himself on his lightning diagnoses. As soon as they both were seated, the surgeon said, "I'll operate on him, but you know the outlook in carcinoma of the stomach, especially one as far advanced as this."

Jake said nothing.

After a moment, Emmerich glanced at him sharply. "You agree, of course."

"No, I don't."

Emmerich gave him the eagle stare. "Every patient is entitled to an exploratory laparotomy if only on the remote chance it might not be cancer."

"Oh, I think he should be operated on, all right. It's just that I don't think he has cancer."

No one had argued with Emmerich in a long time. "What did you say?" he demanded.

Jake almost expected a thunderbolt to come crashing into the dusk from the sunlit avenue outside. "I said I don't think it's carcinoma. I think it's a trichobezoar."

Then he told Emmerich about the hairs in the gastric juice, the trip to the Bronx, the vigil in the furrier's back room, and Mr. Levinson's eighteen-year-old nervous habit. The surgeon, who never left his desk during a conference, stood up and walked to the window, deeply disturbed. After all, he was the Blickarzt, who was supposed to make the dramatic diagnosis at the very first glance. Instead there came to him a dispensary doctor with a theory that fitted the case like a glove, and who had the audacity to throw the glove in his face. The diagnosis was preposterous. He turned around, looked at Jake broodingly, and suddenly knew it was not preposterous at all. This man was no show-off, no sensation seeker. This was a good man, a devoted man, and a very keen man. And, of course, the tumor had been completely movable. He returned to his desk, sat down, and turned toward Jake.

"Whether you are right or wrong, it still is a brilliant diagnosis. I think you are right."

He pressed the button again and the nurse brought the patient in. This time he stood up and helped Mr. Levinson into his chair.

"You are fortunate, first, in not having cancer, and second, in having found a physician who could tell you so in time. Every good doctor is a detective in the world of disease, and Dr. Morelle belongs to our imaginary Scotland Yard." He took his rimless glasses off very carefully and laid them on the desk as if they were irreplaceable. "You are a Talmudist and must use a discipline which requires patience, endless study, and time. But in your present anemic condition, the discipline is exactly the reverse. Speed is imperative. When you leave here, you are to go directly across the street to McKinley Hospital, where all the arrangements will already have been made. On Thursday, I'm taking that thing out."

He stood up and shook hands with the patient.

"This is America," whispered Mr. Levinson to Jake, "where a fur worker can be operated on by an Emmerich!"

He walked out shaking his head. Emmerich patted Jake on the shoulder and said, "A Blickarzt."

When Mr. Levinson reached the secretary's room, he asked politely, "What is the doctor's honorarium?"

"His what?" asked the secretary.

The nurse, who had just walked in, answered, "It's fifteen dollars."

"And he's actually going to operate on me himself for that?" gasped Mr. Levinson.

"Do you know of anyone who would dare to operate on one of Dr. Emmerich's patients?"

"No, no!" Mr. Levinson hurried to explain. "It's just that I think I should pay him more."

"Mr. Levinson," the nurse said severely, "in this office we set the fees. We do not allow the patients to dictate to us."

He smiled and gave her three new five-dollar bills. "I got a son who'll be ready for college in a few years. Maybe some day he'll be a doctor at McKinley. And if he turns out to be one tenth as good a man as Dr. Emmerich, I won't quarrel with God."

That night at McKinley he was given 500 c.c. of matched blood taken directly from the arm vein of a donor lying on a stretcher close to his. In the morning, the gastrointestinal X-ray series was begun, and terminated late that afternoon. Since his hemoglobin had risen only slightly, another transfusion of 500 c.c. of blood was administered the second night. The next morning he was brought to the anesthesia room well ahead of time, since Emmerich always made the incision at the exact moment the schedule called for. Jake, who had arrived in the operating room quite early, found the surgeon and his two assistants already scrubbing up. Nothing was said, for in this place conversation was anathema. Only the surgeon talked; the others never, except in answer to a question.

Emmerich turned his head halfway toward Jake. "They don't agree with us in X-ray. The big filling defect and the crater they interpret as an ulcerating carcinoma." He went on scrubbing his nails methodically. "Do you still stand by your diagnosis?"

"I do," Jake solemnly replied.

Emmerich nodded approvingly.

When the unconscious patient was wheeled in, many people went to work. The anesthetist kept the rubber mask over Mr. Levinson's face with one hand while he dragged along his simple apparatus with the other; an orderly helped transfer the patient from the stretcher to the narrow operating table; the un- scrubbed nurses scurried around; the supervising nurse adjusted the huge overhead light; and the two gowned, masked, and rubber-gloved assistants painted the abdomen with alcohol, ether, and iodine. But when the instrument nurse handed Em- merich the knife, all of them seemed suddenly to fade away. This was no team effort. The personnel were merely the mas- ter surgeon's milieu. Emmerich's incision, as always, was bold, full length, and well through the sparse underlying fat. He was not the man to keep timidly stroking the wound with his scalpel until the proper depth was reached. The ratchety clicking of the hemostats enlivened the utter stillness, but only a few were needed to curb the bleeding, and the severed arteries were rapidly tied off. Many a meticulous surgeon spent more time making an incision than Emmerich took to remove an appendix. Such fussy perfectionists, preoccupied with an almost invisible ooze, would apply more and still more artery clamps until the patient's abdomen looked like a porcupine's back. Emmerich's clamps were few and strategically placed. Today, after their removal, he pushed back the rectus muscles, and was soon down upon the peritoneum, that final tissue, thin as milky cellophane, which encloses and conceals the abdominal organs. After the House Surgeon pulled back the muscles and spread the abdominal wall with his retractors, Emmerich picked up the peritoneum with forceps and nodded to his assistant to do the same an inch away. Confident that the membrane had been pulled up away from the underlying intestines, he nicked it be- tween the two instruments and, inserting a straight scissors into the little hole, opened the belly above and below. With a gentle, lazy, voluptuous motion, he slid his right hand into the ab- domen. His wonderfully sensitive fingers roamed everywhere, five eyes hidden inside the peritoneal cavity. Everyone in the room watched the two eyes above the mask.

"No nodes," said Emmerich in his husky voice. He turned

his face away from the operating table so that he could concentrate better. "It's a big mass but not fixed."

By this time six interns, four surgical attendings, three attendings from the medical service, four visiting doctors, the supervisor of nurses, and one of the men from the X-ray Department had drifted in. Emmerich was used to crowds. He attracted them because his phenomenal speed prevented even a dull operation from becoming tedious. Lap pads were placed in the wound to prevent the peritoneum from becoming soiled, and the stomach was opened. As Emmerich's fingers separated the mass from the mucous membrane, everyone leaned forward. And when he delivered an enormous, mucous-covered ball of matted hair through the incision, it seemed as if a great, silent cheer went through the room. He dropped the trichobezoar into a basin with perhaps a little more noise than was necessary and said, "There's your cancer."

For an impatient man, he closed the stomach with surprisingly meticulous care, growling, "The ulcer will heal by itself," and let his assistant sew up the incision. After the nurses had fluttered up to him and removed his gown, mask, and gloves, he took Jake by the arm and walked toward the doctors' dressing room.

"We could use a head like yours at McKinley."

Mr. Levinson left the Hospital in four weeks. He had gained sixteen pounds and his hemoglobin was 85 per cent. Emmerich warned him to look for another job.

74

FIVE

A SECOND CASE, that very summer, may have proved even more important to Jake's career, because this time his consultant was Rintman, Director of Internal Medicine at MicKinley Hospital.

When Tim Gahagan rang up to ask Jake whether he could come over that afternoon, it was clear that something was really wrong. Tim's ironclad rule was never to bother a doctor unless an illness had lasted at least four days. His wife's had already lasted six. The Gahagans, their three children, and Mrs. Moriarty, Mary's mother, had just moved from a railroad flat into a pleasant six-room apartment on Seventh Avenue, as indeed they had every right to do, since Tim, an enterprising men's clothing salesman on salary and commission, earned as much as sixty dollars a week. When Jake walked into the sunny bedroom, spotless and filled with brand-new Grand Rapids mission furniture, Mary was flat on her back with a wet towel across her forehead.

"I know I should have called you sooner, Doctor, but," here Tim groped for a compliment to pay his wife, "she's built like an ox." He smiled reassuringly. "Oh, she'll get well, all right. Never doubt that."

"The ox has a dreadful headache," said Mary opening her eyes.

Jake sat on the edge of the bed and took a stethoscope from his bag.

"How long have you had the headache, Mary?"

"A good five days."

Jake observed her carefully for a moment. Her face was flushed, her lips cracked, her tongue coated, and the thermometer he slid under it soon registered 103 degrees. But it was her pulse that troubled him. Instead of being rapid, as it should have been with such a fever, it was slow, very slow, only seventy to the minute, full and bounding.

"How long have you had fever, Mary?"

She counted on her fingers, "Six days, only we don't take it regular," she apologized.

"What else troubles you?"

"Just the cramps." She ran her hand over her abdomen. "But they're getting so bad I told Tim he'd have to call you."

"I'm glad he did. How are your bowels?"

"Regular." She thought for a moment. "But the last one was loose."

He fitted the head mirror to his forehead so that he might relay a little sunlight into her throat. On each side of her soft palate was a strange little ulcer. He frowned under the leather band.

"And I've had something of a bronical cough for a few days," she remembered after he had removed the wooden tongue blade from her mouth.

"I'll have to examine you, Mary," he said quietly.

With some difficulty she pulled down her cotton nightgown. Her breasts were young and firm in spite of her having had three children.

"How old are you now?"

76

She glanced at Tim. "Thirty-four."

Percussion and auscultation of her lungs and heart revealed nothing. He covered her chest with the bathrobe that had been lying on a chair next to her bed, and then slowly pulled her nightgown down to the pubic hair. On her singularly white, concave abdomen he could clearly make out five small, rose-colored spots. And that was all. With the exception of some diffuse tenderness in this area, the rest of the physical examination was normal.

He took off his head mirror, closed his bag, and went to the bathroom, where he washed his hands for three full minutes. Then he stuck his head through the doorway.

"Mary, I'd like to speak to Tim."

She nodded as her husband followed him. Mrs. Moriarty was already standing in the parlor, which was filled with images of the Virgin Mary and a few crucifixes.

"Sit down, both of you, please," he said. Then he turned to Tim. "Has Mary eaten any shellfish lately?"

"Only oysters," Tim replied. "A dozen of the finest, two weeks ago at City Island. And what oysters they give you there! There's no taste to them at all, and they slide down as easy as your own phlegm."

Jake thought this over carefully. "I hate to tell you this, but Mary is much sicker than you think. What she's got is another matter. My examination was very crude."

"Please don't be saying that, Doctor. It was a beautiful examination," interrupted Tim.

"We'll have to do some laboratory tests." Jake shook his head. "But, Tim, I'm afraid it looks like typhoid fever."

"The devil you say!" Tim cried out.

Jake turned to Mrs. Moriarty. "The typhoid germs will now be coming out in her stools. For your own protection, and for the children's, disinfect everything that comes in contact with her. Boil her bedclothes and her dishes, and use plenty of

Lysol in the toilet and on the bedpan. And above all, keep washing your hands."

"It shall be done, Doctor," said Mrs. Moriarty, stony-eyed.

"As to her diet, nothing but milk, water, tea, and broth." He turned back to Tim. "We need a consultant. I'd like to get Dr. Rintman of McKinley Hospital. He's the best diagnostician in the city."

"Anyone you say. And don't spare the horses. We've got a little put away."

"I'll send somebody up to do a blood count."

"If I'm not being too bold, what would that show?"

"Well, in most infections accompanied by fever, the blood count is high, but in typhoid it's quite low."

"Now, ain't that clever!" exclaimed Tim. Then he added anxiously, "What are her chances?"

"Let's wait for Dr. Rintman tomorrow, Tim."

At precisely nine o'clock the next morning, the children playing on Seventh Avenue at 118th Street were taken aback by a chauffeur-driven Pierce-Arrow and the man stepping out of it, who continued to write in a red leather notebook until the very second he entered the Gahagans' apartment house. The foundation piles on which Rintman's colossal memory rested were the sixteen filing cabinets in the back room of his house on East 54th Street in which he kept, carefully catalogued and cross-indexed, the notes he had collected on every book, article, event, and person he felt might someday be of use to him. Today, he was merely shoring up the foundations a little. He was a short man who would have loved to be both tall and menacing, but although robbed of his height by cruel genes, he had certainly been endowed with a sinister appearance. His glittering black eyes were quick and penetrating, and seemed to rest on everyone just long enough to say, "I've already photographed you. Move on." Two clumps of black hair above his forehead swirled up to give him the horned, Mephistophelean air he did nothing to discourage. He had a nasty way of pulling his nose and mouth to the left when he sniffed, which was quite often, and of using the left half of his lips when he smiled, which was quite seldom. Today, as always, he wore a black broadcloth suit and a voluminous, swirling black cape. If Emmerich was the Emperor, Rintman was the Sorcerer. Although strictly a clinician, his clever use of blood cultures taken by his own improved techniques, together with endless, imaginative hours at the autopsy table, had enabled him to describe and popularize an important new entity, subacute bacterial endocarditis. And his present investigation of what would someday be known as the collagen diseases was destined to make him famous all over the world. No wife or children had ever entered his lonely life —only disciples, young disciples, all male. He was forty-five and appeared ageless. Although he never seemed to grow older, it would have been as indelicate to tell him so as to have paid the same compliment to Dr. Faustus.

The Gahagans had been on the lookout for him from their second-story window since eight o'clock. The instant the bell rang, Mrs. Moriarty opened the door. He handed his cape to Tim, nodded to Jake, and walked abruptly to the closed bedroom door. Suddenly he whirled on Tim and growled, "I can't work with a cat in the house!"

Actually he was fond of cats, but so much fonder still of showmanship that a little tampering with the truth never disturbed him. The short, apricot-colored hairs on Tim's dark suit had been too great a temptation.

"Glory to heaven and how did you know? But she's not been in the house since last night, Professor," replied Tim, dumfounded.

Rintman smiled his left-sided smile. Then, acceding very ungraciously to Jake's request for a few words in private, he walked briskly to the parlor, sat down on the softest chair, and deliberately turned his face to the window. Jake recited the history, emphasizing the low white count, the Bouveret ulcers in the throat, and the ingestion of oysters. Finally he gave his diagnosis.

Rintman rubbed his knees, never taking his eyes off the window. "Did it ever occur to you that leukopenia is typical of grippe, too? Typhoid is not the only disease with a low blood count. And as for the oysters, the dangers of shellfish have been vastly overrated, especially by our Jewish colleagues in Mt. Sinai Hospital."

He walked out of the parlor, knocked gently on the bedroom door, and without waiting for an answer, went in. Mary was sitting up in bed, her hair freshly brushed. Rintman was so well aware of his deep, concealed hostility to women that he tended to be excessively nice to them.

"They've been frightening you, haven't they, Mary? From now on you must stop worrying." He put his hand gently on her forehead, and exclaimed, "She's cool!"

His examination was extremely thorough and he spent considerable time peering at the spots on her abdomen. At the end, he washed his hands, perfunctorily, and beckoned Jake to the parlor. This time he did not look out the window.

"The trouble with you doctors who don't have inside hospital affiliations," he began with one of his lopsided sniffs, "is that you never seem to think of the simple things. The woman's temperature is normal, her spleen is not enlarged, her so-called Bouveret ulcers are just an ordinary pharyngitis, and your famous rose spots are nothing more than prickly heat. Do you know what she has? She has the grippe, better called *La Grippe*. And do you know why it has the feminine gender? Because like any woman it can make a fool of you."

With this he stalked out and called the family into the bedroom.

"Mr. Gahagan, your wife has the grippe. In two days she will be well. In three days she will be doing the housework." He bowed to Mary, sniffed, and turned to Tim. "My cape, please."

"How much will that be, Professor?" asked Tim, trying to keep up with him.

"Fifty dollars."

Tim pulled two twenties and a ten from his wallet. "Thank you for coming, and thank you for the good news."

But, after he had gone, Tim looked troubled. "He's smart, but do you think he's right?"

"No, I don't," answered Jake gravely.

That night Mary's temperature was 103.4. Sunday morning the diarrhea became profuse. Sunday night her temperature vaulted to 104.2. And Monday morning at ten minutes after six, Tim telephoned Jake.

"She's bleeding something terrible from the rectum. In the name of God, can you come over right away!"

Jake got there in fifteen minutes. Mary was lethargic and very pale. The bedclothes were soaked in blood, and big clots were already on the sheet. Her face looked like the white porcelain face of the statuette Madonna on the shelf above her head, but Jake knew that the light hair streaming on the pillow would have reminded his son of Elaine, the Lily Maid of Astolat, floating on her funeral barge. His examination was brief.

"Tim, she's having an intestinal hemorrhage, one of the worst complications of typhoid fever. We've got to get her to McKinley."

"You'll be treating her there, won't you?"

"No, I'm not on the staff. I just work in the dispensary."

Tim shook his head disapprovingly.

Considering that it was not yet seven, Rintman was surprisingly affable when Jake telephoned him.

"Of course she has to go in, Dr. Morelle, and on the ward service." There was a short pause. "I'll send a private ambulance."

When the ambulance pulled up at the main hospital entrance, between Park and Madison avenues, he was waiting for them inside. The hematologist, five professional blood donors, and two laboratory technicians, all of whom he had driven out of bed, were already hurrying toward McKinley. Three of the donors proved to be group O, and their bloods cross-matched perfectly with Mary's. Although it had been years since Rintman had given a transfusion, his magic touch had not deserted him. A miniature operating room had been set up in the female ward, and there, assisted by the hematologist, he gave Mary 750 c.c. of blood, smoothly and slowly so as not to put a strain on the heart.

Typhoid bacilli grew out of the admission blood culture, and the same organisms were isolated from the stools. Two days later, the Widal test was strongly positive. Pints of salt solution dripping through the big, hollow needles under her skin could not overcome her dehydration, and the cruel ice-water baths were more successful in terrorizing her than in bringing down the soaring fever. Much of the time now she was delirious, mumbling about her own childhood, her honeymoon, and her babies. Rintman came to her bedside three times a day and once at midnight, and directed the ineffectual treatment with a savage persistence. Since Mary was on the critical list, visiting privileges were unlimited and Tim and Mrs. Moriarty were by her side almost constantly. Jake, too, came frequently, although now he had no connection with the case.

"The little professor is here all the time," said Tim to him one day. "I'll be in debt for the rest of my life, I know, but it's worth it."

"She's on the ward service, Tim. He won't charge you a penny."

"Then, why does he do it?"

"Because he's a doctor," answered Jake.

On Saturday morning, Mary had another intestinal hemorrhage, but this time because of a severe reaction the transfusion had to be terminated after only 100 c.c. had been administered. When she began to pick on the bedclothes early that night, Jake knew she did not have much further to go. The priest got there at ten, and she died just before midnight. Rintman had his stethoscope on her chest as her heart stopped beating.

"Poor thing," he mumbled, and walked away dejectedly, looking like a very small professor indeed.

Tim kissed his wife on the forehead and straightened up. "It was God's will," he said, looking away. "She gave me twelve fine years."

"He'll be married again before her grave is hard," said Mrs. Moriarty to Jake.

"I may, someday, at that," answered Tim quietly, "but if I do, it will be only because she taught me how wonderful a marriage can be."

Two weeks later, Jake received the summons. Rintman's waiting room in the big private house on 54th Street was furnished with nothing more than a few wooden chairs and tables, and a thin, black runner that bisected the gleaming parquet floor. Just as unimpressive was the consultation room, with its scratched oak desk and carefully dusted battered oak bookcases. The books, pamphlets, medical articles, pens, pencils, blotters, manila folders, charts, letter basket, and even the telephone were arranged with a compulsive orderliness, as if they were checked every hour to be sure they were in the right position.

"You're prompt, Morelle," said Rintman approvingly. He fixed Jake with his penetrating look. "Dr. Emmerich and I have discussed you at length, and we have both come to the same conclusion. You have the diagnostic touch, and that is something a man is born with, like perfect pitch or a high I.Q. We feel that you would fit in quite well at McKinley. You're Protestant, aren't you?"

Jake nodded.

"Not that I have anything against Catholics, of course. And you are certainly distinguished-looking, handsome, in fact." He laughed, and looked unusually animated. "Besides, you were third honor man at my old Alma Mater, and have worked faithfully in the clinic for many years. A commendable record."

"This talk is getting to sound like the crucial seventh game of the World Series."

"An apt comparison. It may prove decisive for you. Next month one of my adjuncts will be promoted to fill the associateship left vacant by a death. I can keep the adjunctcy open for you for one year, in fact until you return."

Jake looked bewildered.

"Come, come! You know very well that I mean until you return from Europe," Rintman continued. "McKinley has only specialists on its staff. Your transformation from a general practitioner into an internist in one short year can be accomplished only abroad, in Germany and Vienna, to be accurate." He held up his hand when he saw Jake frown. "I know—money." He laughed tolerantly. "But with the inflation that's going on over there now you can get by on almost nothing if you live austerely. And that's exactly how you should live. Then your wife will have nothing to reproach you with. You know, Morelle, it's not a bad idea for a husband and wife to be apart for a while. A man can concentrate on his work much better that way." Resting his elbows on the desk he tented his fingers and looked above Jake's head as if he were trying to see Europe.

"For the first three months you will work in the Department of Pathology of the Allgemeine Krankenhaus in Vienna, where they do twelve autopsies a day—every day, not just on a good day." There was a long pause until he focused on Jake again. "I want you to do autopsies, more autopsies, and still more autopsies! The birthplace of internal medicine is the morgue. The next three months you will spend at the Charité in Berlin for clinical material you never believed existed. They marshal their rare cases over there by the battalion." Rintman's eyes were gleaming. "But I need a few days to prepare your letters of recommendation and to map out the trip for you. In abbreviated form, it will be the same one I took as a young man years ago.

You can leave in June—practice is slow in the summer anyway, and be back the following June. Every year I go to Europe myself from July to September, so perhaps I can be of help to you. My plans abroad are quite fluid."

No woman had ever seen Rintman so excited. Jake hated to interrupt him.

"When you get back, you will have to move your office down here," Rintman warned. "We have no place for Harlem doctors at McKinley. Oh, it doesn't have to be pretentious. Four or five rooms near Lexington Avenue, shared with a surgeon or neurologist, will do. And one nurse for the two of you will be perfectly proper in the beginning."

Jake felt he could wait no longer. "I can't go to Europe, Dr. Rintman. I wouldn't be able to pay the rent back here if I did."

"What rent?" interrupted the internist. "Don't you own your house?"

"No, I don't. All I have to my name is a wife and a son."

"Then, don't be so touchy. Borrow the money from her. That's what women are for."

"There *is* no money—on her side, or mine either."

Rintman was shocked. "No one you can borrow from?"

"Not if I have to start practice all over again, and in a strange neighborhood at that."

Rintman rose, pale with fury. "They call me peculiar because I don't permit my young men to marry. But someday they will all be famous, while you will still be a general practitioner in Harlem. When they're famous, then they can get married." He sat down and pinched his eyes between his thumb and forefinger. "Excuse me, but I hate to see a medical talent strangled, especially by the holy bonds of matrimony. Please do me one favor, although after the way I botched up your diagnosis in the Gahagan case you don't owe me even that. Please think over my offer carefully."

"I have a son who has his heart set on entering Columbia in a

85

few years—premed. If he can win an internship at McKinley, he might turn out to be the Morelle you are looking for."

Jake thought the offer over carefully, but never changed his mind. His status at McKinley never changed either. To his last day he remained a dispensary drudge, forever denied the privilege of working inside the Hospital.

SIX

JIM had no difficulty getting into Columbia College. The fact that his father had been third honor man at the University's College of Physicians and Surgeons was of considerable help in obtaining the approval of the Dean of Admissions. Even more important, perhaps, were his exploits in interscholastic boxing while at a public high school in Manhattan. When he was twelve, he won the affection of "Rightie" Ruber, a childless neighbor on 122nd Street, who in his day had been one of the cleverest lightweights in the world. Almost every afternoon he would dump his schoolbooks at home and race up the block to the brownstone house where the old master taught him everything he knew in the pocket-sized gymnasium in the basement. At eighteen, Jim was six foot two, two hundred and twenty pounds, and as hard as a bronze statue. His mentor often took him down to Stillman's, where he would crawl into the ring and hold his own for three or four rounds with any of the professionals, even the good heavyweights.

As a sophomore he won the first of his three intercollegiate heavyweight boxing championships and was even then recognized throughout the college as one of Columbia's outstanding athletes. Early in June of his second year he was walking across South Field when his attention was caught by a dark-haired little fellow on tennis court number one who was volleying with the artistry of a Cochet and darting everywhere to make impossible acrobatic returns. Seized by the admiration that one athlete feels for another in a different field, Jim peered through the wire netting and then decided to go inside for a better view. Sitting on a bench alongside the court was a slim, pleasant-faced young man who managed to look stylish in an old pair of gray flannel trousers and a faded gray sweat shirt. Jim sat down a few feet away.

"Just like Forest Hills."

"Not quite."

"Did you see that volleying?"

"Oh, yes. But his ground strokes are not tournament quality. He's a volleyer and a scrambler. I'm manager of the tennis team and I know his weaknesses."

"I'm sorry. Tennis is not my game."

"I'm not much of a player either. It was my father's game. He used to play in the tournaments at Southampton and Germantown." He put out his hand. "I'm Albert Huegenon, and I know who you are."

After they shook hands, he shifted his gaze back to the court. "He has a lot of work ahead of him. The coach thinks that if he can make the changes, he may win the intercollegiates some day. But he's very sensitive. His name is Stanley Levinson," he added, as if that explained it.

Stanley shook hands with his opponent, a rangy boy a foot taller than he, and came over to them.

"You're pretty good," said Jim.

"Not good enough. Albert knows what's wrong. But I'm having so much trouble making the changes, you'd think my game was set in cement."

88

"I'll walk you to the locker room," said Jim, waving to Albert.

Neither of them spoke until they were halfway there.

"You're lucky," said Stanley at last. "You've got a heavyweight fighter's build. But it's not so easy to play intercollegiate tennis when you look like a chimney sweep."

"How about Bill Johnston? He weighed one hundred and twenty-four, and there wasn't a man in the world who could beat him except Tilden."

Levinson tightened the screws on his wooden press. "What are you going to be when you grow up?"

"I'm premed."

Levinson stopped and looked up at him. "How about your marks? Or doesn't a heavyweight champ need good marks to get into medical school?"

"They're O.K. How about you?"

"I'm premed, too." Then he added absent-mindedly, "Straight A's so far."

Jim whistled.

"For me it's a must," Stanley said bitterly. "You're a white Protestant. I'm just white."

"Don't get sore at me because your ground strokes are lousy."

Stanley laughed, and suddenly the strain was gone from his face.

Jim smiled. "How about having dinner at my house Thursday night?"

"How will your parents feel when they see that I'm a Jew?"

"They won't be interested. They will probably talk about Wagner all night, either Richard or Honus, depending upon whether my mother or my father gets the floor first. And God help you if you don't know the difference."

"I'm in, then. Richard wrote, but Honus was, "The Flying Dutchman." He went through the motions of attempting to turn the already tightened screws of the racket press. "I don't suppose you'd come to my house for dinner, would you? We're

Orthodox Jews, so Friday night would be the best time. That's the beginning of Shabbos, our sabbath, the Queen of Days, as my father calls it. My mother serves the best food then, gefilte fish, kreplech soup, and Brust. And my father sings the Kiddush, the Sanctification over the Wine. That's the high point of the week in our home. There's another reason why you should help us celebrate the sabbath: Good turns come in threes. Your father saved my father's life years ago."

"Nothing could keep me away. And Stanley," there was a pause, "don't be so damned sensitive."

Stanley shrugged. "I can't help it. That's what it's like to be a Jew."

Within a month the two were close friends, sharing roast beef Thursdays at the Morelles' and Friday evening dinners at the Levinsons', where, seated on Mrs. Levinson's right, Jim wore a black skull cap no one else was allowed to use and beat the others to every "Oh-main!" When, after some hesitation, the friends decided to invite Albert Huegenon into their homes, they were touched to see how happy and grateful he was. Both the Morelles and the Levinsons found him gracious, warm, and meticulously polite, just a shade too polite, perhaps, for a college sophomore. Not only did Albert come to their homes, he joined them in almost everything they did—standing at the opera, climbing up to the theater galleries, listening to concerts at Carnegie and Aeolian halls, taking the Long Island Rail Road to the tennis matches at Forest Hills, and watching the fights at Madison Square Garden.

While his two friends, cashing in on their athletic abilities, were enjoying the coolness of an Adirondack summer as counselors in a boys' camp, Albert was working as a volunteer technician in the heat of McKinley's laboratory. In less than three weeks he was doing blood counts so accurately that the junior interns began to take advantage of him. It was then that the Director of the Laboratory transferred him to the Chemistry Division, not because he was working too hard, but because the interns were now working too little. In three more weeks he was doing the routine blood chemistries without supervision and substituting for the regular technicians when they went on vacation. On his last day, the Director called him into his office.

"You seem to have a flair for this sort of work, young man. Next summer I think we can arrange a small salary."

Albert buttoned the jacket about which Mr. Levinson had once remarked, "He didn't buy that at Moe Levy's," and said quietly, "You're very generous but the salary won't be necessary."

The Director smiled. "I won't insist. And don't forget to come to me in your last year at medical school well before the intern examinations. I might be able to do something for you."

But as soon as college started it was obvious that Albert was not going to get into medical school, not, at any rate, if his marks remained at their C level. His laboratory work in chemistry, physics, and biology was uniformly excellent, but the written examinations did not show him at his best. After a gloomy conference, Jim and Stanley decided to approach him.

"Albert," said Jim gently, "with those marks you're never going to get into medical school."

"I know it. But it's not because I don't study."

"Maybe you don't study properly. Stan and I want you to try it with us."

"Be a barnacle while you sail into medical school?"

"The preamble to our private constitution states that every ship has the right to choose its own barnacles. You're sailing with us."

Under their sympathetic coaching, his work quickly improved and he maintained a B average during his final two years. He remained a mystery man, however, never once returning their hospitality by inviting them to his home.

Early in their junior year while the three friends were studying chemistry in the Morelle library on 122nd Street, the mystery man at last made a revelation. Pointing to a line in the textbook, Albert said, "My father says that this equation made the Bessemer process possible."

"Is your father in the steel business?" Jim asked politely, without being quite sure that his phraseology was correct. Was steel a business, like clothing or hardware?

Albert hesitated a long time. "This is going to sound like the greatest exhibition of snobbery west of the Court of St. James, but I can't help it." He paused again. "He's in everything. It was my grandfather who made the money in steel. My father has piled it up in everything else—banking, oil, shipping, copper, everything. He sits on the boards of at least half a dozen corporations. We know a little girl who always calls him 'Uncle Ty,' although she knows perfectly well that his name is Charles, simply because she's heard him referred to so often as a tycoon." He poured out some sarsaparilla from the big pitcher. "You must have wondered why I've never had you over to my house. Well, my mother is a lovely woman—maybe not quite as beautiful as yours, Jim, but very lovely—and my father is a fine man, a great man, I think, but they could never make dinner at my house as happy as Friday evening at the Levinsons' or roast beef Thursday at the Morelles'."

Jim and Stanley did not move.

"Come to dinner, won't you, any night at all," said Albert at last. "It doesn't matter when, because we'll eat in my room, just the three of us." There was no reply. "How about tomorrow at eight—better still, make it seven so I can put the house through its paces. It's on Fifth Avenue between Seventy-third and Seventy-fourth streets."

"What's the address?" asked Jim.

Albert looked embarrassed. "Why, I don't think it has one. There's nothing else there."

"What are we supposed to wear?" asked Stanley anxiously.

Albert smiled. "Anything you want. But sneakers and sweat shirts are definitely out."

They had no trouble finding the house, startlingly white in

the dusk. Facing Central Park for an entire city block, its low, three-storied limestone structure and lovely, empty grounds proclaimed quite effectively that the Huegenons did not have to get their money's worth by utilizing to the fullest every square inch of space on this, one of the most valuable residential plots in the world. Grandpa Huegenon had vowed, so it was said, to build himself a house that would make Andrew Carnegie's ornate mansion on Ninety-first Street look like a miner's shack. And in the opinion of most New Yorkers, he had. It was built around a slightly sunken oblong courtyard, in the center of which rested a pool only inches deep, utterly still, and everywhere transparent except where the gentle fountains turned it into silk moiré. As a recessed frame surrounds a picture, so a three-stepped oblong stone staircase enclosed the marble walk by the side of the pool, a staircase that led to the cloistered colonnades upon which most of the main rooms opened. Clever architecture had set this entire courtyard indoors by covering it with a curved glass roof, reminiscent on a small scale of the kind seen over European railroad stations. It was here that they both were brought, and here Albert greeted them with an overbright smile that only made them feel uncomfortable.

"Are you ready for the guided tour?" asked Albert.

They followed him into a large circular room with a small stage.

"The theater!" he declaimed. "It holds two hundred and sixty-eight people, of whom approximately fifty will be asleep at any one time."

"What do you put on here?" asked Jim.

"Recitals. My father takes his recitals very seriously. You must have heard of that old bag of Newport snobbery who, after hiring Fritz Kreisler to play in her home for fifteen hundred dollars, asked him not to mingle with the guests. Kreisler's reply was, 'In that case, Madame, my fee will be only a thousand.' My father is just the opposite. He always asks the artist to stay for late supper so that he can find out what makes him tick. In

Carnegie Hall, he says, you learn very little about a great performer. Only something about the composer. The artists all stay. Of course, the acoustics are excellent." He let them linger for a moment and then ushered them out.

"Next comes the ordeal of the East and West galleries. Let's get it over with."

Jim and Stanley were stunned as they walked through the enormous rooms, whose walls were covered with paintings as important as were to be found in any museum in the world. There were no fillers. This house contained only the great masters' greatest creations.

Jim felt that for a man to own a museum was one thing, magnificent certainly, but not so extravagant as it seemed, since it was obviously earmarked for the people; but for him to incorporate priceless masterpieces, segments of the world's culture, into the routine of his daily living just as he would an old pipe, a favorite necktie, or a well-broken-in pair of shoes, for him to pay a milk bill beneath a Titian and read the evening paper between Holbeins, was almost unbelievable.

"I can't decide whether this is a palace or a museum," said Jim.

"It's both," answered Albert. "And it's my father all the way."

Stanley leaned against a chair.

"It's always a tiring tour, and a little oppressive the first time around," said Albert. "Let's recuperate next to the pool."

They walked to the courtyard and sat down together on a stone bench near the water. "Why is it so shallow?" asked Jim.

"My father says that the architect made it six inches deep so that some of the people who come here won't feel out of their depth."

"The pictures alone must be worth ten or twenty million dollars," mused Stanley, "but I suppose this kind of talk is vulgar."

"In my house it would be considered so. Any discussion of my father's money has always been taboo. But there's really no secret about it. My grandfather came over from Switzerland when he was five, and when he died, sixty-five years later, he left my father eighty million dollars. So far, my father has doubled his inheritance."

"Explain me one thing, then, will you?" asked Stanley. "How come we've never heard of him? I'll bet nobody has even tried to assassinate him."

"My father has two passions: art and anonymity."

"Wasn't he angry when you decided on medicine? Didn't he expect you to take over his empire someday?" asked Jim.

"He didn't bat an eye," answered Albert. "You see, my father doesn't have to fulfill any dreams of success through me. He's already been a success in everything he's done—steel, copper, finance, art collecting, even tennis. Once he was ranked twenty-seventh nationally."

Stanley looked impressed.

"And there's another thing," Albert continued; "my mother's father was an illustrious physician, Professor of Medicine at Zurich, in fact. That helped, too."

Albert heard it first—a metallic clicking on the marble floor of the colonnades—and jumped up immediately. Before his friends could follow his example, however, Huegenon had come down the steps and was upon them. He was straight, slim at the waist, and swift, and his gray hair was thick and tightly curled, the hyacinth hair of the Homeric tales. Jim thought not of Odysseus, but of Lorenzo de Medici, and decided on the spot that this must have been the way the Florentine had appeared, standing imperious and impatient in the midst of his power and his art.

"Father, Mr. Morelle and Mr. Levinson."

This was the first time Stanley had ever been introduced to a man in full dress.

"Yes, yes, I knew they were coming." Huegenon waved aside the introduction with a tapering Van Dyke hand, just like the ones in his paintings, nodded to Jim, and turned to Stanley. "Albert tells me you are still having trouble with your ground strokes. Don't despair. I overcame that very handicap when I was your age. You will, too."

He looked at the two guests appraisingly, said, "Good night," and walked out.

"If I ever reach the intercollegiate finals," promised Stanley, "I'll send him the best seat in the house."

"And he'll come," said Albert, "even if they're played in California."

Huegenon did more than reassure Stanley. He arranged to have one of the country's most famous professional coaches remake his game. Largely as a result of this expert instruction, he won the intercollegiate tennis championship in his senior year. Although he played no more competitive tennis once he entered medical school, he never forgot what the Huegenon magic could accomplish. And more than twenty-five years later, when the time came, Jim did not forget either.

SEVEN

It was only after his victory in the intercollegiate finals that Stanley at last felt confident that he would be admitted to medical school. Up to now he could not understand Jim's careless taking for granted that they both would be accepted. Even after their election to Phi Beta Kappa in December, Stanley was still suspicious that religious prejudice might rob him in the end of the fruits of his study. What finally reassured him was the conviction that his athletic prowess would impress a gentile dean. But the two friends grew gloomy about Albert's chances, especially when they heard that only one out of every fifteen applicants would be accepted by the American medical schools. Although they persuaded him to apply to all four New York institutions, deep in their hearts they knew of only one way to insure his success. Jim decided to tell him what it was before it was too late.

"Just to make sure, Albert," he said casually one afternoon after they had left the classroom on Morningside Heights, "why don't you get your father to put pressure on P and S or Cornell? He's a philanthropist."

"He's not a philanthropist. He's an art collector. And, according to him, above even Art there is Competence. He would much prefer me to be an accomplished dilettante than a mediocre doctor. I've got to show him I'm competent by getting into medical school on my own. That was part of the bargain when I decided to become a doctor."

"Couldn't you dangle his name before the greedy eyes of a dean or two?"

An expression of distaste crossed Albert's face. "No. It would make me feel uncomfortable."

"Couldn't your mother influence him?"

"She would never try to influence him in anything. He guards and cherishes her, he loves her, but he would never think of listening to her. I imagine this was part of another bargain, made twenty-five years ago, when he decided to fall in love."

"That's the way to handle a marriage," murmured Stanley from the depths of a great inexperience.

On the first of June, Jim and Stanley received letters of acceptance from P and S in the morning mail. For Albert there were four rejections. Although not surprised, his two friends were outraged. The next day, promptly at 9 A.M., they were in the medical school asking to see the Dean about an admission. The secretary, who knew that they had already been accepted, was temporarily immobilized, but she recovered quickly and walked into the inner office. A few minutes later the Dean was at the door—thin, elegant, saturnine—looking both irritable and curious as he waved them inside.

"Both of you distinguished athletes graduated magna cum laude, but evidently you don't have the brains to let well enough alone."

"We're here for Albert Huegenon. We were hoping you might reconsider him," said Jim.

"I don't know him."

"You turned him down, just the same."

"We had over twenty-three hundred candidates for admission this year. We took one hundred. Do you want me to remember the names of twenty-two hundred rejects?"

"No, sir, only one."

The Dean looked at Jim sharply.

"We think an injustice was done. An unintentional one," Jim hastened to add when he saw the Dean's eyes narrow. "After all, Albert Huegenon can't be anything more than another admission form to you. But to us he is a friend and we hope that some day he will be a colleague. Mr. Levinson and I don't know the twenty-two hundred applicants you've rejected, but we do know at least six of the hundred you've accepted and, believe me, none of them can hold a candle to Albert. He has the quiet virtues that don't get into an examination paper or show in the class standings, and we feel these are at least as important to a doctor as getting an A in calculus, a subject he won't use later on anyway. For the past two years he's had a B average, and he's done something none of your other applicants thought of doing. He's spent two summers in the laboratory at McKinley Hospital, where everybody thinks he's absolutely tops. All we're asking, sir, is for you to give him a chance, to interview him yourself, and to speak to the people at McKinley when you have a moment."

"There's something else," interjected Stanley. "When a Jew with high marks is passed over in favor of a Christian with low ones, the excuse is always that the Christian has the superior personality. Why can't that apply here? Why can't Albert Huegenon be chosen on the basis of his superior personality?"

The Dean, long known as a man of unshakable poise, looked dumfounded. He had been growing paler during the interview, but now his cheeks were flushed and his thin lips seemed a trifle blue.

"I hope for both your sakes that you are unaware of your incredible impudence. Are you trying to tell me how to run a medical school—you, who have never attended one? Are you

99

trying to instruct me in the intricacies of a fair admissions policy after I've been struggling to establish one for twenty years? Or are you trying to get me to throw out a deserving, high-mark applicant so that I can confer on your pal by favoritism what he could not win himself on merit? Well, if you are, your magna cum laude, Phi Beta Kappa brains are even more addled than I thought." He got up, walked to the window, and with his hands in his pockets began to rock back and forth. After a moment he looked up at the sky. "The more I consider your behavior, the more I doubt whether either of you has the mental stability required of a doctor." He kept staring at the sky, and then wheeled around, walked dejectedly to his desk, and sagged into the chair. "That was an improper remark. Actually you've done a very courageous thing, and this Huegenon must be a remarkable young man to have evoked such loyalty in his friends."

"Thank you, sir," said Jim. "I would just like to mention that his father is a very rich man."

"Irrelevant here."

"Oh, yes. I know it is, sir. I didn't mention it because Charles Huegenon is a millionaire more than a hundred times over, or because, converted to philanthropy, he might be a blessing to a medical school. I mentioned it just to illustrate Albert's character. Don't you think it was decent of him, sir, not to have used his father's wealth to try to get into P and S?"

"Charles Huegenon, Charles Huegenon!" mused the Dean. Then he focused on Jim again and said, "Yes, I do. Admirable. And his working at McKinley impresses me. It has an outstanding reputation—that is, for a hospital not connected with a medical school," he added a bit snobbishly.

He sent for the Huegenon file at once, but even before he opened the manila folder he murmured, "Of course, I can't do anything for him this year."

For the next few minutes he studied the application carefully, muttering, "This seems promising," and "I see a few B pluses here in his last year." Then he closed the folder, tented his fingers, and began to teeter back and forth in his swivel chair. "I have a suggestion to make: Why doesn't Mr. Huegenon take his master's degree at Columbia this year, let's say in physiological chemistry. If he does that, and proves half as impressive on his interview as you say he is, I see no reason why he should not be admitted next year."

Three days later, after a short interview, the Dean told Albert he need have no fear about getting in the following year.

Charles Huegenon, chronically skeptical about his son's chances, greeted the news as his most fortunate miscalculation. For years it had been clear to him that the boy would have neither the strength, on the one hand, to preside over the Huegenon empire, nor the weakness, on the other, to agree to its liquidation. Then, all at once, the solution had appeared. Albert's gentleness, sympathy, and basic goodness, the tenderizers that would have made him such a delicious morsel for his father's business enemies, were now to be used for a different purpose. These qualities, transmuted by the alchemy of medicine from business liabilities into professional assets, would henceforth be the driving forces in his chosen career. And he was showing other promising qualities as well, his father thought. His initiative in working his way into McKinley, his ability to inspire loyalty in his friends, his success in getting into medical school, by whatever means and however late, all were very encouraging. Huegenon felt a vague gratitude, unaccustomed and irritating, and a strange satisfaction. He immediately had dinner invitations sent to the Levinsons and the Morelles. And just to be on the safe side, ordered his secretary to go to the Jewish Theological Seminary to prepare a three- or four-page digest—double spaced, of course—on the diet, customs, and religious practices of the Jews.

Mrs. Levinson's hands trembled when she wrote the acceptance note, and she looked behind her more than once as she rushed to the post office to mail it. There would be trouble when her husband came home, she knew. She decided not to tell him until just before they went to bed.

"We're going to Albert Huegenon's parents' for dinner Friday night."

He looked at her as if she had suddenly turned into a heathen. "Friday night! What's the matter with you? Why Friday night?"

"Because I already accepted. We can walk there, and you can eat vegetables and dessert at dinner."

Mr. Levinson shook his head sadly. "And what about Kiddush? Who's going to say Kiddush? In the twenty-five years we been married, there must have been," he thought for a moment, "thirteen hundred Kiddushes. Did I ever miss one yet except when I was in the hospital?"

"So make believe you're in the hospital again. Thirteen hundred Kiddushes! A mathematician I'm married to!"

"Not a mathematician, a Jew. And for a Jew, Shabbos is everything."

"And our son is nothing! You think it was the Phi Beta Kappas and the cum laudes and the Talmudic brains that got him into medical school?" She looked at him with scorn. "It was the tennis. Mr. Huegenon's tennis."

"I don't like it," he said stubbornly. "I don't like it one bit."

As Friday drew nearer, he became more and more depressed, pacing up and down the apartment and muttering, "There are seven nights in the week, only this man has to pick Friday night." Or else some variant on the theme "You wonder why your son is not religious any more."

But Mrs. Levinson became more cheerful by the hour. Her cheeks were flushed, she hummed a little tune while she cooked, and at the last minute even sent out her good dress to be dry-cleaned although it had only one spot on it and that near the hem, where it would not show. It was clear that Stanley had told her what the Huegenon house was like. Just before they left, she patted her husband on the cheek and said, "Papa, you look very nice in the blue serge suit."

"I don't feel nice," he said miserably.

The Morelles were waiting for them in front of the door, and when they reached the indoor courtyard, Albert was there to introduce them to his parents.

Hennie Morelle spoke first. "It's like the pleasure dome of Kubla Khan. It's such a beautiful house."

"It should be," said Huegenon, looking at his wife. "It was built for a beautiful woman—my mother—and always looks its best when beautiful women are here." His bow to Hennie was meant to leave no doubt that she was included in this company.

Mrs. Levinson kept turning around and around, clasping and unclasping her hands and exclaiming, "It's a palace, a regular palace!"

"It should be," said Mrs. Huegenon, glancing at her husband. "It was really built for a crown prince, and always looks its best when crown princes are here." She smiled at her son and at Jim and Stanley.

There was a subdued conversational murmur for a few minutes until she said, "Would you like to go around with us now?" She was still lovely, and though she had faded somewhat, she had done so like a beautiful medieval tapestry.

"What a question!" exclaimed Mrs. Levinson. "This is what we have been waiting for."

Huegenon went out of his way to put his guests at ease. While he did not have a profound knowledge of art, he was sincerely devoted to his pictures in a simple, personal way. He showed them the little Vermeer he had just bought for two hundred and ten thousand dollars with much of the same feeling he would have displayed in demonstrating his favorite cigarette case. By the time the tour was over, Hennie was entranced, Jake deeply impressed, and Mrs. Levinson so elated that she kept clasping and unclasping her hands, and saying over and over again, "It's a museum, a regular museum!"

Only Mr. Levinson, far in the rear, was preoccupied and miserable.

When Mrs. Huegenon led them into the big, oval dining room, they all stood still, subdued, as many other guests before them had been, by its perfect symmetry. Huegenon himself never tired of the tableau. It was always the same—the frozen guests, the six liveried waiters standing stiffly at regular intervals along the curved walls, the grim butler guarding the door into the pantry, and the old man in the center of the room, the head butler for two generations, limping toward them with a little bow. Each guest was unobtrusively shown to his palce. When Mr. Levinson saw the portrait towering above his chair, he turned pale and stopped suddenly in consternation. Even before he looked at the brass name plate, he knew full well whose violent hand was stretching toward him. Yes, it was a magnificent painting, yes, it was undoubtedly a masterpiece, yes, it was, of course, an El Greco, yes, yes, yes, but it was the infamous Estrada just the same, the Burning Cardinal, the murderous Head of the Inquisition, who had sent more Jews to their death than any man in Spanish history. The scimitar nose, the cruel, thin, magenta-tinted lips, the unshaking outstretched arm, and the crazed, coal-black eyes, enjoying what they were about to see, were all just as they must have been four hundred years before, as he sent yet another Jew to the stake. Mr. Levinson squirmed into his chair, trying to forget the eyes that were burning into his back. He had to admit, at least, that when fate placed him beneath the Cardinal's picture he was receiving a well-deserved punishment. He should never in the first place have profaned the Sabbath by coming here. Slowly he bowed his head lower and lower, trying to pull it into his body like a threatened turtle. Through the dreadful silence he could hear the ticking of a clock, the whine of tires on Fifth Avenue, and the moaning of a ship on the East River. But in the room there was not a sound. Why didn't somebody make a little noise, he wondered, rustle a napkin at least, or move a knife?

As from far away, the clock struck eight. Mr. Levinson raised his head. Only then did he see that he was sitting at the head of the table.

"Mr. Levinson," said Huegenon sternly, "aren't you going to say Kiddush?"

A white silk prayer hat with golden stripes, the kind that crowned the Chazan on the High Holy Days, was placed upon his head, and the silver goblet with the blood-red wine thrust into his hand.

"Stand up, Papa, stand up!" his wife whispered from the foot of the table.

With measured tread and as solemnly as if he were leading a religious procession, a liveried servant, bearing a silver tray with two beautiful old silver candlesticks upon it, walked into the room and placed the treasured burden before her. Everyone watched her light the candles. Only then did her husband rise and hold the Kiddush cup before him.

Perhaps, to the impassive servants, the ritual he was performing was a strange one; perhaps his clothes were out of place in this, the most elegant of dining rooms; perhaps the shine on the sleeve of his blue serge suit was just a little too much. But certainly it was no greater than the shining in his wife's eyes, as here, in an alien house under the eyes of the enemy of his people, he sang the Sanctification over the Wine, and prayed deep in his heart for all men, for the great and the lowly, the sure and the perplexed, the healthy and the suffering, the Christian and the Jew. As Stanley stared at the portrait above his father's head, a change seemed to come over the terrible Inquisitor. His cheeks flushed and his eyes widened, as if in the silver goblet held triumphantly below he saw once again the blood of the Jewish martyrs he had long ago doomed, and knew at last that they could never die, that this, the blood he had so cruelly shed, would flow forever, and forever nourish humanity's beating heart. Then the iron arm seemed to fall back, the crazed look was replaced by compassion, and in the glow of the Sabbath lights the magenta-tinted lips seemed to soften and murmur, "Forgive me, forgive me, I knew not what I did!"

"Oh-main!" sang out Jim staunchly, as always the first.

"Oh-main!" said Huegenon crisply as if he were at a board meeting.

Mr. Levinson sipped the wine and then stood there hesitantly until Mrs. Huegenon took the Kiddush cup gently from his hand and drank a little herself. It went slowly around the table as each drank and passed it to his neighbor. Only then did the old butler limp to the head of the table carrying the two lacquered loaves under their silken cloth.

"The Moe-tsuh, sir," he whispered reproachfully, as if afraid that at the last moment Mr. Levinson might forget. But Mr. Levinson did not forget. First in Hebrew and then in English he recited the Benediction over the Bread: "Blessed art Thou, O Lord our God, King of the universe, Who bringeth forth bread from the earth."

Again Mr. Levinson hesitated, and again Mrs. Huegenon held out her hand, this time for a piece of the saffron-hearted twist she knew everyone must eat.

"Mr. Levinson, you need have no qualms about eating here tonight," Huegenon said quietly. "The dishes and silverware have never been used before, the meat is strictly kosher, and the meal has been prepared under the supervision of a rabbinical student who spent the day in this house."

A great silence fell over the room. Not a servant moved.

"You're a good man, Mr. Huegenon," said Mrs. Levinson, wiping her eyes with a lace handkerchief she had saved from her wedding. She thought something over, and then looked into his eyes. "You're sure you don't have a little Jewish blood in you from somewhere?"

"No, I don't think I have," answered Huegenon with a smile.

She smiled, too. "You couldn't be any nicer if you had."

Mr. Levinson cleared his throat, and Stanley could see he was about to embark on a Talmudic dissertation. "The Hebrew for a commandment is 'Mitzvuh.' Most people think that a mitzvuh is a good deed, but that is only because the carrying out of a commandment is in itself a good deed." He began to lapse into the sing-song of the Talmudic discussions. "Now, the Talmud tells us there are six hundred and thirteen mitzvuhs in the Torah. For more than a thousand years, Jews have been deciding on their own and without any divine sanction which are major mitzvuhs and which are minor ones. A revered sage once said that he was not concerned about keeping the major mitzvuhs, they were so obvious. What disturbed him was the thought that he might fail to keep the minor ones. And who can always say which are the more important to God? What seems like a minor mitzvuh to us might result eventually in some incalculable good. In the eyes of the Lord, he who keeps the minor mitzvuhs, who does the little things, is truly righteous. My wife made no mistake. You are a good man, Mr. Huegenon, a good man."

Albert could hardly believe his eyes. His father, usually so cynical, was immensely flattered.

"Really, now," he said, "that's very gracious."

Dinner was superb, and understandably so, cooked as it had been by the head chef of Stiegman's downtown kosher restaurant. This irritable man, unintimidated, in fact unimpressed by the Huegenon fortune, agreed to go, as he put it, "halfway across the world to that house up there," only upon the assurance of a two hundred dollar donation to his synagogue. But he had done well. The gefilte fish contained more white-fish than carp, the chicken soup was filled with kreplech, and the Brust, magnificent by any standard, was the middle cut of a boneless brisket. After Mr. Levinson had said grace, everyone strolled into the study, and there, under the Titian and the two Dürers, they talked about baseball, tennis, Talmud, music, steel, cooking, running a house, and medicine. It was a lovely evening.

Afterward, the Levinsons strolled slowly home. Mrs. Levinson was humming her little tune when her husband turned toward her and said, "You looked very nice in that dress tonight, the one you just got cleaned."

She smiled. Then as they walked side by side toward Madison Avenue, he took her hand. "You were right, mama, perfectly right. Mr. Huegenon is a good man."

His wife reached over and kissed him behind the ear. "Papa," she said, "that's what it's like to be a Christian."

EIGHT

A FEW MONTHS after the dinner at the Huegenons, the three
friends were lounging on the beach at Southampton, where the
financier had his summer place. Jim had just pulled a sweat
shirt over his bathing suit and was looking down at Albert,
stretched on the sand.

"That's a funny-looking mole you've got."

"I've had it for years."

"You mean it's always been coal black like that?"

Albert sat up and stared at the small mole above his knee.
"No, it was never this color before," he said shaking his head.

Stanley kneeled down and examined it, too. "It looks like
one of the eyes in your dining room El Greco."

"Why don't you come back to the city with us tomorrow
night and have somebody look at it," urged Jim.

But Albert only laughed.

Unfortunately, his laughter was singularly inappropriate.
When his parents returned from Europe six weeks later, he
already had an olive-sized lump in his groin. "A regional lymph
node," said the family doctor, busying himself with his bag

and leaving quickly. Two days later he had the Professor of Surgery remove it, together with the mole, at the medical-school hospital. Albert was kept there a few days longer, until the sections came through, and only then was Huegenon summoned by the surgeon, who, since he was a full-time man, had his office in the hospital. He hardly gave the financier time to cross the threshold.

"It was a malignant melanoma."

Huegenon stopped. "That's quite serious, I suppose."

The surgeon nodded.

"He's not going to die," said Huegenon, on an impulse.

"Oh, yes," replied the surgeon.

Huegenon sat down and put his handkerchief to his lips. "You must excuse me. He's my only child."

"I fully understand."

"Isn't there anything you can do?"

"I could do a mid-thigh amputation and resect all the nodes, but none of this would affect the outcome in the least."

How would his wife take it, Huegenon wondered. She would never hold up. "How long do you think it will last, Doctor?"

Now was the time to be expansive, the surgeon decided. A little optimism could do no harm. "I had a case recently that lasted eleven months."

The next day Albert left the hospital, but the mother tumor had already sent its blackhearted cancer cells swarming into his lungs and liver. In less than three months he was beginning to get a little out of breath as he sat up in bed, his emaciation pitifully accentuated by his big, fluid-filled belly. It was then that the family doctor suggested a return to the hospital, but Huegenon just shook his head. That night Albert asked his parents and the nurses to step out of the room a moment so that he might be alone with his friends. It was to be the last time.

"How's medical school?" he asked, lying on his back and staring at the ceiling.

"Lousy," said Jim—and he meant it.

"I don't think I would have minded it. But I'll never find out."

Albert turned toward them and they could see at once that he knew. "Or what it's like to get laid. I had a couple of chances, you know."

"I'm sure you did," said Jim gravely.

"Only, I didn't know then that everything would be over so soon. I think that when God puts a man on this earth, He should guarantee him at least one good lay." He turned back to the ceiling. "I guess I'm supposed to say I'm not afraid, but it hasn't turned out that way. I'm scared. Boy, am I scared! And when I think that in a little while no one will know that I ever lived. . . ." He shook his head.

"You're not going to die," said Jim. "But in case anything should ever happen, Stan and I will see to it that people won't forget you so easily. That's a promise."

With a last great effort, Albert sat up, looking for a moment almost the way he had when Jim first saw him sitting alongside the tennis court in his gray flannel trousers and old gray sweat shirt. "You know, I believe you will at that," he said with a smile. Then he held out his hands to his friends, and lay back again.

The next afternoon, when they raced over from medical school, they learned that he had died in his sleep.

Huegenon had a very small funeral for his son. At the cemetery he asked Jim and Stanley if they would mind dropping in to see him at home for a few minutes later in the day. When they got there, they found him in the courtyard looking down at the pool.

"I'm terribly sorry to put you out," he began at once, "but there is something that has been preying on my mind. Do you think he suffered much the last three months?"

They both shook their heads. "No, I don't think so," said Jim. "He would have mentioned it to us."

Huegenon nodded.

"They certainly did everything they could for him," said Stanley consolingly, after an embarrassing pause.

"On the contrary," said Mr. Huegenon, "they let him down twice. First, they wouldn't let him enter medical school with his class, when just a week there would have meant so much to him. And then, when he needed them most, on the operating table, they let him down again." He turned away from the pool and looked directly at them. "But at least he had three happy years—the years with you."

Just before they left the courtyard, they turned around. Huegenon was sitting on Albert's favorite bench, staring at the still, shallow water.

NINE

THEY HAD NOT LIED to Albert about medical school. Although forewarned by Dr. Morelle, they were finding the first year even worse than they had anticipated. It was the reign of Anatomy. Divided into fifty pairs, each one of which was sentenced to a year's work on the same formalin-soaked corpse, the class, in the very process of steadily diminishing the size of the cadavers by industrious snipping and cutting, only succeeded in increasing the intensity of the smell.

By the end of the term, however, the olfactory nerves of these conscientious dissectors were too exhausted to detect the hideous odor.

At home, still tainted by the ineradicable smell, they studied deep into the stillness of the night, attempting to learn by rote the size, shape, and configuration of all the bones in the body, and every lump, bump, curve, and depression on them as well. Then, driven on by an awareness of increasing fatigue, they tried desperately to memorize the rise, descent, course, origin, and insertion of every muscle and ligament, and the pathways and filamentous branchings of every threadlike nerve besides.

Of the actual workings and purposes of all these structures, they learned next to nothing. And of the great organs that give mankind its life—the heart, the lungs, and the liver, they learned nothing at all. Bones, muscles, and threadlike nerves were evidently all that mattered. Those of them who did not already sense the fact would learn some day that all this cramming would never help them, that even an orthopedic specialist, provided that he had a modicum of sanity, would never think of glutting himself with this senseless rigmarole, and that the one or two who might later need to master some of these wretched minutiae would learn them in a different and better way. Never was so much useless information forced upon so defenseless a few. At least the medieval Scholastics burdened their disciples in the name of the Lord, but there never was a god who demanded that future internists, pediatricians, and psychiatrists memorize the hidden details of every osseous portion of their fellow man. Perhaps it was a god who finally liberated them in the end, a pagan god and one of their own at that, Apollo, the physician of the Hippocratic oath, who, conferring upon them a blessed amnesia, made them forget everything they had learned the moment the final examination was over. In spite of the obvious uselessness of the course, the calcified brains of generation after generation of sadistic anatomy masters had ordained that he who would be a doctor must survive the Ordeal by Rote during the first year.

The Professor of Anatomy, musing over the animal bones in his office on the top floor, did not concern himself with examinations, dissections, curricula, or individual students. He was an old anatomist of the new school. In other words, a comparative anatomist, and famous all over the anatomists' world for his erudite papers on animal osteology. Three times a week he gave his lectures in the amphitheater, the steeply rising, semicircular, wooden tiers of which could easily have embraced the entire school, but which during this period held only the freshman class. The huge room was plunged in darkness, the rostrum brilliantly lighted for that moment, always exactly eleven o'clock, when he would make his entrance dressed in a jet-black, high-collared blouse with trousers to match, looking like the skeletons' clergyman. He dressed this way, first, because he considered it appropriate to Anatomy, the subject of the dead, and secondly, because it showed off his vivid white hair so well. Dead was the subject, dead the presentation, and dead the class. He never saw the students, not merely because, drawing on the blackboard, he so seldom faced the darkened room, but because even when he did, he spoke to another audience, an imaginary audience consisting of the country's top anatomists, most of whom, he slyly observed to himself, did not understand what he was talking about. He demanded only one thing of the students, absolute silence. And he always got it. Stretched out on the curved wooden tiers, their heads pillowed by books and overcoats, the entire class slumbered, snatching from Anatomy in the morning the sleep it had robbed them of at night. During the entire lecture, the professor, with his back to the real and the imaginary audiences, demonstrated the skeletons of strange birds, unheard-of reptiles, and unbelievable mammals, some of which were extinct and all of which should have been extinct in any reasonable world.

Between the unheard lectures, the fetid dissections, and the memorizing of the bones, the class, by the end of the year, had learned everything about anatomy and nothing about the human body at all.

To make a sackcloth-and-ashes course out of anatomy was easy. After all, the subject was not very lively to begin with. But to do the same with physiology, the most fascinating of the basic sciences; to take this medical mystery story and reduce it to a mass of meaningless diagrams and uninspiring numbers, carried to the second decimal place of course, required true anti-genius. This the Professor of Physiology and his colleague the Associate Professor possessed to a remarkable degree. On a medical landscape blazing with colorful investigators, they stood out all gray. It was said that men like these two would never go off half-cocked. The trouble was that they never went off at all. Certainly they were no blank cartridges, for although they had some substance, there was no fire. They were really more like duds. In their lectures, they affected a dry, nasal, monotonous speech, and both added a bit of a cackle as well. The Associate Professor was known as the man who had almost discovered insulin. There was one of these in every medical school. If he had only tied all the pancreatic ducts tightly enough, he would have had it, he told his students. Then he proceeded to methodically bleach the colorful pages of their physiology textbook. It took him the entire academic year, but, then, he had plenty of time. The full Professor had done some work in electricity when electricity was young, and retained the imaginative outlook of the average household electrician. His round, steel-rimmed spectacles glittered with a vast indifference, and if he detected a blooming interest anywhere in the class, he was sure to wither it. When Stanley asked permission to try to pick up a tracing of the fetal heart by applying the electrocardiograph electrodes to a pregnant woman's abdomen, the Professor shook his head and said, "Come down to earth, Levinson." A few years later, the work was done at another institution. Because none of the Professor's publications had ever shown any daring or imagination, he had acquired a reputation as a sound scientist. Actually, he was nothing more than a desert of a man.

The second year was a great improvement. It was what they had expected the first year to be. But not until the third year did the excitement come. Somewhere a long-awaited trumpet sounded, and as the Jericho walls that had imprisoned them crumbled, appropriately enough to dust, their tired eyes could make out just beyond them the glories of clinical medicine. Battalions of great physicians marching into their midst rescued them from their two-year siege. To enrich and illuminate every specialty there were now full-time, part-time, and visiting professors. Among the latter, Emmerich, Rintman, and Hauser gave exciting lectures. Touched by pride when they taught, Jim thought of himself already as a pure-breed, second-generation McKinley man, forgetting for the moment that his father was only a McKinley dispensary drudge and he, himself, not yet an applicant for internship. Soon they were learning medicine not only from an illustrious faculty, but from a complementary mass of clinical material, staggering beyond belief, that was culled from the voluntary and city hospitals affiliated with the school.

No demonstrations impressed them more than those conducted by the Department of Dermatology, which almost extravagantly offered them an endless line of unique and fascinating cases that were the envy of every institution in the land. One biting cold afternoon early in winter, Jim threw his new Rogers Peet overcoat over a chair in the little anteroom leading to the amphitheater and raced up the steps to await another of the great shows. He was not to be disappointed. With an effort to be casual, the Professor of Dermatology brought before the class ten lepers, and followed them with a tertiary syphilitic just as a throw-in. To the students, leprosy was a biblical curse—a medieval bell, stick, and hooded-robe disease—not something to be found in ten ordinary people walking the streets of New York. But there they were, evidently harmless in the temperate climate, although forced to report regularly to the Board of Health. Jim's interest turned to horror when he saw the parade of lepers issue from and return to the little anteroom. But he need not have worried about wearing a contaminated overcoat, for at the end of the period it was gone. As soon as he got home he told his father about the theft, adding reassuringly that since the Department had the names and addresses of all ten lepers, it would be easy to retrieve the coat. Jake shook his head.

"I think now is the time to be magnanimous," he said, "and

to say to him who took it—from a safe distance, of course—
'Your need is greater than mine.' We'll go down to Rogers
Peet tomorrow."

It was more magnanimous than Jim realized, because the
Depression was beginning to hurt his father badly.

The fourth year at medical school was easy and pleasant,
consisting of hospital clerkships, work in the out-patient departments, and practical demonstrations. No formal examinations
were given and no senior had ever flunked out. But a new fear
gripped the class, the fear of getting an undesirable internship
or even none at all. There simply were not enough of those
two-year positions to train the thousands of new doctors who
kept pouring out of the medical schools. To make matters worse,
only a few of the internships were in first-grade institutions.
McKinley, for instance, had only eight openings each year.
In addition to the normal difficulties, Stanley had to face the
handicap of his religion. Because of it, most places would be
closed to him. In the beginning he wanted to apply only to
Mt. Sinai, but Jim kept hammering at him to try McKinley,
since the examinations there were held a week earlier than at
the other hospitals.

"You'll just be building your own ghetto if you don't,"
he warned.

What finally persuaded Stanley was the memory of Hauser's
third-year lectures and an eagerness to work on his renowned
pediatric service.

Soon after the Christmas vacation, the two friends took the
written examinations together. Long before this they had sub-
mitted their letters of recommendation, medical-school records,
and the answers to a few biographical questions—the most
important of which was "Religion?" The examination lasted
five hours, and there were 256 applicants for the four surgical
and four medical internships. Two days later, twenty-five survivors were recalled for the orals, among them Jim and Stanley.

That Stanley was there at all was due to considerable back-tracking on the part of McKinley's highest ruling body.

Two weeks before, word had come down from the Chairman of the Board that again this year no "Hebrews" would be taken. He always called them "Hebrews," as if they were still a wandering Semitic tribe, revealing by this dubious euphemism that he considered "Jew" an insulting term. Not that he was anti-Semitic, mind you, he would say, but, after all, this was a Christian hospital, and once you opened the doors to them you would be overrun. As a matter of fact there were quite a few of them already on the attending staff, and very good types they were, but—"zu viel ist ungesund." He always translated the little proverb for any members of the board who were not of German descent as "too much is unhealthy."

"They're afraid of exposing the hospital to brains," commented Rintman as soon as he heard. "It might start an epidemic."

"Schweinerei!" growled Emmerich.

The third examiner, Hauser, was an Aryan Jew, and he said nothing.

Since the trustees stood in awe of Rintman and Emmerich, and might need their services themselves some day, they retreated, and agreed to accept one particularly gifted "Hebrew."

Four hours after the completion of the oral examinations, Jim and Stanley received telegrams ordering them to report for duty at 8 A.M. July 1.

On the night of June 30, they packed their grips, laid out their best clothes, and went to bed early so as to be fresh in the morning. It took Stanley a long time to fall asleep. He wondered what it would be like to be the only Jew on the house staff, but then he had Jim, and that was like having one's own Praetorian Guard. It would have come as a surprise to him to learn that from now on religion would not play a major role in his life. Jim went to sleep quickly, thinking about McKinley's great surgeons and wondering whether his name would ever be set next to theirs. Then a strange dream came to him. He was staring at McKinley Hospital, which had never seemed so solid and so magnificent. Suddenly, unbelievably, in broad daylight, this great institution rose and slowly sailed away. He would have been astounded had he known that in a very real sense this was exactly what was going to happen.

PART
TWO

"Who shall live and who shall die."

TEN

MᴄKɪɴʟᴇʏ had been designed so that the poor could be treated efficiently by the finest specialists in New York. Of its five hundred beds only one hundred were in the private pavilion. Most of the 400 remaining beds, all free, were housed in high-ceilinged, ancient wards, each stretching for half a block in a building that occupied all of Seventieth Street between Park and Madison. The children's pavilion and a few small structures in the hollow square contained the rest of the patients. Rintman was fond of saying that the wards, with their long, gleaming central corridors, had once been the meeting halls of Valhalla, where the old gods of German medicine assembled each day to recount their battles with disease. The sick were there not only to be treated and cured, but to be utilized, to serve as a means of improving the already formidable skills of the doctors. The word "semiprivate" had not yet been invented. It would not have been understood. How can a patient be half private and half free, the Hospital would have asked.

Every new intern expected to be treated in a scurvy manner. The Hospital had something that he wanted badly, and that something was the free case. For it he would suffer any sacrifice, undergo any humiliation. Soon he knew that he would plunge into a stream of clinical material whose endless flow would heal his wounds, wash away the insults, and momentarily quench his unquenchable thirst for knowledge. The patients would be his, and they in turn would have no other doctor but him. It was he who would see them first, obtain the histories, make the diagnoses, struggle with the decisions, prescribe the treatment, and perform many of the operations. That all of this would be accomplished under the strict supervision of the attending staff would in no way negate his conviction that he had unique possession of the medically indigent. Today, when our society is dedicated to the abolition of the free case, when its slogan is "With charity toward none, with Blue Cross for all," the intern, to keep pace with the disappearance of the ward service, must obtain his medical education more and more by observing the private and semiprivate cases of the attendings. Unfortunately, in medicine, do-it-yourself is not a fad—it is a necessity. So it is obvious that an intern in those days received a full measure of education for his devotion.

The attendings were even more dedicated than the interns. With the exception of a few in the Laboratory and the X-ray Department, they received no salary. A McKinley appointment was a license to work for nothing. Not only that, but the Hospital insisted that its attendings be utterly faithful. No one was supposed to accept a position at another hospital. Like a proud and decorous wife, McKinley decreed that he who would stay wedded to her must forswear all mistresses. A few physicians there were who defied the ban, who had adulterous affiliations with other institutions. Such immoralities might be ignored, but they were never condoned. In return for their sacrifices in preserving the monogamous state, the doctors were given prestige and an opportunity to gain an unparalleled experience. Each had the ultimate responsibility not only for his own private patients but for everyone on his ward service as well. Each had perhaps thirty or thirty-five years in which to study and work through a vast amount of clinical material, integrating and analyzing it, developing new tests, testing new treatments, describing new diseases, and making fresh discoveries about old ones. And each had the opportunity to give to the wards his time, his strength, his freedom, and sometime in the end, his very life. It might well be asked what the free patients offered him in return. They gave him a chance for greatness. It was the ward patient who had made medicine great.

The nurses, too, worked for nothing—or next to nothing—but in spite of miserable wages and inhuman hours, there was no shortage. In those days they were everywhere, not frozen to desks, unseeing and unheeding like Greek statues, not Laocoönlike, struggling with the coils of telephones, not hidden away in conference rooms making up schedules and poring over massed reports like cryptographers, but out in the open wards, moving, always moving, walking among the patients, giving bedside care, reaching and bending, hurrying and swirling, transforming the grim central allée into a choreographer's delight. Their costumes were impressive, and those the students wore were period and pale blue, stretching all the way from the windpipe to the lower ankle and blotting out even the most insistent of feminine charms. As if this were not enough, the novitiate was further encased in a voluminous white skirt and a stiff white bib. The uniform was meant to be a sartorial denial of the fact that disciples of Florence Nightingale had calves, thighs, and bosoms. But it could not conceal the slim, gentle waists, the gardenia complexions, the smooth young lips. Nobody had found a way to do that. The bodies of the graduates were equally well concealed by some master camouflager. Of course, everything a nurse wore had to be heavily starched, and there was much rustling. To a country lad stretched out in bed at night it must have sounded like the forests of his youth.

Not only mobility but public crying was part of the nurse's behavior pattern. Summoned to the office of the Directress for some minor infraction, she was supposed to leave in tears. The operating-room nurses cried because surgeons shouted at them and hurled instruments at the walls. The head nurses cried because Rintman, Emmerich, and Hauser raked them with sardonic broadsides. And the student nurses cried because house physicians and surgeons for whom they had set their newly won caps upbraided them for clumsiness. The news softly spreading through the wards that Miss So-and-So was crying was accepted as an unfortunate but inevitable part of hospital life, like a patient's unexpected rise in temperature or the spread of a pneumonia.

The Hosptial was not cruel. It was authoritative. This was clearly shown by the incident with the beggar that occurred the month before Jim and Stanley began their internships. Those were the days when a city was known by the beggars it kept, the days of the great ones. In London they were gruff and Dickensian, in Berlin thorough and methodical, and in New York so aggressive and grasping that it was customary to say of one or another of them, "I'll bet he owns property." But Vienna, ah, Vienna, no place could equal it. If Cádiz was famous for its young girls (who had not heard "Les Filles de Cádiz" as an encore, of course), and Gibraltar for its Barbary apes, Vienna was renowned for its cunning, its master beggars. The man who had taken up his station in front of the private pavilion the year before had obviously been bred in the great Viennese tradition. One beautiful morning early in June there had appeared before McKinley's private pavilion a middle-aged cripple with the swarthy complexion of a Spanish pirate and the beady eyes of a week-old chick. He wore no hat, because his head was swathed in bandages, and he supported himself by means of a crutch under his left armpit. As motionless as a corpse except for a constant tremor of his extended right hand, he fixed all who approached with his shining avian eyes, and just before they reached the door, chirped piteously, "Help! Help!"

He was never heard to utter any other word, even in response to sympathetic questioning. Taken aback by this appeal, most people would attempt to drop money into his trembling hand, by no means an easy target, but one which in response to the magnetic lure of a coin would in an instant miraculously hold still, only to resume its vibrations as soon as the benefactor moved away. Few could pass him by, and he, in turn, rewarded his patrons' faithfulness by being faithful himself, working seven days a week, holidays included.

At first, the people who ran McKinley regarded him as a mere passing blight, a fly-by-night nuisance, but as they watched him transform himself into a fixture, they became alarmed. For one thing, his head bandage grew filthier, his clothes more disreputable. And dirt and disarray were cardinal sins at the Hospital. As a matter of fact, standing in the snow in January he looked like a member of the once Grande Armée on the retreat from Moscow, a French army at that. But much more important was the fact that he was a poor advertisement for the institution. Would not those who entered the private pavilion and contributed so much toward balancing the budget eventually ask, "Is it likely that a hospital that can do so little for its very own beggar, that ignores his head wound and orthopedic condition so shamefully, is it likely that such a hospital will be able to do much for its patients? And why does the man turn to us for help instead of to the institution under whose walls he stands?" These would be searching questions indeed. The time for direct action had come, and the McKinley authorities made a massive attempt to persuade the man to leave. Singly and in groups, the assistant superintendents, the head nurses, and the supervisors, the housekeepers, the pharmacists, the head clerks, the paymaster, the record-room personnel, and the admission officers used cajolery, flattery, reasoning, offers of medical assistance, and finally threats. To all of these the beggar replied with his little, tweeting, "Help! Help!" The head porter decided to use firmness, and ended by giving the man a quarter. The sergeant from the local precinct, summoned by the Hospital to deal with this emergency, watched the man in action for a few minutes, but after the sixth straight successful "Help! Help!" shook his head and walked away. At a time when millions were unemployed, he was not going to throw a man out of a good job. And now the beggar began to receive help from within. When the winter winds swirling east from Central Park inflamed his eyes, Rintman, long an admirer of his unchanging technique, handed him a package of boric acid wrapped in a dollar bill. Finally, Emmerich, always an implacable foe of sloppy surgery, stopped one day directly in front of him, glared like a disgusted eagle at his filthy bandage, and gave him a new one, neatly encased in a five-dollar bill. The beggar took the hint. He washed and dried the new bandage every night. And he went even further, not because he had been bribed by Emmerich's gift, but because now he genuinely wanted to become part of McKinley. He bought a neat secondhand suit. He shined his shoes. He even waxed and polished his crutch. The higher authorities were appalled. It was obvious that now the man was really dangerous. He was permanently identifying himself with the institution. He was becoming the McKinley type.

One lovely afternoon late the following June, he was summoned to the Superintendent's office. The moment he saw Mr. Stahlhelm's flickering eyes, he knew he had met his match.

"No 'Help! Help!' please," said the Superintendent, raising one hand while with the other he laid hold of the crutch like a victorious general taking his adversary's sword at a surrender ceremony. Carefully placing it in the umbrella stand, he motioned the man to a seat and offered him a cigar.

"You might as well stop the trembling now."

The beggar took the cigar with a steady hand.

"You will have to give up your station in front of the Hospital, I'm afraid," resumed Mr. Stahlhelm. "Captain

Ahearn, the head of the local precinct, had his appendix removed here two weeks ago. He feels very much indebted to us and would, I am sure, do anything for McKinley." He blew an oval smoke ring, a feat the interns credited to his remarkable mustache.

"You can readily see," he continued with a cruel smile, "that the moment has at last arrived when you must say 'Help! Help!' with complete sincerity."

The beggar's eyes clouded as if a nictitating membrane had been drawn across them. He did not move, but the hand with the cigar began to tremble.

"In spite of the fact that we can now easily eject you," Mr. Stahlhelm went on, "I am prepared to make you the following offer—provided you agree to leave voluntarily. From now on, we will serve you a hot dinner at noon every day of the year," here he gave an expansive smile, "as long as McKinley stands."

The beggar leaned across the desk and stretched his scrawny neck like a bird. "The same food the patients get?"

The Superintendent nodded.

"Thanksgiving and Christmas?"

"Certainly."

"Change the clause 'as long as McKinley stands' to 'as long as the recipient lives' and you got yourself a deal."

Mr. Stahlhelm indulged in his second smile. "Why? Do you think you will outlast the Hospital?"

The beggar shrugged. "Just say I'm not taking any chances."

"Agreed." Mr. Stahlhelm handed him his crutch like a magnanimous victor after the surrender.

A minute later people were astounded to see the former fixture of the private pavilion striding along Sixty-ninth Street, bandaged head in the air, crutch tucked under his arm, looking the way he must have looked as a young beggar. It was as much of a shock as if they had seen the Statue of Liberty sail through the Bay out to the open sea.

The beggar now took his stand in front of the Second National Bank at Seventy-third Street and Lexington Avenue— an excellent location. But at night he could be found before the private pavilion of Harland Hospital. It was obvious that hospitals were in his blood. Toward the end of his career, in keeping with the customs of the land, he worked only five days a week, and, finally, he gave up his job at the bank. But he never missed a meal at McKinley and never forgot that it had given him his start. Seventeen years after his interview with Mr. Stahlhelm, he was admitted as a respected semiprivate patient (he had had the foresight to enroll in both Blue Cross and Blue Shield) and died a week later of a massive cardiac infarction. He left his entire estate, valued at twenty-five thousand dollars, to the Hospital.

In the old days, the Hospital was indeed magnanimous and authoritative and no one in it more so, it was said, than the Chairman of the Board of Trustees, August Grund. It was not until one evening late in November that Jim caught his first glimpse of the ruler of McKinley's finances. He did not speak to him, of course. In those days there was too great a gulf between a junior intern and a trustee for any communication to have taken place. A cat might speak to a king, but not at McKinley. He merely stood spellbound behind the main entrance, watching the stately head float slowly upward as if it belonged to one of the major deities in the old mythology book instead of to the old man slowly climbing up the worn stone steps. As soon as he crossed the threshold, Jim could see how tall and ramrod straight he was, and that he was encased in a long, black chesterfield that looked as if it were made of iron— certainly as if it would clang if anyone dared to rap on it. Even before Mr. Grund took off his opera hat, it was obvious that his hair would be a silvery white to match the flowing mustache, and that once the hat was tapped shut, which was done with an extraordinarily loud snap, he would hold it across his chest for a solemn second. For that second, Jim could not remember where he had seen the face before until he suddenly realized it was his childhood image of the face of God, of God with His beard shaved off. Grund nodded gravely, and he felt that he had been recognized, approved, and blessed all in one. Everybody who saw the Chairman of the Board for the first time thought of him as particularly benevolent, but he was not a benevolent man at all. As a matter of fact, he was on his way to the Board Room, on the third floor, for what had become known as the Annual November Bloodletting.

Toward his family, it was true, Grund's attitude was, in the main, one of absent-minded affection. His wife, a plump, placid woman, he regarded as a repository for his sperm; his four daughters as little animals to be stroked like kittens while he read stock reports in the Morris chair no one else was permitted to use; his son as a nice enough boy, but a big disappointment. Only through McKinley, he decided, could he fulfill himself. And so he and the Hospital settled down to a lifetime of exemplary symbiosis. To it he gave not only unfaltering devotion and the deep love other men reserve for their families, but something else, which he felt was much more important—money. From the Hospital he received what his wealth alone could never confer upon him: a position of towering respect in the community. The head of McKinley was looked up to by all of New York.

When he walked into the Board Room that night, the nineteen trustees stood up, some like privates at the call to attention, some grumpily, others so perfunctorily that their rumps rose barely an inch off their chairs. But they all stood up. Although many of them had often complained privately that Grund treated the Hospital as his private preserve, almost everyone admitted that he understood the function of a trustee and saw to it that they did, too.

"Thank you," he said as he sat down at the head of the

long table. "In view of the special nature of tonight's meeting, I suggest that we dispense with all other business."

A motion was made, seconded, and passed by a mumble vote.

"I need hardly remind you that we are here to balance the budget," he began. He smoothed out a piece of paper ominously crowded with figures, put on his steel-rimmed spectacles, and, with a noise like a pistol shot, closed the case, which, according to malicious gossip, was fitted with special springs.

"The deficit for the year 1933 is one hundred and ninety-nine thousand dollars and sixty-three cents. I will contribute one hundred thousand dollars and sixty-three cents." To everyone's annoyance, he took out a huge, black Waterman fountain pen, so old that the originally shining vulcanized rubber had grown dull and gray, and proceeded to do arithmetical sums on the paper as if he were engaged in a problem in calculus. Raising his head at last as if he had just made a startling mathematical discovery, he announced, "That leaves exactly ninety-nine thousand dollars for the rest of you to make up."

When he reached in his pocket for another piece of paper, several of the trustees sighed; almost all the others looked resigned.

"Here are a few suggestions as to how this might be done. "Martin!" he called out like a drill sergeant even though Martin was sitting right next to him, "I've got you down for fifteen thousand. Ewell! You're here for a trifling fifty-five hundred."

One by one he called out the name of each trustee, followed by an assessment none of them had had a voice in determining. At the end, he pocketed the paper and asked, "Are there any comments?"

In his early days he used to ask if there were any objections, but since no one had dared to raise any in a long time, he had modified his question. Tonight, however, it looked as if there was one trustee who was prepared to offer more than comments. Seated in what he imagined was the security of a chair at the opposite end of the table, Shore, a young vice-president of one of the big New York banks, shifted from side to side and finally said rather loudly, "Yes, I have some—some objections, I mean; objections to the cavalier manner with which you ignore all the other services many of us perform. While it's true I don't make the conspicuous contributions each November that you and your friends do, I'd like to know who spends more time at the Hospital, who works harder, who serves on more committees, who writes more reports than I. It's your complete indifference to anything we do—unless it increases income, of course—that I disapprove of even more than the manner in which you casually impose a financial quota on us without even consulting us beforehand. A hospital does not live on money alone, nor is a checkbook its bible. Each one of us serves this institution in his own fashion. I think it's time you realized that in the future there will be two kinds of trustees, the big spenders and the hard workers. I'm serving notice that I belong in the second category."

Some of the men sitting around the table looked bored, some seemed irritated, a few smiled. But no one said anything.

Grund eyed Shore coldly for a moment and then said, "On this board there is room for only one kind of man. A hard-working trustee is a worthless trustee. Hard work is a confession that he is trying to substitute a trivial sideline for his main function. It's a mean little pious evasion. He who gives us service and nothing else pays for his position here with counterfeit coin. We don't need trustees to minister to the sick. We've got nurses for that. We don't need trustees to operate on our patients. That's the surgeons' job. We don't need trustees to run the Hospital, to keep the books, hire the help, and inspect the kitchens. We've got administrators for that. A trustee has only one function." Grund pounded the table with a heavy fist. "To give! and to give in proportion to his

133

importance and the authority he hopes to wield. If hard work and service are what you are interested in, then become a doctor, a nurse, or an administrator. Committee reports don't impress me; only checks. And never lose sight of the fact that it is McKinley that confers prestige on a trustee, not the other way around. Do you think that a man with a failing heart comes to us because he's heard that one of our trustees is a bank president? Do you think that a woman has her gall bladder taken out here because Martin is on the board of six corporations? Do you think a frantic mother brings in a child with pneumonia because she's just found out that somebody on our board once ran for the U. S. Senate? They come to us because of our physicians and surgeons, our traditions, our name. God knows, when we give money, we give little enough, but it's all we can do, and without it there would be no Hospital. And no need for trustees, either."

He unscrewed the cap of his old Waterman, and for the first time smiled. "Shore, Andrew Carnegie had to spend millions to become a philanthropist. You can be one for five thousand dollars."

He handed the pen to Martin, who in turn gave it to his neighbor. There was complete silence as it passed from man to man down to the very end of the table. Shore looked with distaste at the chipped cap and the dull vulcanized barrel, but he reached into his pocket for his blanks and wrote out the check. After slowly screwing down the cap as if he were forever bottling up his rebellious hopes, he sent the pen and the check on the long journey up the row of silent men. Grund studied the check carefully, and waved it in the air like a banner even though it was now perfectly dry.

"Thank you, John," he said quietly. "I would have hated to see an empty place where you are sitting."

He pulled out a thick gold watch from his vest pocket, and pressed on the crown. The lid flew open. Shaking his head reproachfully, he glanced at the dial and snapped the lid shut with a noise that while not quite as violent as the one that had accompanied the closing of his spectacle case, was nevertheless loud enough to be heard all over the room. Ernst Grund called his father the man of a hundred clicks, but not to his face of course.

"I'm sorry about the interruption," said Grund, "but, after all, we did finally fulfill our responsibilities—one hundred and ninety-nine thousand dollars and sixty-three cents' worth of responsibilities, to be exact. I see no reason why we should not adjourn."

He stood up, and once the trustees began to mill around the room, managed to thank each one, reserving a handshake for the more generous contributors. As he walked through the doorway, he flipped open the lid of his watch once more and glanced at the dial. The meeting had lasted exactly eleven minutes.

ELEVEN

JIM REGARDED the second six months of his internship as a courting period leading to the day when as House Surgeon he would finally pledge himself to the Hospital. Stanley awaited July 1 with equal impatience. The House Pediatrician at McKinley could certainly not say, "That's what it's like to be a Jew." Unwilling to lose a day of their precious houseships, they decided to take their vacations during the second half of June.

As Jim was packing one evening in his room in the interns' quarters, Aims Blair walked in, sat down ponderously, and said, "I dropped in to say good-by. When you get back, I'll be at New York Hospital. I decided to accept a two-year obstetrical residency there."

"Congratulations. That's quite a feather in your cap." Jim frowned. "Wouldn't they start the new obstetrical residency here a year earlier for you?"

"I have no idea. I wouldn't have taken it if they had."

It was Jim's turn to sit down. "Wouldn't take a residency at McKinley, and the first one at that!"

"Why should I? I've already got what I want. I'm irrevocably stamped as a McKinley graduate. What more do I need from this place?"

Jim shook his head. "New York Hospital is a university hospital, and you're hardly the scholarly, full-time type."

"It doesn't matter. Half the attendings there are in private practice. Not only do I intend to join them someday, but I'll make damn sure that the prestige of the other half, the full-time scholars, rubs off on me. And you don't think I'm going to let my contacts here wither, do you? Someday I intend to be on the attending staff here, too. At New York Hospital I'll tell them how they do things at McKinley, and at McKinley I'll tell them how they do things at New York. Both places will be in my cross fire all the time."

"I get the picture. A loyal McKinley alumnus."

"You may be closer than you think. My concept of loyalty is different from yours, that's all. With you, loyalty is a physical necessity, like a bowel movement. With me, it's a choice. I feel a man should be loyal only to what's good for him. Anything else is a kind of affectation. We start off by being loyal to our parents because without them we would perish. We're true to our country because if it falls, we fall, too. We're faithful to our friends because then they'll help us over the rough spots. But to anything that prevents us from rising, to that we should never be loyal. With me, loyalty is a road to success. With you, it's a rut."

"The straight and narrow rut, is that it?"

"What else for the Galahad of Morningside Heights? His 'strength is as the strength of ten because his heart is pure.' Sure, so is a ditchdigger's, if by pure you mean simple."

"I thought you came in to say good-by. Why all the gratuitous insults?"

Aims smiled. "Envy, pure envy. I hope unnecessary envy, taking the future into account." Suddenly he looked serious. "I hope you won't be offended by what I'm going to say. It's about your father. He's my horrible example. I can't make him out at all, and I think I know him pretty well from Siberia."

That was the name the interns gave to the Out-Patient Department, because it was so far removed from the main stream of Hospital life.

"An honor man at a good medical school, a top-flight diagnostician, handsome as a king—and he ends up a Harlem G.P. working in a clinic." Aims shook his head. "Some of his diagnoses are strictly à la Rintman. And such a nice man. I wish I knew what it is he lacks: worldliness, ambition, cunning, a readiness to take risks, but whatever it is, you don't have it either." He looked hard at Jim. "Old Faithful, the one-hospital man." He stood up. "I guess there's no point in shaking hands."

"I guess not."

"It will take a few years, but I'll be back. And when I do, I expect to find you in your favorite position, Horatio at a bridge that has long since crumbled, defending the ghostly loyalties everybody else ignores. Pathetic, just pathetic!"

He walked to the door with his slow parade step.

When Stanley returned to the room after having taken a history on one of the pediatric wards, he found his friend disturbed.

"What's the matter?"

"Aims Blair just said a few things that got under my skin. He thinks I'm going to end up like my father."

"Is that bad?"

"Not *being* like my father. *Ending up* like him. Yes, that's bad."

"Tell me the wise man's speech, maxims and all."

After he heard it, Stanley just shrugged his shoulders.

"I get the feeling," Jim concluded, "that Blair thinks McKinley will hit the skids someday. Maybe he's right. After all, what's going to happen when Emmerich, Rintman, Hauser, and that crowd retire?"

138

"Popes come and popes go but the Church goes on forever. Take it from an Orthodox Jew."

Soon after they got back from camping on a little public island on Lake George, Jim found himself in the hands of Stinton, a cold-eyed Canadian, who as Emmerich's favorite associate attending had long since decided that his principal job was to chisel the new house man each summer into something resembling a surgeon, and to do it by the time the chief returned, in the middle of September. As a member of a service that worshipped speed, Stinton was so impressed with the rapidity with which Jim worked that he soon allowed him to do all the ward operations except the most formidable. As far as speed was concerned, Stinton's views were the same as those of his chief's, namely, that if two surgeons could do an operation equally well, but one worked twice as fast as the other, then clearly the one who got through first was the better man. There was, even then, however, another school of thought, headed by Dobbs, the eminent Director of Surgery at Harland Hospital, who felt that speed was unimportant. This was the man about whom it was said facetiously that although he could do a magnificent mastectomy, by the time he got through removing the breast the cancer had already spread throughout the body. Whenever Stinton felt that Jim was operating too slowly, he would fix him with his ice-blue eyes and apply the ultimate insult: "Come on, Morelle, come on! This isn't Harland, you know. You're operating like Dr. Dobbs."

Then Jim would flush under his mask and work faster than ever. At the end of two months he could take out an appendix in fourteen minutes.

Although there was so much surgical material that Jim had to spend most of the day and some of the night in the operating room, he never neglected his duties on the wards. He found that, like his predecessors, he had to order a good many blood counts, which were resented by the new juniors just as much as he had resented them a year before. Fortunately, much of the griping was silenced after he became involved in a scene that endeared him to all the members of the house staff, particularly the younger ones.

One of the features of life at McKinley that irked them the most was the immunity enjoyed by an attending surgeon no matter how outrageously he behaved in the operating room. He might insult an intern cruelly, make fun of him in front of the nurses, vilify him in the coarsest manner; nevertheless, the iron law that had always prevailed decreed that the victim must remain silent. Presumably the justification for this inequitable system was the fear that a sharp retort might endanger the patient's life by upsetting the man who had provoked it. Many of the surgeons treated their assistants harshly; a few took shameful advantage of them. The most sadistic of all was Dormer, a thick-set, iron-haired shell of a man who relied upon bluster, sarcasm, and invective to drown out the fears that were reverberating inside him. The more vulnerable the intern, the more viciously Dormer would attack him, and no one was more vulnerable than a junior called to the operating room. It was in just such a predicament that little Nett, an unusually meek fellow, found himself one afternoon when he was asked to second-assist during a difficult gall bladder operation. Floundering around deep in the abdomen in spite of Jim's help, Dormer transmuted his panic into rage by directing a series of degrading remarks against the defenseless intern. What particularly incensed Jim was the way the attending avoided calling his victim by name, or even by the impersonal "Doctor." Instead, he prefaced each abusive sally by the appellation "schlemiel," a word he had learned from a Jewish patient. After retying a ligature that had slipped off the cystic duct, he turned on Nett and, making sure that everyone was listening, grated, "Schlemiel! You can't even hold a retractor properly."

Jim picked up the retractor and rapped Dormer across the knuckles. "His name is Dr. Nett, not Schlemiel."

Star, who was passing instruments, gasped, her lovely thorax seemingly fixed in permanent inspiration. There was a moment of terrifying silence, and then, to everyone's amazement, a smile crept above Dormer's mask.

"I don't suppose Doctor Schlemiel would satisfy you?" he asked.

When no one said anything, he backed away from the table so as not to contaminate the sterile field, bowed low, and said, "All right, it's Dr. Nett."

For the rest of the procedure he observed an amazing silence. Indeed, relieved of some deep tension, he performed the operation quite skillfully. And he never reported the incident to the Medical Board. From then on no one ever grumbled when Jim ordered a blood count.

The story leaked out, and when Emmerich heard it shortly after his return from Europe in September, he looked grim. But when Stinton told him about Jim's phenomenal dexterity, his expression changed, especially when his associate added, "Some of the old-timers who have seen him operate say he reminds them of you when you were young."

"I only hope he reminds me of you, Stinton, when you were young, not so long ago." He smiled. "Going to the Rockies again this year?"

Stinton nodded.

"I go abroad every year," Emmerich continued, "to eat the food I can't get here, enjoy the art and music we don't seem to have, and to strengthen my blood with a small transfusion of German medicine. You, on the other hand, lie on top of a rock all day waiting to shoot a moose. That's because I am a European at heart, while you are an out-and-out American aborigine."

Stinton smiled. "I'll take the brook trout and venison."

"Brook trout? *Bachforellen?* That's different. Anything that has to do with Bach—trout, music—is good. But venison!" He shook his head in disapproval. "You know, Stinton, I've always identified myself a little with Robin Hood. Taking from the rich and giving to the poor, isn't that what every successful surgeon does? But I never could have eaten all that venison."

Emmerich soon discovered that the reports of Jim's technical brilliance were true, and he responded by spending more time on the other side of the table than he had since Stinton's day. He taught his House Surgeon that a wasted motion was as bad as a wasted opportunity; that fiddling with knife and scissors was not the same as careful dissection; that sometimes in courage and boldness lay the greatest safety; that the hallmark of the true surgeon was the ability to know exactly where he was no matter how deceptively the landmarks were concealed by disease; that his first duty was to get the patient off the table, not to give a virtuoso performance; and finally, the philosophy of the service, which was that speed is the child of perfect knowledge and perfect technique.

He also taught him something about pediatric surgery, a difficult field in which Jim had had little experience. His introduction to it began one evening when Stanley finally stopped pacing up and down their room.

"I've got a bugger of a case of pyloric stenosis on the infant's ward. It's so typical, a medical student could diagnose it," he added, forgetting that he had been one just a year before, "but I can't prove it."

"Why not?"

"You've got to feel the tumor, and I can't. The humiliating part is that Hauser will pick it up the minute he lays his hand on the baby's belly on rounds tomorrow afternoon."

"Maybe he won't. Maybe it's just spasm."

"Not a chance. It's a classical case. A six-week-old baby who has had projectile vomiting after every feeding for a month. The mother says that the milk comes up and hits the wall four feet from the crib. The poor kid, who weighed over seven pounds at birth, now is only five and a half—and looks it. And to gild this pediatric lily there are beautiful peristaltic waves.

All I need is the tumor. No tumor, no operation, is Hauser's rule." He paused. "How about trying it yourself? You might have beginner's luck."

Jim picked up his white jacket without a word.

Since the night nurse on the infants' ward was busy giving out medications, she assigned a student to help them. Jim, whose medical experience had been almost exclusively with adults, was appalled at the baby's size. It was not only small, it was shrunken. And no wonder, he thought. For almost a month, no milk had passed into the intestines, where it could have been absorbed and utilized for growth. The obstruction at the outlet of the stomach had seen to that. Without any warning the baby cried in pain, and Stanley, pointing to the slow undulations on its abdomen, shouted, "There they go!" as if he had sighted a school of whales.

"That's visible peristalsis," he explained to the student nurse. "The abdominal wall is so thin you can see the stomach pushing against the obstruction in waves."

He turned to Jim. "Want to try?"

For ten minutes Jim palpated the baby's abdomen. At last he straightened up. "I can't feel any tumor."

"What kind of tumor are you looking for?" asked the student nurse.

"It's not really a tumor," replied Stanley. "It's just a thick, tight ring of muscle surrounding the outlet of the stomach. Nothing can get through. Once the surgeon cuts through this obstructing ring, the muscle tumor melts mysteriously away and the baby lives happily ever after. The only trouble is that before we can subject a baby as small as this to an operation, we have to be absolutely sure of the diagnosis. The tumor is as hard as cartilage and as large as an olive, and no matter how many you've felt, you always get the same thrill."

"How many have you felt, Doctor?" asked the student nurse.

Stanley sighed. "None."

The nurse looked sad and started to dress the baby. Jim followed his friend to the treatment room.

Stanley was slouching in a chair looking the way he used to after he had lost a tennis match for Columbia. "What annoys me is the idea of Hauser showing me up on rounds tomorrow. You didn't feel it, did you?"

Jim did not bother to answer. "Why don't you ring up my father?" he suggested.

"I can't disturb him for a thing like this, and at night, yet."

"He'd get a kick out of it."

Stanley hesitated, and picked up the telephone.

Jake listened carefully to a description of the case, which was considerably lengthened by Stanley's emphasis on his own inadequacies. At last he said in that nice optimistic voice, which sounded even better over the telephone, "There's an old clinical trick that may bail you out. Get the nurse to feed the baby some sugar water through a nipple with big holes. If he's anything like the others I've seen, he's so dried out he'll gulp down three or four ounces in no time. Then his stomach will rebel and he'll vomit. That's your golden moment. When everything is soft and empty, you'll feel the tumor."

Stanley hurried the nurse so much that she fed the baby a cold bottle, but everything happened just as Jake had predicted. This time it was a soft and yielding belly that Stanley palpated. For a moment he looked disappointed, and then an expression of bewildered ecstasy transformed him.

"Here it is! Hard as cartilage and as big as an olive." He stood there rolling the little mass under his finger, caressing it, getting to know it.

"You look like a man in love with a tumor," said Jim.

"I am, and from the minute I laid hands on it."

Jim put his hand on the baby's abdomen, and the same excitement flashed across his face. "You've got a rival."

On rounds the next afternoon, Stanley presented the case, scrupulously avoiding any mention of the difficulties he had encountered in arriving at the diagnosis. For him to have done otherwise would have been a violation of the intern's code. Young doctors who were seeking to impress their attendings did not wear their professional hearts on their sleeves. Hauser smiled imperceptibly when he heard his House Pediatrician call for a bottle of sugar water with big nipple holes. Although he immediately verified Stanley's diagnosis, he uttered no word of commendation. Praise he regarded as too great a gift to squander on a member of the house staff. He looked down at the baby for a while as if he were gazing at it through the barrel of a microscope.

"I see no reason to waste any more time. Perhaps Dr. Emmerich can operate later this afternoon." He turned to Stanley as if the arrangement had already been made. "And don't forget to wash out the baby's stomach."

Stanley nodded to one of his interns, who walked out quietly to put a telephone call through to Jim.

Fifteen minutes later, as the pediatric staff was about to leave the infants' ward, its collective dignity was ruffled by the sound of a telephone. Hauser frowned. People should know better than to call the pavilion when he was making rounds. After a moment of considerable tension, a student nurse ran up and whispered in Stanley's ear. Dr. Emmerich would operate at five that afternoon.

When the pediatricians entered the operating room at a quarter to five, Stanley was astounded to see that Emmerich had not yet started to scrub. Instead, he was pacing up and down, eyes straight ahead, obviously making an effort not to stare at the clock on the wall. The immobility of the personnel served to emphasize that a black humor was powering this ominous parade. Even Star, who as instrument nurse had the privilege of rattling her hemostats and scissors as much as she wished, even Star was standing next to her Mayo table, a sterile towel covering her hands, quiet and formless. Emmerich turned to Jim.

"And what do you say now? Doesn't your second assistant know that he must be here twenty minutes before an operation to prepare the patient?"

"He knows."

Emmerich took his special operating glasses out of the gold filigree case in his breast pocket and laid them absent-mindedly on the edge of the sink. Only then did Jim realize how disturbed his chief really was. For these were no ordinary glasses. Famous throughout the Hospital, they were made of 18-, rather than 14-karat gold because of the illustrious surgeon's fixed idea that the softer metal would be more comfortable during a long operation. He had gone to Kaertner, the Director of Ophthalmology at McKinley, no fewer than five times before he was satisfied with the fit and the lenses. Although known as an iron man among his colleagues, Kaertner was finally forced to admit, "Herman, I would rather repair a retinal detachment on the King of England than fit you with your damn operating glasses. It would be less of a strain."

From then on they never left Emmerich's person except when he slept. In a sense they became an accessory organ of perception called into play only when surgery was necessary. That was why Jim had a sense of foreboding when he saw them abandoned on the edge of the sink.

At exactly five o'clock, the second assistant came hurrying in on the balls of his feet as if he were carrying his shoes in his hands. Everyone watched him with an anticipatory gloating, everyone except Emmerich, who continued his vigil under the clock as if guarding the little patient against Time—the old, implacable adversary he knew he would have to meet and defeat at the table. But it was not time or Emmerich that interested the second assistant, only the long-armed faucet in the last of the three sinks that rested side by side against the wall—the dear, merciful faucet that would initiate the ritual of scrubbing up so that he could obtain sanctuary while he washed away his sin. But he was not destined to reach the comforting steel. Instead, his hip grazed against the sink and swept the glasses to the floor, so instead of the reassuring hiss of running water he heard the terrifying sound of shattered glass. Sinking to his knees, he began to fit the fragments together like a solemn child trying to solve a jigsaw puzzle.

"Get off your knees!" shouted Emmerich, pale with fury. "Although by rights you should stay there for the rest of your life. You have committed two cardinal sins: You're late, and you're clumsy. Now, leave the operating room."

The youngster walked out crestfallen. Banishment from the operating room was a stiff sentence. A surgical intern became a man without a country.

"Dr. Levinson," said Emmerich, "would you be good enough to act as second assistant!"

It was an order, so Stanley did not even dare nod.

Emmerich walked over to the Supervisor, who had been a student nurse when he was an intern. "And will you be good enough to tell me how I'm going to work without my glasses?"

"Doesn't he have another pair?" Stanley whispered to Jim.

"Does the Louvre have a second Mona Lisa?"

The Supervisor had known Emmerich too long to be ensnared by his rhetorical questions. Instead of answering him, she turned around and ordered the *Diener* to clean up the mess. Always addressed as "Gay-org" (presumably written *"Georg"*), he had never been asked what his last name was. It would have seemed like an invasion of privacy. Cast in the mold of those great prototypes who were to be found in every university hospital and laboratory in Germany, he truly lived up to his title, which could best be translated, perhaps, as "He who serves." And serve he did, lifting patients on and off the table, mopping up the floors, emptying the slop pails, moving the oxygen tanks and heavy equipment around, and carrying out any task a nurse or doctor might set for him. Now he raised the golden skeleton of Emmerich's glasses from the floor, and bearing it like the bones of a saint, laid it in a drawer. It took him just a second to whip off his own steel-rimmed spectacles and stand ramrod stiff before his chief.

"Would the Herr Professor do me the honor of wearing mine?"

Emmerich looked at them with the same disgust he would have shown an unsterile instrument handed him by a nurse.

"Of course, the Herr Professor is a much younger man than I," continued Georg, "but I have very good eyes, too."

Emmerich was at least ten years older than the *Diener*, and his attitude changed at once. Georg crossed to the second assistant's sink, picked up a nail brush, and began to scrub his glasses with green soap and water. After a moment, he rinsed them, doused them with alcohol, rinsed them again, and, raising his head, gave his first operating-room order.

"Schwester!" he said to one of the student nurses, "A sterile towel, please."

Emmerich was visibly impressed.

The nurse popped a striped sterile towel out of its drab brown shell as if she were releasing a butterfly from its chrysalis, and handed it to Georg, who picked it up gingerly by the corner, just as he had seen the surgeons do, and dried the glasses. Wrapping them up in the towel like a bouquet, he handed them to Emmerich, who, once he put them on, knew that his *Diener* had served him well. The first thing he did was to examine his nails curled across his palms. Then, turning his hand around, he looked at them again, now with his fingers fully extended.

"They might do at that," he admitted. "They might do very well."

Taking this as a call to arms, Stanley began to scrub at the second assistant's sink. A moment later, he heard Emmerich mutter, "Clear, remarkably clear," and glancing to his side, saw him staring fixedly at the faucet. Only then did Jim slip between them.

Side by side and bent over slightly, they were soon engrossed in the standard session at the sink. Star sat down on a stool, and, swiveling around, gazed idly at their backs. They looked just like animals at a trough, she decided.

Luckily for her, they were unaware of her thoughts, as with rough wooden brushes they scrubbed their nails and under their nails, their palms and the backs of their hands, their fingers and the webs between their fingers, their forearms and their elbows, scrubbed them doggedly and methodically, over and over again, knowing that only thus could they operate free from the fear of infection. But there was another reason for their diligence. They also feared the irritating forays of the Bacteriologist, who, without warning, would swoop down with his swabs, culture tubes, and petri dishes just before an operation, order them to pull off their gloves, and proceed to take cultures from their palms and the spaces underneath their nails before disappearing into his laboratory vastness like a guerrilla fighter. Four days later, the list would be posted in the doctors' lounge just above the attendance ledger. "Dr. ——, Hands: sterile. Nails: sterile." it would read. And so on down the line until at last the careless or, perhaps, the unlucky offender was reached. Then it would say in red ink, "Dr. ——, UNSTERILE! Hands: Staphylococcus aureus. Nails: Staphylococcus aureus." There for thirty days the man's shame would hang for every attending to see, while he himself roamed the hospital feeling as if he wore the scarlet letter, a scarlet U not a scarlet A, of course.

Brooding over these surprise attacks from the Department of Bacteriology, Stanley washed long and carefully, but since he had started first, he finished first. He barely had time to dry his hands and put on the rubber gloves before the anesthetist, helped by Georg, wheeled the patient in and carried it to the operating table. For such a little thing no elaborate anesthesia apparatus was necessary; just a gauze mask on which the ether dripped from a pin-pierced can. Stanley painted the baby's abdomen with alcohol, ether, and half-strength iodine. As he dropped back, Emmerich stepped forward for his sterile gown.

It was not until he had shrugged into it and held out the waist tape for a nurse to tie behind him that he turned to Hauser, who with his staff was standing behind the anesthetist far from the operative field.

"So you think we'll find a tumor?"

"I know you will," answered Hauser in his contrabass voice.

Emmerich adjusted his rubber gloves over the stockingette cuffs of his long gown. "I'll say this for you. You're usually right."

Hauser found the word "usually" distasteful, but said nothing. He would never have disturbed the sanctified silence of the operating room. It would have been like arguing with the minister while he was delivering the sermon.

As soon as Emmerich and Jim began to drape the baby in sheets, lap sheets, and towels, the atmosphere changed. There was now something of the suppressed excitement that accompanies the dressing of the bride on her wedding day. The supervisor reached up behind Jim to adjust the overhead lights, and instantly a little copper oval gleamed up at them from the mass of white. As was his custom before every operation, Emmerich looked at the clock, only this time, instead of stretching out his hand for the knife, he shook his head, and to everyone's astonishment murmured, "Clear, crystal clear! There is a little speck under two o'clock that I never saw before."

At this the Supervisor whispered to Georg, "And you? Will you be able to get by?"

The *Diener* chuckled. "I think I see better without them."

At last Emmerich stretched out his hand, and Star slipped the scalpel into it almost surreptitiously. She never slapped instruments into his palm the way other nurses did. As always, even on a five-and-a-half-pound infant, his incision was bold and final, with no timid scratching at the ends later on to get more room. So quickly and smoothly did he go through the layers of the abdominal wall that Jim was surprised to find himself picking up the cellophane-thin peritoneum. Emmerich was using the same standard technique as other surgeons, yet in his hands this seemed like a different operation. Jim was reminded of his mother's singing. As much as he enjoyed listening to her at home, the same aria at the Met sounded like a different piece of music. Now he shook his head the way he used to do in the ring to free himself from these obtruding thoughts and from the lulling effect of the operating-room silence, a strange silence compounded of the ratchety clicking of artery clamps, the rustlings of nurses' uniforms, the squeal of the anesthetist's stool as he reached for an airway, the clatter of a shoe against a slop pail, the muted tapping of instruments on the Mayo tray, the gurgling of isotonic saline solutions from the swan-necked flasks, but a silence that in essence was only a blessed absence of words at a time when one might have expected shouts and orders, warnings and alarms. Before he realized it, he was giving Stanley the retractors and Emmerich was slipping his five-eyed hand into the peritoneal cavity. Only then did the friends dare look above the mask into the sightless eyes that were now dreaming, now flickering with excitement, as if the hand were exploring unimaginable, voluptuous delights. For a moment Stanley had to fight down the impulse to cry out, "Is it there?" but his impatience burst harmlessly when out of the incision slipped the hard little, smooth little tumor of pyloric stenosis. Jim was allowed to feel it; Stanley, as second assistant, was ignored. But he was satisfied that his contribution had been recognized when Emmerich broke the silence to announce, "Henry, it's typical. You're right again."

It was not at Hauser that he was looking, however, but at Stanley, and he actually winked.

Then, after putting lap pads in the wound, he severed the ring of thickened muscle that was choking off the outlet of the stomach, choosing the precise area where there were no blood vessels. In a conjurer's pass, the scalpel seemed to change into a hemostat, which he used to spread apart the separated edges until the lining of the pylorus pouted through. It was like slitting the rind of an unusually thick-skinned orange and then pushing the edges apart until the pulp came into view. Convinced that there were no bleeding points, he removed the lap pads, dropped the now unobstructed stomach back into place, and sewed up the abdominal wall in separate layers. The entire operation had lasted just thirteen minutes. Only after the wound had been bandaged and strapped loosely by his assistants so as not to interfere with the normally abdominal breathing of the infant, did he step back from the table and remove his gloves. Everyone froze in anticipation of his summary of the case.

Instead, he shook his head as if denying in advance any argument that might be presented to him and said, "These glasses are definitely better than my other pair, and those others were prescribed by one of the world's greatest ophthalmologists."

He looked around him, but, since no one seemed to have derived any moral from his statement, let the nurses help him off with his gown.

Since Jim and Stanley were the housemen on the case, they were allowed to accompany their chiefs to the surgeons' dressing room and listen to the final conversation. This kind of open eavesdropping was considered part of their education. Hauser and Emmerich sat down on open-backed, white-enamel chairs and faced each other pleasantly. The time had arrived for the exchange of compliments, a custom as hallowed as the exchange of presents beneath the tree on Christmas morning. Jim and Stanley waited until their chiefs looked comfortable, and then sat down.

"I don't see how you pediatricians are able to make the diagnosis in a case like this," Emmerich began. "There's nothing to the operation, of course."

"There's nothing to it when *you're* at the table," commented Hauser. "That's the illusion you always create, Herman. You're like Hofrat-Geheimrat von Haberer of Düsseldorf, the surgical toast of the Ruhr. During the month I spent there, he did fifteen cases of pyloric stenosis, every one in less than fifteen minutes."

"Von Haberer," mused Emmerich. "That's a very nice compliment."

He sat there smiling until he remembered that it was his turn. "You'll take care of the feeding and the formula, of course. That sort of thing is completely above our heads. Personally, I can't make head or tail of it." He made infant feeding sound like quantum mechanics.

Hauser nodded. "But we don't give these cases a formula. They have to have breast milk or they die."

"I had forgotten," said Emmerich, who hadn't forgotten at all. "Where can you get hold of it these days?"

"It's getting harder all the time, but we have our sources."

"How expensive is it now?"

"Forty cents an ounce," answered Hauser, looking at the ceiling as if he were thinking of some rare and noble Burgundy. "And if things go well, we may eventually need as much as twenty ounces a day."

"Eight dollars a day for a five-and-a-half-pound baby! Can the people afford such an expensive menu?"

"The Hospital will pay." Hauser took out a hand-monogramed cambric handkerchief and dusted his nostrils. They handled such things more efficiently at the Children's Hospital in Düsseldorf, he felt, thinking all the way back to a day ten years before, when the Director there, a huge, beer-drinking autocrat, had walked him up to an icebox that was taller than either of them and at least six feet wide, and said, "Can you guess what's inside? Of course not. How could an American understand such things?"

He had yanked open the door, really more like a gate, revealing an interior completely filled with milk in one-gallon jugs.

"I see you're not impressed. Naturally. You don't even know what it is."

Then he had thrown back his head and roared. "You and your flat-chested flappers! It's breast milk, Hauser, all breast milk! Every woman who works in this hospital is a nursing mother. Every maid, scrub woman, cleaning woman, laundress, and clerk serving here has to nurse her own child; otherwise we don't take her. After she finishes suckling her little one (who, of course, boards here all day at our expense), we apply the mechanical pump to her breasts and take off what's left for our own patients. There's always plenty for us because we make sure that every woman we hire is a true German mother."

With that, he had pushed the gate shut with a warrior's thrust, and the crash, together with the clanging of the breast-milk jugs, had sounded like Wagnerian thunder.

"They handled things more efficiently in Düsseldorf," said Hauser out loud.

"Why don't you introduce their system here?"

Hauser smiled one of his rare smiles. "I don't think the American working girl would let us man the breast pumps."

He stood up, and everyone else rose, too. "Thank you, Herman, for operating on our patient."

"Thank you for sending us such a nice case."

To the two interns it sounded as if their chiefs were discussing some wealthy private patient instead of a baby from the free wards.

As soon as the pediatricians left, Emmerich dismissed Jim, took off his white blouse and trousers, and stood there in his shorts, dry and comfortable, close to a mound of bath towels, which he was careful to avoid. He regarded sweating during an operation as a sign of nervous tension. Many of the other surgeons did quite a lot of it, though. The nurses would watch their foreheads like shipwrecked sailors scanning the clouds, and at the first sign of moisture would steal up behind them to collect the drops on little gauze pads they always kept handy. This was to prevent the perspiration from dripping into and contaminating the wound. Emmerich scorned a surgeon's sweat as the secretion of fear.

He dressed quickly, checked his pin-seal wallet, and walked back to the operating room, where the *Diener* and the nurses were cleaning up for the next case. When Georg heard his name called, he walked up to Emmerich and planted his mop between his feet like a sentry at parade rest.

"Would you object if I kept your glasses?" asked Emmerich.

"Object?" exclaimed Georg as if it were a word in a language he did not understand. "It would be an honor for me if the Herr Proessor would wear them."

Emmerich opened up his pin-seal wallet and took out a hundred-dollar bill. At this, Georg turned a dull red, and everyone could see that he was hurt.

"Take it!" cried Emmerich, making it clear that this was an order, not a gift.

Georg stretched out a reluctant hand. "But the glasses are worth only ten dollars."

Emmerich drew himself up to imperial heights. "To you they are worth only ten dollars; to me they are priceless." He looked away. "Please accept my gratitude, which I did not mention earlier because I thought it was so obvious."

Georg turned pale, but he was smiling when Emmerich walked out.

Star started to scrub up. "What happened to his bag of gold?" she remarked to the Supervisor.

The next day, Emmerich roamed through the wards and corridors looking for Kaertner. When at last he came across him in the Doctors' Lounge, he rushed through the story of the shattered glasses so he could have the pleasure of telling the famous ophthalmologist how superior the new glasses were to the old. Kaertner made no answer other than to stretch out his hand and move the spectacles around in larger and larger circles, looking grimmer with each revolution.

"Of course, of course," he said, handing them back as if they were a particularly obnoxious habit-forming drug. "They're too strong for you, Herman, entirely too strong."

Ignoring the remark, Emmerich put them back in his gold filigree case and said as if to himself, "What I don't understand is how an operating-room *Diener* can have a better pair of glasses than a Director of Surgery." Then he put his hands behind his back and, staring at the ceiling, added, "Maybe he had a better ophthalmologist."

And this was the line on which he always ended when he told the story at a dinner party.

Kaertner never revealed that, years before, he had come across Georg waiting in front of the eye clinic and had prescribed glasses for him, the very glasses Emmerich was now wearing. There was something unpardonably petty, he felt, about spoiling a man's favorite anecdote. Emmerich used the glasses during every operation for the rest of his life; only, this pair he never left on the edge of a sink.

It soon became apparent to Jim that the great physicians at McKinley did nothing to conceal their idiosyncracies. On the contrary, they played them up, tending them as carefully as some women tended their hair or their figures. This was the best way, they felt, to make their personalities more colorful, their legends more resplendent, and their divinity more palatable to their friends. A few all-too-human failings would prove a splendid backdrop for their superhuman achievements. Through little weaknesses, they proposed to accentuate great strengths. But sometimes it was hard on their associates.

Emmerich had his seltzer. A good physiologist, he nevertheless claimed that water, plain, ordinary water, disagreed with him. He said it made him feel bloated. But seltzer, gaseous seltzer, ah, that was something else again. That *never* made him uncomfortable. At every dinner party he attended, a waitress was always instructed to set up the big syphon next to his plate. Then, whenever anyone started to say anything he disapproved of, he would pull down the lever so that the stutter and hiss would drown out the offender.

Hauser had his sadism. Although close to sixty, the famous pediatrician remained a highly eligible bachelor. As a fashionable hostess once remarked to a matron who remonstrated with her for pairing him off with a widow of thirty, "Henry too old! Nonsense! Age cannot wither nor custom stale his infinite eligibility."

At dinner parties, his presence always initiated the ritual of the photographs immediately after dessert. Someone would slip out a picture of a child and pass it along the table, while everyone would nod and simper and coo in a kind of imbecilic automatism. As soon as the photograph reached Hauser, however, there would be a respectful silence. After all, a favorable comment from him was better than first prize in the Boardwalk Baby Beauty Contest at Asbury Park, and far less vulgar. All day he had examined children in his office and at the Hospital. Now he had to look at their pictures. And some were far from attractive. He would try to make peace with his conscience by using a euphemism such as *"That's* a baby!" as indeed it was—a baby. But the situation was gradually becoming intolerable. At last he decided to do something drastic. One evening he was invited to a particularly large and distinguished dinner party. Many of the guests were celebrities, but, then, he was one, too. After he had commented patiently on the photographs, he took out one of his own, beautifully mounted in a small Florentine leather case, and confided, "It's a picture of my niece."

Never had there been such a chorus of coos. There was not a couple which did not outdo itself in displaying uninhibited delight. After all, if they praised Hauser's niece, maybe someday he would praise theirs. At the end, he pocketed his photograph and said in that contrabass voice of his that made the words sound as if they were being jerked off the strings by the big bow, "That's not my niece. I don't have a niece. It's a photograph of a Mongolian idiot."

After that, the dinner party petered out. But nobody ever showed him a baby picture again.

Jim was careful not to copy his attendings' idiosyncrasies, realizing that, without the greatness, they would be nothing but empty posturings. But he took care to copy Emmerich's surgical technique, eventually arriving at a point where he was able to perform many operations almost as rapidly and skillfully as his chief. One thing, however, disturbed him. His father had never come up to the operating room to see him work. Actually, Jake's seeming indifference was due to the fear that he might interfere with Jim's surgical education, since he reasoned that a father's presence might cause an attending to withhold the censure and corrections necessary for the son's proper training. But when he was invited by Jim to watch him remove a gall bladder right after clinic hours the following afternoon, he could not refuse. Standing far from the operative field the next day, and trying to look as inconspicuous as a big man could, he was surprised when Emmerich walked up to him after the scrub-up and said, "I'm going to give your boy just as much hell as if you weren't here."

After that, whenever he saw a ward case scheduled for one of his clinic afternoons, he would go up to the operating room to watch his son.

In the spring, while Jim was having dinner with his family in the house on 122nd Street, Jake said, "It's the end of April. Don't you think you ought to find out what you're going to do after July 1? The Great Tradition says you should go to Europe for two years, but the Great Depression says you'll have to stay here."

"I'd prefer to stay on at McKinley even if you could afford to send me abroad. The Hospital established the residency system this year."

Jake's face lit up. "Well, get on the ball, then. Waylay Emmerich."

158

Jim spent a restless night. The next morning he decided to talk to his chief just before he stepped into his car at noon. Although the great surgeon lived across the street from the Hospital, he never walked home in the middle of the day. The chauffeur had been instructed to drive him through the park for exactly half an hour before dropping him at his door. Seated in the sealed silence of the plush-lined passenger compartment, Emmerich knew that there were two places where he was protected from talk, telephone calls, and trivialities—his car and the operating room. As Jim stepped out in front of the private pavilion, shading his eyes and at the same time trying to keep the spring breeze from whipping up his white duck uniform, he saw the famous automobile for the first time, the long, black hood pointed like a cannon at the miles it seemed eager to annihilate, the chauffeur's outdoor section squeezed like a hyphen between the motor and the rear, and the jewel-box passenger compartment, its jet-black roof a glazed blur of sunshine. There was almost no room for luggage. Emmerich believed that a car was designed for people. For consultations, dinner parties, theater, and visits along the avenue, he did not need to carry a trunk. And should he ever decide on a vacation in the country, there was always American Express. Anyway, this was all academic, since he went to Europe every summer.

"What do you call a car like this?" asked Jim of the chauffeur, who, dressed in elegant gray whipcord, was using a feather duster to flick off pieces of lint only he could see.

"A Hispano-Suiza, Doctor."

"Oh, I didn't mean the make."

"A cabriolet."

Jim laughed. "In my neighborhood it was called a frig-the-chauffeur model, because he had to sit out in the rain half the time."

"This one isn't bad. My end has side windows, a leather curtain for the top, and a heater."

Jim walked to the passenger compartment and stroked the lacquered straw that was cleverly plaited over the sides. "What do you call this?"

"A tonneau, a basketweave tonneau, custom built, of course. You don't see many of them around any more. In the old days all the fittings in a car like this were of solid gold and the chauffeur carried a gun. Inside it's really beautiful, though. Take a look. The Professor won't mind."

He opened the door.

"I'd better not."

"Why not?" said a familiar voice.

He turned around and saw Emmerich behind him. "I just want to talk to you for a minute, sir."

"Talk to me in the car. That's the only place around here where you can get any privacy."

Jim tried to hold back until Emmerich climbed in, but his chief motioned him to go first, making it clear that for the moment he was no longer an intern but a guest. He stepped in quickly, not bothering to use the running board, sat down, and proceeded to examine the interior, the soft gray lining that muted the street noises and gave the place its jewel-box atmosphere, the two silver vases high up in the corners in back, the inlaid wood, the wide cloth straps for opening and closing the windows, but above all the long, empty, carpeted floor, that wonderful wasted space stretching out below. This was a car obviously designed for the owner, not for the indiscriminate hauling of passengers. Two seats were folded against the partition in front so that after the guests flipped them down, they would find themselves facing their host instead of sitting disrespectfully with their backs to him. There was a lovely fragrance, and Jim, closing his eyes, took a deep breath. Emmerich took a deep breath, too.

"That's the Vol de Nuit," he said, "not the gardenias."

The chauffeur was already cranking up the glass partition to give them privacy, and Emmerich withdrew to his own privacy, to the day he first met Irene.

It had happened here in front of the private pavilion on just such a spring day as this. He had come storming out of the Hospital in a rage. In those days he seemed always to be in a rage, throwing instruments against the operating-room walls, making nurses cry, shouting irritably at his interns. People used to find some pretext for looking the other way when he passed them in the corridors. He had not yet composed his face after his latest outburst on the ward when he collided with her, sending her little box crashing onto the sidewalk. It was already dripping when he picked it up and gave it to her, and it kept dripping all over her hands. The fresh scent almost stupefied them.

"What's this?" he asked gruffly.

She laughed. "Perfume, of course."

"What kind? I'm a surgeon, not a ladies' man."

"I know. You're Dr. Emmerich, the sad and angry Dr. Emmerich. It's called Vol de Nuit."

Then he looked up and saw the loving-kindness in her eyes, and knew that here at last was an end to hatred and to nagging, to wrangling and despair. She kept the box clasped between her breasts, as grave and smiling they walked side by side along Park Avenue all the way to her home. And at every step on this wonderful, blowy, April morning they were enveloped in a fresh cloud of Vol de Nuit.

The next day he bought her a four-ounce bottle. At twenty-three dollars an ounce, he decided it would be safest to deliver it himself. At least that was how he justified their date for lunch. From then on he saw her every day and sometimes at night, whenever he was supposed to be at a medical meeting or working on some article in his office. And he canceled his trip to Europe. At the end of a few months he realized that he would have to get a divorce. Not once, while struggling to make the decision, had he thought about his wife's feelings. Whatever she had once been, she was now a vicious alcoholic. He was concerned only about McKinley, not because he feared he would be asked to leave, since already he was too powerful for that, but because his action might subtly alter the character of the Hospital. No prominent McKinley doctor had ever been divorced. Of course, a few unimportant members of the attending staff had broken their marriages, but they had quietly resigned and slipped off to practice in the suburbs. Emmerich decided to ask his wife for his freedom sometime during a week-end, when he had found she was most likely to be sober, and to assure her that he would pay any alimony, however high. She never got the chance to fly into one of her terrible rages. On a Thursday night she died in her sleep of a massive cerebral hemorrhage. When Rintman heard the news, he said, "That completely destroys my faith in atheism. There *must* be a God."

Nobody from McKinley went to the funeral, not because they held any grudge against Emmerich, but because they had disliked his wife. But everybody from McKinley came to the wedding six months later. They all loved Irene. After the cere-mony, Hauser kissed her, in itself an unheard of thing, and said, "You've given him serenity without robbing him of his fire. I didn't think it could be done."

But she had. He was a changed man.

The car had already reached Fifth Avenue. "What did you want to talk to me about?" asked Emmerich.

Jim was beginning to feel he had bungled. He should have gone to Stinton months ago and asked him to be his advocate. "I guess it's pretty late to be bringing up the question of the surgical residency. It must be filled by now."

"What did you expect me to do? Wait until June 30, and then ask you whether you had made up your mind?" Em-merich picked up the tube and spoke into the mouthpiece. "Take the East Drive."

Then he turned away and looked out the window. Jim

bowed his head and stared at the floor, assuming more and more of a fetal position as the great womb of a basketweave tonneau moved gently up the park, past the lake, past the castle, Cleopatra's Needle, and the Metropolitan Museum of Art, past the playing fields and the reservoir. Only then did he glance up. Emmerich was laughing at him.

"Certainly you can have the job. I wouldn't consider anyone else as my first resident."

He raised his hand in that Augustan gesture to quell any thanks. "Only, it won't be as easy as you think. You'll have a House Surgeon under you who will feel that every operation you do is stolen from him. He won't have much of a year, and he'll resent it. You'll have to learn to live with that resentment.

"We can always divide up the work."

"You'll do nothing of the sort. I've been watching you. What were you brought up on, anyway, religious tracts? No, now I remember. Your father once told me. Mythology and Arthurian romances. Mythology belongs to the childhood of the human race. It's for children. And King Arthur stories are for children, too, curled up on couches with books and apples while their fathers run around in the rain trying to earn a living."

He fixed Jim with his eagle glare and said, "I want you to give that new man nothing. You will be a surgeon here someday; he will settle in the suburbs." He relaxed. "I was up to Brooke-ville last week to see my old chauffeur. They've just built a two-hundred-and-fifty-bed hospital. It's like all those new sub-urban hospitals. All bricks, no men. Let the new man operate up there when he gets through." He turned his attention back to Jim. "Is there anything else on your mind?"

"Yes. How do I go about getting a basketweave tonneau?"

Emmerich laughed and patted him on the forearm. "Excellent! You're not as bad as I thought. But I am going to take you seriously. You can't, and you shouldn't."

He looked out the window for quite a long time, and when he turned around his face was grave. "Morelle, I have the feeling that McKinley has reached its high-water mark. Maybe I'm pessimistic because I'll have to retire before long."

"You still have quite a few years left, don't you, sir?"

"A few, but there never are enough." He kept silent for a moment, tugging at his thoughts. "Have you noticed what's happening to our little semiprivate division?"

"No, sir."

"Come, come! It's growing so fast we can't keep up with it—and at the expense of the free wards. Don't you see what the trend is? It's toward the abolition of poverty. Do you think this country is going to lie down and let the Depression trample on it forever? This is a rich country, and someday there will be no poor. This is a proud country, and someday there will be no charity. Do you think it will always be that the few ride in basketweave tonneaux while the many go on foot? Or that the free wards will always be with us? A day will come when a doctor as yet unborn will walk through the Hospital and find that they are gone."

He picked up the mouthpiece, but thought better of it. "But unfortunately there is a cloud to this silver lining. Drained of patients by an affluent society, the wards will die. The wards that cradled our greatest doctors! The wards that nurtured and molded them, taught and trained them, and in the end rewarded them not with money but with skill! The wards that lifted medicine out of ignorance and made it into the greatest of the professions! The death of the wards is the price this country will have to pay for abolishing poverty. How will we train new doctors, and on whom? Shall we let them practice on our own private patients? How will we teach an intern to operate? By waiting until ether blots out the trust in some woman's eyes and then handing him the scalpel *we* were paid to wield? How will we give experience and the humility that goes with it to the young physician who has just started out? By encouraging him to prate about the two private patients he is treating in the Hospital instead of reminding him that once he would have had a hundred ward patients to make him wise? I know the new age will be a glorious one, but I am glad I lived in the old. For you it will be harder. You will have to stand with one foot in the age of the great free wards and the other in the age of plenty."

The car was coming out of the park at Seventy-second Street. "I'll take you to the Hospital." Again there was the Augustan gesture to quell any protest.

When they reached the private pavilion, Jim jumped out, and after a word of thanks, closed the door respectfully. Emmerich pulled on the broadcloth strap and lowered the window.

"Kick King Arthur out of your life. Maybe someday you'll have my job."

He reached for the tube, and the car moved toward Park Avenue.

The pediatric residency did not come quite so easily to Stanley. Whenever he tried to bring up the subject, Hauser would dismiss it with a menacing frown. But after both associate attendings had assured him that the position would be his if only he agreed to suffer in silence, he felt more secure. Hauser had to have his daily exercise in sadism. As a matter of fact, he never notified Stanley officially that he had given him the job. Two weeks before going to Europe, he took him aside and said, "When you take over on July 1, I want you to keep a tight rein on the house staff, especially on the new House Pediatrician. Whether he likes it or not, give him nothing."

That was how Stanley learned he would be McKinley's first pediatric resident.

The two friends' lives remained very much the same. They wore the same white-duck uniforms, slept in the same beds in the big corner room on Park Avenue, had the same nights off, ate the same food in the basement dining room, and did very much the same work as before. There was a big difference, though. They had been doctors for two years. Now they were paid. Each received seventy dollars a month.

TWELVE

JIM WAS DESTINED never to forget the first time he heard Star's name. He had been a junior intern a little over two months and had just been electrified by Rintman's first Grand Rounds of the season. That evening, as he was walking along the corridor to his room, he glanced through Kell's doorway and saw the House Physician facing him in his shorts, a towel in one hand and his shaving kit in the other. He looked so friendly that Jim decided to go in.

"That was some performance your chief put on today."

"Wasn't it! Give him a patient and a stethoscope and he's a thousand miles ahead of anyone else. Sometimes he doesn't even need the stethoscope. The physicists who figured out that light travels faster than anything in the universe overlooked Rintman's mind. I guess I didn't look so good though."

"You weren't supposed to look good. You were supposed to be his foil."

"You may have something there. Sit down, sit down!" said Kell, pointing eagerly to a chair. "I don't know why I'm in such a God-damn hurry, anyway."

He put the towel and the shaving kit on the bed and sat down himself. One of the interesting things about Kell was that he looked like an athlete even though he refused to play anything more strenuous than bridge. That was one reason why he admired Jim, who was really the athlete he looked.

"Heavy date?" asked Jim politely.

"Big, very big."

Jim said nothing. That was another reason why Kell liked him. He minded his own business. After a long pause, Kell decided to open up. After all, he had to talk to somebody.

"With Star." He made it sound as if he were going to spend the night with Thaïs.

"Congratulations." Jim leaned back in his chair. "Who is she?"

Kell looked incredulous. "Oh, come on! You know her from the operating room."

Jim shook his head.

"Yes, you do," said Kell. "Her last name is Fawling, so everybody calls her 'Star.'" He smiled at Jim. "Was any guy named Rhodes ever called anything but 'Dusty'? Well, the same goes for her."

"Star," said Jim dubiously. "Well, it's better than 'Dusty'—for a girl."

Kell held out a cigarette, but Jim shook his head.

"Is she hard to date?" asked Jim.

"Let's just say she's very hard to date, but once you date her she's easy to lay."

Jim suddenly came to life. "I know who she is! She's the instrument nurse Emmerich has to have on every case. Figure by Renoir, face never seen; it's always covered by an operating-room mask."

"The brush stroke of the master! And her face is the most beautiful thing about her."

"She's a little old, isn't she?"

"Twenty-five and wise beyond her years, at least in what I'm after tonight."

Kell took a puff on his cigarette, and then tried to flick off ashes that weren't there. "You're not on the grapevine; otherwise you would know that a night with Star is supposed to be a postgraduate course in the arts of love. And the admission requirements are simple. All you have to be are big and handsome. I guess I got in on my size. You remember how Catherine the Great would inspect her bodyguard and then pick out some big lug to spend the night with? Well, that's how Star handles the house staff. Only she doesn't snip off a button and have you shot in the morning. She just doesn't see you again. It's a saying around here that nobody ever spends a second night with Star."

He flicked his cigarette nervously, and this time a little ash came off. "The funny part is that basically she's not a promiscuous girl at all. I don't think she does it more than once or twice a year. But when she does, it's supposed to be the ultimate for her partner, something he can look back on when he's old, like scoring the winning touchdown for Groton or drinking the split-pea soup his mother used to make."

"Only, you don't think she's that good?"

"It isn't that. You see, I've got a theory. I know that if she lets me make love to her tonight, she'll lie there with those long, fuxie legs around me, her beautiful face pressed against mine, and a faraway look in her eyes. But I have a feeling that if I glance over my shoulder just before the big moment, I'll find out she's reading the *American Journal of Nursing* behind my back."

"Maybe it won't turn out that way."

"Maybe it won't."

"Why don't you get a rubdown at Stillman's?"

Kell laughed. "I'm always in shape for this kind of a workout."

Jim stood up. "Well, it sounds better than your mother's split-pea soup."

He went to his room and read up on surgical techniques until he was ready for bed. At one o'clock he was called to hold retractors on a patient with acute appendicitis. When he got back an hour later, he decided to take a shower. There was Kell, gargling with Listerine in front of the mirror. He was the only man Jim knew who rinsed his mouth *after* a date, possibly because he was afraid of catching something. Jim waited until he had dried his lips.

"*American Journal of Nursing?*" he asked.

Kell nodded dejectedly and walked out dragging his bath towel on the floor.

The next morning, Jim was called to the operating room to administer ether-oxygen to a patient with a hernia—and there was Star, looking as fresh and proper as if she had been curled up with a good book instead of with Kell the night before. So routine was the procedure that Jim had plenty of time to watch her work and to see why she was acknowledged to be the finest instrument nurse at McKinley. She had a remarkable flair for anticipating the desires of the surgeon and for being ready with the right instrument before it was demanded. Emmerich, whose favorite she was, used to call her "the mind reader" and would go so far as to reprimand the Supervisor if she was assigned elsewhere when he was scheduled to do something big. Since Jim was having no difficulty with the patient, he began to concentrate on Star herself, noticing particularly how she managed to project her figure through the bulky, all-concealing operating gown. It must be the way she carries herself, he decided. She merely glanced at him from time to time as if she were cataloguing him for the future.

Although Jim came up to the operating room quite often, he never exchanged a word with her. All the same, he found himself watching those operations she happened to have scubbed for. Aims Blair, with a shrewd eye for everything that went on in the Hospital, said to him, "Why don't you make the pass, Morelle? You're the kind she always picks. Or aren't you ready for the major leagues?"

Jim did not tell him that he had yet to play in the minors. Dating, dancing, and necking in taxicabs and living rooms had so far constituted his total sexual experience. His mother had once hinted that his father had been a virgin on their marriage. She had seemed very proud of this. His own upbringing in the house on 122nd Street had emphasized a concept of romantic love that included bilateral premarital purity. In any case, there was little he could do to push back his sexual horizons. The young nurses he knew who had apartments of their own shared them with girls who paid half the rent. He could hardly install a mistress in the East Sixties on an intern's salary of zero dollars a month. And as far as female patients were concerned, a doctor's place was obviously next to the bed, not in it. It looked as if he was going to follow in his father's footsteps.

After he became House Surgeon, he saw Star almost every day, certainly whenever he operated with Emmerich or Stinton. Or, rather, he saw Star concealed by a voluminous sterile gown, a mask, and a white turban. Without fully realizing what he was doing, he would find an excuse to linger in the operating room after a case was finished until she took off her surgical vestments and walked around in the short, sleeveless dress she wore underneath. Afterward he would busy himself in the corridor outside, hoping that she would come out and take off her mask so that he could look at her face.

She reminded him of the women in the book of Greek mythology he had often returned to when he was in college. He would sit in the library of the house on 122nd Street and, turning the pages in the muted excitement of his childhood, enjoy the beautiful nudes. But he never had dreams of making love to them. Too many ancient Greeks had already slept with them for him to have enjoyed such fantasies. His philosophy became "Let the Greeks lay their own goddesses. Someday, maybe, I'll lay mine." Star definitely belonged to the Greeks.

When he became the Resident in Surgery, he spent most of the day in the operating room and saw her even more frequently. But, in two years, the only words he had ever said to her had been the names of instruments.

Saturday had been a searing August dog day. He had just finished taking a shower after a hard afternoon in the operating room and a poor supper downstairs, and now, sheltered by the cast-iron canopy above McKinley's worn stone steps, was watching the summer cloudburst slap and revive the city. He guessed it must be Star the moment she stepped beside him, but instead of turning around to greet her, he kept stubbornly staring at the mushroom drops that were sprouting on the asphalt.

"I like the smell of rain on hot city streets," she said at last.

"So do I. And it has a different smell in every city, just as the same perfume has a different smell on every woman."

"How many cities have you visited in the rain?"

"None, as a matter of fact. I just thought it would be a nice thing to say."

"It *was* a nice thing to say." She lifted her arm toward him. "What kind of perfume is this?"

Very decorously Jim bent down to her shoulder. "It's not Vol de Nuit. I know that, but it's lovely. It's musk."

"I knew you were a faker. I'm not wearing any perfume at all."

"With a skin like that, why should you?"

She smiled, but seemed a little puzzled.

They stood there for a while until it stopped raining.

"Where are you going from here?" she asked.

"I planned on going to the Polo Grounds, but I guess I'll see a movie at Eighty-sixth Street instead."

"I live on Eighty-ninth and I'm taking a taxi. Let me drop you off."

They walked down the steps and along Seventieth Street,

being careful not to brush against each other. When they reached Park Avenue, there was a pool of water in the gutter stretching halfway down the block.

"The sewer must be stopped up," she said.

"Excuse me for not laying down my coat, but it's easier this way."

To her great surprise, he lifted her up and sloshed through the pool into the middle of the avenue.

"Please put me down."

He put her down and whistled through his fingers at a passing cab that swerved to a stop as if frightened by the noise.

After helping her in, he jumped in himself and sat stiffly in the opposite corner without saying a word. In fact, neither of them said anything during the trip. He looked at the back of the cabbie's neck, at the ceiling, at the floor, any place except outside. Maybe that was why he did not see the lights of the movie theaters as Eighty-sixth Street flashed by. Just before they reached Eighty-ninth Street, Star leaned forward and said, "Make a right turn here, please. It's one hundred and eleven."

Jim gave the man a quarter tip, and when he turned around, saw that Star was standing in front of a respectable-looking remodeled tenement with a key in her hand.

"Would you like to come up for a drink before you go to the movies?"

"I'm not much of a drinker."

"Oh, I know, I know. To get punch-drunk in the ring is perfectly fine, but to get plain drunk would be sinful."

He smiled. "I didn't get punch-drunk. They never laid a hand on me."

She took hold of his shoulders, maneuvered him toward the light, and examined his features carefully. Then, to his immense surprise, she kissed him gently on the lips.

"You must have been a wonder. It's true. They never laid a hand on you."

Then, as if she were no longer interested, she turned her

back on him and walked through the doorway. He followed her up the steep, old-fashioned but newly painted stairs, fascinated by the backs of her legs, which remained on a level with his eyes. They made him think of the short lecture on women's legs Emmerich had given to the staff that spring. In Germany, according to his chief, the two kinds most frequently mentioned were Schaumweinbeine, champagne legs, and Moselbeine, Moselle wine legs. To the foreigner, the very sound of the former made them seem by far the more desirable, until he learned, if indeed he ever did, that the descriptions were derived from the bottles, not their contents. Legs like inverted champagne bottles, skinny at the ankles and bulbous in the calves, could never match for elegance the long, slim, tapering legs that looked like Moselle wine bottles. It was obvious that Star's calves and ankles, beckoning through her almost invisible stockings, were magnificent. Kell had said it best—"Those fine, fuxie legs of falling Star."

She lived three flights up, so he had plenty of time to examine them. When she opened the door and turned on the lamps, he found the room far different from anything he had expected. Blazing bright, it was as orderly as the inside of McKinley, and furnished austerely in Swedish modern. Perhaps some of the furniture was not so Swedish, and some was not so modern, but every piece was simple and in good taste. Far in the corner, like a sleeping beast, was a long, black studio couch with three cushions resting straight and obedient against the wall as if they had been spanked into submission. She must get up at half past five every morning, he decided, to keep her place looking like this. He saw that she had already taken off her little jacket, and that standing there in a sleeveless white blouse and dark blue skirt, she was beginning to arrange her hair. "Jesus!" he said to himself, "she doesn't shave under the arms. Beautiful as she is, it's a cinch she doesn't go out much."

She put her hand on the doorknob. "I think I'll change into something more comfortable."

When she came back a moment later, Jim was sitting in the corner as tense as between rounds in a big fight, and she was dressed exactly as before. Only now she was carrying a bottle of scotch.

"I think I'll change into a drunk," she said. "Lady into drunk! But just so you won't be misled, I'll tell you now that I get drunk only once or twice a year. Before the quest."

"What's the quest?"

"It's not for the Holy Grail."

She put the bottle on the table beside him and went into the kitchen. He noticed that although the label had an elaborate design, the printing was a little blurred. When she came back with the ice and glasses, he had unscrewed the top and was holding the bottle to his nose.

"You'll never take a drink if you do that. It smells too much like ether. It must be prohibition scotch."

She picked up a medicine glass she had taken from the Hospital and poured exactly two ounces for each of them. As she bent over the table, Jim decided he liked the faint, exciting scent that came from her body better than all the Vol de Nuit in all the basketweave tonneaux in the world.

"Let's drink it on the rocks," she said, and carried her glass to the other end of the room, where she sipped her drink slowly for a little while.

"Have you ever met Mrs. Emmerich?" she asked at last.

"I was up to the house last winter."

"What is she like?"

"She's like Milton's definition of poetry—simple, sensuous, and impassioned."

"Could you ever care for a girl who was only the first two?"

"I don't believe it."

She looked into her glass. "Is your mother like Milton's definition?"

"I'm sure my father would say she was the inspiration for it were it not for the fact that she doesn't live in the seventeenth century. My own opinion, though, is that sometimes she does."

"Do you think they will keep you on at the Hospital when you get through with your residency?"

"I think they might if somebody on the surgical service drops dead."

They sat there at opposite ends of the room drinking slowly and talking about McKinley, about the obsolete buildings and the old equipment, about the food and the schedules, the doctors and the nurses. But, most of all, they talked about Emmerich. She refilled the glasses once.

"When does he come back from Europe?" she asked.

"The middle of September."

"Not until then? I wish he'd come back sooner. I've got a little lump in my breast."

Jim frowned. "You'd better see Stinton. He's a tremendous surgeon."

"His eyes are too cold."

"What do his eyes have to do with it? This is nothing to fool around with. See him right away."

"I want you to look at it."

"No, no! I couldn't do that. Not here."

But she was already removing her blouse and her brassiere. "Don't you want to examine me? You just said it was urgent."

"Don't you have a bath towel or something so that I can drape you properly?"

"You won't need a towel for this. And you can't do it from the other end of the room."

He walked slowly toward her. She could see that he was struggling to look at her eyes.

"It's right here," she said.

At last he looked down. She smiled. He was trying so hard to be a good doctor.

"I don't feel anything to worry about," he said at last. "It just feels like normal breast tissue to me."

"Is that all it feels like to you? Is that all it means?" She stood up, put her arms around his neck, and kissed him, not with one of those tight, dry little kisses the Barnard freshmen used to give him in taxicabs, but with a wide-open, wonderful kind of kiss he had never had before. He took his hands away from her breast, just as she knew he would, and put them around her waist.

"I don't know much about this, Star."

"You'll see. You will."

She walked to the studio couch and took off her skirt. He started to turn the lamps down.

"Please don't do that! What do we have to hide?"

When he looked at her again, he knew that she was right. To dim the lamps would be as indecent an act as to sneak into the Louvre at night and view the Venus de Milo by candlelight.

He turned up the lamps and solemnly took off his clothes.

Afterward, he lay on his back, relaxed and immensely grateful to her for having made everything go so well. He thought of an afternoon in his childhood when his Uncle Sol had said, "Jake, don't you think sexual intercourse is overrated?" and of the shake of his father's head, his pitying smile. He liked the way Uncle Sol never let the presence of children influence his conversation, and the fact that his father in retrospect seemed always to have been right. He wondered whether Uncle Sol had ever gone to bed with a woman like Star. But most of all he wondered why she had jumped up as soon as it was over, put on a bathrobe, and gone into the kitchen with the drinks. At a time like this, wasn't a woman supposed to lie still, breathing quietly, with filmy eyes and drowsy lids? Wasn't she supposed to be grateful, too? Or was that only in the books? He knew how *he* felt, lying there suddenly alone, when all he wanted was to be next to her, so that he could hold her hand and tell her how beautiful she was. Or just keep his mouth shut hoping that she would sense his overflowing thankfulness.

"Stay where you are. I'll freshen up the drinks," she called from the kitchen.

You're damn right that's where I'm going to stay, he said to himself. I'm certainly not going to put on my shorts and go running around the kitchen freshening up drinks at a time like this. She came back in a moment, set the drinks on a little table, and sat on the edge of the couch. Then, just as if they had not been lovers, she began to talk about McKinley again. How the new girls would not take night duty; how she thought Miss Schneck must be pregnant, she was putting on so much weight; and how they needed a new ether pump for T and A's, the old one was leaking so badly. He lay on his back, staring at the ceiling and sipping his drink from time to time. When she had finished hers, she took off her bathrobe, only instead of lying down next to him, she got up on top of the bed and kneeled over him, barely touching his thighs with the inside of her knees.

"The first time is always the worst," she said.

"It was wonderful, Star. You don't have to make any improvements."

"There are some people who make love over and over again just to forget."

"I'd like to make love over and over again just to remember."

"Even though you know about the others?"

"Do you have to drag them in? But it's going to take a lot to spoil what you've done for me tonight."

"I won't spoil it." She looked down at him, shaking her head as if to reassure him. "When I was a little girl, I used to stand in front of the looking glass repeating over and over, 'Mirror, mirror on the wall, who's the fairest of them all?'" She smiled to herself. "I used to feel so let down when it never answered. But tonight I have an easy question: 'Pillow, pillow on the bed, which one has the handsomest head?'" She took his face in her hands and whispered, "It's you, Jimmy, it's you!"

"Forget it, Star, won't you, just for tonight?"

"I'll try. I'll really try."

"Think of something else." He searched his mind. "Did you know that this was the poet Ovid's favorite position? He said that no Roman worth his salt would make love in any other way."

She smiled. "You're so learned and so absurd. Someday you'll probably be New York's greatest surgeon, but tonight I'm going to make you her greatest whoremaster."

"What do I have to do?"

"Don't cut any classes."

Shortly before dawn, as they were lying side by side, he suddenly sat up. "I haven't let you down, have I, Star? You're not disappointed, are you?"

She sat up, too, and threw her arms around him. "It's no use, Jimmy, it's no use! Even with you." Then she began to cry.

They lay down again and tried to sleep.

He awakened at ten o'clock completely refreshed. Star was in the kitchen looking as regal and innocent as a virgin queen.

"Do you mind if I take a shower?" he asked, jumping up.

"I didn't expect you to take a bath."

"You don't happen to have a razor, do you?"

"I have a little one, but I never use it."

"I'm glad you don't."

When he came out of the bathroom, the studio bed was already made up, with his shorts folded neatly on top. Star was sitting at the table in the kitchen waiting for him to come in. They drank their orange juice slowly.

"I wasn't too forward for you, was I, Jimmy?"

He laughed. "I'm not a baby. I wish I could tell you the story of the Hungarian soldier."

"What Hungarian soldier?"

"It's an old anecdote and a little risqué. I'm afraid you'd be offended."

"After last night?"

"All right. Once there was a simple, young Hungarian soldier, a country boy, really, who went to bed with an experienced lady from Budapest. As she lay beneath him, she perfectly synchronized her movements with his, meeting each of his thrusts with an equally vigorous counterthrust of her own. After a little while, he stopped, tapped her on the shoulder, and said, 'Just a minute, there! Who's doing the screwing, you or I?'"

He took her hand. "You were so wonderful last night that I didn't care who was doing it as long as I was included."

She walked over to his side of the table and gave him the same kind of gentle kiss she had given him on the street the night before.

"After breakfast we'll walk down Fifth Avenue all the way to Forty-second Street. It's lovely on Sunday."

They walked along the park to the children's pool at Seventy-fifth Street, but there were few children about. Instead, middle-aged men with rubber-tipped poles jogged around the edge ready to fend off their magnificent model sailboats before they could scrape against the sides. It seemed as if the rain had kidnapped summer's unwanted child, the miserable humidity, leaving the city ungrieving, cool, and dry. Whenever two sailboats on a parallel course decided to race each other, Jim and Star would bet on the outcome. But the races never materialized, for though the models were designed and built by master craftsmen, they behaved like silly girls, disregarding the orders of their own wise steering devices in their infatuation with the wind, and responding to each puff, each whisper, each breezy prompting by going off first in one direction and then another as if to show their irresponsible lover that they had no other desire than to be ruled by him. Star looked so beautiful that a courtly old man handed her his pole and said, "Don't be afraid, Miss, push it off. In the old days you would have broken a bottle over the finest frigate in the world."

After that, she hated to leave, but Jim was anxious to get to the big lake so that he could row her around. The lakeside boatman looked them over carefully and said, "How about new oarlocks? They're twenty-five cents extra."

Jim took new oarlocks. There was nothing wrong with the old, but it was that kind of a day. He rowed her through the softly winding channels to the bridge and then under it, to the big sequin-covered lake that fitted Central Park like a circus girdle. And there they sat in the very center of the lake, in the very center of Manhattan, shy and silent, feeling as if they were far away in the country and alone for the first time.

"When I was a kid," he said, adjusting an oarlock, "my mother used to take me here. It looked enormous then. I'd run around the edge with a homemade bow and arrow playing Hiawatha all by myself. You know, 'By the shores of Gitchee Gumee, by the shining Big-Sea-Water.'"

"What does Gitchee Gumee mean?"

"Shining Big-Sea-Water, I suppose."

He finished with the oarlock and glanced up at her. "You look just like a Renoir girl."

"A nude?"

"You're beautiful this way, too." He shipped the oars and gazed across the lake. "How would you like to go to the Metropolitan Museum of Art?"

"We just walked past it a moment ago. And it's so lovely here. Why must we go to the Museum?"

He bent down and kissed her hand. "Because you're there on every wall."

She smiled and reached for the oars. "Let me row back."

The old man who had taken the extra quarter was there to pull up the boat and help her out.

"You could have stayed out another fifteen minutes. They'll charge you anyway."

"But we have so many things to do," she answered.

He nodded gravely. "At your age, naturally."

They walked along the narrow, winding concrete paths, never holding hands, never touching, never glancing at each other, but looking carefully at the people on the benches on both sides, at the romping, unmuzzled dogs, the children racing around the KEEP OFF THE GRASS signs, and the policemen with their backs turned to all wrong doings. Jim stopped in front of a little cart on wheels that was shielded from the sun by a red and yellow umbrella.

"Let's have a couple of hot dogs," he said. He turned toward her. "There was a cart like this at the corner of Lenox Avenue and 122nd Street when I was a boy. The man used to sell mushed ice with red syrup on it. I was the only one on the block who wasn't allowed to have any, and I used to stand there with my tongue hanging out while he served everyone else. It seems my father had lost a case of typhoid fever, so he wouldn't let me even taste it."

She looked under the umbrella. "Maybe it's the same cart. There's the red syrup and there's the mushed ice. Let's take a chance. God won't let anything happen to us. Not today."

A woman made her grandchild get off the bench so that they could sit together while they ate the frankfurters and licked the coral frappé.

Afterward they stood up and walked to the museum, a little more slowly than before. As soon as they entered the first room, he knew exactly how it would be. The glowing Titian flesh tints were Star; the coal-black Goya eyes were Star; the stately Sargent beauties were Star. Everywhere he turned, someone had painted Star. She followed him, smiling quietly, glad that he did not talk, satisfied in knowing that no matter where he looked, his eyes would never leave her. After they had wandered through the entire second floor, she said, "Let's go down to the armor room."

She looked around to be sure that no one was there, and kissed him quickly on the cheek.

"You'll be wearing every sword. You'll be in every suit of mail."

Jim had always liked the weapons room. He showed her the

magnificent blade he once had made believe was Durendal, Roland's trusty sword, and told her how in fantasy as a child he had always taken it home with him when he left the museum.

"Would you like to see the finest house in New York?" he asked when they were finished.

She nodded and slipped her hand under his arm. A little closer now, occasionally brushing against each other, they walked on the park side of Fifth Avenue to Seventy-fourth Street.

"Are you tired?" he asked.

"A little."

They sat down on a bench with their backs to the low stone wall that enclosed Central Park, and looked across the street.

"It *is* the finest house," she said. "When I first came to New York, I used to dream of spending a weekend there and sending my mother a book of monogramed matches."

"That's the Huegenon house."

"It is!" She hesitated, a little ashamed to reveal how much she read. "The night before you came, I finished a book called *American Millionaires*. Mr. Huegenon is one of the richest men in the world. And he has never given a penny to a hospital."

"His son died of a malignant melanoma."

She shuddered.

He told her about Albert at Columbia and P and S; about ten million dollars' worth of pictures, and an indoor pool that was only six inches deep; about a state dinner for the Levinsons and the Morelles; and about a young man dying in a home he never loved.

"And you've never seen Mr. Huegenon since?"

He shook his head.

"Oh, Jimmy, you should never have lost a contact like that!"

"Why rouse a sleeping grief?"

She sighed.

"We've had our hot dogs. Now let's have our banquet. At Lüchow's," he said.

"On a resident's salary?"

"I have seventy adventurous dollars in my pocket straining to spend themselves on you."

They took the bus down to Fourteenth Street and walked the four blocks east. When they entered the restaurant, Star was so dazzling that the headwaiter, one of whose predecessors had ushered in Lillian Russell and Diamond Jim Brady, grew soft. Before Jim could say a word, he consulted his list, mumbled, "Oh, yes, you have an early reservation," and waved them in ahead of the line. They sat down side by side on an upholstered bench, and ordered Vichyssoise, roast pheasant, and crepes suzette, things she had never seen before. And beer. She was so thirsty that she gulped hers down, leaving a thin line of foam on her upper lip. And there, in front of a discriminating audience, he took her cheeks between his hands and kissed off the bubbles.

"It's a beer mustache, and like everything else about you, Star, it's delicious."

After dinner, they rode all the way up Fifth Avenue on top of the bus, a trip he had enjoyed ever since he was a boy. Only, now, most of his favorite old mansions were gone, their sites buried beneath massive fifteen-story apartment houses, which he thought of tonight as inhabited tombstones. He wanted to tell her about some of those lovely, long-dead houses, only he noticed that she kept edging imperceptibly away from him, rigid and out of touch, staring ahead with unseeing eyes. Just before they came to Eighty-ninth Street, he reached across her self-consciously and pressed the button that would bring the bus to a stop, but she did not smile up at him as he hoped she would. He tried to help her down the winding steps but she withdrew her hand. And though he looked toward her again and again as they walked the two blocks east, she kept silent. As soon as she reached her house she turned around and faced him. Only, this time there was no key in her hand and she did not ask him up for a drink. Instead, she stood there cold and aloof, mocking him with strange lips. Kell's warning reverberated: nobody, no-body, nobody ever spends a second night with Star! So this is how she does it, he said to himself. Just with an expression. Well, it's better than having a button snipped off by Catherine the Great. Not much better, though. They stood staring at each other while the traffic swished by and people who were careful not to look back skirted around them. With a polite little smile she stretched out her hand to say good-by, and it was then that he noticed that her eyes were moist. Suddenly, as if God had nodded his head, she slid her arms around him and gave him a soft, wide-open, wonderful kiss.

"Would you like to meet me at the same place, on top of the steps, next Saturday night? At seven?" she whispered in his ear.

"I'll be there," he answered huskily. "I'll be there."

After that, he saw her regularly once a week, usually on Sat-urday night. When he pleaded with her to see him more often, she clutched his hands and cried out, "I used to do this once or twice a year. Now it's every week. I'm stretched to the limit, Jimmy. Please don't ask for more."

"I'm not asking for more. I just want to see you more often, that's all. We don't have to make love every time. All I want from you is a chance to take you dancing, to places I can't afford, to smell the perfume on you that you say isn't there, to sit opposite you at a little table with the RESERVED sign still on it while you laugh at me for trying to be a big shot, and later," here he smiled, "to wait in the lobby and watch you coming toward me from the ladies' room, walking like a queen."

A strange, compelling morality twisted her face. "It wouldn't be right, Jimmy. I'd be cheating you."

But even when they made love she felt she was cheating him.

Although he saw her just once a week, they went every-where together, to Carnegie Hall and the Met, to the theater and the Modern Museum, to hockey games and the tennis matches at Forest Hills, to Chinatown and Jones Beach, to night clubs and to church. They danced, ice-skated at Radio City, walked through deserted Wall Street on Sunday morning, went to Coney Island, and took ferryboat rides to the edge of the sea. Afterward, they would go to her room and sit in opposite corners, drinking scotch on the rocks without saying a word. He would lean back, swirling his glass, sipping his drink, examining the ice cubes from time to time as if they were cut from the Cullinan diamond, and then at last glance up as if by chance and say to himself, "How could anyone look more beautiful?"

And then, when she had finished her drink, she would stand up and take off her clothes, and he would know that he had been wrong. When it was over, he would say, "What did I do that was wrong, Star? You won't hurt my feelings. Tell me what I did that was wrong."

And she would take his hand and answer, "Nothing, Jimmy, it's me. I've always been this way."

Perhaps it was because he felt he had something to make up to her that he was always trying to discover the things she liked. She liked skyscrapers and cathedrals, church music, gadgets, photographs, *Porgy and Bess*, Heifetz when he was most austere, figure skating, and rare food. The food in the nurses' dining room was wretched and she hated it. Especially the tapioca pudding. Eventually everything she thought of as inferior, shoddy, irritating, or bad she termed "tapioca." Coloratura sopranos, bawdy humor, football, prizefights, burlesque, farmers, and the past were tapioca. Especially the past. That was real tapioca, and she never talked about it.

From the very beginning, he had noticed that she never took any joy in eating. She would sit at the table chewing slowly and thoughtfully, as if the meal, now that he was committed to pay for it, was something she must dutifully and in good spirit get down. Then one evening when he was thinking of the fun she had had at Lüchow's with the dishes she had never tasted before, he hit upon a way to give her the zest to eat. Naturally,

185

Lüchow's was out of the question on seventy dollars a month, but as they happened to be passing Miyako's, he decided to try out his idea. He announced that he was going to introduce her to Japanese food, and he said it with as much confidence as if he had been there before. She was enchanted with the strange decor, the rapid, slithery service, the waiter's granite good nature and his unintelligible replies, which, they realized, he would never translate into anything they could understand. After he set the heavy black bowl on top of the spirit lamp at their table, raked the greens over the beef slices, and set everything smoking, her eyes grew wide and she exclaimed, "It's just like burning the leaves in autumn."

"It won't taste like burning leaves," he promised, even though he wasn't sure.

"I like this, Jimmy," she said, eating with an unwonted relish.

As he watched her, he said to himself that there was one thing, at least, that he could do for her. He could see to it that she enjoyed her food, that she had better luck at the table than in bed. And he set about to do so, realizing that meals would have to be exotic, or strange, or served in an exciting environment, or superb. How to accomplish this on a resident's salary was the question. She earned four times as much as he, but although she often pressed him to let her pay, he always shook his head. In his family, a man never let a woman pay her way.

Strangely enough, he was helped by the hard times. Those with a little silver in their pockets could make a lining for the Depression's cloud. Prices were ridiculously low, and the initiated could splurge on a pittance. It only remained to find the right places. He took her to the Hotel Lexington Grill, impressive with its maître, assistant headwaiters, plain waiters, busboys, and blue plush rope. Little Jack Little and his band were playing there that winter, and couples not only could dance from seven until nine, but stay an hour longer before the cover charge was applied. The dinners started at a dollar fifteen, but he always insisted that she take one for a dollar and a half. In the summer they dined and danced at the St. Moritz Roof, which had continental food and an atmosphere to match—at a dollar sixty-five each. For special occasions, such as the anniversary of their August cloudburst, he took her to the Hotel Pierre Roof, forty stories high, towering above the St. Moritz and all the places they had shared. Dinner for two was five dollars, but, then, this was the quintessence of elegance. There were much cheaper evenings, such as the ones at the Spanish restaurant in Greenwich Village, where they warmed the bongo drums over a can of Sterno and the trumpet played as if for a bullfight. Jim was doing all this for the first time, too, but he never told her.

Once when she was dancing with him, she said, "If you'll just hold me a little closer you'll be able to feel my heart beat."

But later, after they made love, she said, "I'm always short-changing you, Jimmy, and yet you never complain. Maybe I'm using up my life store of good luck. But it's worth it."

In the beginning she would refuse to see him during her menstrual periods. "Why should I let you take me out and spend money on me at a time like this!" she would insist over the telephone. "You're so chivalrous you simply won't admit there would be nothing in it for you."

He tried to explain his feelings for her, but explanations did no good. Soon, however, he found a simple answer to his problem. On those days of the month, he brought Stanley along. Once the evening was changed from an unfulfilled tryst to a meeting of three friends, she relaxed as if relieved of a duty she could never properly perform. It was on these occasions that she was most gay. Stanley was wonderful, too. He related anecdotes about the Levinsons, told old European jokes, demonstrated the difference between a flat and a top-spin forehand drive, using a soup spoon as a racket, raged against the persecution of minorities, mimicked Hauser's contrabass voice, . . . and all the while never failed to treat her with the deference he showed Mrs.

Morelle. On the one occasion that he felt he had made an embarrassing slip, Star took him to her heart.

Stanley was well able to count, and he soon noticed that there was a peculiar periodicity to the invitations he was receiving. It happened one evening at the Lexington Grill when he was trying to amuse her, Jim having gone out to telephone the Hospital. She was watching him closely because he had just finished his second scotch on the rocks, and she knew he had never tasted anything stronger than Passover wine until recently. Without warning, he hiccoughed and blurted out, "Any day now, I expect to be on display in a florist's window."

"What did you say, Stanley?" she asked anxiously. "Are you all right?"

"Never felt better in my life. I just happened to be thinking of a story, that's all. I'll tell it to you, but only if you're shocked and refuse to hear it."

"I refuse to hear it," she said with a smile.

"All right, under those conditions I'll tell it to you. About a century ago there lived in Paris a girl called Marie Duplessis, Camille, who was loved by the son of old 'Three Musketeers' Dumas. You resemble her, Star, only in that you are so lovely. In nothing else. Whereas you are healthy (*kein ahurra*, as my mother would say, no evil eye should be cast on you), she was already earmarked for tuberculosis. Whereas you are faithful, she was promiscuous. As a matter of fact, that was how she made a living."

He stared up at the ceiling. "Every evening as she walked into the theater or the opera with her white flower, the camellia, pinned over her bosom, courtiers and noblemen would gaze at her from afar, each scheming how best to win favors for the night. But if she wore a red flower instead of the white, then they would turn away in chagrin, knowing, as all Paris did, that the Lady of the Camellias was unavailable because of her monthly cycle."

He turned his eyes to Star. "I'm your red flower. If you ever stop my monthly invitation, I'll know you are pregnant."

He kept smiling benignly and nodding his head. Suddenly, the enormity of what he had said came over him. But instead of apologizing, he raised his hand and took refuge in an old bitterness. "I know what you are thinking. That it's coming out at last. That I'm just a vulgar Jew."

She clasped his hand in both of hers, and he saw that she was laughing. "I've never thought about your religion, but if I did, I'd think of you as a lovely Jew, a wonderful Jew." Then her eyes grew fearful and she clutched his hand even tighter. "Be any kind of a Jew you want, but please never a wandering Jew. Stay close, Stanley, always."

After this she insisted that Jim bring Stanley along at other times of the month as well.

But there was more to Jim's life than Star. The two-year surgical residency was passing rapidly. He was doing not only the difficult but the formidable operations. And just as Emmerich had predicted, the House Surgeon was becoming a mere hanger-on.

"Soon we're going to have to abolish the position," his chief said to him with a sad shake of the head. "Those wonderful old McKinley houseships and the European tours that followed will all disappear. What I like even less is the drop in the ward census. You may think McKinley hasn't changed, but I can see cracks in the walls."

Whenever Emmerich wasn't at the table to help him, Stinton took his place, driving him on to greater speed, greater technical skill, greater virtuosity, driving him on with cold-eyed fury.

"Morelle," he said at last, "I think I detect signs that you are changing from a reasonable facsimile of a surgeon to a real surgeon."

If Stinton or the chief assisted Jim, Star was always there to pass the instruments. At dinner one night, Emmerich was telling Irene about the afternoon's operations.

"When she's the scrub nurse and Morelle is at the table," he said almost in exasperation, "she manages to transform the operation into a lovers' tryst, without, mind you, in any way impairing its efficiency. I don't know what's come over me lately, but every time she hands him an instrument it looks to me as if she were giving him a locket or a ring or plighting her troth. And she seems so happy about it, as if she knew he would treasure the memories forever."

"Maybe he should."

"Irene, I think I'm getting sentimental."

"You always were, dear; that's why I married you. From the beginning I could see the tender heart under the purple toga."

They both knew about Jim and Star. Three times they had seen them together—at Carnegie Hall, at the Theater Guild, and in front of her house. They knew, and they were troubled.

In spite of the fact that his surgical skills were growing, Jim was sleeping badly for the first time. A vague fear began to enter his nights. And then it happened, just as he always knew it would. Only it happened in the spring. That part wasn't fair, he felt. It should never have happened in the spring. She met him one evening, as always, on top of McKinley's worn stone steps. It was two months before the end of his residency.

"Let's sit on the bench across from the Huegenon place," she said.

They walked there slowly and sadly, as if unwilling to come to grips with what had to be done. As soon as they sat down, backs to Central Park, she began:

"I've had an offer."

"I know. I saw him in the corridor with Emmerich this morning. The Giant of the West Coast with the Giant of the East," he said bitterly.

"It wasn't only Dr. Matten. The Chairman of the Board and the Directress of Nursing at Poplars were there, too."

"I've heard."

"They're going to expand. Even in the Depression, movie money is pouring in so rapidly that they're going to modernize and add three hundred beds. They're right next to Hollywood, you know. I almost died when Mr. Almquist, the Chairman, said they had come to McKinley to study the past so that they would know how to face the future. That didn't go down so well with Mr. Stahlhelm."

She sat there, taking in the Huegenon mansion. "You remember Miss Hentz, our legendary operating-room supervisor, who went out there two years ago?"

"Of course."

"She's getting married. At fifty-two! For the past few months she's been pouring my praises into Dr. Matten's ear—he's the real power at Poplars—and when they started to spill over, he wrote to Dr. Emmerich. And he got an immediate answer."

She took a deep breath. "Here's what they are offering. I'm to take over as supervisor of the operating rooms there at once. On July 1, they are giving me an eight weeks' leave of absence to go to summer school at the university. In the fall, winter, and spring, I'm to take night courses toward my B.S. A year from September—and this took my breath away—they are giving me the semester off for full-time academic work at my regular salary. Mr. Almquist assured me that when all this is added to what I already have, a year and a half credit for my work at McKinley, plus the extension courses I once took at Columbia—I used to go there at night before I met you—I will have enough points for my B.S. And he ought to know, because he's a trustee at the university, too. About the time I get my degree, the expansion will be completed and Poplars will affiliate with the medical school. When that happens, I'll also go on the nursing faculty, at three times the salary I get here."

She smoothed down her skirt and smiled. "The Directress of Nursing said after my interview, 'Of course, you realize, Miss Fawling, that you're rather young for the position.'

"To which Dr. Matten replied (he's such a darling old man and he was present while the Directress was grilling me), 'Nurse!' (I liked the way he called her 'Nurse' even though she's the Directress), 'I want it stipulated in the contract that Miss Fawling is always to remain exactly as she is today.'

"Then he turned to me. 'There is one string attached to all this: for a little while you'll have to scrub up with me on the hard cases, just so I can find out what I've been missing all these years.'"

She sat there staring at his profile.

"Go ahead, go ahead, finish it!" he cried out.

"That's it. That's the end." She watched him carefully for a while as they sat silently side by side.

"You're not going to marry me, are you, Jimmy?"

He put his head in his hands and stared at the ground.

"Is it because I don't have any money?"

"Sure! My mother was as poor as a church mouse, wasn't she?"

"Would you marry me if I asked you to?"

"Yes," he answered, "yes, I would."

"But you've never introduced me to your mother and father, never taken me to the house on 122nd Street."

He kept still.

"I could help you in your office. You wouldn't need a nurse." She sighed. "And we could make love every night."

"You would never enjoy it, Star, never."

"Yes, I would. I like to lie beside you and do little things to you and watch your face and feel those wonderful muscles," a cloud crossed her eyes, "and know that no matter what happened, you would never hurt me."

Suddenly she turned around on the bench and faced the park, straining toward the lakes, the winding paths, the museum, all the places they had known together. Then she drew her arm across her eyes and sobbed. "No, I wouldn't, Jimmy. You're right, I wouldn't. I'm just a mechanic who goes to a man's bed to fix him up. I'm an expert on tricks and the forty-nine positions, but when it comes to the real part, the climax and the fulfillment, I'm a nothing, a nothing at all. You're such a golden boy, and look what I have done to you! I've denied you the happiness of knowing what it's like to satisfy a woman. That's something I'll have to account for when I face my Maker someday. But I loved you, Jimmy. I loved you. Maybe He'll take that into account. And I loved what you did for me. You took away a crumbling Nebraska farmhouse, and gave me New York."

She turned toward him and started to cry again. "You're such a big thug, such a big prize fighter, and you were always so gentle. And what makes me feel worst of all is that you never complained, never threw it up to me."

"Of course, I didn't. Would a man spend a night with Venus and then complain because she didn't respond?"

"You and your damn mythology." She dried her eyes. "But I won't do any more harm to you, Jimmy. To you I couldn't. Some day you'll be a king at McKinley, and this would be a morganatic marriage."

She stared at the ground. "What shall I do? What's in store for me? I guess eventually I'll just have to wander around looking for a Pygmalion who will do things in reverse."

"What does that mean?"

"Didn't you teach me all those things? How Pygmalion knelt and wept and prayed before the statue he had created, until the Olympians relented and turned her into a woman. I'll have to find some rich and powerful man past the age of desire who will do the reverse. Some man who will want a showpiece wife with which to impress his friends and make his enemies envious. My wishes will turn inward and lie silent, my hopes will flutter and die, and I will turn into the thing I was supposed to be all along, a fine piece of expensive marble. At night, I'll be placed in the center of the room while his guests walk around me and whisper among themselves, 'Isn't she beautiful!'" She leaned toward him. "Only they won't say it the way you once did."

Suddenly she grabbed his shoulders with both hands and there was a terrible urgency in her eyes. "Let's go home and make love for the last time. Let's do it the first way, and the Ovid way, and all the other ways."

He hailed a taxi and they rode to Eighty-ninth Street, leaning against each other.

"Must you stop for every light!" she cried out.

But the cabbie only nodded and kept still.

As soon as they entered her room she took off her clothes very slowly, while he, in obedience to a fixed ritual, started to turn up the lights.

But she said, "Turn them down, Jimmy. For the last night, let it be dim."

She lay down with him, covered him with her arms, and took him into her. And they made love the first way, the old and the simple way. She saw danger beckon and moved toward it in a strange excitement. And desire came into her loins and a restlessness and a reaching. And she heard herself make a little noise like a creature in the night. And there was the unbearable itching that the closeness would not brush away, and the giving up, and a cry. And then at long last it came, a flutter of wings and the quick, divine seizure God gives to the women He loves. Then she was enveloped in a stillness that seemed to make everything else trivial, and Guilt, her former lover, walked meekly away.

"God sent you, Jimmy," she murmured.

He saw that she was lying still, breathing quietly, with filmy eyes and drowsy lids, just as he had hoped she would be on that first night long ago. When he tried to slip down beside her, she tightened her arms around him and cried, "Don't leave me now! Stay with me just a minute more!"

But soon they stood up while she put on her gown and helped him dress, handing him his tie at the end like a mother sending her little boy to school for the first time. When he was through, she slipped her arms around his neck and gave him a soft, wide-open kiss that was different from all the others and even more wonderful.

"I always wanted you to know what it was like to make love to the right woman, and I always hoped that once, just once, I might be the one."

She took him to the door and closed it without looking up.

All night long he roamed through the city. But not aimlessly. He had a plan: He stood in front of the darkened windows of the Metropolitan Museum and saw her image on every wall. He walked to the children's pond and smiled as an old man with a rubber-tipped pole paid her a courtly compliment. He skirted the big lake and watched her reach for the oars as they sat alone and in love in the heart of New York. He sat in the lobby of every hotel they had ever danced at and lifted up his head as she came toward him, walking like a queen. When he got back to his room at six in the morning, Stanley was awake and worried. And when he started to shave after taking a shower, Stanley was shaving next to him at the row of sinks.

"At least," he thought, "I can keep him from being alone."

The operating room was gloomy without her. Even Emmerich seemed to have lost some of his verve. The next day he took Jim aside and said, "What could I do? Write Matten that she was the worst instrument nurse McKinley had ever trained instead of the finest? Anyway, it's better this way. And better for her, too. Let us know when you feel like coming for dinner. I won't press you now."

But Jim did not feel like going anywhere. Morose and miserable, he roamed through the city night after night, occasionally dropping in unexpectedly at the house on 122nd Street for a silent supper. On duty nights, he would sit on his bed tying surgical knots, just as he used to do as a junior almost four years before. And he never mentioned Star.

Then one night, when he seemed particularly depressed, Stanley closed the door and faced him.

"Speak up, boy, speak up! Say something about her—anything! Because if you don't, I will. Somebody ought to say a word in her honor. I'll tell you one thing. She was beautiful, and no one will ever again be as beautiful. She was faithful, Jim, and no one will ever be more faithful. And she was good, Jim, with her own stern morality. If my father knew all the facts about her, including her reputation before she met you, I am positive he would call her 'Ay-shess High-il.' Do you know what that means? It's the classical Hebrew for a virtuous woman. And do you know what the Bible says about such a woman? It says her children shall rise up and call her blessed. She'll probably never have any children, but I think that we, her friends, we who loved her, should rise up and say it for them."

Jim went to the window, and for the first time in his life began to cry. Stanley turned the key in the lock, and sat with his back to the window holding Holt's Pediatrics on a level with his eyes. After a few minutes, Jim put on his coat.

"I'm going for a walk."

"Mind if I come along?"

"I'd rather go by myself."

"I'm coming along anyway."

They went out through the private pavilion. When they reached the corner, Jim asked, "Where do you want to walk to?"

"I want to walk past the house on Eighty-ninth Street where she used to live."

"You're all right, Stan," said Jim, and his eyes filled. After they had walked a couple of blocks, he turned to his friend and asked, "Do you think I was right to let her go?"

"Certainly I do."

Jim began to talk.

In the days that followed, Stanley noticed that although there was a definite improvement in attitude, Jim still wore despondency like a black arm band. The Morelles were concerned, too.

One night at dinner Hennie turned to her husband. "Was there a nurse?"

"There was a nurse."

"What was she like?"

"Beautiful and brave."

Hennie sighed.

Since Stanley was far from satisfied with his friend's progress, he decided to seek professional advice. He got hold of the Director of Neurology as he was leaving the Hospital.

"This is just a theoretical case," said Stanley, "but I wondered how you would handle it if it should ever arise."

Then he gave a summary of Jim's despondency. But this was McKinley, where everyone knew everything about everybody else. The Director looked at him sharply and said, "Take your friend out and get him drunk every night. Try the Barclay, it's quiet."

The first night they went there, a woman enveloped in a cloud of Vol de Nuit brushed against Jim as she passed their table. He took a deep breath and said, "Twenty-five years from now, if a woman who smells like that passes by, I'll still take a deep breath. My old hag of a wife will probably say, 'I know. Once you were in love with a girl who wore Vol de Nuit.' And I'll turn away and say, 'Once I was in love with a girl who didn't.'"

Stanley poured a third scotch on the rocks into his queasy stomach, and said to himself, "It's not working worth a damn."

But he dragged Jim to the Barclay night after night just the same. Soon he realized that a race was on, a race between the lining of his stomach and Jim's psyche. The question was whether the latter would become whole again before the former rotted away.

Fortunately, two incidents joined with Stanley's ministrations to keep Star from Jim's thoughts. One rose out of the need to establish an office. From their earliest days in medical school it had been understood that they would share one. They anticipated no trouble in finding one. Their problem was to get enough money to equip one. Although Mr. Levinson had done surprisingly well all through the hard times, adding ladies' shoes and accessories to his dress line, he was far from prosperous. And the Depression from the very beginning had dealt harshly with Jake. Each father, nevertheless, promised to contribute five hundred dollars toward furniture and medical equipment. But the sons secretly doubted whether they could start the practice of medicine on such a small sum.

On June 30, 1937, their last night as residents, they went from room to room in the interns' quarters to say good-by, looking out of windows at little views they didn't want to forget, peering in odd places, trading jokes that weren't funny, concealing the heavy heart under the light quip, and staring at Park Avenue as if they would never see it again.

The Medical Resident came in and said, "Somebody is walking around the corridor looking for you guys. My clinical eye tells me he's a butler, and my envious heart asks me how you fellows were able to keep one on your seventy-dollars-a-month salary."

Jim and Stanley found the man standing in their room. After insisting very courteously that they identify themselves, he handed Jim a letter addressed to both and walked out noiselessly.

"What is it, a subpoena?" asked Stanley.

Jim read the note out loud. "One night long ago you saved a useless life. Three equally devoted men, Freud, an analyst, and my husband, collaborated in making it a meaningful and happy one. Joe, my husband, the only one of the five who is not a doctor, joins me in wishing you success in the practice of medicine."

It was signed "Harriet Alternyk."

Inside the envelope were two checks, each for twenty-five hundred dollars.

They went to their beds and sat down heavily.

"I'll bet Emmerich rang her up and told her we were being booted out into the world," mused Jim.

Stanley wore a peculiar smile as he talked. "It seems as if there is always some woman to take care of you. First, it was your beautiful mother, who got you elected to the Round Table. Then it was beautiful Star, who loved you so much she couldn't hurt you. And now it's the morphine lady with these beautiful checks. I can't wait to see what your wife is going to do for you some day. I'm coming along for the ride."

Jim stood up and shook his hand. "You'll be the first passenger."

THIRTEEN

Jim's DESIRE to improve his standing at the Hospital was another factor in driving Star from his mind. The time had come, the two friends now felt, to exchange their Phi Beta Kappa motto, "Per aspera ad astra," for one more likely to bring them advancement at McKinley. "Through *research* to the stars" seemed the appropriate substitute. The incident that precipitated their decision occurred a few months before their graduation from the Hospital, when an eleven-year-old boy on the pediatric ward died in agony of von Recklinghausen's disease of bone. In this baffling condition, calcium is drained from the bones, resulting in fractures, deformities, collapse of the vertebrae, and those characteristic cavities called cysts. Rintman once said on rounds, "The skeleton becomes as soft and full of holes as Swiss cheese." The cause was completely unknown.

Unknown until Parr's article appeared in the *American Journal of Medical Sciences* a month after the boy's death. The New York investigator's attention had become focused on the parathyroid glands, four green-pea-sized bodies under the thyroid, in the neck, because the hormone from these glands removed the small amount of calcium from the bones required by the normal metabolism of daily life. Parr ordered careful neck dissections on all patients with the disease who were autopsied. A small benign tumor of a parathyroid gland was found in every case. After the tumors were analyzed, the cause of von Recklinghausen's disease became clear: They had been manufacturing and still contained enormous amounts of parathyroid hormone, which, cascading into the blood stream, soon decalcified and destroyed the bones.

Next, Parr persuaded the surgeons in his hospital to perform exploratory neck operations on all patients who entered the medical and orthopedic wards with this condition. When the parathyroid tumors were discovered and removed, the bone decalcification ceased at once and the patients recovered.

But strict scientific proof was not yet complete. One question still remained: Could the disease be produced by the injection of parathyroid hormone? Obviously, human experimentation was out of the question. Heineken, one of the greatest bone pathologists in the country, accepted the challenge. He injected large doses of parathyroid hormone into guinea pigs every day, sacrificing them at the end of a month. When the tiny bones were examined under the microscope, the lesions he had produced were seen to be identical with those found in the spontaneous human form of the disease. The last link had been forged.

Stanley, who tried to read every medical article the day it appeared, called Jim's attention to Heineken's work, which had just been published in the *Archives of Pathology*.

"Has it been confirmed?" asked Jim after he had gone through the article carefully.

"It's in the process of being confirmed."

"By whom?"

"By us."

Jim laughed. "The two of us together haven't put five minutes' work into research."

"We'll make up for it with our imagination."

Neither remained satisfied for long with the prospect of confirming another man's work. They wanted to take one step forward on their own. Slowly, during the next few days, the idea emerged. They never discussed who had been the true originator, any more than a pair of mountain climbers roped together for the final assault discussed which of the two had been the first to set foot on a Himalayan summit. It would have been a meaningless distinction.

The plan evolved from facts most physicians already knew. At one time, rickets, basically a decalcification and softening of the bones of infants, had been quite prevalent in New York. It was said that if every baby in the city were carefully X-rayed, 90 per cent would reveal some evidence of the disease. When it was found that the loss of calcium from the bones was due to a deficiency of Vitamin D, rickets was doomed. The synthesis of the vitamin, commercially available as viosterol drops, permitted pediatricians to return the calcium to the rachitic skeleton.

The theory that the two young doctors devised was a simple one: If parathyroid hormone removed calcium from the bones and viosterol deposited calcium into the bones, maybe the two would neutralize each other. Maybe viosterol would prevent the bone damage caused by excessive amounts of parathyroid hormone. Maybe viosterol would prevent von Recklinghausen's disease. Maybe even cure it.

They were careful to discuss the question of controls, the concept on which modern scientific medicine is founded. This iron law proclaims that whenever a group is subjected to a drug, an operation, or a procedure, it must be compared with a similar group from which the drug, operation, or procedure is withheld. If the results are the same, the remedy is worthless. When they asked Rintman for advice, he said with a sardonic air, "You must always use the magic word 'controls' at least three times in any article you write. Let me tell you a story. Once Karl Landsteiner had a young Catholic assistant who had strayed from the Church. Soon after the old man won the Nobel prize for discovering the blood groups, the assistant came to him and said, 'My wife gave birth to twins last night, and I can't decide whether to have them baptized or not.' Landsteiner, always the scientist, stroked his chin and answered, 'Have one baptized and use the other as a control.'"

Stanley did not neglect to use the word in the protocol. "To the Research Committee of the McKinley Hospital:—

We propose to inject twenty guinea pigs with parathyroid hormone daily for a period of thirty days in an affort to produce von Recklinghausen's disease according to the method of Heineken. After the animals are sacrificed, the bones will be sectioned and stained by standard techniques. If we are successful in producing the characteristic lesions, this group will serve as a control. Next, a second group of twenty guinea pigs receiving identical doses of parathyroid hormone will simultaneously be given viosterol by mouth. We hope to demonstrate that the vitamin D of viosterol, by depositing calcium in the bones, will counteract the effect of parathyroid hormone and prevent it from producing von Recklinghausen's disease."

"We'll supply the animals and teach you to cut your own sections," the Director of the Laboratory told them, "but who is going to pay for the parathyroid hormone? It's quite expensive." When he saw how disappointed they were, he added, "Why don't you contact the people who make it?"

A few days later, a representative from Eli Lilly & Co. met them in the laboratory, listened affably to their description of the experiment, and then wrote a few figures in his notebook.

"It will cost about five hundred dollars, and I don't anticipate any trouble getting it for you. We call it parathormone."

"The only thing that worries me," said Stanley, "is that the higher-ups may object to our producing a disease with a Lilly product."

The Lilly representative closed his notebook and smiled. "We're a big company, Doctor. I think we can take it."

At the end of June they started their research project. They learned how to dehydrate tissue and imbed it in paraffin, how to use the microtome to cut it into slices so thin as to be almost transparent, and how to float them on glass slides for fixing and staining. Since they could not afford a technician, they were going to have to prepare the microscopic sections of the guinea-pig bones themselves. Fortunately, they had mastered the technique by the time the first group of animals were killed. These were the ones who had received parathormone alone.

Although the sections were ready at noon, they decided to postpone the examinations until nightfall, reasoning that a deserted laboratory might quiet their excitement and make them more objective. Had they really done what only Heineken had been able to accomplish? But they need have had no fear. The parathormone had done its work well. Scattered throughout the ravished bones like a scientist's jewels were the big, beautiful cysts of von Recklinghausen's disease. There was a moment of magnificent isolation as they stared through their microscopes. They felt like Keats, with Balboa at his side, standing silent on a peak in Darien. Of all the people in the world, Heineken alone had seen this view.

At eight the next morning, unaccountably depressed, they began the crucial experiment, giving viosterol by mouth to a second group of twenty animals who would receive the same amount of parathormone as the first. As the thirty days passed, they worked with less and less enthusiasm. It was sheer folly, they now felt, to expect that the daily administration of a few drops of a baby vitamin would prevent the bone-wrecking effects of injected parathormone. Of course, they did not give up all hope. Perhaps the viosterol would act as a deterrent. Perhaps the slides of this group would show a little less destruction than those of the first. Perhaps the bones would not be utterly laid waste.

Five weeks later, when the bone sections of these animals

were completed, they again waited until nightfall before going to the laboratory. Again they stared through their microscopes, this time hoping that the cysts would be fewer, the decalcification less severe. But the cysts were not fewer, nor was the decalcification less severe. There were no cysts and there was no decalcification. The bones were normal. Viosterol had prevented the occurrence of von Recklinghausen's disease.

"I never expected anything like this," said Stanley, who all along had hoped that exactly this would happen.

They smiled at each other. Science had crowned them with laurel.

There would be no more tricky operations, with surgeons spending hours hunting for tiny parathyroid tumors in the neck. The deformities would vanish; the fractures heal; the cysts disappear; and patients with von Recklinghausen's disease would walk like men again—all because they took a few drops of viosterol daily, like any baby in the land.

But the young doctors' enthusiasm was soon tempered with apprehension. An article rarely appeared in a reputable medical periodical until at least a year after its acceptance. What if one of the hundred thousand doctors in the United States, learning of their results through the grapevine, hurriedly repeated their experiments, and then, through connections and editorial favor, managed to rush his own article into print ahead of theirs? Discoveries had been stolen before. But Rintman, whom they again approached, reassured them. He explained that the prestigious Society for Experimental Biology and Medicine allowed authors of genuinely original work to present their papers at one of the monthly meetings within weeks after the submission of a written summary. The complete report was then published in the society's *Proceedings* in a matter of months. As a charter member, he was able to have them put on the October program.

It was an Indian summer night, and the main hall of the New York Academy of Medicine was completely filled. And not with general practitioners. The audience consisted of surgeons, internists, pediatricians, chemists, physicists, and pathologists, many quite distinguished, who had come to hear the original papers that were to be read on this the first meeting of the season. Jim and Stanley sat motionless in the third row trying to look as if this were the twentieth instead of the first presentation of their careers. Midway through the evening they heard Peyton Rous, the Chairman of the Society and discoverer of the Rous sarcoma, announce their names.

"The paper," he continued, consulting his notes, "is 'The Effect of Viosterol (Vitamin D) on the Occurrence of von Recklinghausen's Disease in Guinea Pigs Receiving Parathormone.'"

He smiled. "Rather a formidable title, I would say, but the work of these two young men should be interesting."

With a great effort Jim climbed the five steps to the stage and read the paper. When the slides from the parathormone animals were flashed on the big screen and cysts four feet in diameter lit up the hall, physicians and pure scientists alike were impressed, because they knew that here was emptiness where once there had been bone. Next came the specimens from the guinea pigs who had received viosterol as well as parathormone. As one slide of normal bone after another came into view, the audience seemed stunned. Everyone was aware of the implications.

The paper's conclusion was modest. "In twenty guinea pigs receiving parathormone, the administration of viosterol prevented the occurrence of von Recklinghausen's disease."

As soon as the meeting was over, most of the people in the audience, Jake among them, shook hands with the two authors as if they were successful candidates on election night. Only one pointedly dissociated himself from the enthusiastic crowd, a gaunt, middle-aged man who stared at them from the other end of the room with cold, unfriendly eyes.

Jim tapped the Secretary of the Society on the shoulder. "Who is that man next to the exit?"

"That's Heineken, the man you quoted five times this evening."

Jim hesitated. "What's he like?"

"He knows more about bone than anyone in the country. And he knows how to strip the hide off a phony better than anyone in the country. Why do you ask?"

Jim just shook his head.

Early the next morning, he telephoned his friend. "I think our results would be more convincing if we repeated the viosterol experiment. Let's use thirty guinea pigs this time with the dosage of viosterol and parathormone kept exactly the same. Nobody can steal our work now. Not after last night."

"You're right, but I wish we didn't have to do it. I hope viosterol comes through for us the second time around."

The Director of the Laboratory agreed to supply the animals. Eli Lilly & Co. sent a fresh batch of parathormone at once. Thirty days later the experiment was completed. The following week the bone sections were ready. Again they waited until nightfall before going up to the laboratory, this time to enjoy in private the triumph they had earned at the Academy of Medicine in October. They placed the slides under their microscopes and began the survey calmly and dispassionately, like old hands. For three hours they searched for normal bone, examining each section over and over again. But their quest was hopeless. Cysts, decalcification, and destruction were all they could find. The bones of every one of the thirty guinea pigs were completely ravished by von Recklinghausen's disease. Viosterol had just been proved worthless. Stanley turned off his little desk lamp and stared at the ceiling.

"It's just tough titty, hard to suck. That's all." There were tears in his eyes. "Anyway, I never enjoyed the screaming of those guinea pigs when they smelled the blood of the others we had just slaughtered. They knew their turn was next." He looked down at his hands, which were still clutching the microscope. "I felt all along that it was too good to be true. But it was beautiful while it lasted."

"Back to the pumpkin and the rags," said Jim.

They stood up, turned off the lights, and left the room in silence.

"I still don't understand why viosterol worked the first time," said Stanley as he closed the door.

The following evening Jim went to a meeting of the Section of Obstetrics at the Academy, where Aims Blair and Grant Phyle, a fashionable old obstetrician with an enormous practice, were presenting a paper entitled "Complications in One Thousand Normal Deliveries," the typically uninspired sort of report doctors write to keep their names before the profession. Anything was better, Jim decided, than sitting at home brooding over the fiasco. A few men were sitting in the hall like those devout souls who, having nothing better to do on a cold day, meditate in church between services. At the end of the meeting Aims marched up the aisle and, much to Jim's surprise, invited him for a drink. They went to the Croydon Bar and ordered scotch on the rocks.

"Phyle is going to retire, and I am scheduled to inherit the practice," said Aims as soon as the drinks came. "If he doesn't quit soon, I'll steal it." He laughed to take the edge off the remark. "By the way, you look awfully glum for a man who was so lucky with his first performance."

"Let me tell you the story of the thirty pigs."

When Jim had finished, Aims said, "Forget the pigs. Mislay the slides. And send your article to the *Proceedings* just as you read it at the Academy last month. Of course, other investigators may get different results when they repeat what you have done. But what of it? When they send in their papers, you're the man they will have to quote. And there is one thing you can be sure of. Somewhere in the country there is a man who will confirm your work. Then the fun will begin. The quickest way for a doctor like you to become well known is to write a controversial article. They do it all the time at the big medical centers. When a piece of work turns out to be a dud, they don't retract. They just sit on the sidelines watching the battle between those who say they are right and those who say they are wrong. It doesn't seem to matter who wins. And looking at it sensibly, how could you possibly hurt anyone by publishing your article as you had planned it until last night. Suppose a doctor in Oshkosh gives a few drops of viosterol to some old crock with von Recklinghausen's disease, how could it do any harm? Doesn't every baby get it today? The old man might be taking a few drops of the elixir of hope before steeling himself for the operation." He took a long swig of scotch and gave Jim one of his best blue-eyed smiles. "I hope you'll take my advice."

There was a short pause. "No, I couldn't stand the stink."

Jim did not sleep well that night. The next morning at McKinley he told Stanley about his encounter with the former obstetrical resident. They decided that it would be best to make a complete confession to Heineken that very afternoon. Since neither of them was eager for an immediate confrontation, they walked the three miles to the Orthopedic Hospital, in upper Manhattan. Nobody in the laboratory paid any attention to them. They entered the pathologist's tiny office unannounced.

He was sitting behind his desk overlooking the bell tower in the park glaring through his microscope. He glanced up quickly, but he did not ask them to sit down.

"Your viosterol miracle is a hoax. My laboratory could not reproduce your work. It is obvious that what you lack in honesty you make up for in effrontery. Even so, I am surprised to see you here." He paused. "But on further reflection, I think I know why you came." He gave them each an elaborate bow. "You came to teach me bone pathology."

"We came," said Jim, "because we couldn't confirm our own work."

Heineken's attitude changed at once. "You couldn't?" he exclaimed approvingly, motioning them to sit down.

Jim presented the findings on the third group of animals and handed him a few of the slides. He glanced at them casually under the microscope.

"We're writing a letter of apology to Dr. Rous," explained Stanley, "and then we're going to try to forget the whole thing."

"Did you send a report to the *Proceedings?*"

"No."

"That makes things much easier. Don't apologize and don't run away from what you have found. You had a good idea. The trouble was that it was too good. I am always suspicious of scientists who start off with champagne ideas. Young men should stick to meat and potatoes. Champagne at the beginning of the meal makes them drunk."

He handed Jim the slides. "Go home, the two of you, and write your article. For one thing, it will be the first confirmation of my own work. For another, it will demonstrate the failure of viosterol to counteract the effects of parathormone. Negative results are important, too. It is valuable to know that vitamin D will not prevent von Recklinghausen's disease. Saves some poor devil the trouble of finding out. But the most important thing is that your work will be honest. After it has cleared the Research Committee at McKinley, send it to the *Archives of Pathology.*"

"I'm afraid, sir," said Stanley, "that a top-flight journal like that would never accept our paper."

For the first time Heineken smiled. "I think it will. You see, I'm the editor-in-chief."

They never discovered what caused the viosterol mirage in the early experiment. But at least they felt a little closer to

Hippocrates, who once sat under the Teaching Tree on the Island of Cos and said in a voice still heard after twenty-three centuries, "Life is short; and the art so hard to master."

The art, of course, was medicine.

FOURTEEN

Jim would always think of the interval between the end of his residency and the entry of his country into war as the beginning of the decline of McKinley. Fortunately and much to their surprise, both he and Stanley were given appointments before the twilight of their medical gods deepened into night. First, however, they were placed on the staff of the Out-Patient Department, an empty honor that did not confer upon them the privilege of seeing patients in the Hospital. They were merely permitted to work for nothing three afternoons a week taking care of routine and, in the main, uninteresting cases. Jim, who two months before had been removing gall bladders and stomachs on ward patients, was now reduced to incising boils and strapping sprained ankles. Their appointments to the attending staff came later. In this they were helped by a defection and a death.

Hauser received one of the greatest shocks of his forty years at McKinley when Pierce, his adjunct attending, told him he was resigning and leaving town.

"Resigning!" exclaimed Hauser incredulously. "If it is a matter of health, a year's leave of absence can be arranged."

"It's a matter of health, all right," retorted the adjunct, "the health of my pocketbook. You are too famous and wealthy to notice it, Dr. Hauser, but in Manhattan, pediatrics is finished. Under one pretext or another, so many young couples with children are moving to the suburbs that our specialty is being bled white. I'm joining a group in Houston, one of the few places in the country with a boom right now. I'm guaranteed twelve thousand for the first year, all expenses paid, and after that the Texas sky is the limit."

"I don't understand how a man can leave McKinley," said Hauser.

"And *I* don't understand how he can stay and still be a man. After half a day every day in the free wards and clinics he's entitled to have a few private patients referred to him once in a while, isn't he? And who can refer patients to him if not the obstetricians? Well, here the obstetricians are about as loyal as rabbits. Besides, most of their practice comes from the suburbs. I can see why they do all right for themselves, though. The women from the hinterland will travel forty miles to be delivered in New York. But they would never think of coming to the city to have their babies examined. That's because they feel their pussies are more important than their children."

Hauser was horrified by the obscenity. But he said nothing. Pierce was known throughout the Hospital as the only man on the pediatric service without a brown nose.

"That's just great for the obstetricians," he continued, "but it is a little hard on us. Another reason why they do all right is that they will do anything to make a buck—obstetrics, gynecology, endocrinology, fertility work and contraception (depending on which way the wind is blowing), internal medicine, and phony psychiatry. They will even do surgery on the male now and then—circumcisions on newborns. For five bucks they would probably change a tire. They seem to do everything except send us decent cases."

He gave his chief a wolfish smile. "I look at it this way. At McKinley the surgeons are the princes of the profession, the pediatricians are the pathetic poohs of the profession, and the obstetricians are the pricks of the profession. I'm getting out."

"Pierce," said Hauser, "you are either a man of vision or a damn fool." Then he decided to make one of his rare excursions into sentimentality. He stretched out his hand. "I'll miss you."

So it was that a notice was put on the doctors' bulletin board announcing that applications would be accepted for the position of adjunct pediatrician. Soon after, Hauser paid a call on the Chairman of the Board of Trustees.

He came to the point at once. "I would like to ask you for my first favor in forty years. I want that position to go to Levinson, one of the finest prospects we have had in all the time I've been here."

August Grund gave him a wintry smile. "As a Hebrew, Dr. Hauser, you must surely be aware that we have a certain quota for your coreligionists. It has always been that way."

Hauser took out a hand-embroidered cambric handkerchief and brushed it across his nostrils twice. "On second thought, I have another favor to ask. Please don't refer to me as a Hebrew. The Hebrews were a nomadic tribe. I've lived in the same house on East Sixty-eighth Street for sixty-four years. If you feel it necessary to refer to my religion, I'm a Jew."

Grund imagined that he saw a cold glow in the pediatrician's eyes. And it was not the glow of anger but of gold. Hauser was a bachelor, and the million dollars he was supposed to have inherited had to go somewhere.

Grund took out the vulcanized Waterman that was turning grayer every year and began to tap on the desk. "I'm forced to admit that your request is reasonable. After all, pediatrics in America was founded by a Jew. It isn't as if the appointment were on the surgical service."

For a moment, he hesitated. Then he said, "I'll talk to the other trustees about Levinson."

"So you think he has a chance."

Grund looked dumfounded. "I said I would talk to the trustees. Just get the Medical Board to vote for the boy and the job is his."

In Jim's case the triumph was sadder. Once, he had told Star that the only way he could get on the attending surgical staff would be for someone to drop dead. Someone did. To the dismay of the Hospital it was Stinton, tough, cold-eyed Stinton, who had turned out to be McKinley's most sensitive political seismograph, registering faithfully the premonitory rumblings of the earthquake that was soon to lay Europe in ruins. He hated Hitler, not with a sackcloth-and-ashes kind of hatred, but with a mean, businesslike loathing he genuinely enjoyed. Whenever he caught one of the defenders of the Thousand Year Reich in the corridors, he would greet him with a shake of the head and say, "You'll never make the Party. You've got no murders, torturings, homosexual relationships, drug addictions, or clubbings to your credit." Then he would look the man up and down with those ice-blue eyes. "But with a Nazi-lover there is always hope."

Many of his victims complained to the Board of Trustees, to some extent still composed of brewers, bankers, and industrialists of German extraction. But Stinton did not give a damn. He knew that someday soon, the America Firsters would be waving the war flags harder than anyone. While it was true that most of the staff were horrified by the Dr. Jekyll to Mr. Hyde transformation of Germany, from Goethe to Hitler, from Heine to Hess, there were still a few attendings who stood up for the Fatherland. They never justified the Nazi crimes; they just denied them. Spiritual relatives they were of the people who all through the war lived close to Buchenwald and Belsen, yet never saw the horrid smoke rise from the chimneys, never wondered why, of the thousands who went in, none came out. To these Nazi apologists Stinton continued to give short shrift.

Deciding that blowing off steam was not enough, he applied for a commission in the reserves. The Army doctors went over him carefully, over Stinton the horseman, the hunter, the fisherman, the tracker, and the crack shot, went over every one of them and found that they all had a blood pressure of 260 over 148. When he came home that night, he did not look like any of those people—just like a tired old man ready to give up.

"When we go to war," he said to his wife, "I think I'll get a nice eiderdown bonnet like my Scotch grandmother used to wear, and sit on my tail, my old wives' tail, while the soft-bellied, sedentary sons of bitches from McKinley parade under my window with bars and leaves on their shoulders and wave good-by."

But he was spared that humiliation. A week later, his stout heart, pumping against an implacable resistance, burst a major artery in the brain. It took him seven hours to die, and for those seven hours it was as if he were at the table exhorting, "Faster, Death, faster! You're operating like Dr. Dobbs!"

McKinley mourned him. Even the America Firsters mourned him. They were relieved, but they mourned him.

At the funeral services, Emmerich murmured, "Why did it have to be my cold-eyed Canadian with the fiery heart?"

Then he turned to Jim and said, "There's another crack in the walls."

So it was that an announcement of a vacancy for an adjunct surgeon appeared on the doctors' bulletin board next to the one for an adjunct pediatrician. At the Medical Board meeting, Jim got eight of the nine votes, Stanley seven. Two weeks later, the Board of Trustees confirmed the appointments unanimously.

Both fathers were stunned by such sudden good fortune. To Jake, his son's success was not only a surprise but a revenge. Going back to his own unhappy interview with Rintman many years before, he felt as if he had outwitted both fate and

McKinley. In spite of a Harlem rearing, a Morelle had won a place on the surgical staff—and before he was thirty. Mr. Levinson, on the other hand, paced around his store, perplexed and bewildered, unable to comprehend how the laws of anti-Semitism could have been abrogated. It was as if the Second Law of Thermodynamics had been suspended. It was against nature.

Since new appointments were rare, a great fuss was made at the Hospital over the filling of the positions, an act that was regarded as something of a fertility rite, a rejuvenation of McKinley.

Jim was unprepared for the disappointment that seized him when his undistinguished and unremunerative practice showed little improvement. Stanley was not only disappointed but positively astounded when his minute collection of Depression patients showed no signs of enlarging. The two friends filled their abundant free time with clinical research in their respective specialties. Jim collaborated with Emmerich in collecting and analyzing more than one thousand gastric resections the illustrious surgeon had performed at McKinley in thirty-five years. A surprisingly large number were for cancer. As master and pupil sat in the consultation room on Park Avenue polishing the article, the older man put down the manuscript abruptly and said, "You are working hard but you're not doing well, are you?"

"Oh, I'm making enough money."

"Don't try to fool me, Morelle. You don't have the talent for elbowing your way ahead." He paused. "In my day, one of the things a young doctor did was to marry a rich girl. They still must be doing it, because your obstetrical colleague, Aims Blair, has just become engaged to the Kirby girl." He pushed the papers away. "And Kirby will be the next Chairman of the Board at McKinley."

"What's happened to Mr. Grund?"

"He's dying."

Jim was so shocked he stood up.

"Sit down, Morelle," said Emmerich. "The German gods are dying. You just happened to come to the Hospital twenty years too late."

Jim kept silent for a moment. Then he said, "What is Mr. Kirby like, sir?"

"He's a live wire, who had the sense to marry into a rich family years ago. He's unbelievably shrewd and bears the same relationship to August Grund that a sharpie bears to a patriarch. Like a great many manipulators, he is a confirmed first-namer. As a matter of fact, he has to know you pretty well before he will call you by your last name. And he possesses an inexhaustible reservoir of vulgarity. Just the same, there must be a big dynamo in this man, because he is on the board of every university, charitable organization, and institution you've ever heard of. He has a harem of worthy causes. Recently, he has become a Democrat, but only, I am convinced, because he is smart enough to see which way the country is moving. A fair evaluation of the man would be that he has brains, wit, money, tremendous drive, everything except integrity."

He stood up and gave Jim his hand. "Forget about him. You and I are starting the New Year in a burst of fame, aren't we? I see our paper is scheduled at the Academy for the first week in January."

Jim left the office haunted by a strange foreboding. His chief was not looking well.

The next day, Emmerich had another visitor, one who came without an appointment. It was Rintman, and he was ushered in immediately.

"I want you to do an exploratory on a carcinoma of the stomach for me. Just for the record," he began at once.

"Of course, of course. How old is the patient?" asked Emmerich.

Rintman gave him a sardonic smile. "It's not exactly a patient. It's me."

Emmerich concealed the shock beneath a brusque irritability. "Since when have you taken to examining yourself? You know the old adage—a doctor who treats himself has a fool for a patient."

"Herman, Herman! A sixty-three-year-old man with a stony hard mass in his epigastrium, what else could it be?" He sat down and said, in a matter-of-fact voice. "It's inoperable, of course."

The surgeon turned his face away.

"Don't look so disturbed. There's a good six months left," said Rintman in the tone he had so often used on consultations, "more than enough time for me to finish my book."

"So! What sort of a book is it?"

"A book on internal medicine, but not one of those run-of-the-mill affairs. This book is a lot of things, a detective story, a collection of anecdotes, a clinician's creed, and a guided tour through the mirages and enchantments of bedside medicine. You're not much of a baseball fan, I know, but there are pitchers who remember every ball they ever threw in their major-league careers. That's how I am. I can remember every case I ever diagnosed or discussed on Grand Rounds. Whoever finishes this book will have walked beside me for thirty years and listened to me as I went from bed to bed on the wards of McKinley. I suppose it's the kind of book Thurston might have written if he had decided to reveal the secrets of his stage magic. You'll never guess what I'm going to call it. It's not a very dignified title. I'm calling it 'A Clinician's Bag of Tricks.' It's not a very modest title, either. But I'll make up for that later. There's nothing quite as modest as a quiet grave."

"Come, come! I haven't even examined you yet."

"Don't interrupt me, Herman. You can examine me at the Hospital. I suppose you could call it a manual on how to become a clinician, like those books on how to become a golfer. I expect it to be popular for a few years, but after that it will have as much appeal for the average doctor as a manual on how to become a knight. For in a few years, genuine bedside medicine will be gone, washed away in the flood from the laboratory."

He held up his hand. "I know, I know! You'll point to the laboratory contributions I made myself. True, true. My generation is like the Sorcerer's Apprentice. We can't turn off what we started. And, of course, we wouldn't if we could. But whether you like it or not, in a few years there will be a laboratory check list for every symptom and sign. If a man has jaundice, the resident will consult his check list like the foreman in a giant auto-repair shop, order the blood studies, X-rays, and assorted tests he sees on it, and, when the results come back, hand the automatic diagnosis to the attending. The diagnostician's eye will become clouded, the laying on of the stethoscope a stylized and meaningless gesture, and the clinical sense will at last wither from lack of use. It will be a great day for the patients, this day of the medical machines, but," here he put his hand on the upper part of his abdomen, "I'm just as happy to take my cancer and go wherever I'm going."

He stood up. "I'll walk over to McKinley now, and let it officially record my fate. Young Levinson once told me that on the Day of Atonement, God sits in judgment and decides who shall live and who shall die during the coming year. It looks as if hospitals are taking over that function."

He walked briskly to the door, with Emmerich just behind him. Suddenly he whirled. "I don't like the color of your lips"; he slipped his fingers around the surgeon's wrist, "or your pulse either. You've had pains in the chest, haven't you? And you've been afraid to tell Irene, huh?"

Emmerich colored.

"Watch out, Herman, watch out!" Rintman warned. "Ease up a little. Or else you'll get there before I do."

Two days later, Emmerich, assisted by Jim, performed the exploratory laparotomy. The cancer was inoperable.

Rintman lashed himself through a quick convalescence. Two weeks after the operation, he was making Grand Rounds again, with less speed and fire than before, but revealing as always that his showmanship was the obstreperous child of genius and wisdom. These were magnificent Grand Rounds, chapters in his hospital life that would remain forever unwritten, but that he hoped instead would be passed along by word of mouth from generation to generation like the Song of Roland and the Nibelungenlied. As soon as the diagnosis of cancer was verified in the laboratory, the Hospital hurried to advance the publication date of his Festschrift, a volume of articles that was to have been prepared in his honor by pupils and colleagues and published on his retirement in two years.

"No matter how fast they work, I'll never live to see it," he growled.

But he saw it being put together. Instead of submitting the usual mediocre articles and standard reviews, scientists, Nobel prizewinners, heads of departments, cardiologists, illustrious clinicians, pathologists, youngsters who were destined to be great, chemists, physicists, and biologists from all over the country worked feverishly on what they considered significant contributions, or else snatched important papers from editors to whom they had already been given. These were the articles that kept pouring into McKinley. And Rintman read every one of them. These were gifts he could understand and enjoy. The introductory biography had been written by Hauser in collaboration with Emmerich. He read that, too, with bowed head, realizing that familiarity, in this case forty years of familiarity, had bred only admiration and affection.

The photograph, which by custom had to appear on page one, posed a problem. Rintman had never had one taken before, and the idea of a picture of a dying man staring at the reader seemed faintly repugnant. The problem was solved by calling in Kartz, the finest photographer in the country, who posed Rintman in a misty chiaroscuro in which the blackness of the old Inverness cape vanished into the blackness of nothing, while the twin Mephistophelean hair tufts of which he was always so proud and the chalk-white countenance he now bore with resignation were suffused with a netherworld glow. When Kartz showed him the proofs, he examined them with a smile and said, "There's the smell of sulfur on the paper." He was delighted.

But McKinley mourned. His loss of weight was not only noticeable, it was appalling. The old magician who had caused so many misconceptions, outmoded treatments, and inaccurate laboratory procedures to disappear from the world of medicine was now disappearing himself. It was his last trick, he said, and it was certainly his saddest.

To Jim this was the unkindest carcinoma of all. After he explained to Stanley why it could not be removed, he said, "Isn't it a dirty trick that in that list of one thousand gastrectomies there could not have been one small slot with Rintman's name." He hesitated, and then added, "I won't tell you what Emmerich's mortality is—I'll have to save that for the Academy—but it is amazingly low."

"Don't worry. I wouldn't miss that meeting even if it were high," said Stanley.

So must the profession have felt, because that night at the Academy the overflow from Hosack Hall had to be sent up to rooms on the second floor, where loudspeakers had been installed for just such a crowd. Jake sat in front, turning around from time to time as if he were counting the gate, and continually consulting the program, where his son's name was prominently displayed.

After the droning introduction by the Chairman of the Surgical Section, Emmerich sighed and strode to the lectern, holding his rolled-up manuscript like a marshal's baton. It took him a long time to read the paper, terse though it was, because he was continually departing from the text to explain, to demonstrate, and to enlighten, clothing a skeleton of facts and statistics with the flesh of his incomparable experience. Toward the end, he began to speak more and more slowly. It was clear that he was having difficulty in breathing. By the time he reached the "Conclusions," Jim could tell that he was having chest pain as well. His shoulders were hunched, and the forehead that had remained dry during the most nerve-wracking operations was demeaned by the perspiration he had always scorned. "Only cowards sweat at the operating table," he had used to say. "Surgeons, never." But he was sweating now, and the audience, which had been listening, fascinated and serene, was beginning to murmur with apprehension. Jim could sense how badly his chief wanted to slide his hand inside his tuxedo to clutch at his heart, and guessed the reason for his restraint, an old fear that he would look like a caricature of Napoleon. At last he finished, slowly and haltingly, but he finished. There was an unbearable hush as he gathered the typewritten sheets together, and then, suddenly, he slumped over the lectern. In a second Jim was beside him, holding him up by the armpits.

Emmerich raised his head and whispered, "Get me to McKinley. I'd like to finish up there."

Then he straightened himself and, leaning on Jim's shoulder, walked to the rear exit as if to a distant funeral march, while the audience, the first in the history of the Academy not to applaud after such a paper, stood up silently instead. When Jim opened the door, Stanley was standing in the empty corridor.

"Call Rintman," Jim said.

Stanley nodded and tossed him his overcoat, which he always kept on his lap during a medical meeting.

"No ambulance, Morelle," warned Emmerich. "A taxi will do."

By the time they reached the street entrance, an attendant was waiting with a cab. Jim placed Stanley's overcoat over his chief's shoulders and almost lifted him in. "McKinley," he said.

The cabbie nodded.

Emmerich leaned back, grunting with each expiration. "I

223

hope you are not cold without a coat. And thank you for calling Rintman. In the Middle Ages they would have said that he had sold his soul to the devil. Now they say he's sold his soul to medicine." His lips were quite blue. "I don't suppose the driver could go any faster."

He leaned forward, but before he could open his mouth, the cabbie said, "Lean back, Dr. Emmerich, I'll take care of everything."

The cab lurched forward and careened down Fifth Avenue.

"Thank you," said Emmerich, and turned to Jim. "Did you know your father out-Rintmaned Rintman on a case of typhoid?" He smiled at another memory. "And he out-foxed me once, with old Levinson." The cab was racing toward Park Avenue. "Do you mind opening the window? That is, if the cold air won't bother you."

When they wheeled him into the corner suite on the eighth floor of the private pavilion, Rintman was waiting, looking more like the Angel of Death than when he had received the nickname twenty years before. The examination was brief.

"How many years has it been?" asked Emmerich.

"Let's see. We interned here forty years ago."

Emmerich tried to chuckle. "We haven't done the Hospital any harm, have we?"

Rintman smiled. "They're not likely to forget us in a hurry."

Emmerich turned to Jim, breathing heavily, a strange look in his eyes. "The walls are crumbling, Morelle. I know that you don't have the stature to save this place, but a man can grow."

Irene came in, calm and beautiful, and immediately the room was filled with the fragrance of Vol de Nuit. Emmerich smiled and stretched out his hand toward her. Without looking at his chief, Jim picked up Stanley's overcoat and walked out. They were pushing the big oxygen tent along the corridor.

Just before dawn, Emmerich died, chin up, eyes fixed on Irene. She gave him an emperor's funeral, and if there had been an Invalides in New York, she would have placed him there. As she left the cemetery on Hauser's arm, she said, "They should have buried him in the courtyard of McKinley's hollow square."

Hauser patted her hand. "Do you remember what I told you at the wedding? You gave him serenity without robbing him of his fire. That's what's important, Irene, not where he's buried."

After this, Rintman never made rounds again. He stayed at home working on his book day and night.

"The last months are reserved for the last chapters," he said with his lop-sided smile. "Besides, I'm not able to do much else. I can't even keep anything on my stomach."

It was true. He was down to one hundred and three pounds. But he had the strength for one last consultation.

It was a spellbinder of a day early in March, the kind New Yorkers believe comes only to New York—a warm, exciting day, a light blue and lovely day, a day when the City seems to shout, "March comes in like a lion, you say? Well, show me the lion now!" and middle-aged men buy flowers for their wives and old people go around saying, "Yes, sir, this is the way it used to be when I was young." Jake came down to breakfast in the basement dining room on 122nd Street in an expansive good humor, eyes clear, chest massive, the fleur-de-lis stickpin carefully placed in the single hole in the center of his blue moiré tie. A man of simple musical tastes, he had especially enjoyed the Philharmonic's all-Wagner program the night before because only the more popular selections had been played. Jim watched him swallow an eight-ounce glass of orange juice, a bowl of oatmeal, scrambled eggs with bacon, and two cups of coffee with the same admiration that had possessed him as a little boy when he saw the young father sitting next to him at Allegretti's down a chocolate ice cream soda with such amazing speed. After rolling his napkin into its silver ring, Jake patted his son on the shoulder and picked up his hat from the coat rack in the hall, while Hennie walked outside to the areaway to give him the bawdy kiss she sent him off with every morning.

He was busy until one o'clock with house calls in the Bronx, Harlem, and Yorkville, all of which he reached by bus, subway, streetcar, and the el. It never embarrassed him to be seen lugging his bulky black bag into a public conveyance. He felt it was as much a part of him as his right arm. And to be unable to afford a car, he had decided long before, was nothing to be ashamed of. What embarrassed him was taking the cash that some patients pressed upon him. Still, it was nice to have money in his pocket, as in the days before the Depression.

He got to the Dispensary early, but climbed the wide, marble indoor stairway two steps at a time. The architect's idea of grandeur eighty years before, it was still impressive, giving rise to the saying that the staircase and the instruments were the only things in the building that were not made of wood. Jake sat down behind his little shelf in the Medical Clinic on the second floor and prepared himself for the cardiacs, diabetics, arteriosclerotics, and tired old women with neuroses who would soon be upon him. Out of the corner of his eye he could see mothers hurrying their children upstairs to the third floor, where discussions of formulas, feeding, and diaper folding usually took place before the Pediatric Clinic opened. As he picked up his pen, a middle-aged woman with the menopause syndrome came in and laid a list of bizarre symptoms before him as if they were heirlooms. All he could give her were open ears and kind words. He smiled imperceptibly. At this moment, he recalled, Jim was doing a hemorrhoidectomy. One Morelle, at any rate, was accomplishing something worthwhile, seeing to it that a grateful woman would walk through life forever free from piles.

"Do you smell smoke, Doctor?" said the Supervisor of Dispensary Nurses.

"I don't smell a thing," her assistant broke in before Jake could answer.

"Oh, Clarissa," exclaimed the Supervisor impatiently, "you have no sense of smell."

They all stopped sniffing and listened. First, they heard a rumbling, a pounding of feet, and an overturning of benches overhead. Then came the crying and the screaming. At this, Jake walked into the hall and saw women and children cascading down the marble stairs. Suddenly they were gone, leaving the staircase like a waterfall that had gone dry. Followed by the two nurses, he cautiously mounted to the third-floor corridor, where a heavy haze was making the familiar furniture look strange and desolate. Turning sharply, he walked past the overturned benches toward the Children's Clinic. The door was open, but as far as visibility was concerned, it might just as well have been closed, so thick was the smoke. Somewhere in the depths, a woman was shrieking, while a child's moaning could be heard in the intervals when she was catching her breath.

"Don't be afraid," yelled the Supervisor in the general direction of the smoke. "Just walk as fast as you can toward the sound of our voices."

But the shrieking continued from the same place.

"Come out this minute, do you hear!" the Supervisor ordered in her most official voice, "You're not supposed to be in there without a nurse!"

The shrieks were interrupted by fits of coughing.

Jake squared his shoulders and went in, stumbling over a chair, tripping over a baby's bottle, colliding with a table, but forging ahead slowly. After losing his way once in the huge cotton-wool room, he found the woman in the far end, one arm hooked around a column, the other supporting a little boy whose face was buried in her neck.

"Just take hold of my hand," he reassured her, "and follow me out."

But she refused to budge. Feet rooted in hysterical immobility, arms curled around the pillar in a catatonic embrace, she foiled all his attempts to free her. And the boy, infected with the maternal rigidity, could no more be detached from his mother than his mother from the post. The smoke was very dense, the temperature rising. Jake sighed, and pinched the woman's buttocks, hard. Her pelvis jerked forward, she gave a scream of surprise, and then, letting go of the pillar, threaded her way to the door with an aggrieved dignity. As soon as she reached the corridor, she bolted for the stairs and ran all the way down without looking back.

"What was wrong with that woman?" asked the Supervisor.

"Hysterical paralysis."

"Then, how in the world did you get her to come out?"

Jake managed to smile, although his eyes were smarting. "That's a lecher's secret."

But the Supervisor was not listening. She pointed toward the other side of the room.

"What is it?" he shouted.

Speechless for once, she stood there like a stuck weather vane. At last she gasped, "There's somebody else in there!"

"I can't see anybody," said the assistant.

"Oh, Clarissa, you know you don't see well."

"Then, why doesn't she scream?"

"Because she's unconscious."

For just a second, the smoke lifted in the far corner of the room, and they all could make out a little figure lying on the floor.

"I can see her curls distinctly," the Supervisor said.

Jake walked slowly toward the doorway.

"Don't go in again, Dr. Morelle," the Supervisor pleaded. "Wait for the firemen."

He hesitated, but then, obeying a more urgent command, crossed the threshold. By now the room was much hotter, the smoke impenetrable. Groping his way along the wall, he collided with a huge wooden locker stacked to the top with cans of evaporated milk, which blocked his progress and made him lose his bearings. He was coughing and having difficulty breathing now, so he got down on his hands and knees, where the smoke was less dense, and began to creep forward. Soon he was sliding his arms about him in desperate arcs, shoving aside chairs and toys in his impatience. Just as he was about to turn in a different direction, he decided to make one last lunge ahead, and in a triumphant moment felt the soft curls he had been seeking. It proved to be a sickening success, however, for when his hand moved down, he realized that this was no child he was grasping but a life-size doll. As he knelt there in a deadly privacy, he could not help thinking of the Supervisor's annual complaint as she watched the children troop into the clinic after Christmas, "There is always money for dolls, but never for a private doctor."

He tucked the doll under his arm and, still on his knees, peered about him, wondering why with all the smoke there was no fire. But clichés are rarely wrong. Fire there was; fire that crept along the floor and seized the front legs of the wooden locker towering above him. Like a ghostly Golem it tottered and fell, striking him on the base of the skull and sending him sprawling. He did not hear the sirens and the clanging of the fire engines. Or the Supervisor's single scream.

Up the stairs came the firemen, monstrous in the haze, grim and implacable, armored and helmeted in black, and brandishing axes and pikes like warriors sacking a burning palace.

"Something has happened to Dr. Morelle!" the Supervisor sobbed, pointing toward the door.

Three of the firemen rushed into the smoke, beating out the embers on Jake's body before dragging him into the hall. There were the thud of axes, the crash of glass. A ladder rose against the wall of the Dispensary as if against a beleaguered fortress. A hose snaked up beside it, and then a shaft of water touched the Children's Clinic like a sorcerer's wand, and subdued the chaos, the crackling and the flames.

The Supervisor knelt beside Jake, who was lying unconscious on the floor near the head of the stairs. "He is so handsome!" she moaned, "Wouldn't it have been terrible if it had gotten to his face."

By the time the fire chief arrived, they had placed him on a stretcher.

"Take him to the Hospital," ordered the chief. "This fire won't spread." He touched the doll with the tip of his boot. "What did he do? Go in after that?"

The Supervisor nodded. "And it's all my fault."

She waited until he walked away, and then picked up an ax and hacked the doll to pieces.

The chief came back and twisted the ax from her hands. "You'd better take her to the Hospital, too," he said to the assistant.

News of the fire had spread so quickly that Jim had already walked to Park Avenue, where a disappointed crowd was watching what was happening to the Dispensary. They had not come to a fire just to see smoke. They wanted flames. And there were no flames, only dirty-gray clouds that hovered around the third story. At last a satisfied shout went up, and people began to point to a faint flickering in one of the windows. There was a crash of glass as a pike came through. In a moment the ladder went up. It was Götterdämmerung, all right, thought Jim, with Emmerich dead, Rintman dying, and McKinley in flames. But then the hoses began to point their white, watery fingers at the old building's shame, and he knew that the Hospital would be saved. For it was clear that the Dispensary was already under an aqueous quarantine. Glancing at his wrist watch, he walked through the police lines in his white operating-room uniform, relieved that his father was not due at the Medical Clinic for some time. But Stahlhelm was standing in the entrance, and the look on his face told Jim that he was wrong.

As they came out with the stretcher, two streams of water overhead saluted it like crossed swords. Without a sound, the crowd parted to let it pass.

Jake recovered consciousness that afternoon, but he was horribly burned.

"Did you see his legs?" asked one of the nurses as she was making up the morphine. "They're like roast turkey."

He was put in the corner suite on the eighth floor of the private pavilion with nurses around the clock. When Trent, the Senior Associate Surgeon, heard the news, he handed his assistant the needle holder with which he was completing a hernia operation and raced downstairs in his gown and mask. The Director of Radiology personally supervised the taking of bedside X-ray films. No resident was considered good enough to give the plasma. The Director of the Laboratory administered it himself, while Stahlhelm hovered outside the door throughout the afternoon. Even old, dying Grund sent a telegram of encouragement. McKinley was taking care of its own.

At midnight, the nurse sent Hennie and Jim home.

The next day, Jake seemed much better. He was rational and was taking fluids by mouth. Trent ushered them outside into the hall and said cheerfully, "He's rallying so well I think he'll make it. Especially with that wonderful physique of his. Of course, he'll be scarred for life."

"I don't care if he's one great scar," said Hennie, "as long as he lives." Then she leaned over and kissed Trent on the cheek.

Early in the afternoon, Jim telephoned Rintman. "I know you're not seeing patients, but could you manage to examine my father today?"

"Of course, I can. There is always room for one last case."

Jim was taken aback by Rintman's emaciation. It was as if the fire which had spared McKinley had consumed him instead. But his voice was as sharp as ever.

"I owe you a good consultation," he said, pointing a finger at Jake as soon as he crossed the threshold, "after the bum one I handed you on that case of typhoid fever years ago."

He was unusually gentle during his brief examination. After it was over, Jim followed him into the corridor, where Hennie was waiting.

Rintman held up three fingers. "He has only three days left. I wish with all my heart it could be otherwise, but I can only prophesy, not change his fate." He smiled sadly at Hennie and inclined his head toward the closed door. "I know. Husbands like that should never die."

He walked quietly away, forlorn and frail, fading into the blackness of the long corridor.

As if to prove the noted internist wrong, Jake awakened the next morning much improved. But at seven o'clock in the morning of the fourth day, his condition began to deteriorate. His temperature soared, his pulse became thready, and he looked toxic. By noon, he was having short periods of delirium. But when he heard the food cart in the corridor, he insisted that Hennie go out for lunch. She kissed him just before she left.

"This is no time for women to be around," he said to Jim in his nice, optimistic telephone voice. He closed his eyes for a few minutes. Suddenly he opened them and asked, "Do you remember the ball games, Jimmy?"

"You bet I do."

"Christy Matthewson was the greatest of them all. You used to think so, too, didn't you, Jimmy?"

"He was the greatest, Pop."

Jake stared at the ceiling. "What was that nursery rhyme I used to recite for you when you were a little boy?"

Jim cleared his throat.

> "Mr. Citron and Mr. Ryne
> Painted their hands with iodine.

When they were cut, they never cried.
When they were caught, they never lied.
Bold as an eagle, brave as a lion
Were Mr. Citron and Mr. Ryan."

Jake nodded. "And you used to say to me, 'Pop, how come Mr. Ryne became Mr. Ryan?' And I'd say, 'People change, Jimmy.'"

He kept staring at the ceiling. "Don't they, Jimmy? Look at me now."

Jim shook his head. "You'll never change, Pop. You'll always be Christy Mattewson, Teddy Roosevelt, and the Charge of the Light Brigade rolled into one. There will never be a day when you couldn't lick Mr. Citron and Mr. Ryne with one hand tied behind your back."

He touched Jake's shoulder, the one that was not burned.
"Bold as an eagle, brave as hell
Was Doctor Jacob John Morelle."

Jake turned his face toward his son and broke into a smile. "Put that on my tombstone, you lobster, you!"

When Hennie returned, he was dead, but the smile was still on his lips.

The poor burned body with the handsome head lay in the house on 122nd Street for three days while wreaths and flowers poured in from everywhere. Mr. Huegenon's secretary left a little box with a single cornflower inside, the only flower Jake ever wore in his buttonhole, and a check made out to Columbia College. On the back was typed, "The Dr. Jacob John Morelle Scholarship Fund. In memory of Albert Huegenon." It was for one hundred thousand dollars.

Mr. Grund's last official act was to authorize the Hospital to pay for the funeral with a fund he especially created for the occasion. On the day of the burial, the city whipped up a gale as if to prevent Jake from leaving the house he had loved so well. But this did not prevent patients, relatives and friends, half the neighborhood, and all of McKinley from coming out in the rain and jamming themselves into the church on the corner; nor the people who could not get in from lining the steps outside just to catch a glimpse of the coffin.

After the service, Irene said to Hauser, "This man and Herman should have been buried side by side in McKinley's hollow square."

Hauser looked up at the sullen sky. "A life of unobserved devotion, a hero's death, yes, he deserves the best. And that, Irene, is to be buried beside his wife."

One month later Grund and Rintman died, strangely enough on the same day. Both would have felt honored by the coincidence.

Without waiting for the regular monthly meeting, Nelson Kirby called the trustees together to discuss what he termed "the unfortunate incident in the Dispensary." While it was true that the fire had caused surprisingly little damage, he pointed out, he was, nevertheless, of the opinion that something should be done to prevent a recurrence. He proposed the installation of a sprinkler system. Shaking with rage, Martin got to his feet and demanded that the disgraceful firetrap that had already cost one life be torn down and a modern building erected in its place. But the character of the board had changed. The old German-American philanthropists were being replaced by cautious lawyers, architects, builders, bankers, and executives, who were willing to donate their time, their names, and their advice to the Hospital but, unfortunately, not their money. To a man, they backed Kirby. And they composed a nicely worded resolution with three whereases for Hennie. The first whereas mentioned Jake's long service; the second, his value to McKinley—this, in spite of the fact that none of them had ever known of his existence until the day of the fire; and the third, his heroic death. There was no accompanying check.

When Grund's will was made public, the trustees were shocked to discover that his fifteen-million-dollar estate had been divided among his wife and five children. Not a cent went to McKinley.

FIFTEEN

THE SIZE of Jake's estate was a shock to Jim. His father's life-insurance policies, which originally had totaled more than fifty thousand dollars, were now, as a result of borrowing, worth less than ten. And there was nothing else. When Hennie heard the news, she smiled and said to her son, "We spent it while we were all together. What would have been the fun of saving it until he was dead?"

"Mother, the neighborhood has deteriorated. It's just a bunch of rooming houses now. I'll get you a little apartment on the East Side with a cleaning woman twice a week. The piano will still be tuned, but only once a year. And a room at the Columbia Club will suit me fine."

She kissed him. "You're as good to me as your father was."

She was remarkably efficient when it came to figuring out how to crowd the furniture from a ten-room private house into her two-and-a-half-room apartment. She simply gave most of it away to the Salvation Army. Only the completely filled Globe-Wernicke bookcases were transported intact. Since there were so many of them, they had to be set up everywhere, making the bedroom easily the most literary in America.

The dreams and the hopes that these books had invoked in Jim during his childhood were not being fulfilled. On the contrary, he was becoming a member of the largest group in his profession, the unknowns. It was not that he was idle; he was operating a great deal both on the wards and on his own patients. It was not that he was lacking in skill; his technique was becoming prodigious, his speed phenomenal. It was not that he was without good judgment; his mounting experience was making him surgically wise. It was simply that his practice consisted almost exclusively of the respectable poor, the unsuccessful and the nobodies. To his office flocked girls from the record room, nurses, young doctors and their families, delicatessen clerks, short-order cooks, cleaning women, obscure cellists and violinists, artists who never sold anything, deadbeats, typists on a three-day-a-week schedule, taxi drivers, bus drivers, garbage-truck drivers, old men who had never done anything, invalids who had not worked in thirty years, house painters who painted three months a year, post-office clerks, waiters, and policemen. Once in a while a schoolteacher. He was doing hernias for thirty-five dollars, appendectomies for fifty, and gall bladders for seventy-five. Some of the patients were so poor, he just charged them a ten-dollar office consultation fee and operated on them for nothing. And there were many to whom he sent no bills at all. Unfortunately, a surgeon whose practice consists only of the faceless and the unknown soon becomes faceless and unknown himself. As far as New York was concerned, Jim did not exist.

His predicament could easily have been foretold. The surgeons at McKinley were not only able but solidly entrenched because of influence, social standing, rich families, or wealthy wives. It would have been unrealistic to imagine that referring physicians would forsake such important men for a newcomer without a reputation just because he could operate so rapidly and so well. Understandably, they kept sending their desirable patients to the same surgeons as before. While Jim had a small group of his own referring physicians, young men such as Kell and Stanley, they were of little help, since they were struggling against the Depression themselves. Unfortunately, he lacked the initiative to go out and make the contacts he needed. But he still dreamed of Emmerich's imperial purple, fees in four figures, the splendor of practicing not only among the poor but among the rich and the mighty, and above all the fame he had fantasied would be his the moment he was chosen to be on the attending staff at McKinley.

Stanley was even less successful. His practice disappeared into the suburbs as fast as he built it up in town. New York was moving out of the city. This was all the more painful, since in his father's early days the migration had been in the opposite direction. On the farms, in the country, and in the little towns of Europe, the restless and the bold, the doers and the dreamers had burst their bonds and streamed toward the metropolis on the Hudson. Today, the descendants of these immigrants were leaving, thrusting their children ahead of them. The children were important. They were the excuse for the getaway.

Pediatricians had become the Danaïds of medicine, their offices sieves, leaking patients into the suburbs as rapidly as they poured in. And no one could say that blacks and Puerto Ricans were pushing them through. Or street crime either. Not in an era when people spent hot summer nights sleeping in Central Park. The white middle class was simply abandoning New York.

But Stanley had a new resource to strengthen him in his hopeless fight against the hinterland. A girl. Adele, orphaned just after she had received her master's degree at Columbia, worked at the New York Institute of Economics. The director had insisted on investing her ten-thousand-dollar legacy himself. So far, she had lost only one hundred and twenty dollars.

238

Since he was a prominent academician and was known to have a little trouble each month balancing his checkbook, she considered herself lucky. She intended to use the money to pay for her wedding, furnish her home, and buy Stanley a car. A doctor had to have a car, she felt. How else would people know he was a success?

Early in the spring, after Jim had done an appendectomy on one of his friend's indigent little nomads, Stanley sat down with him in the tenth-floor conference room near the private operating suite and told him about Adele.

"I'm going to marry her as soon as I earn enough," he concluded. Then he added sheepishly, "We were both virgins when we met."

"Like Romeo and Juliet."

"Juliet was fourteen. Adele was twenty-four. There's no comparison."

The following Saturday, the three had lunch at the newly opened snack bar on the ground floor of the private pavilion. Adele and Jim approved of each other at once. It was obvious that Stanley was quite proud that she was even shorter than he. Had she been taller, Jim felt, she would have found a way to shrink.

Afterward, when she and Stanley were walking along Park Avenue, she said, "He's terribly handsome. He must make a lot of money."

"About twice as much as I do. Maybe eight thousand a year. When I make that much, I'm going to marry you."

"I'll make you marry me before that."

Jim's delight at his friend's good fortune was mixed with sadness caused by increasing signs of the decline of McKinley. His forebodings were reinforced during a casual encounter he and Stanley had with the new Assistant Superintendent. Sam Perkes was six foot eight inches of incredible leanness. When he walked uptown from Grand Central Station every day in his cheap, ill-fitting black suit, with his dark hair swept upward by the breeze, he looked like an umbrella turned inside out by a storm. He lived on the wrong side of Bushy Brook Lane, which he described as the line that separated the serfs from the feudal lords at Brookeville. When asked by some city acquaintance to explain the origin of the thoroughfare's name, he would reply that it was an attempt on the part of the suburban rich to convince themselves that they lived in the country. His father, who had been the janitor of the local high school, had died of a heart attack in Madison Square Garden while watching him sink the winning basket for N.Y.U. in the last three seconds of play. Nelson Kirby, the new Chairman of the Board at McKinley and a Brookeville resident himself, had obtained the athletic scholarship for him, and, when an opening appeared, his present job at the Hospital. Although crippled by arthritis, his mother managed to cook and do the chores in the dilapidated old house in which they lived. He was determined that neither of them would die on the wrong side of Bushy Brook Lane.

The luncheon encounter took place when he and the two friends sat down simultaneously at the last empty table in the snack bar.

"The best way to check on the food and the service is to eat here," he volunteered.

For the next fifteen minutes he tried to pump information from them about the running of their services. Just before he left, he startled them by saying, "This hospital must once have been a paradise on earth for the doctors and the patients. You should know. Now it's a money-wasting anachronism. I hate to say this but I'm afraid its days are numbered. If the trustees and the doctors pored over facts and figures, graphs and census comparisons, and especially the budgets of the past twenty years, the way I do, I'm sure they would agree. The fame of the men you worked under rested on the free wards. But eventually there will be no free wards. Sooner or later those twin bouncers, Blue Shield and Blue Cross, or some kind of state insurance, will throw the free case out of the place and turn it into a private sanitarium, with rich and poor either private or semiprivate patients. Unfortunately, it will be the shabbiest private hospital in town. Most of the buildings are almost a hundred years old. The only thing that's keeping them up is tradition. But tradition won't put in new plumbing and new floors, machines and A.C., laboratories and equipment. You know what happens to an ocean liner when it becomes obsolete. No matter how big and beautiful it once was, if it costs too much to operate, it's junked. One day it's sailing up the Hudson to its pier. The next day they're towing it away for scrap. That's what's going to happen to McKinley."

He put down a ten-cent tip. "The trick is going to be how to get out from under when the crash comes."

As soon as he had left, Jim said, "There's no use arguing with that fellow. His world is made up of bricks. Ours is made up of men. Where we see Frederick Treuler, scalpel in hand, performing the first operation for cancer of the breast, he sees a few house painters plastering cracks and holes in the operating room. Where we see Abraham Jacobi, the founding father, helping a bedridden child by changing the position of the pillow, he sees a hopelessly outdated pediatric pavilion with chipped sinks and ugly plumbing. Where we see the ward corridors as arteries delivering life to the sick, he sees outmoded aisles with patients laid out on both sides like fish on ice. He's one of the new men. An efficiency expert."

"Right. But look around you. Are the doctors in better shape than the bricks? Take my chief. You could put his brain in a walnut shell. And it would rattle. He's not only a nitwit; he's a contradiction in terms—a belligerent Milquetoast. Hauser would have eaten him alive. And your chief? A nice enough fellow, but matching him against Emmerich would be like putting Foo-Foo, the rubber man, in the same ring with Joe Louis. Of course, there wasn't a doctor who could shine Rintman's shoes. But the guy who runs the medical service now couldn't even carry the polish."

"They're going to louse it up even more by expanding the staff. Pretty soon there will be more doctors than patients around here. From an elite hospital it's becoming the metropolitan area's favorite repository for medical mediocrities. You don't have to be above average any more to get an appointment here. All you have to be is a source of patients. What terrifies the trustees more than anything else is the specter of an empty bed. The Hospital doesn't make any money on empty beds."

"Yeh. First the patient can't get into the Hospital for weeks," said Stanley. "Then, if he does, he can't get any care. That's what really depresses me, the decline in nursing service. It was inevitable, of course. You can't expect girls to work twelve hours a day for peanuts, and cap a life of spinsterhood with honored senility. Today the school of nursing is a halfway house between high school and marriage. Just the same, it's a hell of a thing to realize that when a patient on floor care rings his bell, he has about as much chance of getting help as if he were lying on the frozen wastes of Baffin Island. Less of a chance. Up north a friendly Eskimo might just happen to be passing by."

"It's true," said Jim as he paid the check. "Still, there's something about Perkes I don't like. He's shrewd, knowledgeable, and ambitious, all right. And dedicated. Dedicated to getting ahead. He's Kirby's boy. But he's no friend of McKinley's. I have a hunch that someday he's going to cause a lot of trouble for the Hospital."

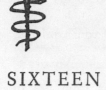

SIXTEEN

By AUTUMN of nineteen forty-one, people at the Hospital began to notice how disinterested and detached Jim had become. It took December 7's radio announcement, which he at first mistook for a hoax cleverer than Orson Welles's description of the invasion from Mars, to jar him loose from his apathy. Almost immediately, he sensed that here was an opportunity not only to strike at fascism, which he detested and had striven guiltily to ignore, but to win his release from a disappointing career. Three weeks later, Stanley and he went down to Church Street to take their physical examinations for commissions in the Medical Corps, an ordeal his friend prepared for by drinking a quart of water and eating six bananas to bring up his weight, while he himself did nothing except dwell uneasily on thoughts of Stinton's unexpected rejection because of high blood pressure. It took only one glance at the physiques of their colleagues, who were stripping self-consciously in the examining room, to convince them of the absurdity of their fears. As soon as they were dismissed, they went uptown in a taxi instead of the subway to celebrate their anticipated acceptance for full duty.

"If they make me a major," Stanley imparted to his friend, "I'll have enough money to marry Adele."

"You ought to marry her even if they make you a private."

"What's in it for her if I don't come back?"

"A son, maybe."

Adele insisted on taking a thousand dollars from her inheritance for a wedding at the Carlyle, which she wanted to be both elegant and orthodox enough to satisfy Mr. and Mrs. Levinson. When the Head of the Insitute, the father of three married daughters, heard that there was no one to give her away but a bachelor uncle in Philadelphia, he called her into his office and said, "For a thing like this you need an old hand. I may not be Jewish, but I'm experienced."

He looked quite distinguished that night leading her down the aisle to the "Hoopah," where Stanley and Jim were waiting in dinner jackets and skull caps. Since her roommate, a good Methodist, was the bridesmaid, there were almost as many Christians under the canopy as Jews.

Stanley would have thought it preposterous to invite as important a man as Mr. Huegenon to the wedding, but he did ask Adele to send him an announcement. In return, he received two pairs of car keys and a grumpy note that read, "This will have to do you for the duration. You should have invited me to the ceremony." It was signed "Huegenon."

Stanley and Adele ran downstairs. In front of the house was a new, baby-blue 1942 Buick.

"And neither of us can drive!" moaned Stanley.

But it did not take them long to learn. By the time his commission as a major in the Medical Corps arrived six weeks later, they were prepared to drive anywhere. True, the opening phrase of his orders, "Proceed at once to Rantoul . . ." gave them a bit of a shock. It sounded so much like Rangoon. But far from being in Burma, it turned out to be in Illinois and the site of an Air Force base with excellent medical facilities for military dependents. This was a welcome surprise. Adele was four weeks pregnant.

Jim's commission arrived at the same time as his friend's. The night before his departure for Fort Monmouth, he put on his olive dress uniform with the pinks, and his overcoat with the gold leaves on the shoulders, and slowly walked around and around the Hospital as if he were a sentry guarding its precious past. Then he went through every ward and department until at last he stood in front of the dark and empty operating room striving to fix everything he had just seen forever in his mind.

After almost a year at Fort Monmouth as Chief of the Surgical Service, he was transferred to the 812th General Hospital, an overseas outfit staging at Fort Devon. The rigorous, infantry-type training proved a hardship for his colleagues, most of whom were fat, frail, flabby, or forty. But not for him. Since he had always kept in condition, the infiltration course, bivouac, forced marches, and rough outdoor life did not bother him. If anything, they prevented him from brooding over McKinley's incipient decline and his lack of success in private practice. To further divert his thoughts, he asked his CO for permission to work out with a Ranger battalion stationed nearby. He boxed with many of the men and found that although they were ten years younger than he and trained pretty fine, he could handle them with ease. Soon he began to show them some of the tricks he had learned from Rightie Ruber. In return, they taught him more judo than any surgeon had ever known.

Then, three months to the day after his arrival at Fort Devon, the gossip seismographers detected a tremor. That night, all leaves were canceled and the unit put on the alert. Three days later, it was transferred to Camp Kilmer, a debarkation center, where it was placed under strict security regulations. No one was allowed to leave camp, write a letter, make a telephone call, or discuss anything but the weather with another unit, and not even that seriously. After a week of complete isolation, they were suddenly booted out on a three-day leave, presumably so that they could impart to the country at large what they had been prohibited from divulging to their comrades in arms.

Jim found his mother much older than he had remembered her, but she kissed him just the way she had used to when he was a little boy.

"Jimmy, there's no reason why you have to be a hero like your father," she warned.

When he returned to Kilmer, security measures were immediately reinstated. Unanswered remained the unit's two most urgent questions: Were they going to the ETO or the Pacific, England being considered a plum, the Far East a disaster? And were they going alone or in convoy? The CO was not talking. A hard-bitten colonel in the Regular Army Medical Corps, he had learned long since that sometimes silence was the wisest form of communication.

On May 26, 1943, he called them together to tell them solemnly that the moment had come, that early the next morning they were leaving for an unknown destination. Again, he warned them that their safety might be endangered by a careless word, a harmless hint, an innocent betrayal of trivial information. There was a silent struggle while he wrestled with his Army conscience. Then the man overcame the officer. He simply said, "I suppose you're all wearing summer underwear. Well, take along some winter underwear, too."

The unit smiled discreetly, trying to hide its jubilation. They were going to England, after all.

The morning of their departure was sunny and sparkling. The one thousand officers, nurses, and enlisted men of the 812th General Hospital rode through the Massachusetts countryside in a long troop train with the shades up, while half the state waved and cheered them on from the fields, towns, and stations along the route, well aware, no doubt, that they were on the way to Boston Harbor, since that was the end of the line. Jim wondered whether this was the best way to conceal troop movements from the German General Staff. But if he had been surprised by the lack of concealment on the trip to the sea, which was conducted more like a publicity stunt than a secret military operation, he was flabbergasted the moment the train stopped to see the old, broad-beamed *Aquitania* a hundred yards away advertising her imminent departure with belching smokestacks and boarding troops. Not only could *he* see the activity on the ship, but presumably any traitor, spy, enemy agent, Bundist, Nazi sympathizer, or psychopath who was willing to spend a few dollars for a pair of binoculars and plant himself on any of a thousand vantage points around Boston Harbor could do the same. Come to think of it, the binoculars were not really necessary. It was a clear day.

Nobody commented on the fact that they had not boarded ship and left in the secrecy of the night. Everyone was too busy scanning the harbor. But there were no comforting destroyers and transports nearby. The old *Aquitania* was going to have to fool the U-boats all by herself.

The hundred yards to the gangplank were to prove the most difficult of the doctors' lives, not because of fear, however, but because of baggage. Each was allowed to bring along four pieces, only one of which, the unwieldy bedroll, was stored for him in the hold. The rest they were forced to carry themselves: the distended duffel bag that only a professional strong man could lift, the Valpac weighted down with everything they imagined their destination would lack, and the bulging musette bag strapped on the back. Their gas masks, tributes to another war, they hardly noticed. Dragging their duffel bags as if they were dead elephants, tugging at their Valpacs, which seemed soldered to the ground, crouching under their clumsy musette bags like Egyptian slaves building the pyramids, they crept forward in single file behind the Colonel, while the British crewmen on the decks above looked down in amazement as if to say, "Are these officers? Then, where are their batmen and their orderlies?" A few shook their heads, and one finally murmured, "Will you look at that! That must be American democracy." It was true. The column looked nothing like a corps of officers, only like what it really was, a group of not-so-young and middle-aged civilian doctors trying to accomplish what no porter had ever done.

When the Colonel reached the foot of the gangplank, a halt was called while they dropped their Valpacs, let their four-foot duffel bags topple over, and examined their fingers and palms, which seemed to have changed both in color and shape.

Jim turned around for one last, encompassing look, raking in memories like a boy scraping together autumn leaves for the burning. Then he closed his eyes. He saw his father sitting next to him at the Polo Grounds, the stiff straw boater tilted just a trifle over one eye, the blue necktie with the fleur-de-lis stickpin stretching over the massive chest, and heard once again that optimistic voice say, "The game is young, Jimmy, the game is young." He felt Stinton's ice-blue eyes boring into him, and heard him mutter, "Faster, Doctor, faster! You're operating like Dr. Dobbs." He saw Emmerich performing prodigious feats of surgical dexterity with imperial disdain, and then watched him slide his five-eyed hand inside the belly in one lazy, voluptuous motion and come out with a benign cyst everyone had thought was malignant. He followed a pair of Mephistophelean hair tufts around the ward until Rintman, obviously communing with the devil, stopped ten feet from a bed to make a black-magic diagnosis that confounded them all. He felt an instrument slipped lovingly into his palm and enjoyed once more the soothing silence of the operating room when Star was there to anticipate his needs. Then everything seemed to change. An exciting fragrance filled the air, and in a flash he saw her standing in an austere room, her clothes at her feet, offering him the Venusberg night whose raptures she could never share. And last, from the mists of long ago, he saw Valhalla rise, saw the dilapidated walls, the obsolete structures, the hollow square, and understood that McKinley had not been a collection of bricks but of men, of men no buildings could ever match though they were designed to pierce the sky.

There was a shuffling along the column. Jim opened his eyes. The Colonel had picked up his Valpac and was standing with one foot on the gangplank facing his officers.

"Gentlemen," he roared, "tea and crumpets will be served in the lounge. Those with dislocated arms will be fed caviar in the Blue Room. Now suck in your bellies and shape up! March!"

For the first time in weeks, Jim smiled. Maybe the 812th General Hospital would not be so bad after all.

PART
THREE

"For Better or for Worse."

SEVENTEEN

The trip across proved to be a routine Atlantic passage, zigzag but pond smooth, and highly satisfactory except to the *Aquitania,* which responded to each change of course by tossing herself sulkily as if protesting the unpredictable commands that kept coming from the bridge. But to Jim and the other members of the 812th sailing through the flat ocean and the revealing May air with no protection from hostile periscopes either by destroyers or waves, these foxy maneuvers were very reassuring indeed. And when anyone grew apprehensive, when he wondered how long they could remain free from underwater attack, he had only to glance up at the top deck, where four sooty pennants told him that he had nothing to fear. No one had outgrown the belief that a sea queen's speed was determined by the number of funnels in her crown, or forgotten the days when a slow tub carried one, a good ship two, and a blue-ribbon champion no more than the *Aquitania's* four.

It was obvious that they were going to have to outrun, since they could never outfight, the enemy. Their armament, a single stern gun, more of a menace than a safeguard, shook the ship so violently during target practice that the first time it went off everyone but the crew thought that a torpedo had found its mark. At night Jim would lie awake in his bunk wondering what would happen if they fell in with a submarine wolf pack or were sighted later on near the coast by a squadron of bombers scouting for prey. Certainly their pathetic top-deck pom-poms could do little more than paw at a hostile high-flying plane, and the little stern gun sticking out behind like a rectal thermometer could never drive away even the greenest of U-boat commanders. But nothing happened. This tempting target, this overworked, obsolete *Aquitania,* with eighty-eight hundred American officers, nurses, and enlisted men on board, sailed north, south, and east on the lonely sea, defying a sun that wished only to betray it and a moon that cruelly revealed it, denied even the short, sheltering embrace of a single fog bank, and protected only by its own modest speed and the wily hand of a British captain.

That it was a British ship was unmistakable if only from the way it treated the American officers. Although the food was meager compared to the profusion found in a cafeteria mess in the States, it was served to them by a waiter in the first-class dining room on snowy linen with silver and glassware that were always correct. Although Jim and five other majors were packed into a room meant for one, sleeping in triple-tiered berths like corpses laid out in a morgue icebox, their bunks were made up every day and kept immaculate by a respectful steward. And although the Colonel refused to reveal their ultimate destination to the doctors of the 812th, the members of the crew showed no hesitation in telling them that the ship was out of Scotland and would undoubtedly return there. To an Englishman an officer was a gentleman. Even an American officer.

Then, early one morning when most of the amateur sailors in the unit had guessed their position as somewhere off France, the *Aquitania* sailed up the Firth of Clyde, putting an end to eight days of fire drills, six to a stateroom, body odors in confined spaces, silent flatus, blackened portholes, and no cigarettes on deck after dark. Glad as the doctors were to see land, and on both sides, they felt a new apprehension. For now, gripped by the green thumb and forefinger of the Firth, robbed of its ability to maneuver and take evasive action, the ship seemed defenseless against aerial attack. Everyone was on deck scanning the skies. Surely, somewhere in the Luftwaffe there must be a man willing to risk his life in order to destroy eighty-eight hundred of the enemy with one nicely placed bomb. Surely, among eighty million Aryans there must be someone ready to brave the ack-ack for the Thousand Year Reich, for Adolf and Eva, for the Brown Shirt pederasts, the degenerates and the goons, for dear old Heidelberg and dear old Buchenwald, for Putzi Hanfstaengel at Harvard, for a rah-rah, a *Sieg Heil* and a *Schmiss*, for the slogan "a suicide a day keeps the Gestapo away," for the good prison commander Buegeleisen and his complaint "Tell them to stop torturing that fellow for a few minutes. I can't read my Goethe because of the screams," for genocide and the massacre of the innocents, for Himmler's eyeglasses and Goebbels' limp, for buggery by night and murder by day, for sadism and mastery of the world.

Major Goldstein, the unit's ophthalmologist, hands on the rails, eyes to the south, wondered what was holding up the planes. There were certainly enough Jews on board to make an attack worthwhile. He smiled bitterly. Evidently it was easier to wipe them out in concentration camps. Jim glanced up at the empty skies and smiled too. "Somebody on our side," he decided, "is doing his job."

At noon the *Aquitania* dropped anchor between Gourock on one side and Greenock on the other. Although debarkation points for hundreds of thousands of troops, both seemed as safe as Hightstown under Coolidge. Jim and his colleagues had to drag their unwieldy baggage to the train, this time under the slightly widened eyes of puzzled Scotsmen. Nothing, Jim thought, looked quite as unmartial as an officer struggling with his luggage. He could not imagine Caesar leading the Tenth Legion with a Valpac in his hand or Napoleon addressing the grenadiers at Austerlitz with a duffel bag across his shoulders. Now he knew why Hannibal had taken those elephants across the Alps. Certainly not just to frighten the Romans.

As soon as he had stowed his things in one of the coaches that were drawn up at the station, and stepped into the corridor just outside his compartment, his embarrassment was replaced by a touch of pride. Hands on the sill, he stared out the window as, two abreast in kilts and tartans, a long column of massive, gray-haired old men made the bagpipes scream. There was a terrifying dichotomy between the wild speed of the notes and the unbearably slow thumping of the marching feet. The ancient melodies grew more barbaric, the blood coursed faster in the veins, as Jim, thinking back to the library on 122nd Street, saw Wallace rise from his grave and Robert the Bruce swirl through Bannockburn on his black charger. Yet, through it all, immune to their own musical stirrings, the granite-gray men paced up and down the platform, their feet beating out a funeral march while their lips called every man to battle. As the train pulled out, Jim raised his hand in a snappy salute. Little Greenock and Gourock were piping the unit off.

Soon the farewell notes were blotted out by the rhythmic clicking of the wheels on the tracks, which sounded to the unit like a stuck phonograph record repeating, "To the front, to the front, to the front!" over and over again. While, as if further to emphasize the imminent peril, the eyes of the young women and the old men who stopped work in the fields to give the "V" for victory sign seemed to belie their digital optimism. "The blood that flows in your veins came from the Old World, and to the Old World it must return" was the message the doctors read in those patient eyes.

Nobody seemed to realize that there was no front—no front except in Africa. And they certainly were not going there, not with all that winter underwear in their duffel bags. And certainly not by rail. After two hours, the train stopped. They had traced a huge circle and were back almost to their starting point. They were in Glasgow.

The unit set up its first hospital in a former RAF rest home ten miles from the city. The day they arrived, the Colonel called a meeting of his officers, not to discuss administrative procedures, as they had anticipated, but to warn them against committing statutory rape. The age of consent in the British Isles, it seemed, was sixteen, and he warned them not to screw anybody younger than that. Although he had never been outside the United States himself, he was able to inform them that British girls matured early. That was the danger, he emphasized. The doctors, most of whom had been comfortably married for years, were immensely flattered to be treated like potential sex fiends.

After six weeks' preliminary training in Scotland, they were transferred to their permanent installation, in Devon, where they set up an eighteen hundred bed general hospital. As Chief of Surgical Service, Jim had twenty officers under him, with all of whom he was on the most pleasant terms. They had been in their new location less than a week when the Colonel called him in and said, "I want to talk to you about your officers, Major. You've got a lot of New York kikes under you, and the rest of them are not much better. They are all sloppy, opinionated, and noisy. I don't know whether they are good doctors or not—that's your department. Remember, I'm the country boy; you're the city slicker. But they are not good officers. They can't keep their wards clean, wear the uniform properly, or even salute. They are a bunch of argumentative individualists who don't belong on a military establishment in the first place, and should never have been given such high rank in the second."

"I don't see what all this has to do with religion, sir."

"Nothing, nothing," answered the Colonel irritably. "I'm no

anti-Semite. There weren't enough of them where I came from in Idaho."

"Maybe that was the trouble, sir."

"Maybe. But I'm telling you this. Unless there is a miraculous reformation at once, I'm kicking every God-damn one of them, Jew and Christian alike, out on his ass. And you know what that means: in three months they'll all be battalion-aide surgeons sweating it out in the line."

He drew his chair closer to his desk. "And to show you I'm not prejudiced, if you have a Moslem on your staff, I'll kick him in the ass, too."

Jim walked to his office and told the sergeant to call a meeting of his officers for noon. Then he went to his room, actually a cell in a cardboard shack, and sat on his cot with his head in his hands. These were colleagues, physicians, men who had always gone their own way, not West Point plebes. Unfortunately he could not even purchase a little popularity by telling them that the storm he was about to unleash had been blown up by the Colonel. This was the Army, and he had to act as if he were responsible. At five minutes to twelve he straightened out his uniform, put on his overseas cap and walked back.

That day and every day for the next three months he hammered them into the mold. He insisted that they stand up when he came in, made them salute over and over again until they had mastered the gesture, prohibited debates with superiors, read them the ARs as if they were the Bible, forced them to wear their uniforms and insignia properly, ridiculed their posture, cautioned them against familiarity with enlisted men and nurses, and inspected their wards day after day for perfect bed alignment, decorum, and cleanliness. Although he was not as successful at picking up dust as the Inspector with the White Gloves, he went through the motions, at least, by sliding his fingers along all the unlikely places. By the fall they no longer behaved like doctors at a medical convention. They

258

were officers even by the Colonel's standards. And not one of them was sent into the line. Jim's reward was loneliness. You could not eat out a captain's ass by day, he knew, and drink with him at night.

The discipline in which he had enmeshed himself proved easy to adjust to. Certainly it was nothing new. Was it not a military brother of the medical system that had molded him when first he came to McKinley? And there was more to remind him of the Hospital than the discipline. There were the wards themselves, unexpected replicas of those on which he had trained, every one with twenty-five perfectly aligned beds on either side and a wide, gleaming alley in the middle. Instead of being under one roof, however, they were scattered over half a golf course, each occupying its own little gray stone building. Jim was in charge of thirty of these wards, and during the Battle of the Bulge they held fifteen hundred patients, three times as many as were in all of McKinley at the time.

He was enormously grateful to the Army for this honor, this responsibility, and these exciting days, which as time went by he feared would have to serve him in lieu of a future. There was really only one thing wrong with the 812th. Its medical standards were high, its operations skillfully performed, its patients well cared for, better than most of them had ever been cared for in their lives. But it was not McKinley—just a wartime sweetheart that could never take its place.

But, then, the old hospital on Park Avenue was not McKinley either any more. Kell's monthly letters were making that clear. Nothing seemed to have changed, and yet everything had changed. The buildings and the Park Avenue location looked the same, but the great names were vanishing. With Rintman, Emmerich, and Grund dead, Hauser and Kaertner retired, and the old German millionaires replaced by flat-walleted, smart managers, McKinley was living off its past. Like a giant liner whose engines suddenly stop in mid-ocean, so McKinley, intact and motionless, lay wallowing in forgotten glories. Only recently had Nelson Kirby started up the engines on cheaper fuel and, backed by his stingy trustees, set sail for less perilous waters.

Since they could not erect new buildings because of wartime restrictions, he announced, they were going to rejuvenate the Hospital by getting new doctors. But it was not the national emergency that made the trustees reluctant to modernize the plant. It was simply their unwillingness to raise the money. "The oyster knife has not yet been honed that can pry open their pockets," Kell wrote. "New blood" became the cry as they brought in men from other hospitals to fill the vacant directorships. "It's one hell of a transfusion," he remarked in another letter. "The blood is new, all right, but it's anemic."

Another letter from Kell about the new regime was more specific. "In our day it was tough to get on the attending staff at McKinley. And when you did, you had to obey a new version of the first commandment—'Thou shalt have no other hospitals but me.' Now it's easy, and the commandment has been repealed. They have recently appointed at least a hundred doctors who are also on the staffs of other institutions. One old McKinley boy with several affiliations is doing particularly well. It is rumored that our house staff mate Aims Blair will be the next Director of Obstetrics and Gynecology. You see, he took the precaution of marrying Nelson Kirby's daughter."

The changes that had come over McKinley were by no means confined to the top echelon. Kirby and his flat-walleteers had flung wide the gates so that a whole army of invaders could enter and assume every rank. In less than two years, Kell wrote, the attending staff had been more than doubled, with the old McKinleyites now outnumbered by the new. No one was naive enough to imagine that this had been done to provide better care for the patients. It had been done for purely monetary reasons. The more doctors on the staff, the more private patients in the Hospital and the less need for the members of the board to dip their hands into their clamshell pockets.

But there were other letters, soothing letters from his mother, in which she enclosed book reviews, notes from the Philharmonic concerts, theater programs, and poems. He had allotted her three quarters of his overseas pay, and she was able to amuse herself as she wished. And warm letters from Stanley and Adele. The baby had been a boy. At the circumcision the mohel had held up a ten dollar gold piece and a prayer book. The baby had put its hand on the book, thus proving, according to Mr. Levinson, that it would grow up to be a scholar.

Some of the devotion that Jim felt for faithless McKinley he gave to the 812th instead. During the first year, he hardly left the post. Early in the second, the Colonel called him into his office.

"Morelle, first comes an apology for the unfortunate remarks I made about your staff. Since then, they've been officers every inch of the way. Second comes a warning. I have repeatedly suggested that you take a week's leave of absence and see some of England. You have not complied. Major, a suggestion by a superior officer is a command. At the moment, the sergeant is cutting an order you'll be forced to obey. I've put in for your promotion to Lieutenant Colonel, a rank that requires that you be interviewed by a general in London. Unfortunately, the general is too busy to come here just to see you. The interview will take five minutes. I expect you to be away five days."

Jim took the hint. He put in for short leaves now and then, came to the monthly dances at the club, treated his officers to dinner at nearby Torquay, and even let the Colonel teach him poker. Kirby's McKinley he tried to forget. And when the allied armies sliced across France early in 1945, he visibly relaxed. It was now just a question of time.

The only thing that disturbed him was the new prisoner-of-war compound, where Nazi privates and noncoms were convalescing from wounds recently received on the Continent. Surrounded by barbed wire and guarded by MPs though it was, it made him feel uneasy. He had a premonition that in some way it would change his life and that of the Hospital he loved so well. When the incident occurred in the middle of April, it was like nothing he had anticipated.

EIGHTEEN

FOR OVER A WEEK his fellow noncoms in the compound had been worried about the big Bavarian sergeant who had been hit at Remagen. His head wound had healed, his physical examination revealed nothing abnormal, but he kept striding up and down, agitated and depressed, jamming his fist into the palm of his hand, muttering and cursing. One afternoon when the three medics of the 812th assigned to his ward were drinking coffee in the kitchen, he walked past them through the short hall and out into the enclosure. The MP at the gate, his back to the prison ward, had taken off his helmet liner to adjust the leather chin strap and was looking at a squadron of B-17s flying toward the continent. Shielded by their thunder, the sergeant ran forward, crouching low and reliving once again the years of triumph. The MP raised his hands instinctively as he felt a big arm curl around his neck, so it was easy for the German to reach down, tear the .45 from its holster, and smash the butt into the unprotected skull. Although the man was already unconscious as he slid down, the big Bavarian struck him a second shattering blow on the temple. Then he wiped the weapon on his sleeve, pushed it inside the waist string of his pants, and walked through the gate into the road.

Three hundred feet away he saw a long, narrow, one-storied, graystone building stretching in the sun. Restless and irritable, he entered the short hall, glanced at the kitchen on the side, and walked toward the surgical ward, a spotless alley with twenty-five evenly spaced beds on either side. Most of the soldiers in the beds were watching a girl in a Red Cross uniform who was writing at a heavy table in the center of the room. The prisoner entered stiffly, jerked out the gun, and shouted, *"Diese verfluchte Allierten haben wieder einen Fehler gemacht!"*

In the sudden silence Corporal Toski, a smalltime mobster whose hand had been shattered by shrapnel, propped himself on his elbow.

"What did he say?" he whispered to a boy from Milwaukee in the next bed.

"He said, 'These damn allies have pulled another boner.'"

"A psycho, huh?"

The German glanced at the two, and in surprisingly good English, said, "This gun holds seven bullets. Who are the seven who will die?" He smiled pleasantly. "You two, certainly."

At this, the girl in the Red Cross uniform stood up.

"Halt!" the German shouted and pointed the weapon at her.

A minute before, Jim, on his way to dress Toski's hand, had spotted the PW entering the surgical ward. So angry had he been that he had raced across the road and reached the hall in time to hear the shouting and see the gun. It took him only a moment to spot a convenient missile on the kitchen drainboard, a large bottle of Nescafé, which he picked up with regret since it was the only coffee in the ETO that did not taste like licorice. Holding it self-consciously in his right hand, he drifted into the ward. An extraordinarily beautiful girl was staring at the prisoner, whose back was turned to him. There will never be a better time than this, he decided, as he shouted *"Achtung!"* and tossed the bottle so that it exploded on the concrete floor a foot behind the man. The big Bavarian turned and stood there, confused and stupid, his eyes on the glass fragments. Then he took a stiff step forward like a robot and fired high. Jim had already dipped, and charging down the alley, slammed him hard against the table. Even before the judo grip cracked his forearm, the German screamed and dropped the gun. When he felt the quick chop on his neck, he slid down and lay flat on his back, half conscious and staring unwinking at the ceiling. It took the MPs almost ten minutes to get there, and by that time Jim had applied an emergency metal splint to the shattered bones.

"How do you like that!" whispered Toski as the stretcher was carried out. "First he breaks the bastard up into little pieces, and then he puts him together again like a jigsaw puzzle." To himself he added, "The boys could use a guy like that in New York."

Jim stood up and turned toward the girl. Her brilliant blue eyes were wide and shining, and not just with the excitement of the moment, he knew. Somehow he was sure that she would always look this way. Then he saw her blue-black hair curled in a Psyche knot behind her neck, and thought at once of the forbidden goddesses in the old mythology book at 122nd Street.

"What a romantic thing to do!" she exclaimed. "It's just like the old days when a lady in distress could always count on being rescued by a knight at arms."

"Well, I couldn't let him shoot up the ward," said Jim apologetically.

"Or me. I hope that's what you mean. I'm certainly going to make believe that's what you mean."

He was looking down at her, obviously embarrassed.

"What are you thinking of?" she asked.

"Of a poem you remind me of."

"Oh, don't look so embarrassed."

He was staring at her now as if she had just risen from the

265

waves. "I don't know where it comes from. I only remember that somewhere Aphrodite was walking through the fields. Bees were humming harmlessly around her head, and she had lyre-shaped hips."

The girl smiled, and the sparkling atmosphere about her became more intense. "Now you're making *me* embarrassed." She paused. "You remind me of a poem, too; only, I can remember every word."

Toski and the forty-nine men nodded gravely in the great silence.

She continued in a low, exciting voice that made Jim think of the way his mother had read to him when he was a little boy:

" 'In peace there's nothing so becomes a man
   As modest stillness and humility.
   But when the blast of war blows in our ears,
   Then imitate the action of the tiger.' "

She added quietly, "As if I needed to tell you."

They stood looking at each other in the middle of the ward as if there were no patients, no war, no world except this little spot in Devon. Then she drew his hand toward her, placed the palm against her cheek, and walked away.

Jim watched her until she passed through the doorway. There seemed to be a strange humming around her head, and she had lyre-shaped hips.

"Colonel," said Toski, and it sounded very loud, "who is Aphrodite?"

"Venus," replied Jim.

Toski thought this over and nodded. "It figures. I know it's none of my business, but in my opinion you handled her A-one perfect."

Jim, his eyes on the floor, walked toward the door between the two rows of beds until he came to Private Muzzy, who was called "Mother" Muzzy because he knew everything and gave advice on everything.

266

"Colonel!" called out Muzzy, "do you know her name?"

"No, I don't," answered Jim.

"It's Gillette. Louise Gillette." He looked at Jim anxiously. "You won't forget it, Colonel, will you?"

Jim raised his head. "Never," he said, "never," and walked out of the ward.

That evening at six, the neurosurgeon drilled a burr hole through the unfortunate MP's skull, evacuating a large collection of blood in an operation that lasted three hours. Only after the man regained consciousness did Jim leave the bedside and walk to the Officers' Club. Like all the other buildings on the post, it was primitive and one-storied, but in contrast to the wards, which were shaped like five-dollar safe-deposit boxes, it was wide and nicely proportioned. Its single large room seemed empty tonight. Nowhere could he find the girl he was looking for among the dozen or two doctors and nurses who were chatting in little groups. He sat down as far from them as he could and watched Major Goldstein, the lonely ophthalmologist, who was standing by the phonograph in the opposite corner playing the unit's favorite record, currently "I'll Be Seeing You," as if he were conducting it. When the Major came to the phrase "The chestnut tree, the wishing well," he lifted the needle expertly, thus making a spectacular contribution to the silence that had descended all at once over everyone. Jim glanced at the door. She had come in out of the night, and her sparkling aura made him think of some famous diamond suddenly revealed when its blue velvet case was snapped open. Without a word to anyone, she walked up to him and sat down.

"I'll never forget the Nescafé bomb, the flash of judo, and the poetic compliment. But tonight do you think we could just sit here and talk?"

Major Goldstein, who knew the grooves in the record as well as he did the anatomy of the eye, placed the needle in the right place, and the machine instantly responded with "The chestnut tree, the wishing well."

"I never mastered the art," said Jim.

"Then, let's just look at each other. Once I prayed for the day when I would never have to see another uniform again. Now I'm a changed woman. Colonel, I could look at you in that uniform the rest of my life."

"I hope I don't have to wear it that long," commented Jim ruefully.

"Cheer up; you won't. Besides, you have something nice coming to you. You saved my life, and you can ask anything you want of me. In your set, it's called a boon, I believe."

"What set is that?"

She looked surprised. "The Arthurian set, of course. You're a member of the Round Table, aren't you? That's what the nurses say."

"A charter member, I'm afraid."

"My father belongs to the Cosmopolitan Club, but yours is a much older organization. By the way, you should be in your element over here. Next door is Cornwall—that's Tristan and Isolde country, and a few miles away, Winchester, that once was Camelot." She smiled. "Well, what's the boon?"

"What do you suggest?"

"Beg me to have dinner with you tomorrow night. At the Imperial, in Torquay."

"Will you?"

"You saved my life, so I must."

But they did not have dinner together the following night, after all. At 6 P.M. a hospital train stopped at Newton Abbott, and soon the field ambulances were pulling into the 812th with three hundred and ten casualties, most of them destined for the surgical service. Working until three in the morning, screening, sorting, and placing the men in the appropriate wards, Jim smiled grimly from time to time as he thought how excited they would have been at McKinley if there had been as many as a dozen surgical admissions in a single night. It was soon evident that the patients were not in bad shape, certainly

nothing like the ones who had arrived during the Battle of
the Bulge, thus emphasizing the old Army saying that the
casualties that come in after a retreat are always the worst. In
fact, he was able to go off duty late the following afternoon,
and, together with Louise, catch the six o'clock truck that went
regularly into Torquay. The Colonel, who would not have
hesitated to sack a nurse who went out with an enlisted man,
or an officer who took his men to dinner, insisted that everyone,
regardless of sex or rank, use the same vehicle. That night
everyone was particularly uncomfortable as the old Army truck,
a covered wagon with passengers separated from the driver by
a barred glass window up front, careened along the skinny,
snaky English roads and threw nurses, Red Cross girls, privates,
and officers against each other like dice in a leather cup. The
enlisted men, who wished to be alone so they could use their
own four-lettered vocabulary, were embarrassed by Jim's rank
and the prohibition that prevented them from dealing appropriately with the nurses who kept bouncing into their arms. But
this was the way the Colonel wanted it. He was a great one for
democracy, the Colonel was. Besides, he had his own private
jeep.

The headwaiter at the Imperial Hotel placed Louise and
Jim at a table near the window so that they could look at the
harbor over gardens filled with bulbs and spring flowers, and
see the palm trees, which, he remarked, were the only ones in
all of England. To their amazement there was roast beef on
the menu.

"I've never heard of an English hotel serving roast beef
during wartime," said Louise. "Those rumors of a German
surrender must be true."

Jim held up a slice of meat that was so thin he felt it must
have been cut with a microtome. But when he put it in his
mouth, his expression changed.

They ate in silence. Suddenly she reached over and touched
his hand. "You remind me of those lines of Keats, 'O what can

269

ail thee, knight-at-arms, alone and palely loitering?' I'm no Belle Dame sans Merci, am I?"

"You're a belle dame, all right. Your beauty is not only conspicuous, it's positively ostentatious."

"It would have to be, to impress you. But why do you look that way? You'll be going home soon."

"I know. And I have a rendezvous with failure."

"Oh, pooh! I've been here a week, and already I've been told a hundred times that you're the finest and the fastest surgeon in the ETO. The Colonel boasts about you wherever he goes."

"What civilian doctors do here doesn't count when they go back home. It's like getting honors in college and flunking in life."

She shook her head. "What else?"

Jim said nothing.

"A love affair?" she asked.

"You might call it that."

"Any woman who turned you down must be psychotic."

"It's not a woman. It's a hospital."

She turned to watch a fishing boat come up the harbor. "How long does it take you to do a gall bladder operation?"

"I've done them in forty minutes."

"I can see where I'm going to end up by falling in love with you." She sighed. "My mother had hers taken out at Harland when I was fifteen. Did you ever hear of a surgeon called Dobbs?"

Jim smiled. "He used to be Director of Surgery there."

"Why did you smile?"

"Whenever I operated too slowly as an intern at McKinley, one of the men who trained me used to whip me on by saying, 'Faster, Doctor, faster! You're operating like Dr. Dobbs!' Dr. Dobbs was my horrible example. But he was a famous surgeon just the same."

"I don't care. He deserved to be your horrible example. They wheeled my mother up to the operating room at half past eight in the morning and they didn't bring her down until half past twelve. For four hours my father and I sat in her room telling each other that everything was fine and that Dr. Dobbs would bring her down in a minute. He finally did. Six days later she was dead of peritonitis." She leaned over and took his hand. "Any man who can do a gall bladder operation in forty minutes shouldn't have a rendezvous with failure."

"Speed isn't important any more."

"It was to my mother. I'll make everybody in New York see that it is." She smiled. "I'm bossy. When my mother died, I decided to move in and take her place—at fifteen. I got very close to my father, traveled everywhere with him, went to concerts, theater, and the opera with him, even pried into his business affairs. As a matter of fact, I did everything but go to bed with him. By the time I graduated from Radcliffe, I was trying to run his life. He was always very kind to me, but he never paid any attention to what I said. I tried, though, and I loved it."

"Why didn't some man carry you off? Even Wotan, king of the gods, couldn't keep his Brünnhilde forever."

"Oh, this was no crummy ring of fire you could beat out with a mended sword. This was charm and good looks and love and protection."

A five-piece English band started to play "I'm Getting Sentimental Over You" in a rather unsentimental fashion. But to Jim, three years away from New York, it sounded as if Tommy Dorsey himself were conducting. They both stood up at exactly the same moment and began to dance in a manner that indicated that they would tear anyone to pieces who dared to cut in. A medley of Gershwin tunes came next. Then the band disappeared, presumably to have some of that refreshing warm beer. Jim and Louise sat down and dawdled over their drinks. After a while she asked, "Have you heard any of the London bands?"

"No."

"But you've been to London?"

"Oh, yes. And I'm going there again in two weeks. The Colonel is sending me to a meeting of military surgeons." He made a great show of consulting a notebook. "May third to the seventh." There was a long and tense pause.

"Well?" she asked, at last.

He looked terribly embarrassed. "Do you think you could bring yourself to come with me?"

She laughed. "Is that the boon?"

Jim flushed. "Of course not! I just thought I'd take a flyer."

"You've been here so long you're beginning to talk like an Englishman." Almost as an afterthought she added, "Certainly I'll go with you. I probably would have suggested it myself. But this way you allowed me to be a lady."

"I suppose we should stay at separate hotels."

"Why? We can stay at Claridge's."

"Claridge's! That's for generals."

"Oh, pooh! My father used to stay there all the time. But there's a charming little hotel called the Mayfair that might be better."

"Don't you think we should have separate rooms?"

"If you want," answered Louise. "But nobody in London cares about things like that any more. The English hotels object to a man bringing a woman up to his room only because he's paid for one. They wouldn't mind if the present Archbishop of Canterbury brought up Thais as long as he paid for two."

"And the difference in centuries could be adjusted."

She laughed. "Naturally. Let me make the arrangements. They know me at the Mayfair, too."

They caught the eleven o'clock truck and walked quickly through the post to the nurses' quarters. Almost at once, Jim shook hands and said good-by. Louise laughed.

After this they saw each other regularly every evening, talking for hours at a time in the Officers' Club, going to the movies in Torquay, having dinner and dancing at the Imperial. The afternoon before they were to go to London, he almost collided with her in front of the Administration Building just as he was going off duty. She was wearing a raincoat.

He looked up at the sky. "Pretty cautious, aren't you?"

She seemed restless. "Let's take a walk. Anywhere except on the post."

They went out through the main gate and caught a Newton Abbott bus that was just pulling into the stop. After they had been driven a mile or two, she decided that they had gone far enough. He helped her out and they walked slowly across somebody's field for a few minutes.

Jim looked around him. "They must dye the grass a permanent green. It's this color even in December."

She held up her palms. "We'll soon see."

They hurried toward a thick copse about a hundred feet away as if they knew it well. Pushing aside bushes and sliding between trees, they came upon a little clearing, well protected by overhanging branches, where side by side they stood listening to the rain tapping on the leaves.

"I feel like a cow, standing up in the rain like this," she said.

They sat down close together and stared at the trees. Soon a breeze sprang up and it began to rain a little harder. After a few minutes she laid her hand on his knee and said quietly, "You don't have to wait until London."

Suddenly they found themselves lying on the grass looking at each other and, after a moment of shyness, making love. A soft, warm rain touched them from time to time but they were unaware of it. Soon her body welcomed his mounting violence, pushing the pain contemptuously aside. And when the moment of fulfillment laid hold of them, it enveloped them so swiftly that they both shared the same surprise.

Jim raised himself off her. She was lying there, breathing

quietly, with filmy eyes and parted lips, looking just the way he once had imagined all women looked after making love.

"This was the first time, wasn't it?" he asked.

"Of course."

He shook his head. "How could I know, with all that fine talk of yours about hotel rooms and the Archbishop of Canterbury?"

"Oh, what difference does it make?"

"It makes a lot of difference to me. I'll marry you, if you'll have me."

They lay in each other's arms for a while. Then Louise sat up, arched her back, and yawned.

"You'll have to marry me. Do you know what will happen if I run all the way back to the post screaming that a brutish, not a British, officer, mind you, dragged me into the bushes and took advantage of me? First they'll court-martial you. Then they will line you up in front of the troops, tear off your silver leaves, cut off your buttons the way they did to Captain Dreyfus, and stamp on them. Have you any idea how ridiculous you'll look without buttons? Your pants will probably fall down. Need I remind you, Colonel, that you will be instantly cashiered from the Coldstream Guards and stricken from the rolls of the Cosmopolitan Club? And even you must realize that they will cancel your charge account at Brooks Brothers."

"Oh, Louise, I just meant that I hoped that you would want to marry me."

She put her arms around him. Her hair and her cheeks were wet.

"If I marry you, will you give me what I want?"

"What *do* you want?"

"The world and all the fruits thereof—but for you, Jim, for you!" She thought for a moment. "That's what Samuel Gompers said the workers should have. Why shouldn't I have it for you?"

"Do you belong to a union?"

"Only the one I just had with you." She leaned back on the palms of her hands. "On the contrary, my father is a capitalist." She smiled. "You raped the right girl."

"He is? I'll bet I know what he does."

"What?"

"He owns the corner candy store."

"Better than that."

"The Gillette razor blade company."

"No, but he must have a lot of their stock." She stood up, fixed her hair, and straightened her clothes. Jim, too, got up and put his uniform in order. Shaking her head in exasperation, she came up to him.

"You don't get the point at all. I'm rich, and my father is very rich. It's what you need, what you've always needed. You'll never make it alone."

He put his hands on her hips. "I'll marry you, Louise. But not because of the Coldstream Guards or the Cosmopolitan Club or Brooks Brothers or the corner candy store or your father. I'll marry you because I never want you to stop loving me. I know I'll never stop loving you."

She slipped her arms around his neck and put her face against his. Her cheeks were wet, but this time when he looked up the sun was shining.

Since she insisted she wanted to walk back to the post, they went the entire distance, side by side, across the fields.

"I'm twenty-nine," she said, "and I'll never let you go as long as I live."

"I'm thirty-seven. That's a little late to start conquering the world."

"I'm only interested in your conquering the fashionable part, dear. Thirty-seven is young. I think I'll hammer my Uncle Ty's favorite motto on your coat of mail: 'Sempre avanti, eterna giovinezza'—'always forward, eternal youth.' It's carved in stone above one of the doors of Rockefeller Center. And on Uncle Ty's heart. He says that since youth has nothing to do with

275

chronological age, he may live long but he can never grow old."

"When I was at college, I had a friend, what was known as a best friend in those days. He used to mention a girl who always called his father Uncle Ty because when she was little, she had been told he was a tycoon."

"Albert Huegenon?"

He nodded.

"Wasn't it terrible about Albert?" she exclaimed. "It happened the year before my mother died."

Jim looked at her in surprise. "What ever happened to Mr. Huegenon?"

"Nothing, really. He's as imperious and elegant as ever. And as lonely. His wife died two years after Albert, and he has no relatives. And very few outside friends except my father. Just money and power. By now he must be worth hundreds of millions of dollars."

"How come he's never in the paper?"

"He's still devoted to his three passions: money, art, and anonymity." She paused. "I wonder where all that money is going."

"Some place like the Rockefeller Institute, probably."

"Oh, no, it isn't! He doesn't like doctors. And hospitals he regards as medical prisons where, to use his own words, 'Fate executes the inmates in a hundred different ways.' He's never forgotten about Albert."

They were approaching the gate. She stopped and turned toward him.

The next morning they took the train to London. The management of the Mayfair was respectful, almost deferential, and not, Jim realized, because of his silver leaves. By now it took stars on an American uniform to impress the better hotels. They were given two large connecting rooms and the door in between was wide open.

While he was unpacking, Louise came in and began to

undress. He walked to the window, and with his back to her began thinking of another time when standing in the same position in his room at McKinley, he had heard Stanley say, "She was beautiful, Jim, and there will never be anyone as beautiful."

"How can you be so silly!" Louise exclaimed. "Will you please turn around!"

He did, and knew at once that Stanley had been wrong.

"This will be the first time I've done it in bed," she said as he came toward her.

Afterward, they fell asleep in each other's arms. When they awakened, Jim said, "As soon as we get back, I'll tell the Colonel that we'd like to get married. They'll yank one of us out of the unit, I'm afraid. They always do."

Louise sat up violently. "Married!" she cried out as if he had suggested that they be tattooed. "Over here in some obscure English town! We're going to be married in New York in the biggest, most ostentatious, and best-publicized wedding I can dream up. And the guests will be chosen with an eye to your career, Doctor. You won't be an unknown any more after the five hundred I'm inviting pass by on the reception line and shake your hand. Do you think I intend to waste a perfectly good wedding over here? It isn't as if we were going to be married every year."

"I can't figure you out, Louise."

"It's better that way. Let me do the spadework." She bent over and kissed him.

"Your skin is remarkably creamy for a spadeworker."

"You'd better listen to me if you don't want it to curdle. Worse is coming. I have an income from money my mother left me. It amounts to about thirty-five thousand dollars a year and it's been piling up since I was fifteen. I want you to use some of it to get started, to pay for a beautiful office, beautiful equipment, and a not so beautiful nurse. I want you to use some of it to furnish and run an impressive home, and for the nice, cold-blooded business entertaining we're going to do in it."

"I can't take money from you."

"I know, I know. The men in your family never take money from women." She took his head in her hands. "I'm not suggesting that I should support you. But you're thirty-seven—you're the one who brought that up, remember?—and the Japanese war isn't over. You're a little late, and you'll have to start big. Everyone talks about your surgical feats, especially your speed. No one has to talk about your looks. What you've never had are contacts and a manager. You're going to have those soon. In a few years you will be supporting me so lavishly that I'll complain about your extravagance, and money will be so plentiful that it will be unimportant to you. If it makes you feel any better, you can start paying me back the day you open your office."

"How can I do that?"

She sat on the edge of the bed. "It's simple. Every night when you come home, I'll be waiting for you at the door. You'll totter in, red-eyed and dog-tired after a day under the hot operating-room lights. I'll be standing there fresh and bold, with painted lips, painted toenails, and a revealing dress. You've never seen me in a dress! I'll tap a little black book I'm holding in my hand and say with a hideous leer, 'Do you know that you owe me twenty-eight thousand dollars and twenty-eight cents?' Then I'll take out my key and unlock the chastity jockstrap I send you out in every morning. 'Get in there and earn your money!' I'll whisper hoarsely, pointing to the bedroom door."

Jim sat up. "You would? You'd go to such lengths to collect?"

"I would."

He put his arms around her. "All right. In that case I'll borrow a little money."

She sighed. "We'll be married in St. Thomas's. They have such beautiful weddings there. Where do you go?"

"I'm a Unitarian."

She laughed. "A Unitarian! That's like being a Jew. But you don't mind St. Thomas's, do you?"

"No. I suppose God must hang around there, too."

"He will, for our wedding. My father will see to that."

They dressed and went downstairs for an austerity lunch. As soon as it was over, she began to question him about his life in New York.

"I have to know even more," she said, "and I'm warning you that I'm an expert at this sort of a thing. At home I'm called the D.A. But don't ever tell me about the girls you've had. I never want to hear that." She shook her head, surprised at her own obtuseness. "As if you were the kind who would."

When he told her more about the library on 122nd Street, she made him pay the check at once so that they could start on a grand tour of London, which she knew almost as well as New York. After he had registered at the meeting of military surgeons, they walked and taxied everywhere for the next three days, turning the pages of the city's history and comparing them with those he had read so hungrily as a boy. At night they went to the theater and to private supper clubs, where they were always welcomed once Louise said a word to whoever was in charge. But on the night of May 6, they stayed at the hotel so as not to miss the official broadcast of the German surrender.

"It's all over but the shooting," Jim said, "in the Far East, I mean."

They went out into the streets to see the city, which was illuminated not by lights, because of the fear that some rogue bomber, some mutinous Nazi squadron, might wreak a treacherous revenge on a target made too tempting, but by a moon and the joy of a brave people relieved at last of a terrible ordeal. In the darkness of Park Lane they could hear rustling and laughter, singing and talking, distant shouts and close-by whispers. Everywhere there were groups of warm-eyed girls pulling buttons and insignia off some embattled American officer whose only protest was an embarrassed smile.

But none of them laid a hand on Jim, perhaps because high up on his shoulders the silver leaves gleamed like a general's stars. No English girl would dare to undress a brigadier. Not in the street.

The next morning, Louise and Jim took an early train back to the post, making a nice connection with an empty truck from the 812th just as it was about to pull out of Newton Abbott. As they climbed down in front of the Administration Building, the Colonel walked by. Conducting an affair on the post he regarded as unforgivable. He called such behavior "fouling the flagpole." But London was something else again. He looked at Jim and Louise approvingly and walked into his office. As soon as he sat down at his desk, he turned to the executive officer and said, "I think Morelle made a connection. The two of them have come back from London looking tired and refreshed. That combination is always a giveaway."

"It's about time," answered the exec.

The week after V-J Day, Louise was ordered home.

"Don't feel so bad," she said to Jim as they stood beside the flagpole in front of the Administration Building. "Somebody has to go back to beat the drums, pull the strings, and tell them what a great surgeon you are." She smiled. "Your speed at the operating table is going to be my sales slogan. Your looks I'll let them discover for themselves. Then I have to make plans for a great, big, vulgar wedding, the kind you hate. It will be the opening gun of your career, dear, so try to think of it as a weapon. And in addition to this, I have to win over your mother, Stanley, and Adele."

Jim looked puzzled. "You make it sound as if you were checking off a shopping list."

NINETEEN

THE DAY Louise arrived in New York she rang up Stanley, who had spent all of the war at Chanute Field. It took her weeks to gain his confidence. She knew she had it when he said to her, "In the beginning there were three strikes against you: You were rich, Christian, and socially prominent."

"I still am," she protested.

"I know. But I don't notice it any more."

He enjoyed the way she told him that she expected him to share the office with Jim.

"Don't let him charge you too much," she lectured. "A surgeon earns five times as much as a pediatrician. Since he's going to make five times as much out of the office as you are, let him pay five times as much rent."

She finally found a place she considered desirable, two blocks from the Hospital—a seven-room Park Avenue suite, which, though lacking the baroque splendors of Emmerich's old palace setup, possessed, as she saw it beautifully furnished in her mind's eye, a simple, impersonal elegance better suited to post-war tastes. To Stanley's enthusiasm she responded with,

"Do you think Jim will approve? Do you think perhaps he'll fall in love with it? They are two different things, of course."

"I think you're more concerned about his feeling toward the office than his feelings toward you."

"Naturally. I *know* he's in love with me."

Hennie's conquest had been even more rapid, helped apparently by Louise's willingness to go to the opera with her and listen respectfully to anecdotes about the singers in the old days.

And Louise always read very carefully and commented very intelligently on the book reviews and poems her future mother-in-law cut out of the *Times* and mailed to her.

Jim came home early in January 1946. One of the first things Hennie said to him was, "Your fiancée knows a great deal about poetry."

From his mother, that was a high compliment, indeed.

"Don't let her fool you," he replied. "It's her body that's poetic. Her mind is prose. And arithmetic."

Already, he noticed, Louise was solidly entrenched among his family and friends.

Less than a month after he returned, she pointed out to him that his mother should move to a better neighborhood.

"You ought to put her in some apartment hotel where everything can be done for her," she said. "She doesn't enjoy keeping house or entertaining. And she's not a very practical person. It can all be arranged quietly. The hotel will send the bills to you, and you can make a monthly deposit to her bank account to take care of her other expenses."

"But, Louise, that takes a lot of money."

"We settled all that in bed one morning at the Mayfair, remember? Let me handle the details." She reached up and kissed him. "Nothing is too good for the woman who turned you loose on the world."

Two weeks later, Hennie moved into the Hotel Stanhope, at Fifth Avenue and Eighty-first Street. And Louise saw to it that everyone was aware of her exclusive address.

Jim hoped he would be as successful with Mr. Gillette as Louise had been with his mother.

"It won't be bad," Louise promised. "I'll take care of everything."

The afternoon he went to have a drink with her father in the big house on Sixty-eighth Street, he felt like an underconfident Siegfried about to meet Wotan, the one-eyed spear wielder, master of the gods. Mr. Gillette, however, had two good eyes, light blue like Louise's but much harder, and the cigarette he was holding in lieu of an ash spear he threw into the fireplace as soon as Jim entered the room. Tall, handsome, and apparently perfectly at ease, he looked to his future son-in-law like a high-ranking British diplomat in the great days of the Empire. Only Louise noticed that the holder was attached to the cigarette he had just thrown into the fire. He walked up to Jim and shook his hand.

"Thank you, thank you, thank you!" he said. "I understand that you have solemnly promised to take this girl off my hands. And that you are of a man of your word. Now, perhaps, I can have a life of my own. Maybe even get married."

"Father," interrupted Louise, "you'll be too busy taking care of your grandchildren."

Jim looked around. "The mother of my best friend would say, 'It's a palace!'"

"Neither envy nor flattery will pry it loose," answered Mr. Gillette. "I like it too much myself. But I promise to give you a smaller version as a wedding present."

He did. And after a beautiful ceremony at St. Thomas's, the big, vulgar affair Louise had asked for, a dinner for six hundred at the Grand Ballroom of the Plaza.

Hennie kissed her son just before they sat down to dinner. With a glance at Louise, she said softly, "Some people might think she's a little bossy. But I love her. She's the only kind of a girl who could ever make you a big success."

Adele kissed Jim, too. "And I thought my wedding at the

Carlyle was the last word!" she moaned, looking around her in bewilderment.

"Well, it was more exclusive," said Jim.

Stanley, who had just recovered from the experience of being best man at a church wedding, sat placidly at the head table, mildly intoxicated, and very much at home because of all the familiar faces around him. Later he realized that it was only as photographs in magazines and newspapers that he had seen them before.

Mr. Huegenon came early and granted a long interview to a cluster of amazed reporters. But he looked far from affable when Louise brought Jim over.

"I approved of this match," he said as if without his consent it could never have taken place, "but not of the way you have ignored me. Why haven't you come to see me all these years?"

"Because I did not want to open up an old wound."

Mr. Huegenon shook his head. "You might have brought back an old happiness." He decided to change the subject. "I'm giving you two a nice wedding present, a Picasso, a Dufy, and a Klee. They may not look like much to you now, but some day they will be important. As I grow older, I find myself becoming more interested in modern art. For my friends, of course," he hastened to add.

The wedding received extensive coverage in the morning papers, with half the space devoted to Mr. Huegenon. "Fabulous financier sheds anonymity for the night," was the way one reporter put it.

Laying down the *Times* at the breakfast table, Stanley said, "I drank so much champagne, Adele, I'm a little confused. Who got married last night, Jim or Mr. Huegenon?"

McKinley was tremendously impressed, especially since of the entire staff only Hauser and Kell had been invited. And Hauser was now merely an inactive consultant.

TWENTY

A FEW MONTHS after the wedding, the two friends were confronted by a case that called upon all the skills the old McKinley had taught them.

For ten years, Stanley had read everything that appeared in the medical literature on icterus gravis, a disease that killed 60 per cent of the newborn infants it attacked and damaged the brains of many of the survivors. Its cause was unknown, treatment almost non-existent. But its conquest was assured when Karl Landsteiner, one of the most illustrious scientists of the twentieth century, was permitted to use his laboratory in the Rockefeller Institute after he had reached mandatory retirement age. Here he showed the world that there was one great discovery left in the old man. In the red blood cells of his Rhesus monkeys he found a new substance, which he called the Rh factor after the first two letters of his animals' name. Racing against time, he was able to illuminate the road ahead for other investigators. And then, when his work was done, God reached down into his laboratory and touched him. He was wheeled through a connecting corridor to the Rockefeller Hospital, where he died as he had lived, close to the scene of his immortal accomplishments. Just before the end he must have known that eventually his last discovery would save the lives and the brains of a hundred thousand infants.

The Rh factor was the solution to the icterus gravis puzzle. Helped by Philip Levine and Alexander Wiener, those giants of blood-group immunology, Landsteiner showed that the red blood cells of 85 per cent of the population contained the Rh substance. These people were called Rh positive. The red blood cells of the remaining 15 per cent lacked it. They were called Rh negative. When an Rh negative woman married an Rh positive man, the baby was usually Rh positive. While in the womb, some of its Rh positive red cells often leaked into the mother's circulation, stimulating her to form antibodies (destroying substances) against the Rh factor. These maternal antibodies flowed back into the baby's circulation, where they wiped out most of its susceptible blood. Not only did a terrible anemia result, but an even more terrifying jaundice, since whenever red cells are damaged, bilirubin, the yellow liver pigment, is formed. In a biological sense the baby was committing suicide, using the mother as the lethal weapon. How did it come about that the mother's antibodies did not destroy her own red cells? It was because they were Rh negative, and, lacking the factor, invulnerable.

At a quarter to eight one morning, Stanley was standing in front of the slanting shelves of McKinley's medical library trying to go through each journal the day after it appeared, when he was astounded to see an article describing a new treatment for icterus gravis. He read it once standing up and once sitting down. In a blazing flash of genius, Dr. Louis Diamond had conceived the idea of removing the newborn infant's Rh positive blood, which was being rapidly destroyed by anti-Rh antibodies derived from the mother, and replacing it with Rh negative blood, which, since it did not contain the factor, could not be harmed. If Stanley was appalled at the radical nature of the procedure, he was dumfounded to read that, in the skillful hand of the Boston investigator, morality had been reduced to less than 5 per cent, and brain damage to almost zero. The new treatment was called an exchange transfusion. To obtain such results it had to be performed soon after birth, before jaundice reached alarming levels.

Dr. Diamond had devised a method of exquisite ingenuity to attain his end. The stump of the umbilical cord was sliced an inch from the navel, revealing a cross section of the vein. A plastic catheter, a clear hollow tube less than a quarter inch in diameter, was inserted into the opening as far as the vena cava, the largest vessel in the body. It seemed to Stanley that in such a blind procedure the end of the catheter would often rest within the heart. A measured amount of the baby's Rh positive blood was removed with a large syringe, and an equal quantity of Rh negative blood returned to the patient. This was repeated over and over again until a pint of blood had been taken out of the baby and replaced by a pint from the bottle. Stanley closed the magazine. He was determined to perform an exchange transfusion at McKinley Hospital.

During the following week he tried to learn everything he could about the technique. He found out that the six-inch catheters were cut from insulating tubing for electrical wiring, which was sold only in hundred-foot lengths. He bought a hundred feet from a Lexington Avenue electrician, who warned him not to do any house wiring on his own. But would this batch behave like Dr. Diamond's? Could it be sterilized? Would it cause irritation? After all, it might go into a baby's heart. He measured off a few catheters and immersed them in antiseptic solution for twenty-four hours. Then, with the permission of the Director of the Laboratory, he inserted an inch from each under the skin of an anesthetized rabbit. A week later, the animals were killed and the tissue around the catheters cultured and examined under the microscope. It was sterile and showed no signs of inflammation. Stanley was ready to go ahead.

He knew that first he would have to gain the co-operation of Miss Grent, the operating room nursing supervisor, whom Jim had once called the Autocrat of the Operating Table. She believed that the old procedures should be performed superlatively, and the new postponed until they had grown old in other institutions. Rarely was anything done in her domain without her approval. Stanley slowly climbed the two long flights of stairs to her office in the main building with a heavy heart.

She was sitting behind her desk writing a report. She looked up but did not rise when he entered. While he was concentrating on what to say, he suddenly realized how unbelievably handsome she still was in spite of her fifty-two years. Her bed had never been empty for long, he felt sure. Without any small talk he sat down and told her in detail what he planned to do.

"First you will have to get written permission from the Director of Surgery," she informed him. Her voice was low and husky.

"Assuming that I do, will you be willing to set up an operating room for me?"

"I would have to speak to him first."

"It won't be as formidable as it seems. In Boston, the transfusion system includes three stopcocks, each of which can be set in three directions. I've figured out that the operator has a choice of eleven different positions. That's all right for a roué doctor from the Champs Elysées, but not for a poor pediatrician from the sidewalks of New York. I'm going to used an open technique without any stopcocks."

Miss Grent laughed, and all at once she seemed a student nurse again. She stretched out her hand.

"Let me have the list."

He handed her a typewritten page on which was written

288

every instrument, syringe, beaker, and piece of equipment that he would need. She read it carefully.

"I'll have everything autoclaved, placed in a large sterile pack and labeled 'Exchange Transfusion.' It will be ready at a moment's notice."

He stood up, thanked her, and walked to the door. Her throaty laughter followed him. As he turned, she said, "Eleven positions!"

Her eyes flickered, and for a moment he thought she was going to offer to teach him a few. Instead she said softly, "Stick to the one you know best, Doctor."

He descended slowly to the first floor in the massive old elevator that creaked like a ship in a storm. He was in no hurry now. All he had to do was wait, wait for an opportunity to do his first exchange transfusion.

It came a week later. At eight in the morning he was examining X-ray pictures in the flickering light box that gave the pediatricians' "Mickey Mouse" room its nickname, when he heard himself being paged on the loudspeakers. He reached over the pile of films and lifted the telephone receiver.

"Dr. Levinson," he said, emphasizing his title slightly.

A dry voice answered, "Charles Huegenon."

Imperial trumpets sounded as they once had when he was an undergraduate.

"Stanley, I've always been in the fortunate position of never having to ask for favors. But I'd like to ask for one now."

"Anything."

"Albert may not have told you this, but until he was nine he was looked after by a very competent governess. Then Mrs. Huegenon decided that she was no longer necessary. That young girl loved him, and perhaps more to the point, he loved her. Early this morning she informed me that her daughter had given birth to a boy in Brookeville General Hospital. He has," there was a rustle of paper, "ictcrus gravis. The doctors up there offer very little hope. They say that even if he survives, he will be severely brain-damaged. The poor mother has already lost two other children to this accursed disease, which must be as bad as Albert's malignant melanoma. Could you do anything for the little fellow?"

Stanley would have preferred another baby for the first exchange transfusion, but he replied, "There is a new treatment. The baby's blood is removed, and replaced with blood of another type. It's never been done at McKinley but I would like to try."

"That's rather radical, isn't it?"

"Yes. Would the parents give their consent?"

"I am sure they would. And I am giving you mine."

"How old is the baby?"

"Three days."

Stanley groaned. "That's awfully late."

"The condition may be too far advanced, you think?"

"Not only that. The umbilical cord, which is what we use for the exchange transfusion, may be so dry that we won't be able to carry out the procedure. In any case, have the baby brought down immediately, if you will. I'll get permission from the hospital for the exchange while it's on the way. And please have twenty c.c. of the mother's blood accompany it. That's for the cross-matching. Can you remember the figure, sir? Twenty c.c."

The famous financier gave a suggestion of a cough. "I have remembered a few figures in my day, Stanley. I think I can remember this."

Stanley raced through the short covered causeway to the main building, hoping to meet the directors of pediatrics and of surgery in the Doctors' Lounge. They usually arrived at this time. Fortunately, they were just walking out of the locker room shrugging themselves into their long white coats.

"May I see you for a few minutes?" he asked.

When they nodded, he continued, "I have a three-day-old

baby with icterus gravis arriving from Westchester soon. I would like permission to do an exchange transfusion."

The widened eyes of the Director of Pediatrics betrayed the fact that he did not know what an exchange transfusion was.

"Let's sit down," said the Director of Surgery, who spent a large part of the day on his feet in the operating room.

Stanley briefly outlined the technique.

"It sounds awfully risky to me," said the Director of Pediatrics, who felt most comfortable while prescribing Pablum, vitamins, and Curity diapers. He turned to his colleague. "You're president of the Medical Board. What do you think?"

"Have they done this anywhere in New York?"

"They've done a couple at Mt. Sinai and the Medical Center."

"The Medical Center is a university hospital. They can get away with it. As for Mt. Sinai, the Jews will try anything." He colored when he realized that he was talking about Stanley's coreligionists. "I meant that as a compliment. They are an adventurous people."

Stanley had learned to smile at times like this.

"I hate to be a crepehanger," the chief surgeon continued, "but it sounds like a crackbrained scheme to me. Removing all the blood from a newborn baby! They'll call you a vampire. And your religion won't be much of a help." He cleared his throat. "Less than fifty years ago the Cossacks unleashed pogroms all over Russia because they claimed that your people were taking blood from Christian babies for use in the Passover rituals." He raised his hand. "It was despicable idiocy, of course. But prejudices like that don't disappear in half a century. They are pushed deep down into the collective unconscious, and emerge whenever the climate is right. If you don't believe me, remember that Hitler just finished killing six million Jews for flimsier reasons." He sighed. "Stanley, you're putting me in an awkward position."

"It's not taking all the blood out of a newborn baby. It's flushing out blood that is being destroyed with blood that cannot be destroyed. And Diamond is a professor of pediatrics at Harvard."

The surgeon hesitated a long time. "All right, you have my reluctant permission." He glanced at his colleague, who nodded. "Our reluctant permission. I suppose that this baby wouldn't be the first patient to die on the table. But I know the Medical Board and most of the trustees. If anything happens to this kid, you're through at McKinley. They'll throw you out on your ear. They would do the same to you if you were a Christian —only more gently." He took off his glasses and polished them. "Get permission from the Executive Officer, too. That's what they call the Superintendent now."

Stanley nodded and walked toward the door. When he reached the threshold, the Director of Surgery said, "Don't think I'm not aware of how far McKinley has slipped in the past ten years. Or of how hard you are trying to live up to your memories of the old Hospital." He smiled. "I'll tell them to lay out the red carpet for you in the operating room. That's about all I can do."

Stanley thanked him and walked briskly to Superintendent Stahlhelm's old office on the ground floor. He was admitted at once when he told the secretary that he wanted to discuss an emergency situation. The Executive Officer listened attentively to the condensed and censored version of his recent conversation.

"I'm not a physician, and I'm not trying to tell you how to practice medicine, but it seems to me that your desire to perform an exchange transfusion without any previous training is extremely unwise."

"There hasn't been time for any training."

"Do you think the Hospital is ready for a thing like this?"

"The baby is."

"Very well. Since the two directors most closely involved

have given their approval, I will add mine—reluctantly. But I must warn you that many members of the Board of Trustees are not receptive to radical ideas. If the baby dies while you are performing the exchange transfusion, there will be two McKinley funerals, I'm afraid. Yours will be the second."

He went back to writing his report.

Stanley walked the few yards to the Seventieth Street entrance and waited for the ambulance. In fifteen minutes it rolled up, sirens wailing. A middle-aged woman stepped out, carrying a small bundle completely encased in blankets. She was followed by a young man holding a tube of blood as if it had just been poured from the Holy Grail. Stanley identified himself, told a messenger to take the specimen to the Blood Bank, sent the father to the admitting office, and guided the grandmother to the children's pavilion. They entered the elevator without a word. It was once claimed that Hauser could arrive at a diagnosis of the most complicated case in the time it took the elevator to go from the ground floor to the Infants' Roof.

"Do you think the baby has a chance?" the woman asked.

"I don't know. I haven't examined it."

"I suppose that as long as there's a God, there's a chance."

Stanley nodded, although he felt far less certain than she.

"Is this a dangerous operation?" she resumed.

"Very. But we have no choice."

After several minutes the elevator came to a thudding halt. A student nurse stepped forward to take the baby, who was to be admitted as a semiprivate patient, while Stanley suggested to the grandmother that she go out for breakfast. He walked to the examining room, where the head nurse, a two-striper, was already undressing the baby. It was terribly pale and stained bright yellow. He lifted the gauze pad that covered the upper abdomen and stared at the umbilical cord. It had completely withered.

"It's like leather!" exclaimed the head nurse.

He grasped it between his thumb and index finger. "It's like a button of bone sitting on the navel."

"You won't be able to do the exchange, will you?"

He shook his head and walked away, shoulders sagging. When he reached the door, his medical discipline asserted itself. He came back and performed a complete physical examination.

"Give him formula number two, as much water as he'll take, and put him in a Gordon Armstrong incubator."

The pediatric nursing supervisor passed him in the corridor. "They're admitting a possible meningitis," she said to the head nurse. "You'd better get the lumbar puncture set ready. One of the residents will be up to do the tap in fifteen minutes."

This time he walked to the elevator with his head up.

He took a series of short cuts to the tenth floor of the private pavilion, where the newer operating rooms were situated, rehearsing all the while what he would say to Jim. He found him stripped to the waist in the doctors' dressing room, calm and dry after an appendectomy. With his flat belly and rippling muscles, he looked, thought Stanley, as if he could still go three rounds with any heavyweight at Stillman's.

"Could you spare me fifteen minutes?"

"All day and all night," answered Jim when he saw the expression on his friend's face.

They went to the little room nearby where surgeons and their house-staff assistants could discuss the problems of a recently completed operation. Before they sat down, Jim quietly closed the door. Stanley told him everything. It took exactly fifteen minutes.

"And after I made such a federal case out of it," he concluded, "it turns out to be nothing but a big dud. The baby will probably be a halfwit, with cerebral palsy thrown in as a bonus."

"Why will it be a halfwit?"

294

"Because the bilirubin will destroy the big centers in the brain."

"If you let it. Stan, you're really not interested in the umbilical cord. You're interested in the umbilical vein. To get from the skin into the peritoneal cavity, it has to follow a certain path. We'll go to the library right now and find out what that path is. When we do, I'll make an incision and pick up the vein for you so you can do your exchange."

Stanley gave a bitter laugh. "For the past week, I've been trying to find the answer to that problem in every book I could lay my hands on. And do you know what I came up with? Nothing. The square inch north of a newborn's belly button is evidently the last unexplored region of human anatomy."

"All right. Then I'll pick it up for you without any help from the books. It's got to burrow under the skin and then rest on the peritoneum. That's where I'll get it."

"The peritoneum!" yelled Stanley. "It's like wet Kleenex at this age. What happens if you tear the peritoneum? The intestines will spill out through the wound."

Jim laughed. "Then do you know what I'll do? I'll put them right back and sew up the hole. A general surgeon lives in the peritoneal cavity, Stan. It's his habitat. That's where he makes a living. Don't fret. We won't let the kid down. Or Mr. Huegenon, either." He stood up. "Just let me know what time you're doing it. I'll be there."

As soon as the door closed, Stanley telephoned the chief technician at the Blood Bank, a gracious lady who had taught him much about the practical aspects of the Rh factor. "There's some fresh Rh negative blood for you in the refrigerator," she informed him. "I bled the donor just two hours ago. And I cheated a little. There are 550 instead of 500 c.c. in the bottle. But I have to get two units ready for a bleeding gastric ulcer. And yours has to be cross-matched against the mother and baby. It won't be ready until one o'clock."

Stanley walked along the corridor looking for Miss Grent. He found her in the supply room demonstrating a Levine tube to a junior intern. A martinet she might be, but she was there when you needed her, he decided. He asked her if he could do the exchange transfusion at one o'clock, and hoped she could get him a nurse anesthetist to administer oxygen if necessary and count the blood.

"How long do you think it will take?"

"About two hours," he replied.

"I'll put you in the main operating room. The hernia can wait."

He notified Jim and then took the long trip back to the Infants' Roof. The head nurse handed him two laboratory slips. The hemoglobin was only 35%; the bilirubin 24 milligrams per 100 c.c.

"Too bad," he murmured. "Anything over 20 makes you worry about brain damage. I hope we're not too late."

"Why don't you go downstairs and get something to eat."

At twelve-thirty he changed into a short white jacket and trousers in the doctors' dressing room on the tenth floor. The telephone rang. "I hate to tell you this," said the head nurse on the infants' ward, "but we may have a case of measles. The resident thinks he sees Kopliks spots all over a baby's mouth. And it's in the same room as your patient."

"He probably forgot to clean his glasses," retorted Stanley wearily. "Don't worry. If it turns out to be measles, we'll give all the kids gamma globulin. Including mine. That is, if he makes it."

He walked to the main operating room, where to his amazement he found four graduate and two student nurses at work, with Miss Grent near the door, hands on her hips, surveying them like a slavemaster on a Roman galley. There was no talking. Some bigshot surgeon must be about to take out an acute gall bladder, he decided. Then he looked at the sheet-

296

covered instrument table. Everything he had asked for was there.

The rumbling in the corridor proved to be caused by the pediatric resident pushing the Gordon Armstrong incubator much too rapidly. "What am I supposed to do?" he asked.

"Pray," replied Stanley.

The seven-pound infant was placed on an operating table designed to hold a two-hundred-pound man. As soon as it was stripped, it was surrounded by towel-covered hot-water bottles. Miss Grent snapped her fingers. Immediately the beam from the powerful center lights was focused on the patient's navel.

"It's like a canary," said the nurse from the infants' ward who had just come in.

"An anemic canary," amended Stanley.

Jim entered, capped and masked.

"They shouldn't make such a handsome man cover his face," a student nurse whispered.

Miss Grent gave her a withering look.

He palpated the baby's abdomen and said, "The usual prep." Then he turned to Stanley and the resident and added, "Let's scrub up."

Masked and capped, they began the ritual washing side by side in the three sinks just outside the operating room.

"I haven't done this since I was an intern," admitted Stanley.

"It will come back to you," Jim reassured him.

At one o'clock the chief technician brought the blood and began the tedious process of removing the rubber stopper from the bottle. Using a long sponge-holder, Miss Grent painted the baby's belly with half-strength iodine. The color of the skin did not seem to change. When the three doctors entered, the instrument nurse held out a sterile gown for Jim.

"Dr. Levinson first," he insisted.

A gracious gesture, thought Stanley, but I haven't paid any attention to operating-room technique in fifteen years. I'm a pediatrician, and I'd like to see how it's done first. He reached forward automatically, and suddenly skillful hands pulled the gown around him from behind and tied the strings. By the time he had adjusted the rubber gloves, Jim and the instrument nurse had completely covered the operating table with towels and lap sheets, leaving only a small square of skin around the baby's navel visible. Behind its head sat the nurse anesthetist, the oxygen tanks on her right.

The chief technician at last managed to remove the rubber stopper from the bottle, and with infinite care poured 550 c.c. of carefully typed Rh negative blood into the sterile beaker. Jim stood at the right of the baby, the two others across the table. He infiltrated a small area just above the navel with Novocaine, and waited a few moments. When he stretched out his hand for the scalpel, everyone glanced at the clock.

As always, the incision was smooth and bold. There was little bleeding. Retractors were hooked under the skin edges and handed to the resident. The fascia, a tough membrane binding the two up-and-down rectus muscles, was split, and the retractors shifted to spread them apart. In the gutter between them was a collection of fat, which Jim gently pushed to both sides. He smiled under his mask, because there, resting on the peritoneum, was a wide gray tube, the never-before-seen umbilical vein. He slid a thin tape underneath it and pulled it to the surface before the retractors were removed.

"There's the little devil," he said.

Everyone looked at the clock. It had taken exactly four minutes.

Using a sharp-pointed iris scissors, he snipped the top of the vessel. The instrument nurse handed Stanley a catheter that had been fitted at one end with a sawed-off needle to allow it to grip the syringe more firmly. Very cautiously the pediatrician inserted the other end of the catheter into the hole and pushed it three inches inside the vein. The resident crossed to the other side of the table and took Jim's place.

As soon as Stanley stretched out his hand, the instrument nurse slapped his palm with an empty 20-c.c. syringe, which he connected to the catheter the resident was now holding. The big moment had arrived at last. He pulled the plunger. Not a drop of blood appeared. After a few seconds he tried again. The piston would not budge. A student nurse wiped away the beads of sweat on his forehead. The baby whimpered.

"Let go of the catheter," he ordered.

The resident pulled back his hand. Stanley pushed the catheter in another inch.

"Hold it in this position."

He pulled the plunger gently, and instantly the syringe filled with blood. There was a soft murmur in the operating room.

"Twenty out," intoned the nurse anesthetist.

He disengaged the syringe and handed it to the instrument nurse, who immediately exchanged it for one filled with Rh negative blood from the beaker. Fastening it to the catheter, he rapidly emptied the blood into the baby.

"Twenty in," recited the anesthetist in a sing-song voice.

"Forty out; forty in," she announced during the next cycle. After he had replaced 100 c.c. of the baby's blood with an equal quantity of the donor's, he injected 1 c.c. of calcium gluconate to prevent the patient from having tetanic convulsions.

"You're on the second hundred," the anesthetist reminded him.

At the 140-c.c. mark Jim said, "You're fast, Stan. Keep going."

But the next syringeful from the baby showed a change in color.

"That blood seems awfully blue," Stanley exclaimed in alarm.

The operating-room silence grew deeper.

"I don't like the way he looks," said Jim sharply.

Stanley discontinued the exchange.

"The baby has stopped breathing," the nurse anesthetist said quietly. "Don't you hear me, Doctor!" she added, her voice rising.

"Bag him," ordered Jim.

She placed the close-fitting mask with its black rubber balloon over the baby's nose and mouth, and turned on the oxygen. When she squeezed the bag, oxygen was forced into the baby's respiratory tract. And when she let go, the elasticity of the expanded lungs forced breath out through an escape valve.

"He shouldn't have died," she moaned. "He was too little. He never had a chance to do anything."

"Keep bagging," barked Jim.

"One grain of caffeine sodium benzoate," Stanley ordered—a little too loud.

Castanets clicked, and a hypodermic was plunged into the patient's arm.

Silence returned to the operating room.

Out of the great quietness, Jim declared, "The lips are getting pink."

After a few minutes of bagging, he repeated, "They're quite pink now." He hesitated. "Take off the bag."

Everyone leaned forward. There was a long pause. Then the baby began to breathe regularly again.

"I've read somewhere," Stanley stated, "that an animal can be killed by the rapid injection of massive amounts of cold blood." He turned to the instrument nurse. "Put your hands around that beaker."

"Even through my gloves I can tell that the blood is ice cold," she answered.

His voice grew stronger. "Miss Grent, could you please fill a tall sterile basin with warm saline?"

As if he had rubbed a sterile Aladdin's lamp, a stainless steel basin appearing on the instrument table was suddenly full.

"Put the beaker of blood in the saline," Stanley ordered the instrument nurse.

After automatically testing the temperature of the fluid with a gloved finger, she lowered the glass beaker into the basin. Everyone stood perfectly still for five minutes.

"Take it out, please," he said.

"It's warm now," she announced.

Stanley flushed out the catheter with isotonic saline and resumed the exchange, this time with warm blood. The procedure went along uneventfully except for the necessity of occasionally changing the position of the catheter. The baby cried lustily a few times. At the 400-c.c. mark Stanley handed the syringe to the resident.

"Would you like to do the last 100 c.c.'s?"

The resident's eyes gleamed. In a few minutes came the call from the anesthetist, "500 c.c. out; 500 c.c. in."

"Don't take any more out," ordered Stanley. "Just put in the rest of the blood. We'll make this kid bloom like a rose."

When the beaker was dry, Stanley slowly pulled out the catheter. Jim tied off the umbilical vein with absorbable catgut, and brought the skin edges together with four silk sutures. They both looked at the clock. The exchange transfusion had taken fifty-seven minutes.

Stanley pulled off his gown and gloves, shook hands with Jim, and thanked the nurses, who, much to his surprise, did nothing to conceal their admiration.

"It looks like a pink canary now," said one of them as she placed the baby in the incubator.

He found Miss Grent seated behind her desk in her tenth-floor office. This time she rose.

"I never could have done this exchange without your help," he acknowledged. "Your department is so far superior to any other in the Hospital there just is no comparison."

"Don't forget, I trained under Dr. Emmerich."

"Besides, your girls treated me as I've never been treated

before. A diaper-smeller isn't used to nurses looking at him with stars in their eyes."

"You were the first, Doctor. And women have special feelings toward the first."

He put his hands on the desk, palms down. "I'd be willing to bet that if McKinley goes under, the operating rooms will be the last to sink."

"I hope so. I've had a few offers, but I will never leave. A captain has to go down with the ship."

What the hell, he thought, no one will see me. He leaned across the desk and kissed her on the lips.

The bilirubin taken immediately after the exchange transfusion was 6.4. The next day it rose to 13.5. But following this determination it dropped steadily until on the seventh day it was 2. The hemoglobin remained firm at 95 per cent. Careful neurological examinations revealed no evidence of central nervous system damage. And when Jim removed the sutures, there was only a hairline scar.

On the twelfth day, as Stanley was sitting at the head nurse's desk in the infants' ward signing the baby's discharge sheet, she handed him the telephone.

"This is Charles Huegenon," said the dry, imperious voice. "Thank you and please send me the bill."

"After those tennis lessons? Never."

"You're very gracious."

"Besides, Jim made the whole thing possible."

"That does not dilute my gratitude. I have always been indebted to you both for what you did for Albert. Now I am indebted to you both for saving this baby's life. It's good to know that an only son with a mortal disease no longer has to die. And there is something else. Once I was very fond of a governess who was kind to my boy."

"That must have been an important person," said the head nurse, looking at him out of the corner of her eye.

"The father of an old friend."

Two student nurses began to wheel the infants out of the room.

"What's the matter?" asked Stanley.

"The painters are coming this afternoon," replied the head nurse.

"Christ! Well, thank God my patient won't be here."

Promptly at ten the grandmother came to take the baby home. She must have been a beauty in her day, he decided. After admiring her grandson, who was lying contentedly in its crib, she turned to him and said, "Thank you for saving his life. He's my first grandchild." She sighed. "I had my heart set on calling him Albert, but his parents have decided to name him Stanley. They asked me to get your permission."

"Permission? It's an honor."

"There is one other thing I would like to say, only I hope you won't be offended. If Master Albert had lived, he would have been as great a doctor as you are today."

"Far greater."

She smiled and shook her head. "A man doesn't have to be any greater than you."

TWENTY-ONE

KIRBY was too shrewd to show his displeasure at not having been invited to Jim's wedding. Besides, he was preoccupied with more important matters, principally with McKinley's failing finances. Convinced that the higher the census, the lower the deficit, he had appointed more and more busy doctors to the staff in an attempt to keep the Hospital filled with private and semiprivate patients. Where once the cardinal sins had been professional mediocrity, poor nursing care, and sloth, today there was only one—the empty bed. His determination to do everything in his power to keep the census up accounted for his coming uninvited to the first postwar meeting of the Alumni Association, late one afternoon in September 1946. Recently the make-up of the group had been altered to include not only former interns and residents, but all members of the attending staff as well. There were over two hundred doctors in Halberstadt Hall, and every one of them was surprised when Kirby walked in. Even the oldest could not remember ever having heard a trustee address the Alumni Association on such an informal occasion as this. With a wave of his hand Kirby silenced his son-in-law, Aims Blair, who, as president of the association, was in the chair, and looked at the doctors with apparent pride.

Jim, who as president-elect of the Alumni Association was behind the same small table as Aims Blair, looked at them, too, but all he saw was a mass of medical mediocrity with old McKinleyites standing out, here and there, like candied fruits on a plain sponge cake.

"The other day I went up to the Columbia Presbyterian Medical Center," Kirby said. "That's a good hospital, too." He could not suppress a smile. "But, for my money, our doctors are every bit as good as theirs."

There was a brisk round of applause.

"They've got a big edge on us, though," he went on, "when it comes to their census. They have a 95 per cent bed occupancy. Ours is seventy-eight. Gentlemen, we have a duty to the community. It is the community that supports us; it is the community that we must serve. Our facilities may be old, but they are time-hallowed. Unless you use them to the full for the benefit of the people of New York, you have failed both as doctors and as citizens. An empty bed reveals an empty heart, a heart devoid of concern for the needs of the city which surrounds us. In this room are scores of eminent physicians and surgeons with practices that are the envy of colleagues everywhere. To them I say, 'You've sent us many prominent patients who were very sick. How about sending us some who are not so sick?' And to those of you whose practices may be a little less wealthy, I say, 'Most of the patients you see in your office have Blue Cross, don't they? How about sending some of them in?' Gentlemen, don't let any of McKinley go to waste. That's an extravagance the community cannot afford."

After the meeting, as they walked toward the courtyard, Stanley said to Jim, "He's a 100 per cent chemically pure hypocritical bastard. I wouldn't mind if he came out and said, 'Gentlemen, the more empty beds, the bigger the deficit. We, the trustees, don't have the money to write off a big deficit, and even if we did, we wouldn't go on doing it year after year.' I'd respect him. But all this crap about serving the community burns me up. Is making a patient wait three weeks for a bed, the way they do in some other hospitals, serving the community? He's plugging for a full house because he's afraid that empty beds in private and semiprivate will mean empty wallets in the Board Room. On the most undignified day of his life, August Grund could never have imagined the Chairman of the Board of Trustees of McKinley Hospital putting on a performance like that."

As they crossed the courtyard, Jim looked around him. "You know the answer. The old gray mare ain't what she used to be."

"Yeah, but you still love her just the same. If I asked you, 'Who was that old gray mare I saw you with last night?' you'd have to say, 'That was no horsie, that was my life.'"

There was another member of the audience whose reaction to the meeting was just as strong, although entirely different. The moment the Chairman of the Board finished his speech, Sam Perkes, sitting in the last row of Halberstadt Hall, realized that the time had come for him to put in motion his scheme to make McKinley vanish.

For the next two years he conducted a relentless campaign, so cleverly that no one was aware of it but himself. As the first step, he decided that he must sell himself, not his plan, to two hard-headed businessmen. Every Monday, Wednesday, and Friday, he caught the eight oh five from Brookeville so that he could sit next to Kirby, who, equally anxious for the meeting, always pushed him into the seat next to the window as if to prevent his escape. For forty minutes, the Chairman of the Board was given key information on income and expenditures, the daily census, outlays for food, salaries, drugs, and equipment, mounting deficits, inevitable depreciation, little corners where inefficiency lurked, payments from Blue Cross, and complaints from patients. As a result of these tri-weekly briefings, Kirby, shrewd and retentive and keeping secret the source of his knowledge, was able to mystify the Board of Trustees, the Executive Officer, and the doctors with his grasp of everything that went on at McKinley. Before long it was generally agreed that he was the best-informed hospital trustee in New York. To his commuting companion he was not ungrateful. He raised his salary twice, telling the trustees each time that their Assistant Superintendent was a living Encyclopedia McKinleya. Sam was careful to be only a purveyor of facts. He felt that his value would go up if he remained cold and without opinions—like a diamond.

But it would take more than Kirby to make McKinley disappear. Sam's plan called for a second participant, a neighbor of Kirby's, Taylor Brooke, Chairman of the Board of Brookeville General, a two hundred and fifty bed suburban hospital lacking wards, research facilities, and a medical education program, but possessing beautiful tree-covered grounds. Brooke, after whose great-grandfather Brookeville had been named, was sixty and looked fifty. But then, according to his wife, he had always looked fifty. He was a man who did not approve of change, either in himself or the world. Or hurrying. Except to catch the seven fifty-seven to Grand Central every Tuesday and Thursday. This was a train neither he nor Sam cared to miss. Brooke, because he could not do without these habit-forming sessions during which his hospital's problems were tackled by someone used to solving far greater ones in New York; Sam, because he did not wish to give up a single opportunity to inspire still greater goodwill in a man who would some day be indispensable to him. Of the two, Brooke was the more impressed. His commuting companion's reputation as a brilliant administrator in a world-famous hospital made him feel a little like a minor-league manager sitting beside a major-league star. Sam remained retiring and respectful, but no longer was he a human vending machine responding to the coin of his employer's approval by disgorging yet another package of facts. Without being officious or overbearing, he became a man of opinions and a dispenser of advice, though only when asked and exclusively in the field of hospital management. So impressed was Brooke with what he heard on the train every Tuesday and Thursday, that one night at a Board of Trustees meeting at Brookeville General, he confessed, with a rare enthusiasm, "What we need is a superintendent like young Sam Perkes. I'd make him an offer, only I'm afraid Nelson Kirby would dynamite my house."

Brookeville General had one problem far different from any with which Kirby had to cope. Its two hundred and fifty beds were no longer sufficient to accommodate the increasing number of well-to-do immigrants from Manhattan who now found it more convenient to seek admission to a hospital nearer their new homes. For two years Brooke had been in the habit of casually mentioning that someday his hospital would have to build a hundred-bed addition to take care of patients they were now turning away, and for two years his commuting companion had done nothing but listen. But when the Brookeville Chairman of the Board announced one morning that at their next meeting his trustees were going to consider methods of financing a building drive, Sam knew that his moment had come.

"I'd like to talk to you for a few minutes some afternoon," he said. "At your office, perhaps, a little after five?"

Brooke turned in surprise as if he had just remembered that Sam came from the other side of Bushy Brooke Lane. "Can't you talk now? You've got almost forty minutes."

"It's not something I'd like to discuss on a train."

"I see. Well, can you give me some idea what it is about?"

"It's about Brookeville and Brookeville General Hospital. Not about me."

Brooke instantly grew more cordial. "Of course, my boy. Drop by the University Club when you finish at McKinley this afternoon."

By taking a taxi, an extravagance he never permitted himself, Sam arrived at the club a little after five. He found Mr. Brooke sitting alone in the big room that ran for half a block along Fifth Avenue.

"What would you like to drink?" Brooke asked.

"Nothing, thank you. I'm afraid what I have to say doesn't go with a drink."

Brooke shrugged. "I can't think of anything that doesn't go with a drink." He pointed to a chair.

Sam sat down gingerly and began at once as if Mr. Brooke were holding a stop watch. "McKinley is finished. A few of the trustees already sense it. Every one of them should know it before too long. Big yearly deficits have eaten up our capital funds until now there's less than three quarters of a million dollars in the kitty. Since this year we will be in the red for over three hundred thousand dollars, it doesn't take a mathematician to figure out how long we can keep open."

Brooke pursed his lips. "I knew McKinley was no General Motors, I mean from the financial point of view, but I had no idea things were that bad."

"It's been a constant struggle against obsolescence. We've won a hundred battles; obsolescence has won the war. Most of the buildings are over seventy-five years old, and you'd be shocked if I told you how much we spend every year just patching them up. And no matter how hard we try to keep the place presentable, the beds are never filled any more. Increasing the medical staff hasn't done the trick." He laughed. "Soon we'll have more doctors than patients."

"I sympathize with you, but why don't you tear down the old place and put up modern buildings?"

"Because it would cost fifteen million dollars."

"What of it? We are going to spend a million next year on the new wing at Brookeville."

"There's quite a difference between one million and fifteen million."

"Go to the foundations. You have to if you want to raise that kind of money."

"We can't. For two reasons: In the first place, it isn't like the old days, when 80 per cent of our beds were on the free wards. Today, less than 15 per cent are. Where's the charity in building rooms for private patients? The other reason is even more important. The first question any foundation asks a hospital that is starting a building drive is this: 'How much have your trustees given?' The sum our trustees would have to contribute to attract foundation money is more than they can afford."

"I find your problems fascinating and your confidences flattering, but where do I come in?"

"I'd like you to listen to a scheme that would solve our problems and yours."

"Mine? I have no problems."

"Yes, you have. Raising that million dollars for the new wing next year."

For the first time, Brooke smiled. "How do you plan to help us do that?"

"It's a simple enough scheme. Quite straightforward. I've been studying real estate values recently. Would you say the ground on which McKinley stands is worth four and a half million dollars?"

Brooke stared at the ceiling as if something were written there in fine print. "A square block between Park and Madison. I'd say it's worth more."

"I think McKinley should close, sell its land, and combine with Brookeville General. With a dowry like that you could build a two hundred and fifty bed addition that would make your institution the pride of Westchester."

Brooke was shocked. "And McKinley would disappear just like that?"

"Not disappear, Mr. Brooke. Move. Everyone is leaving New York for the suburbs. Why shouldn't we? And follow our patients."

Mr. Brooke walked to the Fifth Avenue window, thought better of it, and came back. "It sounds sacrilegious to me. Like moving St. Patrick's Cathedral to Long Island. McKinley is a medical landmark."

"I don't know how much longer the old landmarks will remain, but the people are certainly leaving. You must have heard the current wisecrack—the only permanent residents of New York City are General and Mrs. Grant. McKinley will become a tomb unless we move it to the suburbs."

Brooke glanced at Sam sharply. "And you didn't think I would need a drink!"

"I wanted to keep a clear head, sir, that's all."

"You're clear, all right, though hardly transparent." He ordered a scotch and water. "All I can see at the moment is the destruction of a hospital. It seems like an act of murder."

"Just change the sound a little, sir. 'Merger,' not 'murder.'"

"If it is, it's the most lopsided merger in history." He sipped his drink. "The way I see it is this: we have to raise a million dollars for a new wing. As soon as you hear about it, you come to me and say, 'Don't exert yourself. We'll sell McKinley, the doctors' Old Glory, for five million dollars and give it all to you.' The money will fall upon us like manna from heaven, and we, presumably, will gulp it down greedily like the ancient Israelites." He took another discreet sip. "Only we are not ancient Israelites. As a matter of fact, there aren't any Israelites, ancient or modern, in Brookeville. I feel we're being asked to join that long line of gullible men who bought the Brooklyn Bridge."

Sam smiled. "I can understand why you feel it's too good to be true. You'll be even more suspicious when I tell you that you'll have a five hundred bed hospital without a yearly deficit."

Brooke looked skeptical. "What's that?"

"First," Sam resumed, "there will be no outlay for research. What does a suburban hospital need research for? You've done pretty well all these years without it. You're turning patients away. In the second place, you'll be relieved of the expense of the medical education program for interns, residents,

311

and nurses that every teaching institution in the city has to have. In Westchester the patients are interested in equipment, not teaching a house staff. They want the finest equipment money can buy. And we'll give it to them out of the five million. Third, you'll have that wonderful new equation working for your pocketbook: Blue Cross plus Blue Shield plus well-to-do Westchester equals zero free wards."

Brooke brought his glass down hard on the end table. "But, damn it, what do we do for you? What do you people at McKinley get out of all this?"

Sam took out his handkerchief and mopped the liquor that Brooke had spilled. "You take us off the hook," he said solemnly. "What alternative do we have? Mortgage the property for a couple of million? With our annual deficit we couldn't last five years. Then we'd have to close up anyway, this time under the scornful eyes of a city that would brand our trustees as misers and berate them for allowing one of Manhattan's medical glories to disappear." He took out another handkerchief and wiped his face. "You're giving us more than you think—landscaped acres to put our buildings on; the continuation of our name (it would have to be called the McKinley-Brookeville Medical Center, with Mr. Kirby as Chairman of the Board); convenience —half the trustees live either in Brookeville or nearby; and above all, an out!"

"Don't you think it would be wise to go to the people of New York for the money? To at least go through the motions?"

"Mr. Brooke, you can't build a fifteen million dollar metropolitan hospital on nickels and dimes. Big contributors won't give to an institution unless its trustees do, and our trustees simply can't."

"And you're here to protect their interests?"

"They don't even know I'm here. But since you ask, I think it is my duty to do just that."

Brooke stood up. "Let me get you a magazine. I need a few minutes to think this over."

312

He came back with a copy of the National Geographic. Then he sat down, picked up his drink, and stared at the window. After a few minutes he said, "You can put that magazine away now. I can't speak officially for the Board, but I'm going to anyway. You know, Sam, there are strings to accepting as well as to giving. We have two. First, you'll have to get the ball rolling within a year. We're overcrowded. Our problem is acute. We can't wait. Second, the merger must be put through and the transfer made in complete secrecy. Our trustees come from old families, and they are unusually sensitive to adverse publicity. We don't want to see anything out of line in the papers."

He signaled to the waiter for another drink. "We don't want to be your co-villains. If there has to be any publicity, we'd like it to come late and read something like this (old memories of a college journalism course made him smile faintly) McKinley Hospital to Follow Its Patients. Plagued by financial difficulties and drained of most of its patients by population shifts, the old Park Avenue landmark will close its doors next week. The Trustees of Brookeville General Hospital have offered its sister institution a new home. The two hospitals, which when combined will house over five hundred patients, will be called the McKinley-Brookeville Medical Center and will take care of the growing needs of southern Westchester for some time to come.'"

He signed for the drinks. "I realize that there may be a few men at McKinley who will oppose the merger. That's only to be expected. But if a revolt breaks out, then I warn you that we will drop you like a hot potato."

"Believe me, sir, we're even more concerned about unfavorable publicity than you are."

Brooke stood up and shook hands with Sam. "I suppose I should say, 'Thanks a million,' the way some of the young people do. It would be more appropriate, though, to say, 'Thanks five million.'" He chuckled. "Does Nelson know you are here?"

"No; I'll tell him soon."

Brooke insisted on accompanying Sam all the way to the street door. As he was about to say good-by, he finally asked, "What's in it for you, Sam?"

Sam raised his hands in protest. "That's up to you, sir."

Brooke gave him a shrewd look. "Well, if the merger goes through, I'll certainly do everything in my power to see that you become the first superintendent."

Sam bowed, and walked down the steps to Fifty-fourth Street smiling.

Had he been permitted to attend the next meeting of the Board of Trustees at McKinley, he would not have been surprised by the speeches. His duties were much more menial, however—merely to check the physical arrangements beforehand. At five o'clock, he went up to the Board Room, on the second floor, once used by August Grund for his annual bloodlettings, and laid out eighteen instead of the usual twenty settings, each consisting of a white pad, a brown pencil sharpened to a needle point, and a mimeographed copy of the latest financial statement. Two trustees had died that year and there had been some trouble finding replacements. Then, after looking around to be sure that all the lights were lit, he walked out, leaving the door open. Starting at the turn of the century, the Hospital had decided to leave the door of the Board Room open before each monthly meeting of the trustees so that an awed house staff could have a chance to see the Holy of Holies—the massive, gleaming mahogany table, the oiled, wood-paneled walls, the crystal chandelier that was disassembled and soaked in ammonia water piece by piece twice a year, and the famous painting by Rosa Bonheur that inspired new interns to ask, "That isn't the original, is it?" In Jim's day, no one but a trustee or a member of the Medical Board would have dared to cross the threshold. But the present interns and residents were not so easily intimidated. Recently, they had taken to wandering around the room just before the meeting, filching pencils and pads, and dropping ashes into the ash trays and even on the floor. That was why Sam returned at a quarter past eight. He found ash trays soiled, financial statements crumpled, and three pads and four pencils missing. He sighed. Woodrow Wilson had prevailed. The Hospital's little world had been made safe for democracy. Mechanically, because he had done it many times before, Sam cleaned up and replaced the missing articles. Then he went home to look after his mother.

The meeting was scheduled for eighty-thirty, but, since the old punctuality had long since gone out of fashion, the trustees did not begin to saunter in until just before nine. Kirby let them read the financial report for a few minutes and then tapped on the table.

"Gentlemen, I'm afraid we are being pushed to the wall by rising costs and obsolescence. Seven hundred and ten thousand dollars is all we've got in the kitty, and the deficit last year was three hundred and fifteen. Of course, friends will die this year and leave us bequests. But eating out of coffins is no way for a hospital to live."

He gave them a wry smile. "I admit I sometimes feel guilty, because I persuaded a few of you to become trustees. But on the other hand it hasn't done you any harm, has it? It's helped you socially and it's helped you in business. And it hasn't cost you a dime. You've been philanthropists without a checkbook. That's quite a trick when you come to think of it. Like being a Don Juan without a dick."

He put his palms on the table. "I'm aware of what we ought to do. We ought to tear down the old plant and put up a modern hospital in its place. In the long run it would be an economy. Unfortunately, it's an economy that would cost us fifteen million dollars. I can tell from the way your eyes are fixed on your white pads that you would never seriously consider such a proposition. You know as well as I do that the first question the foundations would ask would be, 'How much have your trustees given?' We'd have to give three million dollars, at least, to make them interested. No reputable professional fund-raising organization would handle the drive if we pledged less. That's a hundred and fifty thousand dollars a man, every man—if we were at full strength." He looked around him and shook his head sadly. "It's out of the question, I'm afraid, simply out of the question. We'll just have to limp along the way we are."

A deep cough came from the nearer of two men seated on his right, two men who seemed set apart from the others, perhaps because of their age, perhaps because they were the only ones who were not doodling on the white pads.

"I'll give a hundred and fifty thousand dollars," said the one who had coughed, "but only to a building fund."

"I'll cover Klaus Martin," said the rickety old man next to him.

Kirby pointed to them and beamed at the others. "Are you surprised? Klaus Martin and Hagenbeck! Upholders of the finest traditions of the old McKinley! Columns on which our Hospital still rests today! When did they ever ignore a call for help? How many times have they kept us afloat during the past thirty years with their timely donations!"

Klaus Martin growled. "Upholders, columns, floats! Milch cows, you mean. Only now we stay dry unless you put up a new hospital."

"And who can blame you?" continued Kirby with a sigh. "Besides," he added in quite a different voice, "we would still be over two and a half million dollars short. No, I think we'll have to work on something less ambitious to stay afloat. I wish we were back in the days of August Grund." He turned to a pale, thin man in his middle forties who looked as if he had been fighting a nameless fear all his life. "Emil, my boy, your father would simply have put on his glasses, read off the amounts his trustees were expected to pay, and walked out of the room ten minutes later with three million dollars in his pocket. Of course, he never had to cope with income taxes."

There was a rustling of papers, and Kirby turned to the man sitting next to Emil Grund.

316

"You want to get in a word, Scud?" he asked, trying to keep the impatience out of his voice.

Scudder Devine, Grund's neighbor, stopped rustling his papers and nodded. He was a man of sixty-one who was trying hard to look fifty, and, in the main, succeeding. The sleeping-child serenity of his face went well with his coal-black hair, kept this color by frequent ministrations of the hairdresser. Why Devine had begun to turn gray even this late was a mystery to most people, since he had never had a worry in his life, except, perhaps, when his wife had lost a little of her money, long since recouped, in the stock market crash of 1929. His fine young hair was matched by a fine young voice. Whenever he spoke, even about trivial things, it was with an amazing resonance, as if he were leading the words lingeringly through his nasal sinuses before allowing them to escape. And the humming words, so often devoid of meaning, rested in their resonance like a cluster of glass jewels in a platinum setting. Hearing him for the first time, almost everyone got the feeling that he was intoning a prayer, a mistake his friends found not too far from the mark, since, from early childhood, he had tried to copy his father's pulpit voice. The voice, not Holy Orders, was what he had desired. He was perfectly satisfied with his own choice of a profession, one that was as old as the bishop's. Scudder was a rich woman's husband. And extremely conscientious about his job. He had resisted since his marriage every temptation to work at anything else. As he now drew some neatly typed sheets of paper from a leather brief case, Kirby looked at him closely, at the smooth pink face, the unwrinkled hands, and the crisp, starched shirt. It's as if a strict but affectionate nanny had just set him down among the grownups, he decided. Somebody must put Johnson's Baby Powder on his buttocks and Desitin on his privates every morning to prevent him from getting a rash. He tried to remember how much Devine had contributed to the Hospital in the past fifteen years. The answer was nothing, absolutely nothing. Reproached with

317

this, he probably would have exclaimed, "Money! Why, I've given you Father's name!"

"I blame myself for not starting earlier," Scudder said. "For the past two weeks I've been making a personal survey of key areas in the Hospital." The familiar resonance was there, the tones soft but worthy of a public prayer. "One of my old professors at Columbia used to say, 'Harness the facts! But never forget that facts are like wild horses. You've got to catch them first.'"

Kirby sighed wearily. "Scud, we're more interested in what you've got to say than in that old Columbia professor of yours."

"Thank you. I've investigated the kitchen, the pharmacy, purchasing and supply, housekeeping, and the record room. This little report," he held up a thin sheaf of papers, "clearly shows that if we discharge 10 per cent of our work force and at the same time raise the salaries of those who remain ten cents an hour—oh, yes, Father always said that the workman is worthy of his hire—we can save five hundred dollars a month. The exact amount is variable. It can all be reduced to a simple mathematical formula."

He held up some figures, smiling like a male Mona Lisa, and regarded the trustees as if they were a kindergarten class to whom he was explaining Max Planck's quantum theory. He had never forgotten the A minus he had received in calculus at Columbia. Neither had his former private tutor, now a very old man.

"Wait a minute, Scud," Kirby interrupted. "This is highly technical stuff. I'd like Sam Perkes to study it before we take it up here. But thanks for all the work you've done."

Devine seemed disappointed but he bowed gracefully.

"Scud has a good idea there," Kirby said in his brassy voice, "but I think we'll get further by tackling the problem from the other end, not by economizing but by raising some dough to keep going. What's the use of talking? It's axiomatic that if you want money, you have to go to the Jews. Things haven't

318

changed much since the Middle Ages. I have a list here of eighteen prominent, and what's more to the point, philanthropic Jewish families. If we are clever enough, I can envision a day when these Jewish St. Bernards will come bounding out of their monasteries, Temple Emmanuel and the Harmonie Club, with flasks of money tied around their necks. And for us, gentlemen, for us!"

"You're not thinking of a Jewish trustee, are you?" interrupted Shore from the other end of the room. "Not after a hundred years without one?"

"Not a Jewish trustee," Kirby answered carefully, "a Jewish Chairman of the Board."

There was an angry buzzing, soothed after a moment by Scudder Devine's familiar resonances. "It's the beginning of one of Nelson's dirty jokes. I only wish I could tell them to my wife."

"You can," answered Kirby, "only this isn't one of them." He turned to the trustees. "He'd collect funds for us from his Hebrew friends. We could even make a couple of them trustees in return for their contributions. That's all there is to it. We wouldn't have to keep them on the Board forever."

Klaus Martin started to rise. He had a little trouble pushing back the heavy chair, but once he did, he stood firm. "I must borrow your vocabulary, Kirby, to comment on your scheme. Your new Chairman of the Board would be the Hospital pimp, chosen for his ability to solicit rich Jews. Their reception here would be somewhat unusual. We'd take their money first and screw them later, thus converting McKinley into a kind of overcautious whorehouse." He hawked savagely, more to clear himself of anger than phlegm. "It's positively shameful."

He had no difficulty sitting down.

A soft murmur of assent ran through the room.

"It's outré, Nelson, really outré," protested Devine, hitting a proper organ tone.

"I'm afraid I can't go along with you on this one," said Shore from the foot of the table.

Kirby looked at the gently nodding heads. "All right, all right, you've convinced me."

"While you're on the subject, Nelse," said Shore, "why don't we appoint someone like Lewis Gillette, Dr. Morelle's father-in-law, to fill a vacancy? Besides money, he has all the qualifications, and he's bound to come across with a tax-deductible contribution. And how about young Krant, Cornelius Krant's son, to fill the other?"

Kirby smiled broadly, "Gentlemen, I think you've come up with something."

But the next morning, when he handed Devine's survey to Sam, he said in quite another voice, "Throw this crap away, will you! We didn't come up with a damn thing last night."

"What's there to come up with?" asked Sam.

Kirby looked up at him sharply. "Sam, that's the first time I've ever heard you express an opinion. I had you filed away as a fact-dispensing machine."

Sam looked around him. "I've got another opinion I'd like to express, sir, but this one needs a grand setting."

"Come up to the Board Room," said Kirby quickly.

After he had turned on the crystal chandelier, he closed the door carefully and motioned Sam to a chair. He, himself, sat down at the head of the table.

"I've already discussed this with Mr. Brooke," Sam began. "I had to. Without him it's nothing. With him it can't miss." He took out his handkerchief and mopped his face. "The property we're on is worth five million dollars. I think you should sell it and merge McKinley with Brookeville General Hospital. They've got the land; we'll have the money. With that kind of money you could add two hundred and fifty beds to the two hundred and fifty they already have up there, making the new McKinley equal to the old. And the yearly deficit of a suburban hospital would be next to nothing."

Kirby's expression had undergone a marked change. He looked like an old lecher who by some glorious mistake finds himself and his spouse at a Greenwich Village wife-swapping party instead of the customary Baptist revivalist meeting.

"What did Brooke have to say?" he asked impatiently.

"He agreed, subject to two conditions. First, we merge within a year. Second, no publicity."

Kirby reached over and patted Sam's cheek. "Sam, I trained you well."

"And, of course, you'll be Chairman of the Board."

"For five million dollars I don't expect to be an orderly."

"If you'll just give me fifteen minutes, I'll outline the plan."

"Don't outline. Don't explain. I'm way ahead of you. You can be Jules Verne. I'll build the submarine."

Sam looked disappointed.

"What did Brooke promise you?" Kirby asked.

"He said he would do what he could to help me become the first superintendent."

"You *will* be the first superintendent. And it's not going to be any pin-money job."

He laughed as he watched Sam's gloom lift. "All you have to do now is see that nothing leaks out." Pushing the chair back, he paced up and down the empty room. Suddenly he turned on Sam. "You see the weakness, don't you?"

Sam shook his head.

Kirby gave a derisive snort. "You're imaginative but not shrewd. You still don't see the weakness?"

"No, I really don't."

"The doctors, Sam, the doctors! What's in it for them? They lose a good hospital affiliation. They're liable to raise so much hell that Brookeville will back out."

Sam thought hard. "Don't most of them have other hospitals?"

Kirby came over and patted his cheek again. "Sure, sure, that's fifteen love for our side. The hundred doctors I appointed certainly do. But that's not what worries me." He sat down at the head of the table again. "It's the old McKinleyites, the ones who are hopped up on McKinley tradition. Like Levinson, that smart Jewish pediatrician. And Jim Morelle." He shook his head. "For an idealist, he's certainly made a hell of a lot of money in the past couple of years. Maybe his wife is responsible. But there is one thing in our favor. He's the kind who does not like to get mixed up in politics." He stood up. "We'll have to handle him with kid gloves, though. Did you ever hear of Ty Cobb?"

"The Georgia Peach? Of course."

"Rival managers used to warn their players not to stir him up. Needling him practically guaranteed that he'd have a good day at the plate. We have to be careful not to stir the old McKinleyites up. If we don't, maybe their professional inertia will take over. Of course, Morelle could be a pain in the ass. Idealists usually are. We'll have to keep an eye on him."

TWENTY-TWO

KIRBY was genuinely impressed by the rapidity with which Jim had transformed his tenement practice into an exclusive and lucrative one. He regarded him with the same admiration one reserves for a quick-change artist who rushes into the wings a beggar and walks out a king. As the Chairman of the Board had guessed, Jim's metamorphosis from a poor man's into a rich man's surgeon had been accomplished by Louise. Among the many devices she utilized to attain her goal, large dinner parties were by no means the least important. Although cocktails were at seven, Jim was never allowed to come home until eight, so that she could have a full hour in which to impress the guests with his importance. During this time he was invariably supposed to be "in the operating room." Not operating. After all, he could have been operating a machine or a vehicle. But "in the operating room," a glamorous phrase which encouraged everyone to figure out for himself just what the doctor was doing there. Certainly not playing potsie, was the insinuation. This "operating room hour" gave her an unrivaled opportunity to discuss his career, his skills, and his miraculous cures. Never once did she mention the celebrities he had operated on. Everyone knew that already. Instead, she emphasized that this patient was a clerk at the A&P, and that one a janitor in a tenement on York Avenue, a kind of reverse no-name-dropping that proved singularly effective. More than anything, she stressed his phenomenal speed.

"Jim keeps telling me," she would say at least twice a week over cocktails, "that speed is unimportant. But I would rather be back in my nice hospital bed forty minutes after he started taking out my gall bladder than lying on the operating table for ages while some slowpoke worked inside me with his scissors and knives. Why, recently Jim did an appendectomy on one of the waiters at the Colony (a ward patient), and the entire operation took less than fifteen minutes."

Lewis Gillette was as successful as his daughter in herding patients to his son-in-law's office, possibly because he looked so much like Honesty in a morality play. When he said, "Jim's the best man in town," everyone believed him. Besides, he had an excellent publicity department, which saw to it that week after week some anecdote about a famous patient appeared in one of the New York papers. People might forget the punch line, but not the name of the celebrity whose life Jim was reputed to have saved.

Once a patient reached the office on Seventy-fourth Street, he was effectively dealt with by Mrs. Westover, the widow of Gillette's former chief accountant, a beaming, big-bosomed lady of the old school whom Louise had persuaded to serve as Jim's secretary. Mrs. Westover greatly admired the Dickensian days, when the poor knew how to treat a doctor, when father and mother, clad in rags and followed by ten equally tattered Tiny Tims, would tiptoe reverently across a Harley Street threshold and intone in unison, "When you saved the little one's life, we thanked God for you, Doctor. When you would not take our pennies, we said Mass for you, Doctor. But when we found the five-pound note you stuffed in the plum pudding, Doctor, all we could do was sit around the table Christmas Day and cry." And Mrs. Westover knew that no properly grateful family would have stopped there. They all would have knelt while each child kissed a finger and the parents worked on the backs of the doctor's hands. Unfortunately, from her point of view, this type of behavior had been replaced by one far less flattering to the medical profession. The new culture required the patient to flip an insurance form on the doctor's desk and say with a grin, "The sooner you fill it out, the sooner you'll get paid, Doc." Mrs. Westover found the vulgarity less distasteful than the idea that there were people who actually depended on insurance companies to pay their bills.

Of these there were now relatively few in her employer's practice. From the beginning, Louise had insisted that the new secretary screen the patients and make up the bills, tasks she fulfilled admirably with the help of Lewis Gillette's credit department. Even long afterward, when such a fee was not unusual, Jim never forgot his amazement the first time she asked his approval before sending out a bill for twenty-five hundred dollars for removal of a cancer of the colon; nor his even greater amazement when the check and a note of thanks were placed on his desk three days later.

In fairness to his secretary, it must be said that she had no prejudices against the poor, provided there were not too many of them. Like an enlightened southern university which admitted a Negro now and then to comply with the federal law, she accepted an occasional poor patient to comply with the Hippocratic oath. Jim had never lost that Pied Piper capacity for attracting the downtrodden, the destitute, and the unemployed. The few she accepted she treated exactly like the rich. She was patronizing, highhanded and unimpressed. And nobody seemed to mind. Even the indigent did not demand special privileges. And she approved of the work Jim still did on the free wards.

It took more than the efforts of Louise, Lewis Gillette, and

Mrs. Westover, devoted and worldly though they were, to make Jim's practice so lucrative. It took consistently good surgery. Few could perform the standard procedures, the appendectomies, the hernia, gall bladder, hemorrhoid, thyroid, breast, and intestinal operations as skillfully as he. None could do them as fast. These, the backbone of surgical practice, he had learned from Emmerich in the days when McKinley was great. The newer operations, those on the heart, lungs, and blood vessels, Jim left for others.

Clinical research, now doubly difficult because of the withering of the wards, he felt was for men such as Stanley. Study of the medical literature, too. He skimmed through just enough of it to keep up with modern trends. His lack of interest in the scholarly medical life certainly did not diminish the size of his practice. Stricken with cancer, gall bladder disease, or appendicitis, the rich of New York cared not a whit about his reading habits, coolness toward research, or penchant for the old procedures. They heard only the tales of his skill and speed; saw only his dramatic cures. On meeting him, they were further impressed by a natural reticence which they considered most appropriate in a surgeon. A man who talked so little, they reasoned, would accomplish much. Within two and a half years Louise's prophecy had come true. He was earning so much that money was no longer important.

She created not only a practice for her husband, but a family as well. The first menstrual period of her marriage, two weeks after the wedding, she considered an affront to her fertility. Nature did not dare to insult her a second time. Ten months later a daughter was born, and named after Louise's mother. She had refused to consult anyone from McKinley.

"One of those midwives!" she had exclaimed. "This isn't the mauve decade."

Instead she chose a young obstetrician and gynecologist from Memorial Hospital whose prodigious technique in removing spreading cancer of the female pelvis had made him famous throughout the country.

"I know I didn't need a man like that for a simple delivery," she confessed afterward. "It's like driving a Ferrari in city traffic. Just the same, it's nice to know that in an emergency the power is there."

She was confined in the Physician's Hospital, a fine private institution where physicians and surgeons from every voluntary hospital in New York sent people who liked a view of the East River. The delivery was uneventful.

Aims Blair, who had just been made Director of Obstetrics, was miffed because the girl had not been born at McKinley. He went so far as to murmur, "It takes a man to make a man," possibly because he already had two sons. And he offered no congratulations. Two years later, when the Morelles had a boy, he did. By then Jim's practice was too important to be ignored.

The baby weighed eight pounds, and according to Hennie, looked a good deal like Jake. A few days after the delivery, Jim walked into his wife's room in the Physician's Hospital as she was diapering it.

"I don't seem to be able to get used to his little organ," she said.

Jim ignored his wife's excursion into anatomy. "I'd like to call him Albert. Albert Huegenon Morelle. And ask Mr. Huegenon to be his godfather."

Louise looked down at the diaper to conceal her approval.

"It should be Jacob John Morelle," he continued, "but Pop would understand."

At the christening, Mr. Huegenon said to Jim, "Thank you for the second April. Your father was a generous man. I think he would have approved."

Although Jim now had a daughter and a son, a devoted wife and a fashionable practice, he often wore what Louise called his Belle Dame sans Merci look. At the bottom of his uneasiness lay an inability to reconcile himself to the changes that were taking place at McKinley. He often recalled a dream that had come to him the night before he had started his internship. Sleep, opening his inner eye, had shown him McKinley rising incredibly from its eternal roots and dissolving in the mists of the future. The dream had been prophetic. The Hospital was growing unfamiliar and blurred. The McKinley of the present had become less vivid than the McKinley of the past.

The wards were disappearing. Gone were the gleaming central allées, each guarded by twenty-five meticulously spaced beds on either side. These once great halls had been cut up into semiprivate rooms, where the needs of a prosperous America could be more suitably satisfied. No longer was the doctor lord of a hundred free cases. Instead, he peddled his services to Blue Shield patients in the semiprivate bazaars. Jim would have much preferred treating the poor for nothing rather than selling his skills to them for an insurance company pittance. But he also realized, though rather sadly, that while Robin Hood medicine with wards full of charity patients was ideal for the education and training of doctors, for the people themselves the new system was better than the old.

Unfortunately, the new-system house staffs lacked the priestly devotion of the old. Less than twenty years before, not only were such groups limited to celibate young physicians, but marriage after acceptance was tantamount to dismissal. It was felt that since an intern's wife was properly the Hospital, a flesh and blood union was little short of bigamy. Now, however, McKinley was forced to adopt a different attitude. Two thirds of its young doctors were husbands on arrival, having chosen the connubial state at age twenty-four, perhaps because they were under the impression that the only way to obtain a sexual partner was to marry one. This was a medical generation evidently too naive to have heard of fornication. Children were so frequently the result of such legalized intercourse, that if an intern did not produce a baby within a year, he was regarded as something of a homosexual. In addition to his fertility he usually came equipped, not only with the wife and child to prove it, but a car, an apartment in town, and, of course, no chance of paying for all this for years. Responsibilities at home diverted him from his main task, which was to learn medicine, and conferred upon him a spurious maturity he was yet to earn. In effect, he was a student, though not a scholar, masquerading as a family man. The stethoscope and whites, long the symbol of his calling, he had abandoned during both extremes of the working day for a sack suit and an attaché case. Every morning at nine the interns would straggle into the Hospital in street clothes, brown leather cases in hand, fresh from a night of diapering and baby cries. Every afternoon at five, interns similarly disguised would hurry out to take up once more their unfinished chores at home. Jim often wondered what instruments were inside these attaché cases, which for some time had been the badge of the house staff. He later discovered that each contained a set of underwear and a pair of socks.

The attending staff had deteriorated, too, its distinctive essence of devoted McKinleyites diluted by wave after wave of mediocre new appointees, men who had so many other affiliations that they could properly be characterized as hacks in all hospitals, masters in none.

If the attending staff suffered by being too many, the nursing staff's weakness lay in being too few. No longer were young girls willing to spend three years studying the medical sciences, stare death in the face without trembling, handle pus, blood, and feces without showing disgust, work at night and sleep by day, only to find themselves after years as R.N.s earning a dollar and a half an hour while a truck driver made two. Nor were they willing to forgo marriage for a decade so that, dedicated and unencumbered, they might follow in the footsteps of the great head nurses of the past. A year after graduation, many of them, though not heavy with knowledge, were already heavy with child. Jim had to get used to not only the father-intern, but the pregnant nurse.

Frequently as he stood in the corridors of McKinley waiting hopelessly for someone to help him dress a wound, perhaps an intern already at home taking care of his own sick baby, or a nurse pursuing a more academic education in the classroom, he realized that Louise's designation of him as the knight-at-arms in *La Belle Dame sans Merci* was singularly appropriate. Only he knew what ailed him as he stood there "alone and palely loitering." He was yearning for the old McKinley. And wondering what Emmerich would have done if he had been alive and young.

The deterioration of McKinley was mirrored not only by the nurses, attendings, and interns, but by the trustees as well. No longer did the members of the Board sit brooding over the budget, aloof and inaccessible like Norse gods in Valhalla. No longer did they offer themselves up to the May bloodletting while August Grund looked at them with his terrible eyes. Now they gave advice instead of money, raised objections instead of funds. At all hours of the day, while other men were working, they stalked through the Hospital like butterfly hunters, ready to impale on their criticism any minutiae that came within their reach. A member of the Board of McKinley no longer practiced philanthropy. He indulged in a hobby. But whereas golf, yachting, even religion could be expensive, a trusteeship did not cost a dime. Just time; and the trustees at McKinley were rich in time. Sam Perkes once said, "It's good the by-laws limit them to twenty; otherwise they would roam through the Hospital in packs."

In spite of this deterioration, life without McKinley would have been unimaginable to Jim. It was his other wife as well as his Hospital. He had loved it in health; he would not forsake it in sickness. But Louise was becoming contemptuous of the relationship. It seemed to her more an example of necrophilia than high romance.

As they were dressing for dinner one evening, she said to him, "You'd be easier to live with if you would only give up your McKinley moods. You really can't expect it to be as exciting as it was when you were an intern. That's like expecting a woman to look twenty after she's been married for thirty years. Why don't you float with the current? You might become Director of Surgery some day. That's what your father would have wanted, isn't it?"

He nodded.

"I can't understand why you are so moody, anyway," she complained. "Isn't a doctor's main duty to treat patients? You're certainly doing that."

"There's more to medicine than private patients. There's the Hospital, the only place where you can work in the clinics, tramp the wards, and teach the interns and residents. A doctor without a hospital is like a minister without a church."

"Oh, no! Now you're the good Father James! Well, *my* father is coming to dinner tonight. You can tell him your philosophy." She sat down in front of the mirror. "By the way, Kirby has asked him to be a trustee."

Dinner turned out to be as relaxing as ever. Afterward, Gillette drank his Irish coffee appreciatively. Liqueurs he found too sweet, brandy soapy and overrated.

"Nelson Kirby has just asked me to join your club," he said to Jim. "For the other vacancy, he's tapped young Krant. The boy is completely irresponsible, but they are after his father's money. I'm not too flattered to be bracketed with Krant, but I've decided to accept. The initiation fee is supposed to be thirty thousand dollars."

"Isn't that a little high?" asked Jim.

"I suppose so, but Louise wants you to be Director of Surgery some day."

"Oh, father," interrupted Louise, "you know that you'll have a wonderful time outwitting those nineteen ninnies."

"They're not all ninnies, my dear. But you're right about one

331

thing. I'll enjoy outwitting them. May I have some more of your excellent Irish coffee?"

Louise lifted the silver coffeepot while Jim reached for the decanter.

"They remind me of an outfit," continued Gillette, "that's gone to a lot of trouble to conceal plans for bankruptcy. I get the feeling that I'm being asked to buy a co-operative apartment in Valhalla a couple of months before it's scheduled to go up in flames. I won't be in a hurry to write that check."

TWENTY-THREE

STANLEY was delighted when Adele told him that they had received a dinner invitation from the Morelles. Serene and peaceful, with every disquieting topic for the moment put aside, dining with Louise and Jim was the divine opposite of meals at home when he was a boy. In those days the Levinsons' table was a magnifying glass that gathered in heated issues, emotionally charged opinions, and violent prejudices, and focused them in one burning point on the collective heart of the family. Suitable subjects for discussion were considered to be the baby's bowel movements (introduced when Mr. Levinson asked in an anxious but nonetheless menacing voice, "Did he make, today?"), anti-Semitism, mixed marriages, staying out late, and any school mark under ninety. And if a single member of the family, wounded perhaps by a telling remark, failed to eat with Falstaffian zest, Mrs. Levinson would put down her knife and fork and cry, "All day long I work my fingers to the bone over a hot cookstove! And for what? So you can play with the food!" Here she would flip her hands as if she were shooing chickens, and deliver the *coup de grâce*. "I'll give everybody the money. Better you should all go out and eat in a restaurant!"

That was why Stanley was so enchanted by the tranquillity of dinner at the Morelles', especially when Mr. Gillette was there. The one Adele and he were attending was even calmer than most. Not once was the Hospital mentioned. But a little later, as they sat in the living room, Gillette said, "I have very bad news for you about the Hospital. You would be wise to steel yourselves. At the Board meeting last night, the deadheads voted to close McKinley and merge with the Brookeville General Hospital. They are getting a good price for the land—five million dollars. The money from the sale will be used to build a two hundred and fifty bed wing that is supposed to make a first-class institution out of this new McKinley-Brookeville Center. Sam Perkes, a young manipulator, will be the Superintendent, at thirty-five thousand a year." He shook his head. "It's a damned outrage. Great institutions should never be entrusted to the faint of heart. Leaving Klaus Martin and Hagenbeck aside, if you did an autopsy on the entire Board of Trustees (which might not be such a bad idea at that) I'm convinced that you would find a lily in every liver."

"You tried to block the move, of course," said Jim.

"Certainly. I talked for twenty minutes. I pleaded with them. I even dragged out my old Virgil pun, 'Arma virumque cano,' I sing of *a-l-m-s* and the man. But there wasn't a man or an alm in the place. Then Kirby called for a vote. It was seventeen to three for relocation. At least old Klaus Martin and Hagenbeck voted right."

"Father," said Louise, "you weren't up to form."

He turned toward her, obviously hurt. Anger put an edge to his voice. "If every man in that room had been willing to contribute as much as I, a new hospital would be rising on Park Avenue within a year."

After this, there was little conversation. The guests left early. The following night Jim and Stanley met at the Barclay

334

cocktail lounge to plan their strategy. Over their bitter cup, scotch on the rocks, they decided to visit the important men at McKinley, and by a combination of logic and sentiment, persuade them to fight the move.

Hauser, whom they had chosen to visit first, received them at the end of the week. As he rose to greet them, they remembered that, once, he had been the only doctor at McKinley who would get to his feet when a nurse entered the room. In those days it was the nurse who was supposed to rise for the doctor, not the doctor for the nurse. Hauser used to stand up not to confirm the nurse's standing as a lady, but his own as a gentleman. Today, he looked quite young, dressed in a beautifully tailored tweed suit that did everything for him except what he desired most, conceal the fact that his great body was slowly shrinking.

Jim and Stanley waited until he was comfortably seated. Then they sat down themselves and looked at him steadily. That was the way he liked young men to behave. They noticed that his eyes, once a crystalline blue, were now like onyx. As soon as he nodded, the two friends launched a review of the glories of the old McKinley, revealed the scheme to move it to the suburbs, and finally attacked the merger with considerable heat. Hauser listened, as unimpressed by their arguments as the wall of a handball court would have been by the clever shots of two players. After they had finished, he took out a dazzlingly white, monogramed cambric handkerchief, and dusted his nostrils.

"Why do you come to me?" he asked in his contrabass voice. "I reached the mandatory retirement age years ago. Or do you expect me to shout down the proposal in the corridors of McKinley?"

"You might rumble a little," Stanley suggested meekly.

Hauser smiled.

"We came to you," declared Jim in a burst of boldness, "because you're a rich bachelor who once loved McKinley. A generous contribution from you, coupled with the prestige of your name, might be the financial shot heard 'round the world. It might arouse people from their lethargy and start a drive to save the Hospital."

Hauser put the handkerchief in his back pocket, in a wrinkle-proof compartment, Jim presumed. Then he looked at him as if he were an intern.

"I wouldn't give you fifty cents to buy a popgun. The McKinley I knew and loved is dead. You don't try to revive the dead, you bury them. And Brookeville will make the perfect cemetery. Think of all those spacious lawns."

He turned his face to the window. "In a sense, I suppose we old-timers are to blame. The oaks cast too big a shadow for the little trees to grow under. Perhaps we were so busy training young men that we forgot to develop them." He turned back to them. "It's the old story of the present devouring the past. You two can't save the Hospital all by yourselves. Give up the idea. Or, if you can't, tackle somebody younger and less cynical than I."

Stanley was so shaken by the visit that he refused to go to see Kirby, the second man on their list, claiming that it would be best not to arouse his latent anti-Semitism. Jim met the Chairman of the Board alone late one afternoon in the trustees' room of the Hospital, he himself sitting under the crystal chandelier while his adversary took his usual place at the head of the table.

"I think it's a crime to move McKinley out of New York," Jim began with considerable heat. "My father-in-law says, 'It's worse than a crime. It's a blunder.' The trouble with this place is that it's been taken over by a bunch of trustees who are too stingy to contribute a dime and too lazy to go out and raise one. They think they've got it made, with all the joys and none of the responsibilities that go with the job. Well, there are a few of us who don't like the setup. If you actually put this thing over, we're going to raise such hell . . ."

"Jim!" Kirby interrupted, "don't make a speech. You'll only

feel like a damn fool afterward. You're a fast man with a knife; don't be so fast with a conclusion. We're not going to move anywhere," he held up his hand, "in spite of what your father-in-law says. One meeting doesn't make him an expert on hospital management—or in collecting information, either. I'll admit that occasionally I have to consider the possibility of a move. After all, the Hospital runs at a deficit, and I can't be caught with my pants down. But I'll tell you one thing. If you want to make sure that we move, just go around spreading rumors."

"Will you give me your word of honor that you haven't amalgamated with Brookeville General?"

"Yes. And I'll do better. I'll say it before the entire Hospital. You're the president of the Alumni Association now. Call a meeting any time, any place. I'll be there."

"All right. I'm going to do just that."

"Hell, my own son-in-law was just made Director of Obstetrics. Do you think I want him to lose his job after a year?"

The moment Jim left, Kirby picked up the telephone and asked that Dr. Blair come to the trustees' room as soon as possible. When he walked in ten minutes later, the somber, mechanical quality of his gait reminded his father-in-law of a sentry at Buckingham Palace.

"I'm sorry I took so long," said Aims, sitting on the edge of the table in his operating-room suit. "I've got a woman in labor."

"I've got a Hospital in labor," retorted Kirby. "It's going to deliver a big, bouncing bankruptcy right here on Park Avenue and incriminate me as the father unless I can get it quietly out of town. The merger is supposed to be top secret, but Sir James, the surgeon knight, knows all about it from Gillette. He wants to lead a crusade to keep the Hospital in New York. It seems McKinley is Holy Ground, and at fifty dollars a square foot maybe he's got a point. I'd let him enjoy himself, but he'd attract so much attention that the trustees at Brookeville would

337

call the deal off. Then I'd be faced with the choice of sinking my last cent into this place and have it close up anyway, or just letting it close up and be branded a stingy prick. If your wife wants to inherit some money, you'd better find a way of keeping Jim Morelle quiet."

"That's not the problem, Nelse. He's naturally quiet, passive almost. But he's a loyalty bomb with a nostalgia fuse. Perhaps his wife has de-fused him. She's made his present so successful that maybe he doesn't need the past."

"I hope so. I don't want him to explode during the next few months. I need a little time. The old Germans who wrote the by-laws wanted the Hospital to stay where it is. Before it can move, a relocation committee must be appointed and hold two meetings at least a month apart. Following this, a sixty-day period must elapse before the Board of Trustees can vote on the measure. I haven't even appointed the committee yet."

"You'd better."

"I know, I know! I didn't want to make it look as if I were railroading anything through. I'm not worrying about the votes. A two-thirds majority is necessary for a move or a merger, and I've got seventeen of the twenty trustees in my pocket. Everybody except old Klaus Martin, old Hagenbeck, and now Gillette. I've got the plan, I've got the votes, I've got the Brookeville trustees. All I need is a little quiet—no talk, no arguments in the Doctors' Lounge, no publicity. And, above all, time. The next three months will tell the story. By the way, how do you think the Medical Board will react when they find out?"

Aims crossed his knees. "I don't think they will get their bowels in an uproar. In the first place it's really a money matter, not a medical matter. You can always tell them that a financial emergency made a quick merger imperative. In the second place, every one of them has another hospital affiliation. And in the third place, not a single member of the Medical Board is an old McKinleyite," he gave his father-in-law one of his blue-eyed smiles, "except me."

338

Kirby smiled back at him. "An old McKinleyite is fine, but a disinherited McKinleyite wouldn't be so good, eh, Aims? Your job will be to keep Morelle, Levinson, and the other old McKinleyites from screaming their heads off during the next three months. Rock them to sleep. Sing them lullabies. Or mug them. I don't care what you do as long as you keep them quiet. This is a five-million-dollar deal." He stood up. "I hope you do a better job on them than you do on those women in the labor room."

Aims slid to the edge of the table, put his feet down carefully, and walked to the door with massive dignity.

"Aims, my boy, can't you do something about those women?" asked Kirby irritably.

His son-in-law stopped and turned around with a smile. "If you don't mind, I'll concentrate on Morelle and his friends."

He proved singularly adept at dispelling the rumors, although it would have been difficult to decide which was the more effective, his diction or his bearing. He marched through the Hospital shield-chested and confident, flashing his blue-eyed smile everywhere. He was the pukka sahib, Clive at Plassey, Kitchener at Khartoum, the old brigadier reassuring the women and children that the natives would not attack at night. When one of the young obstetricians mentioned hearing through the grapevine that McKinley was going to combine with Brookeville General Hospital, Aims laughed and said, "You heard through the grapevine! I live in Brookeville and my father-in-law is Chairman of the Board. I'm so entangled in the grapevine that Morelle calls me the McKinley Dionysus. And I haven't heard a thing."

After a week he became a bit disenchanted with his success. He was finding most of his colleagues surprisingly indifferent to the fate of the Hospital.

There were only a hundred of them in Halberstadt Hall the day of the special meeting of the Alumni Association. Kirby walked in as brisk and blustery as the March afternoon that was

339

mauling the city, nodded to Jim in the chair, and without waiting for an introduction, began, "I'm sorry I'm two minutes late."
The effect was that of a man so considerate that the trifling
delay had been preying on his mind.

He took off his camel's-hair coat and draped it across a chair.

"Somebody around here has been spreading rumors that
McKinley is shutting down and combining with a suburban hospital"; he made a searching movement with his hand; "Brookeville General, I believe. They probably decided on Brookeville
because I live there. Now, isn't that one hell of a thing? Here
are your trustees working their asses off to keep the place going,
and somebody is trying to cut the ground from under their feet.
Oh, I don't deny that occasionally when things look black—that
is, when we're deep in the red," he paused, "didn't somebody
once write a book called *The Red and the Black?*" There were a
few nods from doctors who remembered Stendahl from college.
"I don't deny that at times like this I toy with the temptation
of closing up. I'd be crazy if I didn't. But that doesn't mean I'm
taking the idea seriously."

He looked around him furtively and lowered his voice. "I'm
going to tell you something behind closed doors, something I
don't want mentioned outside this room. Every couple of years
I hint to the Board of Trustees that we may have to close up or
amalgamate with another hospital because of our financial position." He glanced at Jim out of the corner of his eye. "You've
never heard of this, because the trustees are not supposed to let
it leak out. I'll bet none of you can figure out why I pull this
stunt." He waited for a moment. "I do it so I can milk a few
dollars out of my colleagues on the Board. My son-in-law tells
me that fright makes the human body secrete adrenalin. I use
fright to make the governing body secrete money. It's an old
trick," he gave a rasping sigh, "and most of the trustees are wise
to it by now. Sometimes a new trustee will fall for it, though."
He glanced at Jim again. "It's always worth a try." He shook
his finger at them and raised his voice. "Now, listen to me. If

any of you are anxious to have the Hospital move away, just go around New York telling people that we're leaving. Then we'll *really* have to get out. Let me ask you a question. Would anybody in this room like to be operated on by a dying surgeon? Well, patients don't like to be treated in a dying hospital. Don't make it harder for the trustees. It's hard enough already."

He paused. "If you doctors want to make a contribution to the welfare of McKinley, let it be this—don't go around spreading false rumors."

He looked over the audience, toward the back of the room, where a table had been laid out with sandwiches and liquor. "I haven't had a thing since breakfast. If you would like to save another life, Jim, make a motion to adjourn."

Before the motion had been seconded, he was walking toward the food. Jim caught up with him as he was biting into a roast beef sandwich.

"You kept your word, Nelse," he said. "I'd feel a lot better, though, if Lewis Gillette hadn't told me about Sam's plan."

"Sam's plan! I know all about Sam's plan! A brilliant fellow, all right, but as expansive as a hard-on. He must have picked Brookeville for his little scheme because he lives there. A big shot, all of a sudden, he wants to be superintendent of two hospitals! Can't you see the boy is simply trying to feather his own nest?" He laid the sandwich on a paper plate. "Stick to surgery. Politics are not your line."

At home that night, after a roast beef dinner whose appeal the afternoon's roast beef sandwiches had done little to diminish, Kirby jotted down the names of the four men he had decided on for the relocation committee, and notified them by telephone that they were to meet in the trustees' room at 5 P.M. the following day. That an even number might predispose to a tie, he did not for a moment consider. Shore, Devine, Krant, and Grund, the four men he had chosen, would vote unanimously for the merger, he felt sure.

Kirby could see Julia Devine supporting her husband, but

341

not a philanthropy she had never been interested in; young Krant enjoying a trustee's prestige, but not bearding his stingy father for the money to increase it; Emil Grund sitting passively under the crystal chandelier the great August Grund had once made shine so brightly, but not helping to rescue an institution he considered a monument to a cruel and tyrannical old man. As for Shore, the Chairman of the Relocation Committee, it was hardly likely that a man who had once had the audacity to tell the elder Grund that the function of a trustee was to give service, not money, would abandon such a position now that it had become fashionable.

Of all the possible arguments, the most telling, Kirby felt, was the fact that the trustees could relieve themselves of the burden of making any financial contributions in the foreseeable future simply by voting in favor of the motion. To Krant and Grund, both of whom lived in Brookeville, the move would actually represent a convenience.

Kirby's logic proved flawless. The members of the committee met the next day and exchanged clichés. At the end of twenty minutes a vote was taken. It was four to nothing in favor of the merger.

To Jim, unaware of the vote or even of the existence of the Relocation Committee, Kirby's speech to the Alumni Association had had the force of a reprieve. McKinley might languish, but she would never die. An invalid she might be, but never a corpse. That Kirby might be dissembling occurred to him once or twice, but he dismissed the suspicion as unrealistic. No one, he concluded, especially a hard-headed businessman who depended on credit for his financial life, would jeopardize his honor before a hundred men. Now that he was convinced of Kirby's good faith, his McKinley depression lifted. Louise sensed his change of mood at once. For three days he held out against her questions. But on the night of the fourth as they were undressing for bed, he put on his bathrobe, went downstairs to the kitchen, and came back with a cold bottle of Piper Heidsieck. "If we drink it fast, we won't need an ice bucket," he explained.

He aimed the cork at the lamp by the side of the bed, and almost at once there was a pop and then a ping from the china base.

"You're like a little boy," she said as he took a glass to her on the chaise longue.

He smiled and sat down on a low-backed decorator's chair, long his favorite because it reminded him of the stool the coach used to shove toward him as he walked to his corner at the end of a round.

"What are we celebrating?" she asked.

"We're celebrating McKinley. It's not moving. It's not amalgamating. It's not disappearing. It's staying right where it is. I got it straight from the Chairman of the Board."

"And you believe all this just because Kirby told it to you?"

"He did more than tell me. He gave me his word before a hundred witnesses. I kept it from you as long as I could because it makes your father look a little naive. It boils down to this: Whenever Nelse thinks the deficit is getting too high, he tells the trustees that McKinley may be forced to close. It's shock treatment, Louise, pure shock treatment. An attempt to raise some money. By now, almost everybody is wise. The only ones who believe him are the green peas like your father. The scheme was aimed at them, and he fell for it. He wasn't supposed to let anything out, though."

Louise sat up on the chaise longue, her face red, her eyes frosty.

"What's the matter?" he asked. "Red cheeks, white shoulders, and blue eyes. You look like the American flag." He drained his glass. "Long may you wave."

She gave a little laugh. "I'm not laughing at your silly joke. I'm laughing at you. My father is as shrewd as a fox; you're about as worldly as a kindergarten teacher. He was rich *before* he got married. And he didn't make his money by being an easy mark. But all of a sudden you feel competent to instruct him in the ways of sharpies. That's like a rabbit telling a fox how to steal a chicken."

She walked to the window and stood there in her slip with her back to him. "He's warning you. Only you can't see it or do anything about it because when you read *Morte d'Arthur* it didn't tell you how to rescue a hospital." She shook her head. "I don't care what they do to McKinley. But I don't want them to make an ass of you."

He went to her and put his hands on her hips. "Your father may have been rich before he got married, but so was I. I was rich the moment I laid eyes on you."

She sighed and pressed the back of her head against his chest. "What can I do with you? Nothing, I suppose, except try to protect you."

He took her hand and led her back to the chaise longue. They sat on the edge.

"Kirby gave me his word of honor that McKinley wouldn't move," he said solemnly.

"Oh, what's so special about a word of honor! You make it sound like some contract a battery of my father's lawyers just drew up."

"When I was a boy, it was as binding as a contract. It still is a pretty serious business as far as I'm concerned. Just the same, to this day I always associate it with St. Honorés, those old fashioned, glacé-domed pastries covered with candied fruits and maraschino cherries. On summer nights my father would take us all to Reid's, a big ice cream parlor on 125th Street, because it was the only place in the neighborhood that served them. There was an illuminated fountain in the middle of the room, and the kids would all rush up to it to watch the goldfish swimming in the basin. My mother and my aunts, with their strict, beautiful faces, would be perched on wire-backed chairs on one side of the table, looking like Gibson girls in their shirt-waists and lace jabots. My father, Uncle Sol, and a friend called Lep would be on the other side talking about Three-Finger Brown and the Chicago Cubs. And all the while the big wooden blades of the ceiling fans would move slowly through the air like the oars of lazy rowers. One evening Lep told a funny story about a landlord who lost a lot of money because a contract hadn't been signed and a lawyer hadn't kept his word. It must have been funny, because my aunts laughed. I still remember the sudden give as my fork went through the crust of the St. Honoré, and my father leaning over me and saying, "A good man always keeps his word, Jimmy, especially his word of honor."

She kissed him absent-mindedly on the lips. "You're still back in Reid's ice cream parlor. It's hopeless, hopeless!"

"I think you ought to take back one of the things you said about me tonight."

"Which one?"

"That I'm a rabbit."

"You would be if I didn't wear a diaphragm." She leaned over and gave him a far from absent-minded, open-mouthed kiss. It made him think of Star. "That's not such an insult," she said. "A rabbit can be a father to a hundred sons."

"Would you like to try for one now?" asked Jim.

"I'd love to. Putting in that diaphragm is such a production."

TWENTY-FOUR

THE MONTH that followed was a particularly gratifying one for Jim, first because his fears for McKinley had been laid to rest, and second, because he managed to save a child from a surgical catastrophe that, though fortunately quite rare at the time, had been far from uncommon when he was an intern. Late one morning, Mrs. Westover's big-bosomed serenity was shaken by a woman who appeared at the office without an appointment. "She'd never think of going to a good restaurant without a reservation," the secretary said to herself disapprovingly. "Why doesn't she behave the same way here?" But in a few minutes she ushered her into the consultation room after having first told Jim that a Mrs. Emil Grund, the wife of a McKinley trustee, insisted on seeing him.

"Your nurse thinks I'm rude for barging in like this," said Mrs. Grund even before she sat down, "but I have a son who is dying, and time is running out."

Jim pulled out a chair for her and went back to his desk. "Please start at the beginning. I hope I can do something for your boy."

346

"He's eleven, and his name is Jimmy, the same as yours."
She started to cry. "You've got to save him, Doctor, you've got
to! It would be like saving a little piece of yourself." She took
out a handkerchief and dried her eyes. "It started four weeks
ago, right after his birthday party. I only hope none of the
children caught anything from him. He was fine when he went
to bed, but he woke up at eleven that night with a bad cough
and a temperature of one hundred and five. I screwed up my
courage and rang up Hettrick as soon as I looked at the thermometer, and he promised to come over in the morning."

"Who is Hettrick, Mrs. Grund? You make him sound as if
he were on the cover of this week's *Time*."

"He's the pediatrician. There are only two in Brookeville, so
he's very important. He knew what it was at once. It was
pneumonia. He came faithfully every day to give the penicillin
shot, but Jimmy did not get better."

"In the suburbs, penicillin is the opiate of the masses."

"I never thought of that. I've always taken it for granted that
it was good for everything. It certainly didn't help Jimmy. One
night a week later he woke up with a pain in the stomach. After
a while it traveled down to his right side and he vomited."

"You're sure the pain came first?"

"I'm positive. Hettrick said it was from the lungs. In two or
three days it stopped, and the temperature dropped to normal.
We thought he was well, but then everything started all over
again: the pain, the fever, and the vomiting. Especially the
vomiting. And his stomach became terribly tense and bloated.
Hettrick called it paralytic ileus."

"That's a paralysis of the intestines."

"Eventually Jimmy couldn't keep anything on his stomach,
so he had to be taken to Brookeville General Hospital for intra-
venous feeding." She buried her face in her hands for a moment. "All that's left of him is a little heart of a face and a big
balloon of a stomach. Now Hettrick thinks he has cancer. He
had a surgeon remove a gland from Jimmy's groin this week,

347

and although it did not show anything, he still thinks it's cancer. A retro- something or other."

"A retroperitoneal sarcoma. That's a malignant tumor deep in the abdomen." He looked at her sharply. "But that doesn't mean that Jimmy has it."

"Hettrick is going to ring you at twelve. He doesn't think Jimmy should be disturbed by another examination, but I insisted." She started to cry again. "Help me, Doctor, please help me! Go to Brookeville and try to save my son. And when you see what's left of him, please remember that that's not my real Jimmy. That's my dying Jimmy."

"I'll go this afternoon."

"Thank God. I feel as if New York's sheltering arms were already reaching out for him."

Jim handed her a cigarette and lit it. "Mrs. Grund, why isn't your husband with you?"

"Oh, he couldn't. That would be giving in to McKinley. And by implication to his father. To Emil, August the Great *was* McKinley."

"Then, why does he keep up his association with the Hospital? Why is he on the Board of Trustees?"

"So he can have the last laugh. He's the McKinley trustee now; his father isn't. The fact that his father has been dead for almost twenty years doesn't seem to spoil the taste of victory." She shook her head. "Sometimes I think famous men use the same drive to ruin their children that they do to get ahead in life. You knew August Grund as the master of McKinley. I knew him as Emil's father. He was a horror. When I was a little girl, there was a comic strip about a boy who was run over by an asphalt roller. It didn't seem to hurt him. He walked around quite well, but he was completely flattened, like those little figures cooks cut out of dough for the children. That's what August Grund did to Emil. He made him a two-dimensional man. Only after Jimmy was born, did he begin to live in three dimensions. I know I shouldn't wash dirty linen in your office, but I must tell you this. It explains so much. When Emil was at Columbia, he was a very good painter. He never bothered anyone at home; he always cleaned up his mess; and he kept his canvases neatly stacked in his bedroom. But his father felt that there was something disreputable about painting, something that would eventually drive a boy to cut off his ear, or disappear in a South Sea island, or pick up a venereal disease. So, one Sunday afternoon when Emil was looking at an exhibition at the Modern Museum, Mr. Grund told the butler to slash every one of his canvases to ribbons. When he got home, his mother told him what had happened. He locked himself in his room and didn't come out until the following night. He could have taken it if his father had stalked into his room in a rage and smashed a few canvases. But sending in the butler to systematically slice them all up was shattering. Emil never said a word about it. He just went on hating his father even more. And he never painted another picture. To this day you can't get him to visit a museum." She tried to smile. "You represent the old McKinley. That's why he couldn't come."

"Then, I'll go to him."

"I know deep in my heart that it's too late to do anything for Jimmy. But you've got to try, Doctor, a kindness from one Jimmy to another."

"I'll try."

He got up and took her to the door. Then he walked across to Stanley's office. "You busy?"

Stanley looked up from his book.

Jim sat down and stretched. "I've got fifteen minutes to kill. Ever hear of a Brookeville pediatrician called Hettrick?"

"Never heard of him."

"At twelve he's supposed to ring me and ask me to see Emil Grund's boy in consultation. I have a hunch he's pulled a terrible boner. I just thought you might know him."

"I do know him, even though I've never laid eyes on him. Can't a police artist draw a picture of a suspect from descriptions supplied by witnesses? Well, I'll reconstruct a picture of Dr. Hettrick from things I know about suburban colleagues. They're all the same, you know. You must realize that a doctor is marked by his environment the way a polar bear is bleached by the Arctic snows or a tiger striped by the branches of the jungle."

"Stan, I think you are as eloquent about the suburbs as you are about anti-Semitism."

"More so. I have to be. The suburbs are growing. People today have a passion for ownership. They must own a house, an acre, a pool, a lawn, a barbecue, a garage, and a mortgage. Their slogan is, 'No ownership, no security.' And why not? They are just fulfilling their destiny as Americans. To be a 100 per cent American in nineteen fifty you must meet four specifications: You must have a car, a house in the suburbs, a kid in camp with braces on his teeth, and a fifteen-hundred-dollar orthodontist to service them."

"I'm only 25 per cent American. The car, you know," said Jim apologetically.

"To get back to Hettrick, what effect do you think all this has on a suburban pediatrician?"

"I can see it's not going to be good."

"Looking back through the years, wouldn't you say that half my time has been spent in the free wards and clinics of McKinley? And a good hunk of the rest devoted to teaching the interns and residents? Throw in the innumerable conferences and the medical meetings at the Academy, and you've got a lot of effort put into *not* making money. Now, you really don't think the suburban doc goes through anything like this, do you? There are no free wards and clinics in a place like Brookeville, or a house staff either. If a pediatrician up there feels a little education would make him look good, he takes a few days off to go to a convention—income tax deductible. He's got it made. It's the parents who are in a dilemma. They can't admit, openly at least, that they moved because city rents are high, private schools expensive, and ownership a passion. So they blame it on the kids. You know—'New York's a great place to visit, but I wouldn't bring up a kid there.' As if Al Smith, Senator Wagner, and George Gershwin were raised in Levittown. But if the health of the children is paramount, how can they justify giving up the children's doctors, the best in the land, for suburban counterparts who are pretty low on the professional totem pole? There's the rub. The parents solve their dilemma with typical South-Yankee ingenuity. (That's Westchester ingenuity, son.) They glorify the suburban pediatrician. True, all his patients are private patients; he doesn't set foot in a free ward or a free clinic; he does no teaching and is a stranger to research.

"But these things don't bother the parents at all. He's busy. And they long ago decided that the busiest doctor is the best doctor. Of course, he's smug, too. He has a captive practice. Since he may be the only children's specialist in the community, where else can the patients go? I think you will find Dr. Hettrick not only smug but snotty."

Mrs. Westover came in and announced that a Dr. Hettrick of Brookeville was on the telephone. She made the word "Brookeville" sound slightly indecent.

"Do me a favor," said Stanley as Jim stood up. "Be a little snotty, too. And don't forget Rintman. Do a rectal on the Grund kid."

Jim walked to his office and picked up the telephone. The voice on the other end was deliberately faint, as if to tell him, "If you want to understand what I'm going to say, strain, you bastard, strain!" It said, "Morelle?" and when Jim acknowledged the name, "This is Cal Hettrick of Brookeville. Mrs. Grund wants you to see her son with me this afternoon. I don't think it's necessary but she's very persistent. It's a terminal malignancy. I'd like to be able to tell her you will be up at four."

"You can," said Jim.

"There's just one thing. I'm pretty busy, so I'm not sure

that I'll be able to get to the hospital. But the chart is complete, and there is a good nurse on the case."

"All right," said Jim, "I'll start examining the boy promptly at four. And if I think I can help him, I'm going to have him transferred to McKinley."

There was a long pause. Suddenly Dr. Hettrick's voice was loud and distinct. "You'll call me first, of course, before you do anything like that."

"No," said Jim, "I'll have that good nurse let you know." He hung up.

That afternoon, Jim drove to Brookeville on a parkway bounded all the way by synthetic countryside. Dr. Hettrick and Mr. and Mrs. Grund were waiting for him just inside the main entrance to the hospital. Grund looked chronically anemic, as if the blood had been pressed out of him while he was being flattened into two dimensions by his father.

"I should have come to your office this morning, Dr. Morelle," he apologized, "but there are feelings I can't always control."

"Your wife explained them," answered Jim reassuringly.

Brookeville General was only two stories high, with most of the rooms on the first floor. Since it owned plenty of land, it had decided to make itself into a kind of ranch-house hospital. Jimmy had a particularly desirable room, facing a group of old trees, which, Mrs. Grund reflected, though beautiful, did not seem to be effecting a cure. She and her husband stayed in the waiting room while Dr. Hettrick took Jim down the corridor to an alcove where the chart racks were kept. Jimmy's chart was two inches thick and contained the results of a formidable number of tests—X-rays, blood counts, blood cultures, blood chemistries, sedimentation rates, electrocardiograms, and liver-function tests, most of which Jim considered irrelevant.

"It's a terminal malignancy of some kind," Dr. Hettrick explained. "I haven't bothered to go over him myself in the past couple of weeks. No use adding to his misery."

Jim looked at Hettrick with disgust. Evidently the laying on of the hands and the stethoscope's feather touch constituted medical cruelty in this part of the world, while probing needles and laboratory machines were considered kind. Hettrick read from the chart in a dry, unemotional voice. At frequent intervals during the consultation he was called to the telephone. Although he attempted to show his irritation at these interruptions by means of suitable cricket noises, Jim could tell that he was secretly delighted at this demonstration of his popularity.

"I think I'll examine the patient before you get any more phone calls," said Jim after the third interruption.

When they reached the room, he knocked twice, waited respectfully, and then opened the door.

"I'm Dr. Morelle," he said, filling the threshold and blotting out Hettrick, who was standing just behind him.

The boy lifted his head from the pillow. "I didn't think you'd be so big." He stared for a minute. "You were the champ at Columbia, weren't you?"

"I used to box there, but that was long ago."

"But you were the champ, weren't you?" There was an urgency in the boy's voice as if he had decided beforehand that Jim's surgical ability was somehow dependent on his athletic prowess.

Jim picked up a chair with one hand, carried it to the bed, and sat down.

"Yes. For three years. An old pro taught me how to fight."

He motioned to the nurse, who slipped off the boy's hospital gown. When he saw the poor, emaciated body, the pipe-stem arms and thighs, the skeletonized chest, and the waxy, bloated belly, he found it hard to suppress a sigh. He placed his hand flat on the left lower corner of the abdomen. Then his gently pressing fingers began to follow the traditional croquet-wicket path of examination, upward and across to the right. When he reached the right upper corner, Jimmy's mouth tightened, and when at last he pressed down on the rigid right lower quadrant, the boy moaned. He took his hand away.

"Jimmy, I'm going to do a quick rectal examination. My finger slips in like a thermometer, only it doesn't stay in as long."

He stood up, took off his coat, and unloosened his gold cuff links so that he could roll up his sleeves. "I'll be careful."

"I've already done a rectal," interposed Hettrick.

"I know. Two weeks ago."

The boy looked fixedly at the cuff links as if to take his mind off the rectal examination from which Dr. Hettrick was obviously trying to protect him. "They're like big, gold dominoes," he exclaimed. Then he smiled at Jim, a weak, that's-a-good-doggie smile. "Just the right size for you, though."

The nurse pushed a rubber glove over Jim's extended hand and ceremoniously anointed his index finger with lubricant. He sat on the edge of the bed.

"Bend your knees and breathe in and out, Jimmy."

He slid his finger past the anal sphincter. The rectum contained no feces. On the right there was a bulge in the wall, a huge, inverted dome, firm but not hard, smooth and tense.

"Does this hurt?" he asked, sliding his finger all the way to the left, well beyond the mass, and pressing.

"A little."

"Does this?" He brought his finger back to the center of the inverted dome and pressed. Jimmy uttered a terrible groan and tried to jerk away.

"That's all," said Jim, and withdrew his finger.

He walked to the sink, rinsed the glove before taking it off, and washed his hands. A quotation careened crazily through his mind. "In Xanadu did Kubla Khan a stately pleasure dome decree." He felt like saying, "Coleridge, you old dog, there are more domes in heaven and earth than are dreamt of in your philosophy." But the nurse was watching him. He walked back and sat down by the bed.

Jimmy was trying to hold back the tears. "I'm supposed to be brave, but I can't be. I'm going to die, and I'm scared."

Jim laughed. "You don't have to be brave. You're not going to die."

"I'm not?" Astonishment crowded out joy.

"Of course not. I'm going to operate on you."

"You mean I'll be as good as new when you get finished?"

"Better. After I get you on your feet, we'll put on the gloves a few times and I'll make a fighter out of you. I might even belt you a couple in the jaw to toughen you up. On the other hand, after I get through training you, you just might belt me."

The boy smiled, and this time the smile was real. "Maybe, but you look pretty rough to me."

Jim squeezed his leg. "I'll be back."

As soon as he got Hettrick in the alcove, he said, "The pneumonia threw you off. A week later the boy got appendicitis. The appendix ruptured, and now he has a big peritoneal abscess."

Hettrick was shaken. When the nurse came up to him and told him he was wanted on the telephone, he waved her away. He thought for a moment and raised his head. The Grunds were approaching.

"You're not going to tell them a thing like that, are you? You'd really be crawling out on a limb."

"I'm not only going to crawl out on that limb. I'm going to describe the view."

Emil Grund quickened his pace. "Is there a chance, Doctor?"

"There certainly is. The boy had pneumonia, but it was a viral pneumonia, judging from the low blood count at the time. That's why the penicillin didn't work. It has no effect on viruses. The midnight abdominal pain later on was appendicitis. And it couldn't have come at a worse time, from the point of view of diagnosis. The inflamed appendix broke, and now there is big, pus-filled abscess in the peritoneal cavity."

"Peritonitis is very serious, isn't it, Doctor?" asked Emil Grund anxiously.

"Yes, but this is a localized peritonitis. I want to drain that abscess tonight. At McKinley. We have to get that pus out."

"I think you'd be taking a chance," warned Hettrick. "It's a long trip, and we have excellent surgeons here."

"No one but Dr. Morelle will operate on Jimmy," said Mrs. Grund.

Jim turned to Hettrick. "I didn't expect the boy to walk to New York. Don't you have an ambulance up here?"

"He'll go by ambulance," said Mrs. Grund. She looked at her husband.

Emil Grund turned his back on Hettrick and smiled bitterly at his wife. "I guess it's back to McKinley, after all."

Jim excused himself and went to the boy's room, still in his shirtsleeves. "You've got appendicitis, Jimmy," he explained. "I'm going to operate on you tonight. It won't hurt, and you'll be asleep when it happens."

"I know. And it won't be dangerous, will it? I mean real dangerous."

"Duck soup, my boy, duck soup. I'm not going to do it here, among the hicks. I'm going to do it in the big town, in New York, in my own hospital, McKinley." He rolled down his sleeve. "All right?"

"Sure." With a tremendous effort Jimmy raised himself on his elbows. "But New York is far away. How do I know that I'll ever see you again?"

Jim sat down by the edge of the bed and took the cuff link out of his right sleeve. "These were a present from my wife, the first thing she ever gave me." He pointed to the lettering: "L.M. to J.M., with love." Very gently he laid the boy on his back, and put the cuff link in his palm. "Give it back to me in New York."

He rolled up his right sleeve again, slung his coat over his shoulder, and pushed open the door. Hettrick was waiting for him in the corridor. He wanted to say, "For a medical pygmy that was a giant mistake. How did you ever manage it?" Instead he growled, "Get that ambulance rolling, please."

Jimmy Grund reached McKinley at six-thirty that evening, and was immediately taken to a corner room on the ninth floor of the private pavilion. Jim introduced him to Stanley, who had been waiting to give him an infusion of 5 per cent glucose. The needle slid into a vein in the bend of the elbow easily and almost painlessly.

"Gee, no fishing around!" the boy exclaimed.

An hour later, he was being wheeled into the operating room.

As always, Jim's incision was firm and bold. There was little bleeding and no fuss, probably because he regarded abdominal wall hemostasis, the tying off of vessels in the skin and underneath, not as an end in itself but as a means of getting to the trouble. In four minutes he was down to the peritoneum. He lifted the thick gray membrane with forceps, and the resident copied him a half inch away.

"Suction," he ordered, and a second later a warning hiss filled the room.

The moment he cut the peritoneum between the two instruments, thick, yellow, foul-smelling pus welled through the opening.

"E. coli pus," he grunted.

Silence clutched the room again. He slipped the perforated suction tube into the abdomen while Stanley watched the bottle to which it was connected fill halfway up.

"Over a pint," he informed his friend.

Jim enlarged the peritoneal opening so he could slide his hand into the cavity. "There is a tremendous abscess. It's going to be in and out for me."

Stanley saw the same dreamy expression steal over his face as used to possess Emmerich's when he had his hand in the belly.

"I've got the stump of the appendix," Jim announced.

He tied it off, carbolized the edges, put in the drains, and sewed up. The entire operation had taken sixteen minutes.

Jimmy Grund's recovery was so rapid that he was sitting up on the third day and walking around the room on the fourth. In three weeks he gained fifteen pounds. At eight o'clock the morning of his discharge, Jim found him completely dressed, sitting patiently in his room. He walked up to the boy and stuck out his cupped hand.

"Let's have it," he growled.

"What?"

Jim took off his coat and pointed to his rolled-up right sleeve.

"Oh!" said Jimmy weakly. He searched in all his pockets before coming up with a wallet, badly deformed by a large cuff link. Jim took it out, rolled down his sleeve, snapped it in place and put on his coat. From his side pocket he lifted a blue-velvet jewel box and pulled back the lid. Inside rested two great gold cuff links identical to his own except for the inscription. He pointed to the letters: "J.M. to J.G." Then he laid the box on the boy's knees and walked away. When he reached the door, he looked back. Jimmy's head was bowed. He was trying to say "Thank you," but the tears were running down his cheeks.

"You'll grow into them," said Jim and closed the door.

He stared up and down the empty corridor. Suddenly it was as if he were standing in the central allée of old Male One with a procession of nurses gliding between the perfectly spaced beds on either side. Rintman was looking up at him with his twisted smile and saying, "You learned something from me, after all, didn't you, Morelle?" He took a step forward, and in the distance saw Emmerich marching toward him like a Roman emperor at the head of his legions. The husky voice sounded once again, "You don't have the stature, Morelle, but a man can grow." It had been a great case, a wonderful case, and an old McKinley case, but Emmerich had been right. The Hospital had made him a slick surgeon, Louise had made him a fashionable one, but he just did not have the stature.

At six that evening, Mrs. Grund telephoned him. "I'm sorry to disturb you at home, but I had to tell you how happy Jimmy is. He treasures his scar and his cuff links. And he wants to live in New York."

"Maybe he'll lead the trek back."

"I hope so. I'm so grateful I feel I ought to do something for you besides just paying the bill. As far as that goes, we'll pay anything, anything at all."

"I'm not finished with the case yet. In a couple of months, I'm putting on the gloves with him."

"You ought to put on the gloves with the trustees." There was a long pause. Then, in another voice, Mrs. Grund said, "I really rang you up to warn you. The trustees are going to sell McKinley and move the name up here to Brookeville. Don't be too hard on Emil, please. He's just one of twenty. And he didn't agree to it because he was afraid that McKinley would make him poor, like the others. He did it for revenge. Maybe he is a little crazy, but at least he's not petty, like the others. His philosophy is simple: If McKinley is destroyed, his father will be destroyed with it. Blotted from the face of the earth. And from the hereafter, too. That's quite a trick, because Emil is ambivalent. He thinks of his father as being in both places, a sort of celestial suburbanite commuting between Heaven and Hell. The only way he can get back at him is through the Hospital." She sighed. "Maybe you can rally some support."

Jim's voice was low. "I'm not very good at that, but I'll try. How much time is there?"

"About a month."

Jim thanked her and hung up.

TWENTY-FIVE

HE TOOK the three-passenger elevator to the bedroom, where
Louise was dressing for dinner, and sat on the edge of the little
decorator's chair.

"Madame Aesop," he said, "your fable of the rabbit and the
fox has come true."

He told her what Mrs. Grund had said. "I think I'll call a
mass meeting of the Alumni Association and get them to pass a
motion condemning the merger," he said, looking at his knees
as if he were in the ring waiting for the bell. "That ought to
slow up those bastards."

"I don't see why you have to take it so much to heart," Louise
remonstrated. "Your world isn't coming to an end just because
McKinley is closing. All you need is an operating room.
Why don't you work at some other hospital? They all have
operating rooms."

"How does that help McKinley?"

"I don't know and I don't care. You can't expect me to have
your obsession."

"I don't expect you to. But I took McKinley for better or for worse, and I'm not going to let her down now."

"Oh, all right!" She slipped off her evening gown and put on a street dress. "I'll give the tickets to your mother. It's *Tristan*. You know, of course, that nothing you do will have any effect on Kirby and the trustees. If my father couldn't stop them, you certainly can't. But maybe you'll learn something. Maybe you'll grow up. I just hope they don't make a fool of you." She took a coat from the closet. "Ring up that girl who runs the mimeograph machine at McKinley, dear. You took her appendix out for nothing. She should be willing to do something for you. And please get Stan, Adele, and her to meet us in the Hospital in an hour. If we all work steadily, we should be able to get the notices of your meeting off by midnight."

Everything went faster than they had expected. By midnight they had mailed a notice to every one of the 526 doctors on the Alumni Association roster. The all-night post office on Lexington Avenue and Forty-fifth Street had only five hundred special-delivery stamps, so 26 of the letters had to go by regular mail. On the way home in the taxi, Louise and Jim sat silent until they reached Fifty-ninth Street. Then he leaned forward and told the cabbie to drive through the park. He turned to her.

"Naturally, I don't expect all five hundred and twenty-six to show up. We'll be lucky if we get four hundred."

Louise laughed. "Grow up, dear, grow up! You'll be lucky if you get a hundred. Can't you see that nobody really cares? Nobody except you. And Stan."

He put his arm around her and touched her breast.

"Jim! We have two children! Last month you were a little boy in Reid's ice cream parlor. Tonight, you're a college boy necking in a taxi. Oh, dear! I suppose it's a step in the right direction."

Five days later, on April 10, 1950, at a quarter to five in the afternoon, he sat in the presiding officer's chair looking across an empty Halberstadt Hall at the sandwiches heaped on a long table in the back of the room. Soon there was a slow trickle of doctors, seemingly sealed off at five-thirty, when Kirby, Shore, and Aims Blair entered together and sat down in the first row. Jim counted sixty-four in the audience. He rose with a heavy heart, and began the speech he had prepared for four hundred.

"If I may be permitted an unpleasant metaphor directed at the captain of the ship and his crew, who must have hatched this plot in the Board Room, the seemingly harmless merchant-man has pulled down its colors and hoisted the skull and cross-bones at last. They are going to sink our Hospital. After denying the accusation, the trustees are about to sell McKinley for five million dollars and build a new wing for the Hospital in Brooke-ville, where so many of them live. It's called a merger, and it will become final and irrevocable at the trustees' meeting four weeks from tonight. They say they are moving McKinley to Brookeville, but all they can move is a name."

He swept the room with his eyes. "I see about twenty old McKinleyites in the audience. They know that for a century this Hospital has been a refuge for the sick and the troubled of New York. Tearing it down would be as abominable an act as dismantling the Statue of Liberty and casting it into the bay. McKinley is not a piece of real estate to be sold to the highest bidder. It is an institution that has been indispensable to the life and health of our city for a hundred years. Imagine what the old Germans who made it great will think of us as they watch their Valhalla go up in flames because seventeen stingy men have calculated that a match costs less than a brick!"

He looked at the audience. A few of the men were whispering to each other. Disregarding them, he went on, "I hear it said on every side that the old Hospital isn't what it used to be. If our Hospital is really dying, we must search for a cure. We must not abandon it. Too many lives have been saved on its wards; too many discoveries have been made in its laboratories; too many masters have walked through its halls. It is up to us to come to the rescue of the Alma Mater. It is up to us to take care of her in her old age the way other and better men took care of her in her youth. It is up to us to make her what she used to be and what she was always meant to be, the pride of New York."

He lowered his voice. "I will entertain a motion to condemn the action of the trustees."

There was a short silence. A fat doctor in the back row directly in front of the sandwiches cupped his hands and called out through them, "Hey, Morelle, when do we eat?"

There was a burst of laughter. Aims leaned sideways and murmured in his father-in-law's ear, "Morelle would have been the sensation of Parliament in the days of the elder Pitt. Angels rush in where bankers fear to tread, don't they?"

"Oh, he's just jerking off in public," growled Kirby.

Stanley stood up. "I move that the Alumni Association condemn the proposed merger and instruct, no, change that to 'appeal to'" he added, although nobody was taking down his motion, "the Board of Trustees to set their financial affairs in order so that McKinley Hospital may remain on the site it has honored for a century."

Kell and two old McKinleyites seconded the motions simultaneously.

Jim announced that the floor was open for discussion.

"I'd like to speak to the motion," Stanley began. "I've known Jim for almost twenty-five years, and this is the first speech I've ever heard him make. It was worth waiting for. He talked about the glories of the past. I would like to dwell on the sellout of the future. My friends, don't be the prisoners of an illusion. You can move the people to the suburbs; you can move the houses to the suburbs; you can move some of the money to the suburbs. But you can't move great medicine to the suburbs. The discoveries which transformed us from a band of witch doctors into an army of scientists were not made in Ho-ho-kus, Mamaroneck, or Brookeville. They were made in the cities of the world and in the centers of learning which copied them. Not that the people of the hinterland show any gratitude toward the mother city which gave birth to them. Every day they stream into Manhattan, choking it with their traffic, fouling it with their refuse, deafening it with their clatter, and then, having sucked it dry, return to their ranch houses at night to revile it. Let us consider what would happen if in some grand swirl of magic the cities were made to disappear for a year. What would remain? Practically nothing, my friends. Just a thousand panic-stricken suburbs rushing around frantically in search of a tit. Let us at least render unto the cities that which belongs to the cities. To the bankers I say you can't move Wall Street to the suburbs. To the builders I say you can't move the skyscrapers to the suburbs. And to the doctors I say you can't move McKinley to the suburbs. We are being asked to approve the sale of a first-rate hospital so that a third-rate hospital may be enlarged. The philosophy behind this reminds me of the woman who had two chickens, a healthy one and a sick one. She killed the healthy one to make chicken soup for the sick bird." He cleared his throat. "Instead of standing around like children sucking their thumbs, the members of the Alumni Association should get busy and save their Hospital." He looked around uncertainly and sat down.

The fat doctor in the last row rose and shouted, "Hey, when do we eat?"

"Yeah, how about it," seconded his companion, "when do we eat?"

There were a few guffaws.

The back of Jim's neck turned red. He stood up and looked at the fat doctor. "If you don't pipe down, I'm coming back there with a Murphy tube, shove it up your ass, and feed you by rectum. And as a special concession to your friend, I'll make it a 'Y' tube so he can share your meal."

This time the laughter was heavy. Kirby's eyebrows arched. "Say something," he ordered his son-in-law.

364

Aims stood up, and without asking Jim for the floor, faced the audience.

"I feel quite humble following two such orators, Jim, the William Jennings Bryan of our Hospital, and Levinson, the young Demosthenes. You will remember that Demosthenes learned oratory by standing on the seashore with pebbles in his mouth, declaiming to the waves. I think Levinson still has some pebbles in his mouth. At least I didn't get half of what he said. According to him, a family changes its identity when it moves to the suburbs. I can assure him, however, that people remain just what they were before, Americans with a vision. They make the move in order to give their children a better life. That this cultural pattern has deprived Levinson of a practice is as obvious as it is unfortunate. But he cannot expect the rest of us to stop progress just to provide him with patients. He has my sympathy. And for an entirely different reason, so has Jim."

He poured himself a glass of ice water from the pitcher on the little table in front of Jim, and took the traditional de-bater's sip. "Eventually a child must be told that there is no Santa Claus. This process of de-Santa Clausation is a painful one. So, although I would tell a child that there is no Santa Claus, I would not be so cruel as to tell him that there had never been one. Let him believe deep down that once when he was very little, there had been a Santa Claus, a wonderful old Santa Claus who was taken away from him by the grownups. That is the way Jim, here, should be treated. If he wants to create a McKinley mythology for himself, that's fine. If he wants to sit in his private, dilapidated Valhalla holding séances with his old German gods, that's fine. But I refuse to foist his imaginary hospital on you. I hold your intelligence too high. Overpraise of the past demeans the present. I served on the same house staff as Jim, but I saw no Valhalla. Maybe I was less of an adolescent than he. I saw surgeons hurling instruments at pock-marked walls, interns bullied, nurses abused, and flim-flammery rampant. One of Jim's gods used to make his famous snap diagnoses on the wards by secretly reading through the diagnosis book in the admitting office fifteen minutes before rounds. True, most of New York called him in consultation. The trouble was that half the time his consultation diagnoses were wrong. Jim, of course, remembers only the times that they were right."

He chuckled, and the audience smiled.

"Don't be intimidated by the past. To the surgeons here today, I say you can perform operations never dreamed of by your predecessors. To the internists here today, I say you can effect cures never imagined by your predecessors. And to everyone here today, I say you are better doctors than your predecessors."

There was a fine round of applause.

"Jim admits the old Hospital isn't what it used to be." He paused dramatically. "Well, maybe it never was. From this merger you will lose less than you think and gain more than you dared hope for. I can envision a day when on the rolling lawns of Westchester there will arise a new McKinley that will put the old to shame."

He gave the audience his most impressive blue-eyed smile and sat down.

When the applause stopped, Kirby stood up and nodded to Jim. "Some of you must think me less than honest because last month in this very room I told you we had no intention of moving. At the time, it was true. But a financial crisis arose which made it necessary to either amalgamate or close our doors. Brookeville General came to our rescue by offering us a home. I have been asked whether the rumors which had been floating around the Hospital put the idea of the merger into my head." He gave them a crafty smile. "I refuse to answer the question."

He walked to the center of the floor and stood directly in front of Jim. "The speeches I just listened to were worthy of the Democratic National Convention. But you know as well as I do that they were just talk, fine talk, sentimental talk, noble talk, but talk just the same. And we can't keep this Hospital running on talk. It takes money. Our plant is obsolete. I'm surprised it hasn't been condemned. A new five-hundred-bed hospital would cost us fifteen million dollars. You have to go to the foundations and the big corporations for that kind of dough. And to get them interested we would have to raise five million dollars ourselves: you, the two hundred doctors; we, the twenty trustees. The quota would be two and a half million from the docs, two and a half million from the trustees. That's over twelve thousand dollars from each of you. Look at the man on your right. If he defaulted, you would have to come up with twenty-five thousand bucks. Do you have that kind of money? Do you, Dr. Levinson?"

Stanley blushed and looked at his feet. But the question was rhetorical.

"Well, we, the trustees don't have it either," Kirby continued. "Not to the tune of one hundred and twenty-five thousand dollars a man; not with income taxes what they are today. And even if by some miracle the fifteen million were dumped into our laps, how could we operate the new hospital afterward? We have no endowment fund. We'd be running an expensive plant on a shoestring."

He paused and smiled reassuringly. "This is not the end of our Hospital, it is a beginning. I pledge you my word that the new McKinley will carry on the traditions of the old. No one will lose his job. Everyone from scrub women to doctors will be welcome in our new home. Brookeville is not in Siberia, you know. It's only fifty minutes from Forty-second Street. Some wise guy is sure to whisper that the only place that's fifty minutes from Forty-second Street is Forty-third Street. Well, I've made it from Brookeville to Times Square in thirty-five."

He gave the audience a hard stare. "I can't quote the classics. I never knew Demosthenes or Valhalla or those old German gods. I go for the homely saying. The one that applies here is this: 'Shit or get off the pot.' Get me five million dollars and we stay in New York. Otherwise, I think you should put your shoulders to the wheel and make the merger a success."

He waved his hand at the audience and walked to his seat.

There was a long silence. Then Shore cleared his throat and said, "May I have the floor, Dr. Morelle? Although, like Mr. Kirby, I'm not a member of the Alumni Association, I have served on the Board of Trustees for thirty years."

As soon as Jim bowed, Shore rose stiffly. "I think the time has come for us to put away recrimination. Let us concentrate not on what should happen in an ideal world, but what is bound to happen in this one. Income taxes and the shift of the middle class to the suburbs make the scrapping of the Hospital inevitable. McKinley reminds me of the old *Aquitania*, which took me to Europe a dozen times and Dr. Morelle once. It was a brave ship with a splendid tradition. And it weathered every storm except the last, the storm of time, which in the end sweeps everything away. Last month the *Aquitania* was sold for scrap."

He cleared his throat again, obviously without success. Then he went to the little table and drank an entire glass of water.

"Gentlemen, we must come to terms with the inevitable even though we abhor it. I don't like growing old. As a matter of fact, I am actively opposed to it. But," and he smiled sadly, "I have learned to accept it, gracefully, I hope. We must not turn away from the fact that McKinley is old, feeble, and failing. Its condition is incurable. We must face the death of our Hospital as we would the death of a loved one, with fortitude and dignity, not, if I may be permitted to say so, with emotional demonstrations like Dr. Levinson's and Dr. Morelle's. We cannot expect to ride the wave of the future. It is going to engulf us. If the old ship is doomed, then let us go down with flags flying. Like men!"

Jim waited until Shore was comfortably seated before turning to the audience. "We have just heard from three of the top brass. Let's hear something from the privates."

He probed the audience with his eyes, but not a man rose.

"In the old-fashioned books I used to read when I was a boy, somebody would have said, 'Will no one break a lance for Old McKinley?' "

After the experience of the fat doctor in the last row, no one dared to laugh. There was only a mocking silence.

Kirby growled in Aims's ear, "I don't know whether anybody will break his lance, but I bet nobody will break his ass for Old McKinley."

Jim sat waiting for the miracle, for Caesar to march in with the Tenth Legion, for Matty to come from the bullpen and strike out the side. But nothing happened.

"Then we'll vote," he announced at last. "We have to vote. All those in favor of Dr. Levinson's motion please rise."

It did not take long to count them. There were nineteen, and they sat down at once.

"Those opposed." He made an upward motion with his hand.

This time there was a great deal of noise from the shuffling of feet and the scraping of chairs. Forty-three men stood up.

"The motion is defeated," he announced, not so much to the doctors as to an inhumane reality.

For no one was listening. Without waiting for a motion to adjourn, the audience was streaming toward the sandwiches.

When Louise saw the expression on his face as he entered the living room a few minutes later, she said immediately, "I suppose you want scotch on the rocks?"

He nodded.

"Why is it," she asked, "that whenever you're troubled, you always take scotch on the rocks?"

He shrugged.

"It has something to do with a girl you once knew, doesn't it?" she persisted.

"I refuse to answer. I'm a Fifth Amendment husband."

"Then, tell me about the meeting instead."

"I made my first speech. Kirby was right. I should stick to surgery."

He told what he had said, and then summarized each of the other speeches. After a long pause, he gave her the attendance, and last of all the vote.

"You don't seem very disturbed by what I just told you," he concluded.

"Why should I be? And I'm certainly not surprised. You're a knight in a world of connivers. You came to that meeting straight from the Round Table instead of a smoke-filled room on Capitol Hill. And I don't sympathize with you one bit. You're so good, Jim, it hurts! If this wicked world would just let you stay good, you would be perfectly happy. But you are not nearly as righteous as you think you are. You're just passive. If you really want to fight for something you love, you have to do more than go through a few romantic motions. You have to close with your enemies, and then some of their dirt rubs off on you. You have Reid's ice cream parlor. I have my story of the French Revolution that I read as a girl."

She stood up and arranged her hair. "Would you like to hear it? A woman whose lover had been sentenced to death traveled all over Paris looking for the one member of the Revolutionary Tribunal who could save his life. At last she found him. He was standing in a little clearing, ankle deep in blood from the corpses which had been brought from the guillotine. With tears streaming down her cheeks, she pleaded with him for her lover's life. He took a silver goblet from his coat, bent down, and filled it to the brim with the blood that covered his feet.

"'Drink it,' he said as he handed it to her, 'and your lover goes free.'

"She put the cup to her lips and drained it."

Louise walked up to her husband and put her hands on her hips. "Of course, she went somewhere afterwards and vomited. But she saved her lover's life. I don't care one way or the other about McKinley. I think you're ridiculous to get involved. But if you want to save the Hospital, you'll have to do things that will make you vomit. You'll have to take off your surgeons' gloves and get your hands dirty. And you're not going to like it a bit."

Neither said very much for the rest of the evening. At night they lay at opposite sides of the big double bed, close to the edges, with their backs to each other. Louise fell asleep at once. Jim stayed awake until four. Only then did he go to the medicine cabinet for a Seconal capsule.

At seven-thirty he was jarred back to consciousness by the telephone. The brassy voice at the other end seemed a continuation of the ringing. It was Kirby asking to see him in the Board Room at nine.

Although Jim was ten minutes early, he found the Chairman of the Board already waiting for him in his customary place at the head of the long table. Kirby thanked him for coming on such short notice, and then set to work.

"Jim," he began, "your friend Levinson is going around calling me 'half-a-shoe Kirby, the heel without a soul.' It's a a good crack, but I wonder how he would handle things if he were in my shoes. You see, it's not a question of moving or staying. It's a question of moving or disappearing. Oh, we could stay open another few years, rolling up a bigger and bigger debt as we went along. But in the end we would have to sell the land anyway to pay what we owed. Then we would wind up with nothing. That makes sense, doesn't it?"

"It seems to."

"My way we wind up with five million dollars and a new home. Do you know what a hunk of money like that is? It's muscle. We can tell the people in Brookeville just how we want the new hospital run. And believe me, it's going to be run the McKinley way. And it's going to be called McKinley, no McKinley-Brookeville crap."

He shoved a pack of cigarettes across the table, but Jim shook his head.

371

"Still in training," said Kirby, and Jim smiled.

"Jim, Jim," Kirby went on, "we're not going to use the five million dollars to build a string of whorehouses across Westchester. We're going to use them to treat the sick, probably the children and the grandchildren of the very people who used to come to us here on Seventieth Street."

Jim shoved the pack back, and Kirby lit a cigarette.

"This plan to save McKinley," Kirby went on, "has a few weak links. I'm referring to the trustees at Brookeville General, a group of conservative old farts who regard publicity as they would sodomy or incest. If a stink is raised about the merger, they will drop us like a hot potato."

He walked over to Jim and stood above him. "Just keep on making speeches and rousing the doctors, and before you know it, the story of the fight will be splashed across every newpaper in town. Then we'll all be sunk."

He sat down on the other side of Jim. "I'm going to work out a deal with you, a deal that will be good for you, good for me, and, above all, good for the Hospital. For three hospitals, as a matter of fact: McKinley, Brookeville, and Harland. You'll admit that Harland has always been the closest thing to a sister hospital. It's never been a McKinley, but how many hospitals have? And it's heavily endowed. The fact that it's on the West Side instead of Park Avenue shouldn't bother you. You've got a car."

He stubbed out his cigarette. "Ed Harnett, the Chairman of the Board at Harland, is an old friend of mine. He looks up to me, and has always come to me for advice. Not because I'm any great shakes, but because I'm head of McKinley." He gave Jim a hard look. "You know about the Director of Surgery at Harland. He's brilliant, everyone admits that, but a first-rate troublemaker. Something like your friend Levinson. For five years he's been a thorn in their sides. Last night they asked for his resignation. They're looking for a new Director of Surgery, this time a man they can get along with. If I recommend you to

Ed Hartnett and a couple of others on their board, the job is yours."

He put his hand on Jim's shoulder. "Here's the proposition: Give me your word that you will do nothing to jeopardize the merger and I guarantee that you will be the next Director of Surgery at Harland Hospital."

Jim took a deep breath.

"On the other hand," said Kirby, taking his hand away, "if you throw a monkey wrench into the works here, you'll never have a chance at Harland. I'd be forced to tell them that you were a troublemaker. And remember—they just got rid of one."

"How long do I have to decide?"

"Take all the time in the world," answered Kirby benignly. "Jim, Jim, isn't this what your father would have wanted? If he couldn't see you Director of Surgery at McKinley, wouldn't he have wanted to see you hold down the same job at Harland? And it wasn't I who gave him the dirty deal. That was the work of your old German gods. You know, Jim, I've appointed a few doctors to the inside staff here in my day, over a hundred, in fact, and if I had been Chairman of the Board when your father was young, you can bet your bottom dollar he would have been on the inside staff, too."

He stood up, and so did Jim. "Your conscience should be clear," said Kirby gravely. "You've done everything a man could do. You worked on Gillette, but the trustees voted overwhelmingly against him. You went to Dr. Hauser, but he gave you the bird. An eagle, I presume. You laid your case before your colleagues, but they rejected it. Now you have to think of yourself. I'd like to see you in a position that would make your father proud of you." He paused. "In the meantime, let's see what we can salvage from the old McKinley to give to the new."

As Jim walked out of the Board Room, he thought back to the days of his childhood, when he used to sit on his stoop on 122nd Street to work out his problems. He had an urge to go back to that house and sit on those steps until he came to a

373

decision. But it was too far away. And too far away in time, too. Instead, he strolled up Fifth Avenue to Seventy-fourth Street, and sat on a park bench facing the Huegenon mansion. He remembered with a pang that this was the very bench on which Star had said good-by fifteen years before. She had been so beautiful then. And since he would never again see her, she would remain forever fixed in the moment of her greatest beauty. But she was gone now. And his father and Emmerich and Rintman and Albert all were gone. And the elegant old man in the house across the way would one day be gone, mercifully with a sudden heart attack or cruelly with a stroke or a spreading cancer. And he himself was worse than gone. He had never even arrived. Certainly he would never be what he had hoped to be, the heir to Emmerich's imperial purple. The long leap forward from Harlem had turned out to be just a shuffle. A fashionable surgeon he was, and a fashionable surgeon he would remain, adroit and quick at the operating table, but never to be touched by greatness.

What was the use of kidding himself? He could no more restore McKinley's past than he could bring back to life the great men who had created it. All he could do was make the gesture. The question was, Which was more important, the Don Quixote gesture or the Harland plum. Plum, hell! The Golden Apple. Well, he was not going to worry about it now. When the time came, he would make the decision.

He stood up in the pale April sunlight and stretched. Thank God for the eleven o'clock operation. That ought to take his mind off the merger. He was going to remove Mrs. Schuyler's piles for a thousand dollars and give them to the government. The dollars, unfortunately, not the piles. Well, it was better than being a bum.

TWENTY-SIX

EVER SINCE the night they had helped mail notices to the members of the Alumni Association, the Levinsons had been trying to think up an idea big enough to save the Hospital. From the trustees, they felt nothing could be expected. It was obvious that they would neither donate the money nor raise the funds to keep McKinley in New York. Besides, after selling the land and handing over the proceeds to Brookeville, they would be hailed as the master builders of the new institution. The doctors were largely indifferent, although it would have seemed that of all those involved they had the most to lose from the merger. But they were butterfly men now, flitting from hospital to hospital and spending just enough time in each to insure reappointment the following year. In this way, if their favorite institution was full, they could be sure of getting their private patients into one of the others. At last, prodded by Adele, an old admirer of Henry Wallace, Stanley came to the conclusion that they would have to go to the people. Over the weekend the two talked constantly of trusting the people, listening to the people, accepting the verdict of the people. The only question was how to *get* to the people. Adele suggested that their friends should write letters to the *Times*, but Stanley protested that this was a job for cranks. He felt that they should write to their congressmen, but she retorted that this would be going to the servants of the people instead of to the people themselves. They both agreed it would be nice if they could get some prominent figure to present their case on television, but such a venture would entail the purchase of a half hour of prime time, and the cost would be prohibitive.

One Sunday morning as they were lounging in the living room halfheartedly reading the *Times*, he in flannel pajamas although the weather was mild, she in a filmy nightgown that did little to conceal the thoracic architecture the birth of their child had made even more formidable, the solution to their problem suddenly came to them. Not token, but massive, publicity. They would enlist some well-known columnist to lead their crusade. They first thought of Walter Winchell, but were forced to admit that his importance might make him inaccessible. After considering several others, they decided on Bill Tuck, not only because he was talented, dynamic, and enormously persuasive, but because, six months before, he had successfully launched a fund-raising drive for the Heart Association with a twelve-hour telethon. Not everyone was as favorably impressed by him as were the Levinsons. What his fellow journalists thought of him could best be judged by an expression they had coined, one that they used on people who particularly annoyed them. It was, "Oh, go Tuck yourself!" But, of this, Stanley and Adele were unaware.

At one o'clock Monday afternoon Stanley took the subway downtown, got off at the eighth floor of the building where Tuck had his office, and handed his card to the first person he came across, a young girl with a bosom that reminded him of Adele's. In response to her "So what?" he stated with some embarrassment that he wanted to see the columnist. She returned in a moment without the card, and pointed to an open door at the end of the corridor.

He had expected Tuck to be sweaty and irritable in shirt-sleeves and a green eyeshade, rummaging through a mound of papers. But the man on the other side of the desk was a cool Ivy League type in a well-cut three-buttoned tweed, and seemed to have nothing to do but listen. Stanley introduced himself and said he was from McKinley. Tuck replied that he knew McKinley well. His two children had been born there, Aims Blair officiating. As a matter of fact, he was quite friendly with the Chairman of the Board. They belonged to the same country club. Although Nelse was a first-rate raconteur, he confided, he was a lousy golfer. He expected Stanley to laugh.

But Stanley, obsessed by his mission, plunged at once into the story of McKinley's past glory, present poverty, and imminent disappearance. He pleaded with Tuck to save the Hospital for his readers, who were, in effect, the people of the City of New York. With his column, his contacts, and his influence, he could raise the money to keep McKinley where it was.

Tuck nodded and smiled benignly, but the expression in his cold gray eyes never changed. This is a genuine shnook, he said to himself. Not only is he trying to louse up a perfectly good merger, but he expects me to get him fifteen million dollars. Nelse Kirby must love this guy! He should be put out of his misery, he decided, not so much because he's a nuisance, but because he's an idiot.

He waited until the Roman candle of Stanley's rhetoric had fizzed out and then stood up.

"I'm going to send up a trial balloon, or in the language of Broadway, put the show on the road and see what the reaction is. I'm going to find out how much I can raise from the boys in the office. When I did this for the people from the Heart Fund, I came back with three hundred and eighty dollars."

He handed Stanley a copy of *The New Yorker* and walked out.

But he did not go to the boys. Not until later. He went to a little office at the other end of the corridor and rang up Kirby. They were on the telephone a long time.

Forty minutes later he returned beaming, and handed Stanley a long white envelope.

"Five hundred and thirty dollars the first crack out of the box! That's a hundred and fifty dollars better than I did for the Heart Association. As you would say, Doctor, the prognosis is good."

Stanley smiled and counted the checks. There were twenty-two, and every one was made out to "Stanley Levinson, M.D." He frowned.

"What do you think I ought to do with these? Open up a special account?"

Tuck laughed scornfully. "For five hundred and thirty bucks? Put it in your own account. You have a bank account, don't you?"

Stanley flushed. "Of course I do."

"When the fund grows to a few thousand," Tuck continued in a matter-of-fact tone, "we'll decide what to call our organization—'Friends of McKinley, New York for McKinley'—something like that. Then you can open an account under that name and transfer the money." He gave Stanley a quick look. "How much time do we have before the merger becomes official?"

"Until three weeks from Friday night."

"I'll get in touch with you this Friday. And if you take my advice, you will deposit those checks at once. The boys were paid today, and by the end of the week some of them may be a little short."

Stanley was so elated with his success that after describing it to Adele, he telephoned his mother.

"It's like I always say," she informed him as soon as he stopped talking. "If you want to get something done, go to a busy man. He always has time."

But he did not hear from the busy man on Friday. Instead, at five in the afternoon he received a telephone call from Kirby ordering him to come to the Board Room at once. Thoroughly frightened, he went to the Hospital in a taxi, a means of transportation he reserved for emergencies. He found the Chairman of the Board already seated at the head of the conference table, and slipped into a nearby chair.

Kirby gave him a hard look. "The trustees want your head."

"You don't mean they want me to resign."

"Oh, you'll have to resign all right. I mean they want to bring you up before the District Attorney."

"The District Attorney!" Stanley exclaimed in a high-pitched voice, "For what?"

"For this." Kirby took a long white envelope, filled with checks, out of his pocket and slid it along the table.

Stanley opened the envelope, looked at the canceled checks inside, and said, "I'm collecting money for McKinley. Is that a criminal offense?"

"I don't see McKinley anywhere on these checks. I see your name in front and your signature in back. You know damn well that you deposited every one of them in your own account." He drummed on the table with his fingers, accentuating the beat with his thumb. "Did anyone give you the authority to solicit money for the Hospital? Did the trustees? The Medical Board? The Executive Officer? Well, did they? Levinson, you're caught with your pants down."

Stanley turned pale. "Do you really think I would steal, Mr. Kirby? And if I did, do you think I would drag McKinley into it?"

"Of course, I don't. It reminds me of an old routine of Weber and Fields. It wasn't very funny, but neither is this." He pointed to the envelope. "The big one, I think it was Weber, tried to get Fields to enter a house which was guarded by a ferocious dog. He kept repeating to Fields, 'I'm telling you the dog won't bite, the dog won't bite.' When he got through,

Fields shook his head and said sadly, 'You know it, and I know it, but does the dog know it?' It's the same here. 'You know it, and I know it, but do the trustees know it?' I'm afraid the answer is 'No!'"

"May I ask where you got the checks?"

"From Bill Tuck. With the donors' written requests in his pocket, he must have persuaded the banks to let him have the canceled checks before they went out with the regular monthly statements. Or else the boys did it for him. He thinks you're a phony. You've got to admit that the whole thing looks fishy." He threw up his hands. "We need fifteen million dollars to keep McKinley in New York, so you come up with five hundred and thirty! And don't give me any crap about 'great oaks from little acorns grow.' Did you expect to see a tree shoot up in three weeks? The trustees think you were going to collect some dough, turn a little over to the Hospital, and keep the rest for yourself—for expenses. I'm not naive enough to think that they can send you to jail. You'll probably get a suspended sentence. But your license may be revoked. And your career will certainly be ruined."

Stanley wanted to light a cigarette, but his hands were shaking. "What do you advise me to do, Mr. Kirby?"

Kirby sighed. "I'll gladly go to the trustees for you, but give me something to bargain with. Your greatest asset at the moment is your nuisance value. Trade it in! Empower me to tell them that from now on you will forget about the merger, and you can be damn sure that from now on they will forget about you. Well, how about it?"

Stanley bowed his head, once again a little Jew-boy from Walton Avenue, the Bronx. Kirby put the envelope in his pocket, walked to the door, and waited. As soon as Stanley came within reach, he put his hand on his shoulder.

"Once all this blows over, I'm going to ask Ed Hartnett to find a place for you at Harland Hospital. I may be 'half-a-shoe

Kirby, the heel without a soul,' but you will have to admit I have a heart."

Stanley opened the door and walked out without uttering a word.

"Don't forget to send Bill Tuck a check for five hundred and thirty dollars," Kirby called after him. "And please mail me your resignation tonight."

The moment Stanley reached his office, he began to pace up and down the hall waiting in vain for Jim's door to open. The patient inside, a medical Sheherazade, had thought up a thousand and one complaints. Unfortunately, unlike the sultan's beautiful slave, she wanted to tell them to her listener all in one night. When at last she emerged, purged of a few, Stanley slipped past her, and without bothering to close the door, sank into the easy chair in front of the desk.

"I have a little story for you," he said to his friend. "It's called 'The Tale of Two Golfers,' or 'He Who Gets Screwed.'" Then he poured out his heart.

When he was through, Jim put his hands on top of the desk and began to flex and extend his fingers the way he used to do before going into the ring. After a long silence, he looked up. "Don't worry, Stan. The game is young."

"Sure, sure! With three weeks left and me thumbed out of the ball park."

"You'll be back." Jim got up, picked up his hat, and went home.

The moment he entered the living room, Louise said patiently, "I see it's scotch on the rocks again."

He settled himself comfortably in his favorite chair and replied, "No, this time it's the cup of blood." He recited Stanley's story quite calmly, but it was obvious that he was enraged.

"Poor Stan!" Louise said. "He's pathetic! A kitten in a den of rats! Jim, why don't you give it to Kirby and his miserable trustees! The way you did to that Nazi PW in the 812th." She smiled. "I'd love to see you do something that my father couldn't do." She thought for a moment. "I'm surprised they didn't try blackmail on you."

"They tried bribery instead. Kirby offered me the directorship of surgery at Harland if I would keep my mouth shut. I hadn't reached a decision, as a matter of fact, until tonight."

They looked into each other's eyes. "I'll have to get the Alumni Association to reverse that vote," he said.

"But not with any more of those speeches. Please!"

"No, it's going to be person to person after this."

Gillette dropped in at nine o'clock, more for the Irish coffee than for anything else, he insisted.

"Jim," he said after the first sip, "I'm completely briefed on what happened to Stanley. When Louise lived with me, she was an expert at tying up the phone, everyone's phone. She hasn't changed a bit since then. May I ask you this? Of the five hundred and twenty-six doctors on the Alumni Association roster, how many have their offices in the suburbs?"

"Oh, I should say at least two hundred."

"That's going to make it difficult, because you're going to have to visit them, too. As well as the ones in Manhattan."

"Yes, I've already accepted that."

"You won't be offended if I make a suggestion, will you? When you talk to these men, hammer home just three points: One, it's a damn shame to see McKinley disappear. Two, they really owe something to the old place. Three, it won't cost them a penny to vote to keep it here. They are not financially responsible for the Hospital. If they start to argue, tell them the trustees are trying to railroad the merger through. You're just stalling for time."

"You won't like doing this, dear," Louise broke in. "The Knights of the Round Table never had to do any door-to-door selling. It's quite a comedown, I know, from King Arthur's Galahad to McKinley's Fuller brush man."

"We'll be glad to send out the notices from the Wall Street

office," said Gillette. "We'll map out your itinerary and make the appointments for you, too."

"I can't impose on you like that," Jim protested.

Gillette laughed. "Last week a friend of mine asked me how many people worked at Gillette and Company. I answered, 'About half.' This will give the other half something to do."

"Thanks. How about publicity for the meeting?"

"I assure you that there will be a reporter from every newspaper in New York at your meeting. And, by the way, why don't you make it at night, so that more of the doctors can come? As far as the trustees are concerned, you've got three votes already: Klaus Martin's, Hagenbeck's, and mine. All you need are four more."

He stood up quickly, went to the foyer, and put on his topcoat. "Good luck, Jim. Long ago Charles Huegenon gave me some advice: 'Be nice to people, but never let them forget that you can be a bastard.' I'm passing it on to you."

He kissed Louise on the top of her head and walked to the little elevator.

The Morelles stayed in the living room until one o'clock. With the Alumni Association roster spread before them, they worked out an itinerary for the weekend that Jim planned to spend in southern Westchester. In addition, he telephoned Mrs. Westover to cancel all elective operations for the next two weeks and tell Kirby's secretary the first thing Monday that he was not interested in becoming Director of Surgery at Harland. Last of all, he arranged for a young surgeon to temporarily take over his practice.

The next morning was cold and pitiless. At the door, Louise said to him, "You've got that look again. Jim, when you talk to these men, don't be a poet. Be a traveling salesman, or a ward heeler, or the man in the smoke-filled room. And afterward, when you come up against the trustees, don't invite them to joust with you in the great tournament at Camelot. Just clobber them."

She kissed him on the lips and closed the door.

The next ten days were trying. During the first few interviews he felt like a detail man from a drug company. A doctor in Mamaroneck kept him waiting an hour. The secretary of another, this one in Larchmont, had him come back three times. Several refused to see him at all. But he quickly learned how to maneuver. He instructed the people at Gillette's not to remain anonymous over the telephone any more. Soon they were announcing, "This is Gillette and Company calling for Dr. Morelle." And they made it quite clear that there would be no solicitation of funds. After this, there were no more refusals. He mastered the art of name-dropping. When it was all over, he told Louise that if there was an epidemic of sacroiliac disease among the doctors in the suburbs, it would be the result of their efforts to pick up the glittering names he had dropped during his tour.

Most important of all, he realized that the soft sell was the smart sell. He neither extolled McKinley's past nor castigated the trustees for betraying her future. Instead, he mentioned Gillette's three points in a diffident sort of way. To his amazement, he found that almost everyone agreed with him. But the doctors were stale from overwork. At night they wanted either rest or amusement. It was not going to be easy to make them leave their comfortable homes to go to a meeting at the Hospital.

He shifted his attack. There would be a crowd of over four hundred, he promised them, old friends they had not seen in years, important men they would want to talk to, people from all over the country. If they voted to cut off debate, the business meeting would be finished in five minutes. Then there was going to be one hell of a shindig. Enough liquor to sink a battleship. And entertainment, too.

Casting his thoughts back over his practice, he remembered a bull fiddler years before who had recovered so rapidly from an appendectomy that he had rejoined his jazz sextette in two weeks. With the bull fiddler in mind, he promised the doctors he visited one of the hottest combos in town. He also recalled the patient the man had sent him, a stripper with an amazing figure, who had been very grateful to him for removing a polyp from her rectum. So grateful had she been, in fact, that he felt sure she would cancel any engagement to strip for the doctors after the Alumni Meeting in Halberstadt Hall. Of course, he did not know how seductive she would appear to such a sophisticated audience, but at least her scar would not show. It was a good six inches up her rectum. He promised them a stripper. And a good comedian, too. Mrs. Westover cross-indexed all his patients under "occupation." Somewhere in the past he must have operated on a comedian. "Yes, sir," he always added before he left, "the old McKinley greats will roll in their graves that night—in time to the music, I hope." He felt cheap after that, but they laughed.

In the end he realized that of the ten days devoted to gentle persuasion, he had spent the last six away from home. When he returned Tuesday to preside over the meeting that night, he felt like a publicity man for a traveling burlesque show. But he had visited two hundred and fifty-six doctors, spoken to eighty more on the telephone, and had two hundred and seventy votes in his pocket.

The ten days that had shaken his turn-of-the-century world were not yet behind him. But, successful as he had been in fishing for votes in city and suburban waters, his greatest catch, he felt, had been made with the long-distance lines. John Despard of New Orleans and Harry Shapiro of San Francisco had both promised to come to New York. Both had served on the house staff a few years after him. Despard was reputed to be the biggest intern, both longitudinally and horizontally, ever to train at McKinley. But he was no slob, the boys soon discovered. So well cut were his suits, even his made-to-order uniforms, that he looked exactly what he was, every inch—and there were many of them—the southern gentleman. No more impressive man could have been chosen to present the motion condemning the merger. That Shapiro should have agreed to come all the way from the West Coast was not surprising. During their intern days the huge Louisiana aristocrat and the little Bronx Jew had been inseparable. Evidently each had qualities the other admired and lacked. Their appearance together had certainly been startling. They were referred to everywhere as the minnow and the whale. But Shapiro did not need size to make him formidable. His piercing high-pitched voice was enough. He had been nicknamed "Soprano" Shapiro, and no one had ever been known to shout him down. No better man could have been chosen to present the motion to cut off debate.

When Jim entered Halberstadt Hall at twenty-five minutes after eight, there were over four hundred men in the audience. Not only was every seat taken, but doctors were standing in back and leaning against the walls on the sides. Many were waving and shouting at friends they could not reach. The long table was buried under liquor bottles, untouched only because of the vigilance of the five bartenders. Jim noticed that not a trustee was present. It would have been surprising if any had come. The notices had pointedly stated that only doctors were invited. As if to make up for their absence, Aims and the other nine directors walked in together at half past eight. They had to stand on the side. Jim ignored them. After waiting a few minutes, he called the meeting to order.

An enormous man rose at once from the back of the audience and asked, "May I have the floor, Mr. Chairman?"

Eighteenth-century eloquence is out, Jim said to himself. It doesn't work any more. He took a deep breath and announced, "Gentlemen, the fattest man ever to graduate from McKinley, and the most elegant. All the way from New Orleans—Jack Despard! How about a big hand!"

There was a good deal of applause, followed by a good deal of talking.

"I'd like to make a motion," Despard began in a nice southern drawl.

The talking stopped at once.

He bowed, took a piece of paper out of his pocket and read, "We, the members of the Alumni Association, condemn the attempt to merge McKinley Hospital with Brookeville General and exhort the trustees to keep our Hospital" (the "our" sounded like "ah") "right where it is." He folded the paper and put it back in his pocket. "It doesn't sound very legal, suh, but, believe me, it's from the heart." He sat down at once.

Jim put his hands on the little table in front of him and leaned forward. The silence was now absolute. The next moment would decide everything, he said to himself. "Do I hear a second to the motion?"

Nothing happened. Suddenly a tremendous roar went up from the audience. He leaned back.

"The motion is now open for discussion."

A little man next to Despard stood up. Jim nodded. Farewell to Burke and Demosthenes! Now was the time for all good vaudevillians to come to the aid of their country! He pointed to the back of the room.

"All the way from San Francisco, 'Soprano' Shapiro, the man with the world's highest voice. But he's got five children back home, and every one looks like him. Do I hear a hand for the 'Soprano'?"

Shapiro got a good one. He bowed and said, "I didn't come all the way from California to perform. I came to make a motion."

The audience smiled, not at what he had said, but at his absurd voice.

"I move that all discussion be closed," he cried out as loud as he could, using his upper register.

From everywhere came shouts seconding the motion.

Jim glanced at the side door near him and nodded. The combo entered. The saxophonist and the clarinetist each carried a folding chair as well as an instrument. The pianist, sweat pouring down his face, pushed a miniature piano into the room. A giant Negro just behind him bowed and lifted a contrabass with one hand. In a minute the drummer staggered in, dragging his paraphernalia. He was champing ostentatiously and making a splendid effort to appear under the influence of drugs. Mrs. Westover had not let him down, Jim was forced to admit. The boys certainly *looked* good. The drummer went out for more folding chairs, and when he came back, everyone sat down behind Jim.

He nodded toward the side door a second time. The stripper walked in slowly and sat down next to the band. The effect was electrifying. Perhaps she was a little top-heavy, but her figure was still superb. She was fiddling with her dress, and no one could figure out whether she was buttoning or unbuttoning it. When Aims Blair took the floor, nobody paid any attention to him.

"May I have your attention!" he cried irritably. "This isn't a meeting. It's a circus. Since we are not in Russia, I have a right to be heard, and so has everyone else in this room."

"There is a motion on the floor, a motion to shut off debate," Jim reminded him.

"There are two motions on the floor."

"Yes. But the motion to shut off debate takes precedence. I would ask you to sit down, Aims, but there is no place to sit."

Jim rapped for order. "All those in favor of cutting off debate, please raise their hands."

A forest of arms appeared before him. After the hands were lowered, he said, "Opposed."

He did not bother to count. There were fewer than thirty.

When the shuffling stopped, he stood up and placed his hands on the table. "Then we will vote on the first motion, a motion condemning the proposed merger with Brookeville

General Hospital, and exhorting the trustees to keep McKinley where it is. All those in favor, please rise."

Almost four hundred stood up. Nobody knew why, but the orchestra and the stripper stood up, too.

"Opposed," he stated, after everyone had sat down.

This time he counted. There were twenty-eight on their feet.

"The motion is carried. There will be a half-hour intermission while we liquor up. Then the entertainment will begin."

The audience applauded and slowly moved toward the rear. Jim walked through, backslapping and shaking hands. At last he reached Despard.

"Thanks for starting the steamroller."

"If the people of New York ever get around to building a new McKinley, Jim, maybe they'll remember that we laid the first brick here tonight."

Most of the doctors had just come through a backbreaking winter. During the first hour and a half they finished one hundred and six bottles of liquor. And they applauded the entertainers enthusiastically. Especially the stripper.

When Jim got home, he found Louise sitting on top of the bed in a short nightgown reading the *Saturday Review of Literature*. She put down the magazine immediately, not, he noticed, on her lap, but on the end table. He knew that meant she was in the mood.

She smiled. "How did it go?"

He made a circle with his thumb and forefinger, and began to take off his clothes. "I'll tell you after."

Later, as they lay side by side in the darkness, he told her about the meeting. Then he said, "Tomorrow morning I'd like you to set up an appointment for me with Mr. Huegenon."

"With Uncle Ty? Why don't you ring him up yourself?"

"Because I want to see him tomorrow, and you're the only one who can get me an appointment on such short notice. The trustees meet a week from Friday."

"All right, dear."

"And I'd like you to fly to Philadelphia," he went on, "as early as you can, to see Scudder Devine's sister. You're still friends, aren't you? Get me every scrap of information you can about him and his father. And write it all down."

"But she hates Scud. She never sees him. And she didn't think much of her father, either."

"I know that. I'm counting on it. I'm after anything in their lives that might damage or compromise them. If it's scurrilous, so much the better."

She turned on the lamp, raised herself on her elbows, and looked down at his face. "You're getting to be quite the wheeler-dealer."

"Business is bad in Camelot. They haven't held any tournaments lately."

The next morning there was an account of the impending merger, and the doctors' reaction to it, on the front pages of the *Times* and the *Tribune*. The stories were remarkably similar. They contained a short history of McKinley and sketches of Emmerich, Rintman, and Hauser, followed by the total number of patients treated, babies born, and operations performed in the Hospital since its founding over a hundred years before. There was a brief statement from Kirby on the reasons for the merger—the hopeless financial picture, the migration of former patients and their families to the suburbs, and the generosity of a sister institution in offering the Hospital a new home. The evening papers gave the story greater coverage. On the first page of the *World Telegram* was a picture of McKinley with its flag at half mast (evidently taken shortly after the death of Franklin D. Roosevelt). The caption read, "Old Glory."

The reporting was all factual, Jim noticed with considerable sadness. Nowhere, he was disappointed to find, was there a condemnation of the move or a call to the people of the city to rise up and preserve the Hospital. This was the stuff of which editorials were made, he supposed. And there were no editorials. The doctors' vote was regarded as a sign of loyalty, quite appropriate under the circumstances, the move unfortunately inevitable, and the union with Brookeville General a stroke of good fortune.

Of all the columnists, Tuck alone mentioned what he called the "goings on" at McKinley. He urged the big New York hospitals to open branches in the suburbs the way Macy's and the other department stores were doing.

TWENTY-SEVEN

JIM found it hard to concentrate on the newspapers, so absorbed was he in his coming appointment with Huegenon, which Louise had arranged for six-thirty that very evening. When he entered the glass-dome atrium of the great house on Fifth Avenue, it was as if nothing had changed since the day of Albert's funeral, twenty years before. The financier was sitting on a stone bench by the pool in the same position as then, one hand on his knee, his eyes fixed on the shallow water. When he looked up, they held a hint of that coldness that, Jim supposed, must be common to all men who wield enormous power.

Huegenon had him sit down beside him, asked a few questions about Louise and the children, and then nodded to him to begin.

"McKinley is in trouble. I need your help," said Jim, "your financial help."

"I read the newspapers, Jim. But I never give to hospitals."

"This would be a very small donation, only a half million dollars. And it might not even be accepted."

"What could you hope to accomplish with a half million dollars?" asked Huegenon skeptically.

"I want to use it for bait. According to the by-laws of the Hospital, seven trustees can block a move or a merger. We've got three who are committed to keeping McKinley where it is. I'd like you to give the money on condition that the Hospital does not move for at least three years. There must be four trustees who would be tempted."

Huegenon gave a cynical laugh. "No one would be tempted."

"Then, you would still have your money," answered Jim, "plus your unblemished record of never having contributed to a hospital."

The financier frowned. "You, of all people, should know why I haven't."

He took out the same thin solid-gold case that had once fascinated Jim and tapped a cigarette on its mirrorlike surface. "What would you do at the end of three years?"

"Mr. Huegenon, until recently a child with leukemia had about two months to live. Now, by using three new drugs one after another, because each in turn soon becomes ineffective, a pediatrician can keep it alive for as long as three years. To help a child of four live until seven may not seem like much. But pediatricians struggle to do just that, not only because every day in a child's life is precious, but because they hope that before the last of the three drugs becomes ineffective a cure for leukemia may be discovered. It hasn't happened yet, but someday it will. Perhaps before three years are over, something will happen to save McKinley."

Huegenon lit his cigarette, inhaled, and stared at the water.

"There are some things that were not in the papers," Jim continued. He described his vote-getting trip. Huegenon was amused. Then Jim told him how Stanley had been trapped.

The financier's mouth tightened. There was a long pause.

Then he said, very softly, "Uncalled for! He will have to be reinstated, of course." But his words had the force of a royal decree. He looked at his guest. "Does he play much tennis now?"

Jim shook his head.

Huegenon turned toward the pool. "Albert used to be exasperated with his game. 'Nerve, serve, and verve' was the way he described it. But all that changed when we took Stanley in hand, didn't it? He could have gone on to Forest Hills after he won the Intercollegiates."

"Half of that cup belonged to Albert. He did a lot for Stan."

"And Stanley did a lot for him. So did you, Jim, so did you. I've never forgotten how you two bearded the Dean at P and S. It has always been a comfort for me to know that my boy would have been admitted to medical school if he had lived."

A butler suddenly stood at his side. The genie of the ash tray, Jim imagined. Huegenon stubbed out his cigarette and the butler disappeared. There was a long silence.

"Is there anything new for malignant melanoma, Jim?" the financier asked at last.

"Nothing that would have saved Albert. But today a surgeon excises all the lymph nodes that drain a melanoma as well as the melanoma itself. If he finds at the operating table that the nodes are not involved, the patient has a 50 per cent chance of making a complete recovery. Even if the microscopic examination later reveals that the melanoma has spread to the lymph nodes, the patient still has a 50 per cent chance of recovering completely."

Huegenon looked up sharply. "That's a great deal, Jim, a great deal."

He turned back toward the pool and thought for a moment. "All right," he said finally, "tomorrow morning a half million dollars will be deposited at the Chase National Bank. At the same time, your Board will be notified that the money has been contributed by an anonymous donor to help defray the running expenses of the Hospital. Acceptance of the money will indicate acceptance of two stipulations: One, that neither a merger nor a relocation will be initiated for at least three years. Two, that Dr. Stanley Levinson will be reinstated at once." He looked Jim in the eye. "It is understood that you will not disclose my name. I don't want to be bothered by the American Hospital Association. It must have a few thousand hungry members on its list."

He brushed aside Jim's thanks and escorted him to the entrance hall himself. Then he walked briskly to his favorite room just off the atrium and sat down at his desk directly under the picture of St. Jerome by El Greco. He looked back at the picture once, and rang for his secretary. The man opened a stenographer's notebook as soon as he entered, but Huegenon shook his head.

"Twenty years ago," he said, "just before my son died, I asked you for a résumé on the customs of the Jews. The résumé was satisfactory, the punctuation was not. I want you to have another résumé made, this time on everything that is known about McKinley Hospital, starting with the day it opened. Put as many people to work on it as you like. In nine days the trustees are holding a meeting that I am interested in. I want the report on this desk in seven." He took out another cigarette. "You must have learned something about punctuation in twenty years."

The secretary smiled. He knew that Huegenon had provided very generously for him in his will.

It took Jim less than five minutes to walk home. He found Louise on the couch in the living room, a thin manuscript in her hand. Lewis Gillette's private secretary was at the desk near the window putting the cover on her portable typewriter. As soon as she left, Louise jumped up and asked, "What did Uncle Ty say?"

Jim smiled, but shook his head.

"Then I shouldn't tell you anything about my talk with

Lydia in Philadelphia," she said as they sat down on the couch, "but I will."

"Did you fly both ways?"

"Yes." She glanced through a few pages. "I didn't get anything very shocking from Lydia. Scud played with dolls until he was four. Wet the bed until he was five. He managed to get by at Browning, no one knows how. One night after reading his report card, the Bishop chipped off a piece of his front tooth with a backhand swipe. Usually he was more methodical in his punishments. He would make Scud take down his pants and drawers in front of Lydia, lay him across his knee, and spank him—Stanley would love this—with a Jewish prayer book presented to the Devines by a rabbi during interfaith week." She turned a few pages. "Scud flunked out of Groton. It took three tutors to get him through Columbia. There was a little difficulty with the Dean about cheating during a chemistry exam, but Scud always denied that he had. After graduation he worked for a brokerage house, but they dropped him in six months. Then, in quick succession, came a private banking firm I've never heard of and a real estate company I have. Both let him go within a year. He's never been able to earn a living, and what's worse, his wife doesn't seem to mind."

She read through a paragraph quickly. "The old man used to practice his sermons in a T-shirt and shorts before a mirror. He was impotent during the last twenty years of his life, but continued to pinch the maids' behinds just the same. Mrs. Devine used to call him the Red Bishop, not because he had Communist sympathies but because of the color he turned when she reminded him of his marital inadequacies and his extramarital excesses. I think what embarrassed him most was the fact that his excesses were confined to pinching."

She arranged the typewritten sheets so that none of the edges protruded. "It's all like this. Nothing very horrifying. Just dirt under the laquered fingernails. What is really sad is that the Bishop was such a towering success and Scud such an abysmal failure."

She handed him the manuscript and went upstairs to dress for dinner. In fifteen minutes he joined her.

"Can you use any of it?" she asked.

"I can use all of it. It's just what I wanted."

When Jim got to his consultation room at eight Thursday morning, he found a memorandum from Mrs. Westover stating that the appointment he had asked her to set up with Mr. Shore was scheduled for two o'clock that very afternoon, in the trustee's Wall Street office. Stacked neatly on his desk were six charts, each with the words "Occupation: Writer" typed on the bottom of the manila folder. Mrs. Westover's cross-indexing system, Jim reflected, was paying off again. Since he was doing only emergency surgery and postoperative work, he had plenty of time to read the charts, and in the case of the four patients who were listed in Who's Who, the articles about them, as well. After carefully considering the six, he decided upon John Riding as most suitable to his ends, because he had written a series of "Profiles" for *The New Yorker,* possessed a distinctive style, and had never forgotten that bitter New Year's Eve when, down and out and moaning with the pain of a ruptured gastric ulcer, he had won back his life under Jim's hands on an operating table in McKinley Hospital. When Mrs. Westover knocked on the surgeon's door promptly at nine o'clock, he asked her if she thought she could persuade Riding to come to the office quite late in the afternoon to allow plenty of time for the trip back from Wall Street.

The meeting with Shore started well. The old trustee seemed determined to recapture his youth by embracing the McKinley of thirty years before. He talked of Emmerich and Rintman, of single interns and unmarried nurses, of the pride that came from being known as "Shore of McKinley," and of sitting at the right hand of August Grund like the Son of God. Jim guessed that an uneasy conscience was catalyzing his memory.

397

"I'm either rude or senile," said Shore suddenly, "the former, I hope. I forgot to ask you why you came."

Jim waited until Shore had swallowed a little pill he had just taken out of a silver case. "Mr. Shore, someone once said that the cleverest wile of Satan is to convince people that he does not exist. Kirby and Aims Blair have borrowed the idea, improved on it, and applied it to a great institution. They are trying to convince people that McKinley *never* existed. I'm glad to hear that you were not taken in."

"Of course I wasn't. Belittling the past merely impoverishes the present."

"Mr. Shore, I came to ask you to change your vote. The doctors have just changed theirs. They voted fifteen to one to keep the Hospital where it is. That ought to impress you."

"It certainly does."

"I think Kirby is getting desperate. Here is how he treated Dr. Levinson." When he finished the story of Stanley's entrapment, he gave Shore a hard look. "That ought to impress you, too."

"I'm appalled."

"I'm saving the most impressive piece of information for the last. It's the name of the anonymous donor. Since I am not supposed to reveal it, I'll have to ask you to keep it a secret."

Shore smiled. "I will be more honorable than you, Doctor."

"It's Charles Huegenon."

Shore stopped smiling at once. "Well, well! And Kirby called the money chicken feed."

"It is. If I can find seven trustees with courage enough to reject the merger, I'm going to Mr. Huegenon again. And this time I'll ask him for something big, for a medical center on Park Avenue in the very heart of New York—for a new McKinley on the site of the old, for a medical school and a group of laboratories dedicated to research."

Shore digested this information. "My boy, have you any idea

398

how much such a venture would cost? At least a hundred million dollars."

"Don't you think Mr. Huegenon has it?"

"Of course he has it. He has four or five times that much. He's one of the wealthiest men in the country. But do *you* have it? Do you have a commitment from him, or a promise, or even a sign that he might be interested in such a grandiose scheme?"

"No. But I would rather fail trying to get a hundred million dollars to save McKinley than succeed in pirating five million dollars by wrecking her. In that speech of yours, you pleaded with us to go down with flags flying. Which flag, Mr. Shore, the skull and crossbones?"

He waved aside the cigarette that Shore offered him. People had a way of trying to divert you just as you were approaching a climax. "My friend, Stanley Levinson, often quotes a saying from the Hebrew. It is 'Shaar yashaav,' 'The remnant will save.' There isn't much of a remnant left at the Hospital, just Stan and myself and a few old McKinleyites and Mr. Hagenbeck and Mr. Klaus Martin and Lewis Gillette, in spirit, at least—and you. But the remnant *must* save. And if you will only join us, Mr. Shore, the remnant *will* save."

Shore stood up behind the desk and smiled. "Morelle, you should have been an insurance salesman. Certainly you have my vote!"

Jim thought of everything he had once wanted to be—Launcelot at Camelot, Kitchener at Khartoum, Chinese Gordon leading his irregulars with a little bamboo cane, Matty coming in with his fadeaway when the count was three and two, Ty Cobb stealing home with a hook slide under a high throw, Siegfried slaying Fafnir with Nothung the incomparable sword, Emmerich at the operating table. Somehow, he had never thought of being an insurance salesman. He took Shore's hand and shook it warmly.

Without rushing, he was able to see two postoperative

patients at the Hospital and still get to his office ten minutes before his appointment with Riding. He found a big change in the writer since he had operated on him that New Year's Eve three years before. Riding had put on twenty-five pounds, an expensive suit, and a serene expression which, considering the psychogenic component of his gastric ulcer, Jim could only hope reflected a serenity within. Since he knew that the "Profile" expert read all the newspapers completely and methodically, he wasted no time in describing McKinley's plight. Instead, he explained that seven of the twenty trustees could defeat the attempt to move the Hospital to Brookeville simply by failing to show up at the meeting a week from the following night. Already, four had promised that they would oppose the merger. All he needed were three more. He was going to tackle Scudder Devine next.

Riding laughed. "That parasite! He's worse than a tapeworm. At least a tapeworm doesn't talk."

"I know. His life is devoted to sponging on his wife and cashing in on his father's name." He rose from behind the desk, the manuscript in his hand, and walked up to Riding. "Why don't you write a series of 'Profiles' for *The New Yorker* called 'Fathers and Sons'? It would be about sons who never measured up." He handed him the manuscript. "Here is the material for the first."

He went to one of the examining rooms and dressed an appendectomy wound. When he came back fifteen minutes later, he found Rider looking grave.

"I'm very grateful for your having saved my life, Doctor," he said, tapping the manuscript against his palm, "but I can't write this. It's libelous, and *The New Yorker* would never publish it."

"Who said anything about publishing it?" Jim exclaimed. "I want to use it to blackmail Devine. I'm asking three things of you. One, write this 'Profile' in your own distinctive style, the famous 'high-Riding' style. You don't have to sign it. Two, put the article in an envelope that has your name and address printed in front. Three, get it to me by noon Monday. I realize it's going to be a lot of work."

"It's not the work, it's the anxiety," said Riding, who had just started his analysis. "You're sure you won't send the article to *The New Yorker?*"

"A week from tomorrow night I'll destroy it. I'll even burn it and send the ashes to you."

Rider smiled. "All right. And I've never missed a deadline yet."

As soon as he left, Mrs. Westover telephoned Scudder Devine, who agreed to come to the office Monday afternoon, but only after he had consulted his wife's appointment book. Next the secretary rang up Emil Grund. When she asked him if he could drop in the following morning, he replied that she had only to set the hour.

Grund looked almost three-dimensional as he walked into the consultation room Friday morning, shook hands warmly with Jim, and sat down.

"I suppose I'm here because of the bill," he said with a smile. Jim nodded and smiled back.

Grund took out two long, blank checks folded on each other, tore off one, and said, "Don't spare the horses, Doctor."

"Oh, there is no money involved. This is strictly a quid-pro-quo deal. A life for a life. McKinley's life for your son's."

Grund seemed stunned.

"You saw what happened to him at Brookeville General," continued Jim, "you saw what was done for him at McKinley. If he ever gets sick again, where would you want him treated? Do you think five million dollars will make a McKinley out of a Brookeville? Do you think money can buy the hundred-year-old tradition, the accomplishments, the men? You may feel you will be dealing your father a second death blow by helping to destroy the Hospital he served for thirty years, but you will be destroying only yourself. And not like Sampson, either.

When you pull down McKinley, you'll be buried in self-contempt. I don't see how you will ever be able to look your son in the eye again if you join Kirby and his band of nonentities. Why don't you build yourself up instead of trying to tear your father down, and by copying his good qualities, excel him? He saved McKinley in his day; you will have a chance to save it in yours. I'm not asking you to vote against the merger. I only want you to keep away from the meeting Friday night."

Grund put the two checks in his pocket. His color came back. "Doctor, I pay my bills just as promptly as my father did. I'll be at the meeting a week from tonight, and I'll vote to save McKinley just as he would have done."

After he had gone, Jim wanted to raise his hand and shout, "Two!" like the Count of Monte Cristo. But whereas the counting Count had had plenty of time to get the three people on his list, Jim had only a week left to get two.

Over the weekend he set about to complete his task. He visited eight trustees, persuaded none. With one exception they all reacted identically. Perhaps, he conjectured, they had been coached by Kirby. They listened politely, refused to be drawn into an argument about the merits of the merger, and stated flatly that they were already committed. They could not go back on their word. The exception was young Krant. Obviously disturbed and on the verge of becoming abusive, he shouted at Jim and accused him of being a troublemaker.

At ten minutes to twelve Monday morning, Riding handed his "Profile" of the two Devines to Mrs. Westover. At two, Scudder Devine walked into the consultation room as if he were ascending the pulpit, his touched-up black hair going nicely with a face that had just been massaged back to a temporary youth at his wife's beauty salon. She was very generous about anything that concerned his appearance. He sat down, already relaxed before his plump buttocks touched the chair, discussed the weather from the meteorologist's point of view, and finally asked Jim how he could help him.

"You might be able to help me out of an embarrassing situation," Jim began hesitantly. "I have a grateful patient who is convinced I saved his life once. His name is John Riding. You may have heard of him."

"Of course, I've heard of him," said Devine, using the "M" sound to achieve a fine sonority. "He's had a series of 'Profiles' in *The New Yorker*. Quite a remarkable style there."

"He is starting a new series of 'Profiles' called 'Fathers and Sons.' It's about famous fathers," here Jim looked discreetly at his hands, "and sons who never made the grade. The first article is about the Bishop and you."

He glanced up suddenly and saw that Devine had turned pale. "Riding knows how I feel about McKinley. That's why he showed me the manuscript before sending it in. It's scurrilous, but it's clever, too."

He handed a long white envelope to Devine, who carefully examined the name and address in the upper-left-hand corner, and then ran his fingers absent-mindedly over the lettering to see if it was raised. In an effort to appear unconcerned he lit a cigarette before opening the envelope and flipping back the beautifully typed pages. Suddenly he turned red.

"I hope your patient is proud of this!" he exclaimed bitterly. Then he read out loud, "'Mrs. Devine once told a friend, 'My sex life has always left much to be desired. The Bishop was never the man to soil the sheets.'"

He put the manuscript on the desk for a moment. "Do you mean to tell me that any reputable magazine will print that?"

"No. I'm sure it will be blue-penciled. So will a dozen other sentences. But a week after the 'Profile' is published, people will be saying that the stuff that was taken out was better than the stuff that was left in. And quoting it all over town, too."

Devine was puffing so rapidly on his cigarette that he began to cough.

Jim went to the window, opened it wide, and came back to his seat behind the desk.

"I'm sure I could stop Riding from sending in the 'Profile,'" he said with assurance. "All I would have to do is remind him that once I saved his life. He certainly owes me something. But, of course, that would be unethical."

He pushed an ash tray toward Devine, who stubbed out his cigarette and stopped coughing at once. Jim closed the window and returned to his chair.

"I would do it, though, if I felt it would save the Hospital." He paused while he observed Devine narrowly. "Mr. Devine, vote against the merger a week from tonight and the manuscript will never leave this desk."

He added that he would be with a patient for the next fifteen minutes, and walked out. When he returned, he found Devine staring at the article as if it were his own obituary.

"Well, Mr. Devine, do I have your vote?" he asked pleasantly.

"I am afraid you do. I was not brought up to deal with blackmail."

"Where is the blackmail?"

"Where, indeed!" replied Devine, shaking his head sadly.

Jim leaned across the desk, took the manuscript out of Devine's hand, and put it in the top drawer. "May I remind you that I am getting nothing out of this? But, because you are so bitter, I will give up one of my demands. You don't have to go to the meeting and vote against the merger. All you have to do is stay away."

He stood up and escorted Devine to the lobby. "Take a night off from work," he advised with a straight face. "Go to a concert." He smiled broadly and closed the door.

Three down and one to go, he said to himself. Suddenly he stopped smiling.

TWENTY-EIGHT

WHERE WOULD he find the seventh trustee? That was the stumbling block. The time had come for him to do some elementary arithmetic, he decided. He sat down at his desk, took out a pen, and began to write on a prescription pad. Of the twenty trustees, six were committed not to vote for the merger: old Klaus Martin, old Hagenbeck, Lewis Gillette, Shore, Grund, and Devine. Over the weekend he had approached all but five of the rest—unsuccessfully. It was obvious that he would have to get the crucial vote from one of the remaining five.

By the next night, Tuesday, he was forced to admit that his quest was hopeless. Three of the five trustees had refused to see him or even discuss the situation over the telephone. Reluctantly he had rung up each of the three a second time. Two of them had cut him short. The third had hung up while he was still talking. The final two were more cordial. One let him come to his office. The other met him at the Racquet Club. Both explained patiently that they were already pledged to vote for the merger. As long as such a pledge absolved them from spending money, Jim reflected, they would hold to it as stubbornly as his father would have held to his word of honor.

Tuesday night, after he returned from the Racquet Club, he said to himself, "The game is young." But he knew that the game was practically over. What else could he do to block the merger? Kidnap a trustee? Break one up the way he had broken up the Nazi PW who was about to shoot Louise and Toski, the mobster with the shattered hand? He knew only too well that he could no more lay a finger on any of the fourteen honorable men who were committed to the murder of the Hospital than he could send them to the electric chair.

Most of the fourteen did not return his dislike. Only one, Cornelius Krant, bore him any personal animosity. However, this was an animosity so intense that its possessor would have rejoiced if the surgeon could have been sentenced to be buried alive under the ruins of McKinley. The reason for this hatred was understandable. Young Krant regarded Jim as standing between him and the merger. And the merger had become the breath of life, the breath of his new life.

Long regarded by his father, a wealthy builder, as the gray sheep of the family, he had been forced to submit to periodic inspections of his pelt to see if any of the hairs had turned black. So far, none had. Irresponsible, erratic, and unpredictable though young Krant may have been, he had not yet done anything to disgrace his name. Nothing, that is, except fail in every venture he had undertaken. When Kirby offered him a trusteeship, his father had smiled. It might be a good thing for the boy, he reasoned. It might well keep him out of trouble. Old Krant's philosophy of wealth was that it was like a stockpile of atomic bombs. Security and power lay in the hoarding. To his son he said, "Be a philanthropist if you want. But remember not to spend any money."

For the first time in his life young Krant was a success. He attended every Board meeting, worked hard on his committee assignments, drew up comprehensive and accurate reports, mastered the financial details of the running of the Hospital, and became something of an expert on Blue Cross. He did all this not because he loved McKinley, but because he loved the job. When, in the beginning, Kirby told him that the trustees expected a handsome contribution from his father, he had been thrown into a panic. Everything, his first success, his newly won self-respect, his chance to impress the family, might all be lost because his initiation fee in this most wonderful of clubs was not forthcoming. In the relocation, he saw his salvation. The five-million-dollar price on the head of the old McKinley would, when claimed and pocketed, make it unnecessary for a trustee ever to have to contribute to the new. As a resident of Brookeville he was entranced by the prospect of a lifelong trusteeship in an institution so close to his home, and one that would never call upon him for a donation. He was beginning to forget the past, take pride in the present, and savor the future, when Jim made his first attempts to block the move to Westchester. These were so ineffective that Krant at first regarded him as a harmless meddler. But, after the last meeting of the Alumni Association, he became alarmed, all the more so since he sensed that the redoubtable Chairman of the Board was alarmed, too. It was easy to guess why. The trustees of Brookeville General Hospital had informed Kirby that they were displeased at the recent publicity and would seriously consider withdrawing their offer unless the relocation was accomplished quickly and quietly.

Quite correctly, Krant saw in Jim the cause of his troubles. When he learned that one McKinley trustee after another was being asked to change his vote, he became enraged. His new career, his new life, his new personality would all be obliterated if his enemy was successful. Slipping back to the old days of strange thoughts and irresponsible behavior, he decided that he would have to discredit Jim in order to render him impotent. Soon he evolved what seemed to him the perfect plan. All he needed was some shady character, some minor underworld figure to carry it through. Suddenly he thought of just the man. He remembered that many years before, his father had used a petty mobster called "Donnie" for strong-arm jobs in the construction industry. He got one of the firm's old secretaries to call him up and ask him to come to the office as soon as he could.

At ten o'clock Wednesday morning, a middle-aged little man, with cold, unblinking eyes, arrived.

"Please sit down, Mr. Donnie," Krant said.

"No mister. It's a first name."

Krant was impressed by the bulge in the mobster's suit just in front of the left armpit. He was sure it was a holster gun. Actually, Donnie, a sufferer from chronic sinusitis, always stuffed a thick wad of tissues in his left, upper inside coat pocket before he went to work in the morning. As he used them up during the day, his appearance became less and less menacing.

"Donnie, you know I'm on the governing body of McKinley Hospital?"

"All I know is that I once did a few jobs for your father."

"Donnie, McKinley is falling to pieces. We've got a once-in-a-lifetime opportunity to sell the land and use the money to build a new hospital out in Westchester. One man stands in the way, a doctor. He's got to be neutralized. And I am going to neutralize him."

Donnie's concept of the word "neutralize" was not the same as a chemist's. He suddenly became interested.

"How you gonna do that, Mr. Krant?"

"By discrediting him. By compromising him with a woman patient. By framing him. Get it?"

Donnie sniffed.

"What's the matter?" asked Krant suspiciously. "Don't you like the idea?"

"I got a sinus condition," Donnie muttered.

"All right," Krant grunted. "I want you to get a woman over to the doctor's office tonight sometime after his nurse leaves.

Be sure he's alone. How the woman gets an appointment is your worry. As soon as she undresses for the examination she'll tear her clothes, scream that she is being raped, and run outside half dressed to rouse the neighborhood. At the station house she'll charge that the doctor took advantage of her. A few days later she can drop the charges. I just want a little newspaper publicity before the trustees meet Friday night."

"Can this guy be for real?" Donnie asked himself. "He must be some kind of a kook." Out loud he said, "You sure you want to push this, Mr. Krant?"

"Certainly."

"It's no skin off my teeth," Donnie decided. "A buck is a buck."

He thought things over for a moment, and then announced quietly, "Mr. Krant, it will cost you a thousand."

"A thousand!" echoed Krant. "That's pretty high, isn't it?"

Donnie shrugged. "Inflation, labor costs; you know how it is."

Krant frowned. If you wanted to be a trustee of a hospital, you had to be prepared to spend some money once in a while, he supposed. "How do you want it, in small bills?"

"Any way, as long as it's a thousand. You can even mark it," Donnie added.

He returned at noon with a rather elegant-looking woman whom he introduced as Miss Charlotte Given. She looked so elegant, in fact, that Krant decided to lecture her on the technique of framing a doctor for rape. When he finished, she said in a high, hard voice, "It takes me back to the time I tried to shake down an old doctor—he must have been seventy if he was a day—back home, for some stuff he kept in his office. I wasn't a user. This was for a friend. I told him that unless he handed it over I'd rip my clothes and run out into the street screaming that he had raped me. I'll never forget the look in his eyes. 'Will you, Miss, will you?' he begged. 'I'll give you fifty dollars if you do!' "

Donnie laughed hoarsely.

"This is no laughing matter," said Krant severely.

He gave her Jim's name and address, and then handed her ten one-hundred-dollar bills.

During the entire interview Donnie had seemed interested only when Jim's name was mentioned. Once outside the office, he took five of the one-hundred-dollar bills from Charlotte and dismissed her. He had decided to see Toski immediately. Ordinarily, he would not have bothered a family head in Cosa Nostra over a grand. But he remembered something about Toski's hand. In this business, you did not live long if you had a poor memory.

He found Toski sitting in his beautiful office, polishing his nails one by one with an old-fashioned chamois buffer. In the dignified and elegantly dressed man behind the desk no one would have recognized the beat-up corporal who, propped up in bed on a surgical ward of the 812th General Hospital, had watched stony-eyed as Jim disarmed the crazed PW who was about to slaughter him.

"I'm sorry to bother you about a little thing like this, Mr. Toski," Donnie whined. Then he told him about Krant.

Toski went on buffing his nails. He had not asked Donnie to sit down.

"I'm glad you came," he said at last. "Let me put it another way. It would have been bad if you hadn't."

Donnie wanted to sniff but he did not dare.

"I'm obligated to the Colonel," Toski continued. "I owe him two things: This." He held up his right hand. Then he went back to his buffing. "And my life."

Donnie was afraid to move. Toski was obviously approaching the end of his labors. He was carefully working on the little finger of his left hand.

"I never liked that woman," he said, inspecting his fingers with a satisfied air. "Once, before I went into the Army, she tried to double-cross me. But we never could pin anything on her."

He put the chamois buffer in the top drawer and looked at Donnie for the first time. "Let her go ahead with this. I may want to pull something myself."

He dismissed Donnie, and rang up Jim's office at once.

"A Mr. Toski, a notorious underworld figure, wants to talk to you," said Mrs. Westover over the intercom, and her disapproval filled the consultation room.

Jim thought for a moment and then picked up the telephone.

"Colonel, this is Corporal Toski," said a smooth voice at the other end of the wire. "You don't remember me from a hole in the wall."

"How's your hand, Toski?" Jim snapped.

Toski was taken aback, but he recovered quickly. "Stronger than the other one, Colonel. Maybe that's because it's my right hand."

Jim laughed.

"I hear there's trouble at McKinley," Toski continued. "How important is a trustee called Krant?"

"To me he is very important. There's a struggle going on to save the Hospital, and he holds the deciding vote."

"Oh, he'll vote your way, Colonel," said Toski reassuringly. "This morning he made a mistake. He got hold of a little punk friend of his father's to frame you with a woman. The little punk friend came to me." He paused. "You won't have to do much, Colonel. When a Miss Charlotte Given gives your office a call to try to make a seven o'clock appointment today, see that your nurse gives it to her. At six-thirty a man will call at your office. As soon as he does, clear out. Your nurse, too. That's all."

"There's not going to be any rough stuff, is there, Toski?"

"I hate rough stuff as much as you do," answered Toski reproachfully.

"Sure, sure! Well, thanks."

"Don't say 'thanks,' Colonel. I never said 'thanks' to you. You're just making me feel cheap."

At five o'clock a Miss Charlotte Given telephoned Mrs. Westover complaining of the classical symptoms of acute appendicitis. Dr. Morelle, it seemed, had been recommended to her by one of his prominent patients who had left for Europe that very morning. Since she was in Greenwich, she couldn't possibly get to the office before seven. No, she did not want to meet the doctor at the Hospital. Hospitals terrified her. Reluctantly, Mrs. Westover agreed to have the doctor wait. Since it was her Philharmonic night, she would not be there, she regretted to say, to assist with the examination.

At six o'clock Stanley got an emergency call from a woman in Riverdale who claimed that he had been recommended to her by one of Dr. Morelle's prominent patients who had left for Europe that very morning. He took his bag and went off at once. The "patient's " address proved to be a vacant lot. Mrs. Westover left at six-fifteen.

Promptly at six-thirty the bell rang. Jim let in a big man dressed in a well-tailored, dull-gray suit, a Brooks Brothers button-down shirt, a blue-and-gray-striped Guards tie, and pebbled black English brogues. In one hand he carried a gray Cavanaugh fedora, in the other a small, brown paper bag.

He had pepper-and-salt, crew-cut hair, rugged features, a shy smile, and looked, thought Jim, like a full-time professor of surgery at a medical center. Except for the eyes, which were muddy-brown, flat, and expressionless. Jim took his own hat, also a Cavanaugh, and left. The man quickly explored the office, closing all the windows, turning on the lights, and leaving the closet doors half open. Then he sat down behind the desk in the consultation room, put the little brown paper bag to one side of the blotter, and began to drum on the arm of the chair with his fingernails.

At five minutes to seven, Charlotte Given strolled slowly

412

through Seventy-fifth Street in a simple black silk dress she had bought the year before at a Saks Fifth Avenue sale for a hundred and nine dollars. She was tall and wide-chested, with unusually narrow hips, which did not swing up and down even though she wore no girdle. Her face was quiet and dignified, but her lips, which once had been showy, were now thin and mean. For a woman of thirty-nine her legs were remarkably good, long and elegant, with only an occasional varicose vein. This she attributed to the fact that she had never had a child. Charlotte disliked doctors intensely. She had regarded her single vaginal examination as a disgusting intrusion of her privacy, the position humiliating. Her resentment had increased when the gynecologist refused to perform an abortion—not, she felt, because he disapproved of the procedure, but because he had been afraid of being caught. Luckily, she had miscarried three weeks later. When she pressed the doorbell, her thin-lipped smile was sincere.

"Dr. Morelle?" she asked the big man.

He politely ushered her in.

"What a beautiful office!" she exclaimed. She walked quickly through the hall and looked into all the rooms. When she was satisfied that no one was there, she followed him into the consultation room. He motioned her to a chair next to the desk, sat down behind it, and stared fixedly at the brown paper bag.

"Dr. Morelle, the pain has traveled from the pit of my stomach to way down on the right side," she complained softly.

When he said nothing, she stood up and slipped the black dress over her head. Although she hated the sexual act, undressing and exhibiting sometimes excited her.

"I'd better take these off, too."

She dropped her slip and her brassiere on the chair, and stood in front of him in black chiffon panties. This was the moment, she knew, when he would order her gruffly into the examining room. But instead, he just sat there motionless, staring at the

413

brown paper bag. Impatiently, she picked up her slip and ripped it.

"Doctor, don't do that!" she screamed as loud as she could. "Stop it, please stop it! Take your hands away! I don't want it!"

He looked up at last and examined her carefully. "For a middle-aged broad you got a great pair of tits," he said with deliberation.

Miss Given stopped screaming at once and stepped back from the desk.

"Who the hell are you? You're not Dr. Morelle, you bastard!" she exclaimed, and her voice was shaking.

"Did I say I was?" he answered softly.

He stood up, walked to the door, and peered up and down the hall. For the first time, she noticed how big he was.

"What are you going to do?" she asked anxiously.

"Rape you," he answered in a matter-of-fact tone, his back to her. "Isn't that what you want?" He continued to look up and down the hall. "When I was a little boy, I used to rape little girls. But always in a dark cellar. I gotta have a dark cellar before I can rape anybody." After a moment, he turned around. "Isn't that one hell of a thing? No cellar!" He walked toward the center of the room. "All right; no cellar, no rape."

He picked up her clothes and tossed them at her. "On your horse!"

She dressed quickly, even though her hands were shaking. As soon as she was finished, he picked up the brown paper bag, crooked his other arm for her, and asked, "May I have the honor?" They walked down the corridor as if she were the bride at a church wedding. The moment they reached the foyer, the doorbell rang. The man opened the door and two thugs walked in. The tall one was young, but already his face was disfigured by acne scars. The short one was middle-aged, with a peaches-and-cream complexion and an ominous bulge in his right coat pocket. The big man nodded toward Charlotte and said, "Miss Given."

414

Both thugs bowed.

"Miss Given just made an unfortunate mistake," said the big man. "She tried to frame a friend of Mr. Toski's."

Charlotte turned pale.

"A good friend?" asked the acne thug, and there was awe in his voice.

"A very good friend," answered the big man.

"That's too bad. What do you think we ought to do?" asked the acne thug.

"It's not what we ought to do," answered the big man. "It's what we gotta do." He took an unusually small pineapple out of the brown paper bag and held it up by the stalk as if it were a bouquet. "She screams a lot. We gotta take her someplace where nobody can hear her scream, and shove this up her ass."

Charlotte began to sag. The acne thug stepped behind her and held her up by the armpits.

"That's too bad," said the peaches-and-cream thug, shaking his head. "She's so refined."

There was a long silence.

"Couldn't we do something else?" the peaches-and-cream thug asked at last.

"Like what?" countered the big man.

"Like having her sign a paper."

"What kind of paper?"

"This kind of paper," said the peaches-and-cream thug, taking a single sheet out of his coat pocket and handing it to him.

The big man held it up to the light and read aloud. "I, Charlotte Given, of 1296 Third Avnue, was called to the office of Mr. Cornelius Krant at twelve noon today. Mr. Krant wanted me to go to the office of Dr. James Morelle tonight and frame him for rape. He handed me ten one-hundred-dollar bills to do this. Tonight, I went to Dr. Morelle's office complaining of pain in the stomach. I undressed, ripped my clothes, and began to scream that he was raping me. At no time did the Doctor molest me. I was thwarted by some of his friends.

I am very sorry that I agreed to carry out this scheme for Mr. Cornelius Krant."

"What does 'thwarted' mean?" asked the acne thug.

"It's some kind of a foreign word," explained the big man with a shrug.

No one said anything for a full minute. Charlotte kept her eyes closed.

"Well, what do you think?" asked the big man.

"I think we ought to let her sign the paper," said the peaches-and-cream thug. "She's very refined."

The big man hesitated. "All right." He put the pineapple on a small table and handed Charlotte first the paper and then a fountain pen. "It's a Parker 51," he added with apparent pride.

She bent over the table and signed her name. The signature was barely recognizable. The moment she straightened up, the peaches-and-cream thug reached into his coat pocket. Charlotte tensed, waiting for the gun. Instead, his hand come out with a thin, imitation-leather case containing a notary public's kit. He pressed the seal into the lower portion of the paper, inked in his name with a little pocket stamp and stamp pad, and finally added his signature.

"It's not legal unless it's notarized," he said by way of explanation.

The big man handed her the Parker 51. "Compliments of Mr. Toski," he said graciously.

The acne thug opened the door. They all bowed, and Charlotte tottered out into the night. It was ten minutes before she realized that she was walking in the wrong direction. She took a taxi home and fell into bed. Two Nembutal capsules could not bring her sleep or even the comfort of drowsiness. She lay under the covers with all her clothes on, chilly and frightened. Just before dawn, as she finally lost consciousness, she thought of the pineapple again. It was really very small; maybe it would have been possible . . . ?

When Mrs. Westover entered the office Thursday morning, she found a crumpled brown paper bag, and an unusually small pineapple on the foyer table. She never heard from Charlotte Given again.

A few minutes later, a boy arrived with the confession. On a piece of paper clipped to it was typed, "You know what to do, Colonel."

"I know what to do, all right," said Jim to himself as he tossed the slip of paper aside. "The question is, can I put on a good enough performance while I'm doing it."

He picked up his hat, walked to the corner, and took a taxi to the building where Krant worked. A little blond secretary was standing in front of his private office. Jim picked her up by the armpits and set her down to one side. Then, without bothering to knock, he opened the door, closed it quietly behind him, and locked it. With a glance at Krant, who was sitting frozen to his chair behind the desk, he took off his coat, laid it carefully on a couch, and rolled up his sleeves.

"Before I send you to jail, I'm going to beat the hell out of you," he whispered.

Slowly he advanced on the desk. When he was a foot away, he reached into his back pocket, took out the confession, and laid it carefully on the blotter. Krant sat there, jaw slack, staring at him.

"Read it," Jim ordered.

Krant's eyes focused on the paper. After a minute, he raised them.

"Now read it again," said Jim.

Krant looked down again.

Jim sat on the couch and stared at his fists for a little while. "You got any children?" he asked at last.

Krant looked up and nodded.

Jim scratched his jaw and digested the information. Then he stood up, picked up the paper, and put it in his pocket. With a final glance at Krant, he rolled down his sleeves and got into his coat.

"Stay away from the trustees' meeting tomorrow night," he warned. "If you don't, you'll spend a couple of years in jail."

He unlocked the door and walked out. The little blond secretary was standing just where he had left her. He picked her up under the armpits and set her down in front of the door. They smiled at each other.

TWENTY-NINE

THE NEXT DAY, Friday, each of the seven trustees who had agreed not to vote for the merger prepared for the meeting in a different way. Krant took a plane to Florida. Devine got tickets for the Flonzaley Quartette. Old Klaus Martin and old Hagenbeck slept all afternoon. Shore pored over the annual Hospital reports from the time of August Grund to the present. Gillette arranged for the press to be waiting downstairs at McKinley when the meeting was over.

Just before dinner, Emil Grund asked his wife where she kept his father's things. She returned in a few minutes with a large metal box shaped like a sugar cube. Emil lifted the lid and, one by one, examined the articles inside. After some hesitation, he put the watch and the eyeglass case in his pocket. Then he went into the bedroom. Not until he had closed the door did he press the crown of the watch. The gold lid snapped open with a ping he remembered from childhood. And the click when he closed it was as loud as it had been in his father's day. The eyeglass case was even more effective. It shut with a report like a pistol shot. He was not surprised to find it a bit large for his glasses, but they fitted inside well enough.

At eight-thirty that night, eighteen of the twenty trustees sat grimly around the long table in the Board Room. The crystal chandelier no longer twinkled. Since it had not had an ammonia bath in two years, its teardrop pieces were coated with an oily scum. And the wood-paneled walls, which once had gleamed like a seal in the sun, were now, through lack of polishing, as dull as toast. Only the Rosa Bonheur landscape remained the same, immense and impressive and wonderfully old-fashioned. It seemed to be saying, "So I'm not a good picture! I'm famous, and that's more important."

Kirby was careful not to call the meeting to order. He told two long stories and a few one-liners. But, all the while, he was looking around him counting the votes. With Gillette, Klaus Martin, and old Hagenbeck in opposition, he figured that he still had fifteen of the eighteen trustees in his pocket. He only needed fourteen to pass the merger. But to a cautious man a one-vote margin was not enough. He continued to wait for Devine and Krant.

At ten minutes after nine, he went outside and rang up their homes. When he returned, he was chuckling, but there was a wary look in his eyes.

"Scudder Devine and young Krant must have forgotten about the meeting." He looked like an indulgent father. "But it really doesn't matter. This is just a formality."

He turned toward Gillette, who was sitting with Klaus Martin and Hagenbeck. "Let's make it unanimous."

Gillette took out a gold case almost as long and thin as Huegenon's and tapped a cigarette on its polished surface. "You forgot to announce that an anonymous donor has given us a half million dollars on condition that we stay where we are." He coughed discreetly. "And reinstate one of the doctors."

"All right, I'm announcing it now," said Kirby with a touch of irritation. "It's penny-ante stuff anyway. A half million

420

dollars if we promise to wither on the vine here, as against five million if we pack up and set up a going concern in the suburbs. Besides, the question has already been decided. The Relocation Committee has voted unanimously in favor of the merger. We are here tonight to confirm what they have done."

He placed his palms on the table and said in a sing-song voice, "All those in favor of the merger with Brookeville General Hospital please raise their right hands."

Twelve of the eighteen trustees complied.

Kirby smiled patiently. "Just a minute, there," he said, "I see twelve. With mine that makes thirteen. Something must be wrong with my arithmetic. Let's go at it another way. All those opposed please raise their hands."

Gillette, Klaus Martin, Hagenbeck, Shore, and Emil Grund raised their hands. Kirby's face turned gray. He looked at Shore.

"What kind of a dirty double cross is this?" he shouted. "You were Chairman of the Relocation Committee, weren't you? You'd better change your vote back again or you'll go down as the man who sold out McKinley for a lousy five hundred thousand dollars."

"Kirby, I once stood up against August Grund," replied Shore icily. "What makes you think I'm going to knuckle under to a little man like you?"

Kirby turned away from him and looked at Emil Grund. "Your father crapped over you from the day you were born until the day he died, and you still won't climb out of the chamber pot! What do you do, pay rent?"

Emil Gund stood up, took out his father's watch and pressed the crown. The gold lid snapped open with a familiar ping. The click when he closed it was startling in the hushed room. After replacing the watch in his vest pocket, he took out his father's eyeglass case and very carefully placed his own glasses inside. Waiting a moment in order to enhance the

421

effect, he closed it with a report like a pistol shot. Nothing like it had been heard in the Board Room in twenty years.

"You're right, he almost destroyed me," said Grund at last. "But I think he loved me in his own way, too. I haven't amounted to much, I know, but I'm going to do one thing tonight that I'll be proud of for the rest of my life. My father built up this Hospital and I'll be damned if I'm going to let it go under."

He sat down. Old Hagenbeck pounded on the floor with his cane in lieu of applause, which he felt should be given only to entertainers.

Kirby took a deep breath. "All right, all right! We're not getting anywhere this way. All we are doing is blowing off steam. Let's regard this as a preliminary meeting. Let's sleep on the merger. When Devine and Krant get back, we can vote on it again. That's reasonable, isn't it?"

Gillette gave a contemptuous laugh. "It's reasonable, but it's crooked. Under the constitution and by-laws of the Hospital, this was a final meeting called to vote on the merger with Brookeville General. The merger has now been rejected. Downstairs, there are reporters from every paper in town waiting for me to tell them the results of this meeting. If you try to pull a fast one, Kirby, I guarantee that there will be enough publicity to make the Brookeville trustees throw both you and the merger to the wolves."

Kirby scooped up some papers from the table and put them in his pocket. He was deathly pale. "All right, *you* take over, Gillette. I'm through being the keeper of this white elephant. And I think you'll find I'm not the only one who's had enough."

He walked out, a somber little man, followed by his twelve trustees. Gillette thought of a painting of Napoleon's retreat from Moscow popular in his youth. All that was needed now, he felt, were a few dead horses and some dirty snow. Only Grund, Klaus Martin, Hagenbeck, Shore, and himself remained seated at the table. Old Hagenbeck smiled. He had not smiled in years. He smiled again, this time just for the hell of it.

Emil Grund rose and walked up to the full-length portrait of his father that hung on the wall opposite the crystal chandelier. The old man looked as if he were about to enter the lobby of the Metropolitan Opera House. His full-dress suit was covered by the famous straight black overcoat reputedly made of cast iron, and his right hand was raised to the brim of his high silk hat. Emil held back a tear. Through the mist it seemed as if the hat were being lifted toward him in a silent salute and the frosty blue eyes were widening in loving admiration.

Leaving Emil Grund to commune with his father, Gillette went downstairs to brief the reporters. As soon as he had finished with them, he telephoned his son-in-law and told him exactly what had happened in the Board Room.

"So McKinley stays alive at least until tomorrow afternoon," said Jim. "That's when I have my second meeting with Mr. Huegenon."

At two o'clock the next day, the financier received him in his study. He was standing behind his desk under El Greco's St. Jerome, the McKinley report in his hand.

"My congratulations," he remarked affably. "I see you are now able to revive the dead. At least a dead board."

"Only part of a board."

The old man took out the thin gold cigarette case, motioned his guest to a chair, and sat down. The case was so beautiful that Jim wondered why people did not use things like that any more.

Huegenon lit a cigarette and said, "In this instance the part was bigger than the whole." He smiled and added, "I never thought you would be able to put it across."

"The cause was good."

Huegenon laughed cynically. "In this world the cause is nothing, the advocate everything." He looked Jim in the eye. "What did you come to me for, more money?"

Jim nodded.

"I see," said the financier, "you think a philanthropist and his money are soon parted." He put the cigarette to his lips, and inhaled deeply like a man about to make love. "I suppose you are going to persuade me to leave some money to the Hospital. In return I would be guaranteed a limited immortality." He glanced through the McKinley report and then looked up. "I have never failed to be surprised that the men who have promised me immortality have invariably been fund-raisers rather than clergymen." He smiled at Jim. "What figure did you have in mind?"

Jim waited a moment to heighten the effect of what he was about to say.

"Not a figure—a foundation, the Charles Huegenon Foundation, created for the purpose of building and administering a medical center in the heart of Manhattan. On Park Avenue, on the site of the old McKinley; in fact, just a few blocks from this beautiful home. And built by the living, not by the dead."

The financier was stunned. "You've caught me by surprise, Jim. Elaborate. Exactly what do you want?"

"I want the Charles Huegenon Medical Center. It would consist of three divisions: first, a new McKinley Hospital which would do honor to your name; second, a group of research laboratories whose discoveries would keep your memory alive; and third, a medical school. One side of the medical school would be a wall of smooth, unbroken granite into which would be chiseled forever the words, 'THE STONE THAT THE BUILDER REJECTED HAS BECOME THE CORNERSTONE.' And underneath, in smaller letters, 'THE ALBERT HUEGENON MEDICAL SCHOOL.' Its bronze doors would be open upon a stone chapel that would contain no furniture, no pictures, no decorations—nothing except a photograph of Albert on the far wall. And not just because he was your son. But because he wanted so desperately to get into medical school. And because he would have made such a good doctor if he had."

The old man was shaken. "It's an ambitious project," he said as if to divert his thoughts from his son.

"Yes, it would cost at least a hundred million dollars." Huegenon brushed the remark aside with a wave of his hand. "The money is nothing any more. It's the idea that is so formidable."

"For me, too, sir. McKinley would be transformed, unrecognizable. The directors and key doctors would be professors in the medical school. They would have to be physicians and surgeons without private practices, full-time men, salaried employees. When I was young, I never dreamed that this could ever happen to McKinley. But it's the wave of the future. And the future is often unkind to the past. Above all, the medical school must become part of a university. Otherwise it will be a motherless child."

Huegenon hesitated. "I don't mean to be rude, Jim, but I have to have time to digest this. Come back in a week. I'll see you at eleven o'clock next Saturday morning."

As soon as Jim left, the financier telephoned Louise and asked her to see him as soon as possible. A request from Huegenon was a command. She arrived in twenty minutes. He motioned her to a seat opposite him, facing the El Greco, and said, "Louise, I have to make a decision. I think it is the most important decision of my life, and I've made some big ones. I want you to tell me everything you can think of about Jim as far as it relates to McKinley."

She talked into the tape recorder on the desk for an hour and ten minutes. When she walked out, she was smiling.

By the middle of the following week, Jim had become quite moody. Wednesday night, as he and Louise were going to bed, she said, "You've worn that look for days. What's bothering you? Don't you think you impressed Uncle Ty? He's bound to give you something, dear."

He sat on the decorator's chair in his shorts and stared at the carpet between his feet. That's the way he must have looked when he boxed for Columbia, she thought.

"I can't win," he said. "If Mr. Huegenon were to build the center I want him to, there would be no place in it for me."

Louise walked up to him and kissed him on top of the head. "Stop fretting," she urged. "You have a distinguished practice, and at least twenty-five more good years in bed."

Saturday turned out to be a clear and heady May day. Jim got home from an emergency appendectomy at ten, took a short second shower, and put on a fresh set of clothes. He chose his favorite tie, an old blue-silk moiré from Sulka's.

When he entered the glass-domed atrium of the great house on Fifth Avenue promptly at eleven, he found Huegenon beside one of the stone benches, looking years younger than he had the week before. He stood there as slim and erect as in the old days, with a healthy glow replacing the gray on his cheeks. Taking Jim by the elbow, he guided him around the shallow pool toward Albert's favorite stone bench. Huegenon never wore rubber heels, and a slow, martial clicking filled the huge room.

"I am very grateful to you, Jim," he said at last. "Suddenly I find that I am not ready to die." He lifted his eyes to the glass dome. "I like your plan. I am going to build a medical center that New York and my son will be proud of." He made it sound as if Albert were upstairs studying for his exams. "I don't know why I didn't think of it myself years ago." He smiled ruefully. "But maybe it would not have been as much fun then. A spring day in December is always more precious than one in May."

He touched Jim's elbow again to make him sit down. "I'm going to start the fund with a hundred million dollars."

Jim's athlete's heart beat faster. "Thank you, sir, but there is one thing that is troubling my conscience. Suppose we get socialized medicine here someday; suppose the government takes over the doctors. What would become of your Center then?"

"The government would take over only the private practitioners, Jim. The Center would be safe, a fortress of knowledge like the monasteries in the Dark Ages. You don't understand this country, my boy. America may socialize people, but it will never socialize property."

He took out the beautiful, thin gold case and tapped a cigarette on its unblemished surface. Jim wondered whether it was polished every morning, like the Rolls-Royce.

"McKinley itself should cost about forty million dollars," Huegenon went on. "I'm going to let the people of New York pay some of that. If they contribute to the Hospital, they will take it to their hearts."

"I hope you will take an interest in the running of the Center," said Jim politely.

Huegenon gave him a look of cold amazement. "I intend to take more than an interest. I intend to shape the policies. For one thing, I expect the full-time doctors at McKinley to be exactly that. It is the great paradox of American medicine that the only doctors who do not work full time are the full-time doctors. Their hours are a pleasant nine to five, Monday through Friday, while the rest of you work seven days a week, and often all night, too. They not only work the laity's hours—they live the laity's life—a job in New York and a home in the suburbs. I intend to change all that by paying them high enough salaries to make my wishes stick. I intend to detach these full-time men from gypsy America, that great mass of our fellow countrymen who move from the city to the suburbs and then from one suburb to another. I will expect all McKinley doctors to live within walking distance of the Hospital. McKinley, not their car or The New York, New Haven & Hartford, will be their second home. There will be no gypsy dances by McKinley doctors on the five-fifteen to Westport every night."

He let Jim light his cigarette for him. "I may sound like a despot, but I hope to be a benevolent one. I have extensive property holdings on the East Side. McKinley doctors and their families will be welcomed in these apartment houses, and at rents in keeping with their salaries. And there will be scholarships in good private schools for the children."

"You're very generous, sir."

"Not at all. It will be worth it. Perhaps some spring night when a McKinley full-time doctor is bored with television or too much *Time*, perhaps for something better to do he will walk a few blocks to the Hospital to hold a fevered hand, help a bewildered intern, or give courage to a frightened child. You can't do that from Mamaroneck, you know."

"You're preaching to the converted, Mr. Huegenon."

"Always the best audience. And there will be a new Board of Trustees for McKinley. Although I would like to keep Lewis Gillette, Shore, and Grund. And those two desiccated old Germans as reminders of the past."

"I am sure they would all be happy to serve."

"I want Sam Perkes on the administrative staff. His rascally plan had daring and imagination. He was the only one in the place with a big idea. He can be reformed—as long as there is something in it for him."

"He has his own set loyalties—to Kirby and to efficiency. He'll just transfer them to the new board."

Huegenon nodded. Then he put his hand on Jim's shoulder for a moment. "Where the dilapidated old Dispensary now stands, I am going to put up a magnificent new building which will house all the out-patient clinics of the Hospital. It will be called the 'Jacob John Morelle Clinic,' more, really, to honor McKinley than to honor your father. On the third floor,

428

where he met a hero's fate, will be a silver plaque with this epitaph, the nursery rhyme you recited to him as he lay dying,

BOLD AS AN EAGLE, BRAVE AS HELL

WAS DOCTOR JACOB JOHN MORELLE.

Jim had bent over, and was staring at the marble between his feet. "I hope there's a hereafter, so that he can look down and watch the building rise."

"The picking of the staff I will leave to the experts," Huegenon continued. "They can choose anyone they wish. Except the Director of Surgery. That's going to be you."

There was a long pause. Jim looked up. "Thank you. I'm grateful. But I can't take the job."

"What's that!" exclaimed Huegenon. "Don't you want to be Director of Surgery at McKinley?"

"Of course I do. I always have, ever since I was a boy and sat in my father's office and listened to his stories about Dr. Emmerich and the Hospital. But I'm not fit for the job. I'm the wrong man. I don't have the qualifications."

"Jim, don't be tiresome. Someone once defined a bore as a man who tells everything. I define a bore as a man who tells nothing. You have not mentioned your training under the old German masters, your unsurpassed skill, your speed at the operating table, and your remarkable cures."

Jim shook his head. "You're just painting a picture of a fashionable surgeon in private practice. McKinley needs a different breed, a full-time salaried surgeon from some university hospital. And you don't become one of those over-night. A man like that starts training for an academic career the day he becomes an intern. It's something that occupies an entire medical lifetime. You can't suddenly become converted at forty-two."

"Why not? I've heard of people becoming converted to Catholicism in their seventies."

"I know. But the university is less charitable than the Church. It wants none but the pure of heart, while the Church welcomes sinners. It is inconceivable that a university would ever accept a doctor who has been seriously tainted by private practice. The head of a department in a great university hospital must be a scholar whose scholarship has been honed to a fine edge by years of study, a master of the medical literature, a research scientist, an educator, an administrator, and an innovator. I simply don't measure up."

Huegenon looked grave. "What about Stanley?"

"He really is a scholar. Like his father. But as far as a medical school is concerned, he is just a doctor with a little black bag who runs all over New York making house calls even on the well-to-do for ten dollars. After he leaves, he is followed by the television man, with a bigger black bag, who makes house calls for fifteen. And he in turn is followed by the plumber, with the biggest black bag of all, who won't come out for less than twenty-five. Maybe Stanley should get a big, black valise in a luggage store." He laughed bitterly. "A university hospital would never accept a man like that as head of a department."

"It seems a pity that you didn't take the king's road to academic medicine when you were young," said Huegenon sadly.

"How could we have known? Why, in my father's day, full-time teaching in a medical school was considered a confession of failure. A doctor who chose such a career was said by his colleagues to be a man who 'couldn't make a go of private practice.' When Pop went to P and S, the full professors and heads of departments had magnificent private practices. That was one of the reasons why they were chosen. But there has been a complete reversal in the past thirty years. They're all full-time now, and have been since the day they finished their residencies. Stan and I are not the first to be swindled by time."

Huegenon seemed puzzled. "You will send your private patients to the new Hospital, of course. But, damn it, what role will you play, what position do you want?"

Jim smiled. "Chief Admirer."

Huegenon shook his head. "A sort of Moses to McKinley's Promised Land."

"I'm afraid I could do very little to develop the real estate. Let me ask you a question, sir. Suppose the Lord had allowed Moses to set foot in the Promised Land; do you really think he would have been fool enough to enter?"

Huegenon gave Jim a sharp look. "Then, why did God order him to stay out?"

"It was an act of kindness, sir. He wanted to spare His loyal servant the ordeal of temptation."

Huegenon sighed. "All right, Jim, I won't tempt you. But your father would be troubled."

"Yes, but he'll understand. We'll both be written off as failures."

"He sired a faithful son. You saved McKinley. Failures? Nonsense."

Jim bowed his head. "Thank you. All the same, I hope I haven't let him down."

"Never," said the financier. "You've made him the proudest father in Heaven. He certainly was that on earth."

He stood up, and they walked side by side through the atrium.

"Someday," said Jim, "when the Huegenon Medical Center is the greatest in the land, maybe people will say, 'The new McKinley could never have become what it is today if it had not been for the old.'"

"They will," said Huegenon. "I promise you that they will. I have a dead son who says that they will. They will never forget."

The door opened. Jim walked slowly toward Fifth Avenue. The May air was soft, the sunlight shimmering. His heart was a little heavy, but it was a wonderful day.